BULGAKOV'S FEUILLETON

101 feuilletons by Mikhail Bulgakov

Translated by Mila Sanina and Michael Wagner

FOREWORD

Mikhail Bulgakov (pronounced bool-GAH-kuf) is one of the world's great writers. His works are considered 'top-shelf' in the countries of the former Soviet Union, along with those of Pushkin, Tolstoy, Dostoevsky, and Gogol.

Bulgakov's earliest published works were feuilletons (pronounced fey-yea-TONES), a genre of the short stories. *The Big Soviet Encyclopedia (1970)* offers one of the better definitions for this somewhat ineffable genre:

> "Feuilleton (Fr. *feuilleton* from *feuille,* a leaf or small piece of paper) – an artistic-journalistic genre with an inherently critical, often comical, including satirical, character. Its general characteristics are the currency of the subject and the fluidity of the message and narrative; the apparent "planlessness," lightness, and unpretentiousness of composition; and the parodic use of artistic and supra-artistic genres and styles. The uniqueness of the feuilleton lies mainly in that it belongs to a mixed artistic-journalistic style by virtue of [its] methods for processing facts, its treatment of facts, and its goal … [feuilletons] violated official seriousness and the stereotyped and abstract governmental style, although they often gravitated to slick character study."

The feuilleton was wildly popular in Europe during the 19th and early 20th centuries, so much so that newspapers created sections for them, often entitling the sections "Feuilleton."

Bulgakov's Feuilleton presents 101 feuilletons written by Bulgakov between November 1919 and March 1926. These feuilletons were published in a variety of newspapers and magazines, under Bulgakov's own name and pennames such as *Ol 'Wright, F.S-ov, M. Bull, Emma B.,* and *G. P. Ukhov* (of the ear). Only two of these feuilletons have ever been published in English translation.

The period 1919–1926 is of historic interest. Russia was recovering from the combined effects of WWI, the Russian Revolution, and the Russian Civil War; and it was engaged in a massive experiment in social engineering under Communism. During this period, writers experienced increasing censorship and repression, which culminated in the purges of the 1930s.

Bulgakov's Feuilleton offers a unique perspective on this period, beginning with the story "Future Prospects," which is Bulgakov's first published work. "Future Prospects" is unusual. It is written in the first person and it is devoid of humor. In it, Bulgakov paints in the large about the implications of the Revolution and the wars for Russia. From that point on, Bulgakov paints in the small. He depicts ordinary people in ordinary settings who are struggling with problems of existence—hyperinflation, bureaucracy, corruption, travel delays, incomprehensible regulations, cronyism, nepotism, red-tapism, drunkenness, wife beating, the housing problem, education, pointless day-long meetings, and encounters with "the healthcare system." He draws hundreds upon hundreds of characters, with a psychological perspicacity that we in the West have come to expect of a Russian master.

Bulgakov's feuilletons stand in the same relationship to his major works, as do the sketches of any great artist to his masterpieces. And the reader can see the precursors of characters, settings, and plot elements found in *The Heart of a Dog* (1925) and *The Master and Margarita* (1940) taking shape in them.

Bulgakov's Gogolian imagination and his playwright's ear for dialogue are abundantly on display in these stories. The action moves quickly. There are twists and turns. But always a poetic ending.

MilSan and MikWag

In the broad field of Russian letters in the USSR, I was the one and only literary wolf. I was advised to dye my fur. Absurd advice. You can dye a wolf, clip a wolf—he still doesn't look like a poodle.

From Bulgakov's letter to Joseph Stalin
May 30, 1931

Cowardice is the most terrible character flaw.

From "The Master and Margarita"

CONTENTS

BULGAKOV'S FEUILLETON

1919

Future Prospects (Грядущие перспективы)

Now, when our wretched country finds itself at the very bottom of a pit of shame and disaster to which the "Great Social Revolution" has driven her, one and the same thought has begun to appear more and more often to many of us.

This thought is perseverant.

It is dark, gloomy. It arises in the consciousness and powerfully demands an answer.

It is simple: What will happen to us next?

Its appearance is natural.

We have analyzed our recent past. Oh, we have very well studied practically every moment of the past two years. Many have not only studied it, but cursed it as well.

The present is before our eyes. It is such that one wants to shut those eyes.

To not see it!

There remains the future. The mysterious, unknown future.

Indeed, what then will happen to us?..

Recently, I happened to peruse several issues of an English illustrated magazine.

For a long while I looked, as if spellbound, at the wonderfully executed photographs.

And long, long I thought, and then...

Yes, the picture is clear!

The colossal machines in the colossal factories feverishly, day after day, gobbling up coal; they growl, they pound, they pour out jets of molten metal, forge, repair, build...

They forge the might of the world, replacing those machines that not long ago, sowing death and destroying, forged the might of victory.

In the West, the Great War of the great nations has ended. Now they are licking their wounds.

Of course they will recover; they will very soon recover!

And to all who have finally a mind that has cleared, to all who do not believe the pathetic lie that our malignant disease will spread to the West and infect it, the powerful rise of the titanic work of peace will become clear, which will raise the Western countries to an unprecedented height of peacetime power.

And we?

We will be late...

We will be so very late that none of the modern prophets, perhaps, will say when we will ultimately catch up with them, and whether we will catch up at all.

For we have been punished.

To us, it is inconceivable at this time to build. We have before us a heavy task: to win, to re-seize our own land.

The reckoning has begun.

Hero—volunteers are tearing the Russian land inch by inch out of the hands of Trotsky.

And everyone, everyone, including those who fearlessly perform their duty, and those who now huddle in the southern cities in the rear, in a bitter illusion thinking that the matter of saving the country will move itself along without them; all of them eagerly wait for the liberation of the country.

And she will be liberated.

For there is no country that didn't and doesn't have heroes, and it is a crime to think that the homeland has died.

But it is necessary to fight a lot, to shed a lot of blood, because as long as there are madmen behind the sinister figure of Trotsky, duped by him, still hovering armed, there will be no life. There will be a deadly struggle.

One must fight.

And while in the West, the machines of creation will be chattering, with us, from one edge of the country to the other, the machine guns will be chattering.

The insanity of the last two years has prodded us along a terrible path, and there is no stop for us, no breather. We started to drink from the cup of punishment and we will drink it to the end.

There, in the West, uncountable electric bulbs will blaze, aviators will drill through the conquered air, there they will build, explore, print, learn...

And we... We will fight.

For there is no force that could change that.

We will be conquering our own capitals.

And we will conquer them.

The English, remembering how we covered the fields with bloody dew fighting off Germany, dragging her away from Paris, will lend us more overcoats and boots, so that we more quickly will reach Moscow.

And we will reach it.

The scoundrels and fools will be expelled, scattered, annihilated.

And the war will be over.

Then the country, bleeding, devastated will begin to stand up... slowly, heavily, to stand up.

Those who complain about "fatigue," alas, they will be disappointed. For they will have "to fatigue" even more...

It will be necessary to pay for the past with unbelievable effort and severe poverty of being. To pay in its literal and figurative senses.

To pay for the insanity of the March days, the insanity of the days of October, for the separatist traitors, the dissipation of the workers, for Brest, for the insane use of the machine for printing money... for everything!

And we will pay it off.

And only then, when it is already too late, will we begin again to create something, to attain equal rights, so as to be admitted back to the halls of Versailles.

Who will see these bright days?

We?

Oh no! Our children, maybe, or maybe even our grandchildren; for the sweep of history is wide and she reads decades just as easily as she reads individual years.

And we, the representatives of the unlucky generation, already dying in the ranks of the wretched bankrupts, will have to tell our children:

Pay, pay honestly, and forever remember the Social Revolution!

Translators' note

"Future Prospects" is noteworthy for its anti-Communist content. For this reason, Bulgakov glued a newspaper clipping of this—his first publication—facedown in his album.

He begins and ends the story with ironic reference to the "Social Revolution." He refers to Communism as "our malignant disease." He says that future generations will have to pay for the damage done by a litany of events and groups: the March and October 1917 Revolutions; hyperinflation caused by printing of paper money; the 1918 Treaty of Brest-Litovsk, which ended Russia's involvement in WWI and allowed the Red Army to focus on defeating the White Army in the Russian Civil War (1918-1921); and the Ukrainian separatists, led by Petliura, who fought against both the Red and White Armies.

Bulgakov wrote this story on a train, while accompanying wounded White Army soldiers to Vladikavkaz, a city controlled by the White Army. He described its writing in *Notes on the Cuff: Early autobiographical prose*:

"Once at night in 1919, in the dull autumn, riding in a loose train, under the light of a small candle inserted in a bottle of kerosene, I wrote the first short story. I brought the story to a newspaper in the city to which the train dragged me. There it was published."

A bit more about Bulgakov: Mikhail Bulgakov was born in 1891 in the city of Kiev, Russian Empire. He graduated from the First Imperial Alexander Male Gymnasium in 1909 and the Kiev University Medical School in 1916. He was drafted to work in a hospital in World War I and as a field surgeon during the Russian Civil War. He also practiced civilian medicine in Kiev (venereology) and single-handedly ran a rural hospital.

A translation of "Future Prospects" can also be found in the book *Manuscripts Don't Burn: Mikhail Bulgakov A Life in Letters and Diaries*, by J.A.E. Curtiss. Overlook Hardcover, New York, 1991, p 16.

This map positions Kiev, Vladikavkaz, and Moscow—the three cities in which Bulgakov resided during his life—relative to each other, and within the Soviet Union (black rectangle within the inset map of the USSR). The lines connecting the cities represent rail lines (the connection between Kiev and Moscow is not shown). The city of Sochi, on the Black Sea, is the site of the 2014 Winter Olympic Games.

1920

"Kavkazskaya gazeta" (Caucasus Gazette), Vladikavkaz, January 18, 1920

At a Café (В кафе)

A café in a city in the rear.

Floor covered with dirt. A tobacco fog. Sticky, dirty tables.

A few military men, several ladies, and a lot of civilians.

On the stage, a piano, cello, and violin playing something rollicky.

I thread my way among the tables and sit down.

A young lady in a white apron approaches the table and looks at me quizzically.

— Be so kind as to bring me a glass of tea and two cupcakes.

The young lady disappears, then returns with a look as if she is granting me a favor, puts a glass of yellow liquid and a plate with two dried cupcakes in front of me.

I look at the glass.

The liquid in appearance remotely resembles tea.

Yellow, murky.

I try it with a spoon.

Tepid, slightly sweet, a little disgusting.

I light up a cigarette and look around at the public.

At the next table a group sits down loudly: two civilian gentlemen and one woman.

The woman is well dressed; she rustles in silk.

The civilians make the most positive impression: tall, rosy-cheeked, well fed. At the prime age for the draft. Dressed exquisitely.

On the table in front of them appear a plate of cupcakes and three cups of coffee à la Warsaw.

They start talking.

Snatches of conversation from the civilian sitting closest to me, the one in patent-leather shoes, drift my way.

An anxious voice.

I hear:

— Rostov... can you imagine... Germans... Chinese... panic... they were in helmets... one hundred thousand cavalry...

And again:

— Rostov... panic... Rostov... cavalry...

— It's horrible, — the lady says languidly. But it is obvious that the one hundred thousand cavalry and the helmets bother her little, if at all. She, squinting, smokes a cigarette, and with shiny eyes, looks around the café.

Patent-leather shoes continues his whispering.

My imagination begins to play.

What would happen if suddenly, as in a fairy tale, I were granted authority over all these civilian gentlemen?

I swear to God, it would be great!

Right here, in this café, I'd get up and approach the gentleman of the patent-leather shoes, I'd say:

— Come with me!

— Where? — the gentleman would ask in astonishment.

— I heard that you worry about Rostov; I heard that the invasion of the Bolsheviks worries you.

— It does you honor.

— Come with me. I'll give you a chance to enlist immediately. There you will instantly get a rifle and a full opportunity to go to the front at the government's expense where you can take part in defeating the hated-by-everyone Bolsheviks.

I can imagine what these words would do to the gentleman in the patent-leather shoes.

He would in a moment lose his charming rosy cheeks, and a piece of cupcake would get stuck in his throat.

Having recovered a little, he would begin to mumble.

From this disconnected, but breathless babbling it would become clear, first of all, that looks can be deceiving.

It turns out that this as-fresh-as-a-daisy, rosy-faced man is sick... Desperately, irreparably, terminally ill to smithereens! He has heart disease, a hernia, and the most terrible neurasthenia. It can be attributed only to a miracle that he is sitting in a café, absorbing cakes, and is not lying in a cemetery, being absorbed in his turn by the worms.

And finally, he has a medical certificate!

— It means nothing, — I would say sighing, — I myself have a certificate, and not just one, but three. And yet, as you may have noticed, I have to wear an English overcoat (which, by the way, doesn't warm one up at all) and every minute have to be ready to report to the troop train, or for any other eventuality of a military nature. Spit on your certificates! Nobody takes them seriously! You yourself were just now painting the situation so drearily...

Then the gentleman breathlessly would go on babbling and would start to prove that he, in fact, has already registered and has already been working for the defense at such and such.

— Is it really worth talking about registration, — I would say, — to get registered in the rear is difficult, but to unregister and end up at the front takes a split second!

As for defense work, you... how to put it... are mistaken! From all outward indications, from your behavior, it is clear that you are working only on padding your own pockets with royal and Donsky notes. That's for starters. And then, secondly, by hanging out in coffee houses and movie theaters, by sowing confusion and fear with your stories, which infect everyone around you, you are working on the destruction of the rear. You must agree that nothing but dirty tricks can result from this kind of defense work.

No! You are certainly not suited for this work. And the only thing remaining for you is to go to the front!

Here the gentleman would start to clutch at a straw and would say that he enjoyed exemptions (the only son of a dead mother, or something of this sort), and finally, that he couldn't even hold a rifle in his hands.

— For God's sake, — I would say, — do not tell me about any exemptions. I repeat, nobody wants to hear about them!

As for the rifle, it is a triviality! I assure you that nothing is easier in the world than to learn how to shoot a rifle. I tell you this from my own experience. As for military service, there is nothing you can do about it! I wasn't in the army either and look what happened... I assure you that the war, along with the troubles and sufferings associated with it, does not attract me at all.

But there is nothing you can do about it! It isn't good for me personally, but one has to adjust!

I love, no less than you and perhaps even more, the calm peaceful life, movie theaters, soft sofas, and coffee à la Warsaw!

But, alas, I am able to enjoy none of these things to the fullest!

And nothing remains for you and me other than to take part in the war, one way or another, otherwise the red cloud will wash over us, and you yourself understand what will happen then...

That's what I would say, but, alas, I would not convince the gentleman in the patent-leather shoes.

He would begin to mumble or finally would have realized that he didn't want... wasn't able... didn't desire to go to war...

— Well, then nothing can be done, — I would say sighing, — since I cannot convince you, then you will just have to submit yourself to circumstances!

And then, addressing myself to those surrounding me and quickly executing my orders (in my dream, of course, I imagined them as an essential element), I would say, pointing at the totally slain gentleman:

— Escort the gentleman to the military commander!

Having dealt with the gentleman in the patent-leather shoes, I would address the next one...

But, oh, it would turn out that I was so carried away by the conversation that the sensitive civilians, having heard only the beginning of it, silently, one after another, would have forsaken the café.

Every single one of them, absolutely everyone!

....

After an intermission, the trio on the stage started "The Tango." I abandoned the reverie. The fantasy ended.

The door of the café banged and banged.

The crowd grew. The gentleman in patent-leather shoes tapped with a spoon and demanded more cakes...

I paid 27 rubles and, wriggling my way through the occupied tables, exited to the street.

Translators' note

The Red Army occupied Vladikavkaz at the end of February 1920. Bulgakov obtained a discharge from the White Army and left the practice of medicine. Soon after that, he obtained a position as head of the Literary Section of the Arts Sub-department of the Vladikavkaz Revolutionary Committee. He turned 29 on May 15th.

1921

The newspaper "Kommunist," Vladikavkaz, April 1, 1921

The Week of Enlightenment (Неделя просвещения)

One evening, our commissar visits our company and says to me:

— Sidorov!

And I respond:

— Sir!

He looks at me piercingly, and asks:

— You, — he says, — what's going on?

I say to him, — nothing...

— Are you, — he says, — illiterate?

I, of course, say to him:

— Yes sir, Comrade Commissar, illiterate.

Then he looks at me again and says:

— Well, if you are illiterate, I will send you this evening to *La Traviata!*

— Excuse me, — I say, — what did I do? It's not our fault that we're illiterate. They didn't educate us under the old regime...

And he responds:

— You fool! What are you frightened of? It's not a punishment, but a benefit. There you will be enlightened. You will see a show and it will be a pleasure for you.

But me and Pantelayev from our company had taken aim on the circus that evening, for a visit.

I add:

— But would it be possible, Comrade Commissar, to be granted a leave to go to the circus instead of the theater?

And he screws up one eye, then asks:

— To the circus?.. Why this?

— Yes, — I say, — it is irresistibly amusing... They will show an educated elephant, and again the red-haired clowns, Greco-Roman wrestling...

He wags his finger.

— I will, — he says, — show you an elephant! You lacking-in-social-consciousness element! Clowns... clowns! You yourself are a red-haired clown. Elephants are educated; but you, to my dismay, are uneducated. Of what benefit to you is the circus, huh? But at the theater they will enlighten you... It's nice, it's good for you... No further discussion, soldier... Take the ticket and march!

I have no choice. I took the ticket. Pantelayev, he's also illiterate, got a ticket, and we set off. We bought three cups of sunflower seeds, and made our way to the First Soviet Theater.

At the gate where they let people in, we see that it is a Babel of Babylon. The crowd breaks on the theater like a wave. And there among our illiterate are the literate, mostly young ladies. One of the young ladies reached the ticket taker, shows a ticket, and he asks her:

— Excuse me, — he says, — Comrade Madame, are you literate?

And she obtusely got offended:

— What a question! Of course, I am literate. I studied in a lyceum!

— Ah, — says the ticket taker, — in a lyceum. Very nice to meet you. In that case, let me bid you goodbye!

And he took away her ticket.

— On what grounds, — screams the lady, — how dare you?

— That's how it is, — he says, — it is very simple, because we are to admit only the illiterate.

— But I also want to listen to the opera or a concert.

— Well, if you want to, — he says, — please go to the Kavsoyuz. All your literates have been assembled there; the doctors are there, pharmacists, professors. They sit and drink tea with molasses because they aren't given sugar, and Comrade Koolikovsky sings romances to them.

And so the young lady left.

Well, Pantelayev and I were let in unimpeded, and led to the parterre, and seated in the second row.

So we are sitting there.

The show had not yet started; therefore, out of boredom, we each chomped through a cup of sunflower seeds. We were sitting like that for about an hour and a half; finally, the theater darkened.

I see someone is climbing to a main fenced-in place. Wearing a sealskin cap and a coat. Mustache, beard streaked with gray, and he looks so serious. He climbed up, sat down, and then the first thing he did was put a pince-nez on himself.

I ask Pantelayev (although illiterate, he knows everything):

— And who is this going to be?

And he responds:

— It's the con, — he says, — doctor. Here, he's in charge. A serious gentleman!

— Well, — I ask, — why is it then that they place him behind a barrier?

— Because, — he responds, — here he is the most literate in opera. So, they exhibit him here as an example for us.

— So why do they exhibit him with his behind to us?

— Uh, — he says, — this way, it is easier for him to lead the choir in a circle-dance!..

And this very conductor unfolded before himself some kind of book, looked into it, and waved a white stick. Immediately, under the floor, violins began to play. Plaintively, thinly, well, really making one want to cry.

So, this conductor, in literacy, indeed proved himself to be not the least of men, because he does two things at once: reads the book and waves the stick. And the orchestra is cooking. Hotter and hotter! After violins come fifes, after fifes come drums. The thunder walks around the entire theater. And then from the right side comes a roar... I looked at the orchestra and yelled:

— Pantelayev, may God strike me dead if it isn't Lombard, the supply master from the regiment!

And he also looked and said:

— That's him! No one but him can lay into the trombone like that!

Well, I got excited and yelled:

— Bravo, encore, Lombard!

And out of nowhere here comes a policeman, and right away he approaches me:

— Please, comrade, do not disturb the silence!

Well, we became silent.

Meanwhile, the curtains parted, and on the stage we see a party cooking at its peak! Those who are in jackets are gentlemen, those who are in dresses are ladies, and all sing and dance. And, of course, the cocktails are right there, and the playing cards are there too.

In short, the old regime!

Well, here, y'know, among the others, is Alfred. Also drinking and eating.

And it turns out, my brother, that he is in love with this very Traviata. But he doesn't explain this in words, but only in singing, all singing. And she responds to him in kind.

And it turns out that he cannot escape marrying her, but has, it turns out, this very Alfred, a dear father with last name Lyubchenko. And suddenly, out of nowhere, in the second act, he sneaks onto the stage.

In height he isn't tall, but he is so imposing, gray hair, a voice strong, thick, baritone.

And then he sings to Alfred:

— How could you, such-and-so, forget your dear land?

Well, he sang, sang to him, and he sent Alfred's entire machination to the devil. The drunken Alfred got drunk with grief in the third act, and he arranges, you my brothers, a huge scandal to this very, his, Traviata.

He gave her hell in front of everyone.

He sings:

— You, — he says, — and this and that and, in general, —

he says, — I do not want to have anything more to do with you.

Well, that, of course, sends her into tears. Noise, scandal!

And from grief she falls ill with consumption in the fourth act. They sent, of course, for the doctor.

The doctor comes.

Well, I see, although he is wearing a frock coat, by all indications he is our brother: a proletarian. Long hair and a healthy voice, like from a barrel.

He goes up to Traviata and starts singing:

— Rest in peace, — he says, — your disease is dangerous, and certainly you'll die!

And he didn't even write a prescription, but just bid farewell and left.

Well, Traviata sees she has no choice; she should die.

Well, here come both Alfred and Lyubchenko, ask her not to die. Lyubchenko gives his permission for their marriage. But nothing comes of it!

— Excuse me, — says Traviata, — I cannot, I must die.

And indeed, they again sang a little more, the three of them, and Traviata died.

And the conductor closed the book, took off his pince-nez and left. And everyone went home. That's all.

Well, I think, thank God, we got enlightened. And that should be it from us! What a boring story!

And I say to Pantelayev:

— Well, Pantelayev, let's go to the circus tomorrow!

I went to bed and the whole time I see dreams with Traviata singing and Lombard quacking on his trombone.

So, the next day, I report to the commissar and say:

— Please, Comrade Commissar, may I get a leave for the circus tonight...

And he bellows abruptly:

— Still, — he says, — you have elephants on your mind! No circuses! No, brother, today you will go to the Council of Trade Unions' concert. There, — he says, — Comrade Blokh and his orchestra will play "The Second Rhapsody" [1] to you!

I sagged. "So much for the elephants!" I think to myself.

— What is this, — I ask, — more of Lombard cooking on the trombone?

— Absolutely, — he says.

It's a curse, forgive me Lord, wherever I go, there he goes with his trombone!

I look at him and ask:

— Well, how about tomorrow?

— Tomorrow, — he says, — no. Tomorrow I'll send all of you to a drama.

— Well, the day after tomorrow?

— The day after tomorrow, no, to the opera again!

And in general, he says, enough hanging around circuses for you. The week of enlightenment had set in.

His words bedeviled me! This way you will be doomed forever, I think. So I ask:

— What is this, will everyone in our entire company be herded around like this?

— Why everyone? — he says. — The literate won't be herded. The literate are fine without "The Second Rhapsody!" It's only you, the illiterate devils. Let the literate go wherever they please!

I left him and pondered. I see that we're screwed! Since you're illiterate, it turns out you must forfeit all pleasures...

I thought and I thought and I finally figured it out. I went to the commissar and said:

— Permission to report!

— Report!

— May I be permitted, — I say, — to go to the literacy school?

The commissar then smiled and said:

— Well done! — And he ordered me into the school. Well, I attended it, and what do you think they educated me! And now the devil isn't my brother, because I am literate!

Translators' notes

This feuilleton is based on an actual Week of Enlightenment that took place in Vladikavkaz in March 1921. Bulgakov wrote the following about this story: "I published a feuilleton in the local paper and received 1,200 rubles for it and a promise that I would be detained for mockery in a special facility if I printed anything similar..."

1. Bulgakov loved the "Second Hungarian Rhapsody" by Ferents List, which he often played on the piano.

ARE YOU HELPING TO LIQUIDATE ILLITERACY? [top and right]
THE TESTAMENT OF ILYICH [Lenin]—BY THE XTH ANNIVERSARY OF THE
OCTOBER REVOLUTION THERE SHOULDN'T BE A SINGLE ILLITERATE—
[left]
BRING EVERYONE INTO SOCIETY "ERADICATE ILLITERACY" [bottom]

1922

The magazine "Rupor" (The Loudspeaker), № 4, Moscow, July 1922

Spiritualistic Séance (Спиритический сеанс)

> It isn't worth summoning him!
> It isn't worth summoning him!
> *The Recitative of Mephistopheles*

I

The fool Ksyushka reported:

— A guy came for you...

Madame Luzin blushed:

— In the first place, how many times have I told you to address me as 'Madame' and not 'you!' Which guy is that?

And she floated into the foyer.

In the foyer, Xavier Antonovich Lisinevich hung his hat on a deer antler and smiled sourly. He had heard Ksyushka's report.

Madame Luzin blushed again.

— Oh, God! Excuse me, Xavier Antonovich. This peasant fool!.. She is like this with everyone... Greetings!

— Oh, for pity's sake!.. — Lisinevich fashionably threw open his arms. — Good evening, Zinaida Ivanovna, — He set his legs in the third position[1], inclined his head and brought the hand of Madame Luzin to his lips.

But just as he was preparing to throw Madame a long and gooey glance, husband Pavel Petrovich crept through the doorway. And the glance extinguished.

— Aa-a, — immediately began the bagpipe of Pavel Petrovich, — 'A guy' ... heh-heh! Sa-vages. Mature savages. I think: There is freedom... Communism... Good heavens! How can one dream about Communism when such Ksyushkas are all around us! A guy ... Heh-heh! Please forgive us, for God's sake! A guy...

"The fool!" — thought Madame Luzin, and interrupted:

— Yes, what are we doing in the foyer?.. Come to the dining

room...

— Yes, my dear friend, please to the dining room, — affirmed Pavel Petrovich, — After you!

The entire group, bending over, passed under a black pipe and into the dining room.

— As I said, — continued Pavel Petrovich, embracing the guest by the waist, — Communism... indisputably, Lenin is a genius, but... would you like to try this from our ration... heh - heh! Today I received it... But Communism is such a thing that it, so to speak, by its nature... oh, is it broken? Take another, from the other side... By its path, it requires a certain development... Oh, is it wet? Oh these cigarettes! Try this one if you will... By its content... Wait a second, until it lights... Oh these matches! Also rationed... a certain consciousness...[2]

— Just a moment, Paul! Xavier Antonovich, tea before or after?

— I think... er-eh, before, — answered Xavier Antonovich.

— Ksyushka! The primus stove! Soon everyone will arrive! Everything is terribly interesting! Terribly! I also invited Sophia Ilinishna...

— And the table?

— We found one! We found one! But... it is made with nails. But I think it will be OK, right?

— Hmm... Of course, it isn't good... But somehow we'll manage...

Xavier Antonovich cast a look at the tripodal table with inlays and his fingers quivered.

Pavel Petrovich said:

— I must confess that I do not believe. No matter what you say, I do not believe. Although, in truth, in nature...

— Oh, what are you saying! It is insanely interesting! But I warn you: I will be scared!

Madame Luzin's eyes shone with life. She ran to the foyer, hastily touched up her hair in front of the mirror, and flew into the kitchen. From there one could hear the roar of the primus and the slam of Ksyushka's heels.

— I think, — began Pavel Petrovich, but he did not finish.

There was a knocking in the foyer. The first to appear was Helen, then a lodger. Sophia Ilinishna, a middle school teacher, didn't keep the others waiting. And immediately after her came Boboritsky with his fiancée Ninochka.

The dining room filled with laughter and tobacco smoke.

— For a long, long time we should have planned something!

— I, to be honest...

— Xavier Antonovich. You will be the medium! Say yes. Yes?

— Ladies and gentlemen, — demurred Xavier Antonovich, — I am, you know, in fact still among the uninitiated, although...

— Eh-eh, not! You had a table rising up into the air!

— I, to be honest...

— I swear, Manya saw a greenish light with her own eyes!..

— What a horror! I don't want to see it!

— With the lights on! With the lights on! Otherwise I won't agree to it! — screamed the sturdily built and materialistic Sophia Ilinishna, — otherwise I will not believe it!

— So be it... We give you our word...

— No, no! In the dark! Like when Julius Caesar tapped out to us our funeral dates...

— Oh, I can't! I can't ask about death! — cried Boboritsky's fiancée, and Boboritsky whispered languidly:

— In the dark! In the dark!

Ksyushka, mouth open in amazement, brought in the teapot. Madame Luzin rattled the cups.

— Quickly, ladies and gentlemen, let's not waste time!

And they sat for tea...

...On instruction from Xavier Antonovich, they covered the window completely with a shawl. They extinguished the lights in the foyer and ordered Ksyushka to sit in the kitchen and not to stomp her heels. They sat down, and it became dark...

II

Ksyushka immediately became bored and worried. Some kind of devilry... Darkness everywhere. They locked her in. First silence, then quiet measured tapping. Hearing it, Ksyushka froze. It was frightening. Again the silence. Then an unclear voice...

— Lord?..

Ksyushka shifted on the greasy stool and strained to hear... Knock... Knock... Knock... sounds resembling the voice of a guest (the sturdily built cow, forgive me, Lord!) mumbled:

— Ah, ha, ha, ha...

Knock... Knock...

Ksyushka on the stool, like a pendulum, rocked from fear to curiosity... Sometimes from behind the black window a devil with horns loomed at her, and other times she was drawn to the foyer...

Finally, she couldn't take it. She closed the door to the illuminated kitchen and ducked into the foyer. Feeling her way along with her hands, she banged into chests. She squeezed through further, groped, discerned the door, and nestled up to the keyhole... But in the keyhole was a hell of darkness, through which one could hear voices...

III

— Gho-ost, who are you?

— A, b, c, d, e...

Knock!

— E! — the voices sighed.

— A, b, c, d...

— Em!

Knock, knock, knock...

— Em-pe-ro!.. Uh-oh! — Ladies and gentlemen...

— Emperor Na-po... Knock... Knock...

— Na-po-le-on!! Oh my God, how interesting!..

— Quiet!.. Ask him! ASK HIM!

— What?.. Yes, ASK!.. Well, who wants to go first?..

— Ghost of the Emperor, — haltingly and excitedly asked Helen, — tell me, should I change my job from GovChem to RailCorp?[3] Or not?..

Knock... Knock... Knock...

— Bi... bimb-bo, — clearly answered Emperor Napoleon.

— Shee! — the impudent lodger chokes down a laugh.

The choke went around the chain.

Sophia Ilinishna whispered angrily:

— Are you really asking such nonsense!

Helen's ears burned in the darkness.

— Don't be angry, kind ghost! — She pleaded, — if you are not angry knock one time!

Napoleon, controlling the hand of Xavier Antonovich, who had contrived to do two things at once: to tickle the neck of Madame Luzin with his lips and to spin the table, swung the table leg and stuck it on a corn growing on Pavel Petrovich.

— Ss-s! — hissed Pavel Petrovich painfully.

— Quiet!.. Ask!

— You don't have strangers in the apartment, right? — asked the cautious Boboritsky.

— No! No! Speak boldly!

— Ghost of the Emperor, tell us, how much longer will the Bolsheviks be in power?

— A-ha... This is interesting! Quiet!.. Count!..

— Ta-ak, ta-ak, — tapped out Napoleon, pressing on one leg.

— Th... r... ee... three... months!

— A-ha!..

— Praise the Lord! — cried the fiancée. — I so hate them!

— Shh! Are you nuts?!

— No one is here!

— Who will overthrow them? Ghost, speak!..

They held their breaths... Ta-ak, ta-ak...

...Ksyushka was bursting from curiosity... Finally, she

couldn't take it. Recoiling from her own reflection flashing in the haze of a mirror, she squeezed her way between the chests back into the kitchen. Seized a handkerchief, darted back to the foyer, shaking a little before the door lock. Then having decided, she quietly opened the door and, freeing her heels, raced to Masha Downstairs.

IV

Masha Downstairs was found downstairs on the main staircase in front of the elevator, together with Duska from the fifth floor. Masha Downstairs had, in her pocket, 100,000 rubles worth of sunflower seeds.

Ksyushka poured it all out.

— They locked themselves in, girls... They take notes about an Emperor and about the Bolsheviks... It is dark in the apartment, a nightmare!.. The tenant, master, mistress, her stud, schoolmarm...

— No way! — exclaimed Ms. Downstairs and Duska, and the mosaic floor got covered with sticky shells...

The door to apartment № 3 slammed and Comrade Courageous, wearing unusual pants, moved down the stairs. Duska, Ksyushka, and Masha Downstairs watched from the corners of their eyes. The pants were cut normally to the knees, but from the knees they expanded, expanded, and became like bells.

A square bronzed chest was bursting out of a jersey, and at the hip a sharp-nosed barrel dimly and darkly peeped out from a leather thing.

Comrade Courageous, dashingly throwing a head with golden letters on the forehead, striding easily, bells dangling, descended to the elevator, and, having burned all three with a fleeting glance, headed for the exit...

— They turned off the lamps so that I, y'know, wouldn't see... Hee - hee!.. and they're taking notes... to the Bolsheviks, they say, kaput... The Enpirater... Hee! Hee!

Something happened to Comrade Courageous. The lacquered boots suddenly became steel-cleaved to the floor. His step slowed. Courageous suddenly stopped, searched in his pocket as if he had forgotten something, then yawned, and suddenly, obviously reconsidering, instead of going to the front door, turned, and sat on a bench, hiding from Ksyushka's view behind a glass protrusion with the title *Concierge*.

Apparently, a cracked red Cupid on the wall interested him. He fixed his eyes upon the Cupid and began to study him...

...With a relieved heart, Ksyushka stomped back. Courageous yawned dispiritedly, looked at his wristwatch, shrugged his shoulders, and seemingly bored of waiting for someone from Apartment № 3, got up, and, freely swishing the bells, set out on a march just a step behind Ksyushka...

When Ksyushka, trying to not slam the door, disappeared into the apartment, a match flashed in the dark of the landing under the white unit number '24.' Courageous was no longer steel-cleaved to the floor, or yawning.

— Twenty-four, — he said to himself intently, and cheerful and animated, he flew through all six floors like an arrow.

V

In the smoky darkness, Socrates, who had replaced Napoleon, worked miracles. He danced like a madman, predicting the Bolsheviks' imminent demise. A sweating Sophia Ilinishna incessantly repeated the alphabet. Everyone had numb hands, except for Xavier Antonovich. Murky white silhouettes flashed in the haze. Just as nerves were strained to the limit, the table with the-sitting-within-it-wise-Greek fluttered and floated up.

— Ah!.. Enough!.. I'm scared!.. Please! Dearest! Ghost! Higher!.. No one is palming it with his feet?.. No, no!.. Shh!.. Ghost! If you are here, play 'A' on the piano!

The Greek dropped from above and thundered with all fours on the floor. Something inside him burst with a crack. Then he floundered and, stepping on the feet of the shrieking ladies, began to advance towards the piano... Spirits, knocking foreheads, dashed after him...

Ksyushka jumped up in the kitchen like a scalded cat from a calico blanket. Her squeak: "Who is this?" went unheard by the delirious spiritualists.

Some kind of new, evil, and spooky ghost took possession of the table, throwing out the dearly departed Greek. With his feet thundering menacingly, like a machine gun, he rushed from side to side pouring down some kind of gibberish:

— Dra-too-ma... bwe... ee... ee.

— Dear spirit! — moaned the spiritualists.

— What do you want?

— The door! — burst at last from the berserk spirit.

— A-ha!.. The door! Do you hear! He wants to run to the door!.. Release him!

Knock, knock, knock, — limped the chair to the door.

— Stop! — shouted Boboritsky suddenly, — you see what kind of power he has! Let's see if he can knock on the door from here!

— Spirit! Knock on it!!

And the spirit surpassed expectations. From the outside, he thundered so hard, as if with three fists at once.

— Aii!! — yelped three voices in the room.

And the spirit was indeed fleshed with power. He began drumming in such a way that the spiritualists' hair stood on end. Suddenly, breaths froze, silence descended.

In a trembling voice, Pavel Petrovich shouted:

— Spirit! Who are you?

And from behind the door, a sepulchral voice replied:

— The *Cheka*.[4]

...The ghost cravenly vanished from the table, in a split second. The table, leaning on a damaged leg, stood still. The spiritualists petrified. Then, Madame Luzin moaned: "Oh my Go-o-d!" and quietly swooned in an unaffected faint on to the chest of

Xavier Antonovich, who hissed:

— To hell with this idiotic venture!

The shaking hands of Pavel Petrovich opened the door. Instantly the lamps lit up, and a ghost appeared before the pale-as-snow spiritualists. He was leather. All in leather, starting with his cap and ending with his briefcase. Not only that, he wasn't alone. An entire procession of demi-ghosts loomed in the foyer.

A square bronzed chest flashed, polyhedral barrel, gray overcoat, another overcoat...

The ghost cast his eyes on the chaos in the spiritualistic room and, grinning ominously, said:

— Your documents, comrades...

EPILOGUE

Boboritsky went to prison for a week; the lodger and Xavier Antonovich: 13 days; Pavel Petrovich: one and a half months.

Translators' notes

Bulgakov based characters in "Spiritualistic Séance" on his acquaintances, Ivan Pavlovich Kreshkov, Vera Fedorovna Kreshkova, and their maid Ksyushka. Kreshkov tried to beat up Bulgakov after the story appeared.

According to Bulgakov's first wife, Tatyana Lappa, Bulgakov once suggested that they host a spiritualistic séance in the apartment of the Kreshkovs. "He was supposed to give me signals with his leg and I was supposed to do as he said. And make some kind of noises."

1. The *third position* is both a ballet pose and an ideological stance. The ballerina stands with right foot in front of left, heels together, toes apart. The ideologue stands neither on the right nor on the left—he dances neither the Marxist March nor the Capitalist Tango.

2. In this paragraph, Pavel Petrovich interleaves his opinion on Communism with a courteous offer of a rationed cigarette to his guest. Minus the courteous offer, the opinion about Communism reads: *As I said, Communism... Indisputably, Lenin is a genius, but Communism is such a thing that it, so to speak, by its nature, by its path, requires a certain development; by its content [requires] a certain consciousness.*

The courteous offer reads: *Would you like to try this from our ration? Heh-heh! I received it today. Oh, is it broken? Take another, from the other side. Oh, is it wet?*

Oh these cigarettes! Try this one if you will. Wait a second, until it lights. Oh these matches! Also rationed.

3. GovChem and RailCorp are abbreviations for government-owned industries. In the original, the names are *Glavkhim* and *Jeleskom*. *Glavkhim* is an abbreviation for *Glavnoye upravlenie khimichekoy promishlennosti*, the Central Administration of the Chemical Industry. *Jeleskom* is an abbreviation for *Komitet lesozagotovok i oborudovaniya dlya jeleznikh dorog*, the Committee on Wood and Steel Supply for Railroads.

4. *Cheka* is an abbreviation for *Chrezvychaynaya kommissiya*, the Extraordinary Commission, which was the first Soviet state-security organization. *Cheka* was created by decree of Lenin on Dec. 20, 1917. It committed tens of thousands of political murders. In 1922, *Cheka* became part of *NKVD (Narodny kommissariat vnutrennikh del)*, the People's Commissariat for Internal Affairs, and was renamed *OGPU (Gosudarstvennoye politecheskoye upravelnie)*, the Political Directorate of the NKVD. *OGPU* was directed by aristocrat-turned-communist Felix Dzerzhinski. In 1946, it became *MVD (Ministerstvo vnutrennih del)*, the Ministry of Internal Affairs. In 1954, *MVD* became *KGB (Komitet gosudarstvennoy bezopasnosty)*, the Committee for State Security; and, in 1995, after the collapse of the USSR, *KGB* became *FSB (Federalnaya sluzhba bezopasnosty)*, the Federal Security Service.

The Russian-language newspaper "Nakanune" (On The Eve), Berlin, September 24, 1922

The Escapades of Chichikov (Похождения Чичикова)

A poem in N paragraphs
with a prologue and epilogue

— Hold on, hold on, you fool! — shouted Chichikov to Selifan.

— I'll get you with a sword! — shouted a galloping-towards-them courier with 28-inch-long moustache.

— Can't you see, the devil take you, this is a public carriage.

Prologue

An outlandish dream... It was as if Satan the Jester had opened the doors in the kingdom of shadows, over whose entrance flashes an inextinguishable lamp with the inscription *Dead Souls*.[1] The dead kingdom began to stir and from it stretched, in an endless stream...

Manilov, in a fur coat astride large bears, Nozdryov in an appropriated carriage, Derzhimorda on a fire truck, Selifan, Petrushka, Fitinya...

And the very last to set off was He, Pavel Ivanovich Chichikov, in his famous *britchka*.[2]

And the whole gang marched on Soviet Rus' and after that, astonishing incidents happened there. Concerning these incidents, several points follow.

I

In Moscow, having exchanged his britchka for a car, Chichikov, while flying in it through the ravines of Moscow, cursingly cursed Gogol:

— A plague on him, the devil's son, the plaguesome brat! He trashed and messed up my reputation so that there is no place I can snoop my nose into. If they find out that I am Chichikov, naturally, they will throw me out! And it would be good if they would only throw me out, rather than the worst case in which I would have to spend my days, God forbid, in *Lubyanka*.[3] And all of it because of Gogol, a plague on him and his relatives!

And thinking thusly, he drove through the gates of the very same hotel that he had left a hundred years ago.

Positively everything in it was the same: cockroaches peeped out of the cracks and even, it seemed, there were more of them, but there were certainly some changes. For example, instead of the sign *Hotel*, there hung a poster with the inscription: *Dormitory № such and such* and it goes without saying that the dirt and mud would have been hard for even Gogol to imagine.

— Room!

— Paperwork please!

Not for a single second was the brilliant Pavel Ivanovich rattled.

— The manager!

Capital! The manager turned out to be an old friend: bald Uncle Pimen, who once ran *Akulka*, and has now opened a cafe on Tverskaya Street in the grand style with German amusements: flavored rum drinks, herbal liquors and, of course, prostitutes. The guest and the manager embraced, chatted for a bit, and, without any paperwork, the matter was resolved in an instant. Then Pavel Ivanovich had a bite of whatever God provided, and flew off to enter the workforce.

II

He appeared everywhere and enchanted everyone with his bowing, slightly slanted to one side, and with his colossal erudition, which has always distinguished him.

— Fill in the questionnaire.

They gave Pavel Ivanovich a questionnaire more than two feet long, and on it one hundred of the trickiest questions: Where was he from? Where had he been, and why?..

It didn't take Pavel Ivanovich even five minutes to scribble over the entire questionnaire. When he was submitting it, only his hand quailed a little.

— Well, — he thought, — they will read it now, this treasure, and...

And absolutely nothing happened.

First, no one read the questionnaire, and secondly, it ended up in the hands of a young lady, the registrar, who disposed of it as usual. Instead of placing it as *incoming*, she put it as *outgoing* and then immediately tucked it away somewhere, so that the questionnaire disappeared as if sunk in the water.

Chichikov grinned and entered the workforce.

III

And then it went easier and easier. At the outset, Chichikov looked around. He saw that wherever you spit, you find one of your own. He flew to an institution where they issue rations. There, he overheard:

— I know you chiselers: you take a live cat, scalp it, and then pass it off as rations! Give me steak with my pasta. Because I would not place your ration's frog into my mouth, even if sugar-glazed, and your rotten herring, I will also not take.

He looked closely. It was Sobakevich!

As a first order of business, Sobakevich, as soon as he arrived, had begun to demand a ration. And he got one! He finished it and then requested a supplement. They gave him a supplement. Not enough! Then they gave him a second ration; the first was regular size, the second was a knockout dose. Not enough! Then they gave him an armored dose. He gobbled it up and demanded more. And then screamingly demanded. Cursed everyone as Christ-sellers, said that here the swindler swindles the swindler and is punched by the swindler and that there is only one decent man, a clerical assistant, and he, truth be told, is a swine!

They gave him an academic portion.

As soon as Chichikov saw how Sobakevich finessed the rations, he immediately joined him. But of course, he outdid Sobakevich. For himself, he received a ration for a non-existent wife and child, for Selifan, for Petrushka, for his own uncle whom he told Petrishchev about, and for an old mother that he didn't have. And for all of them, the academic portion. So much that a truck had to deliver the products to him.

Having settled the question of nutrition, he traveled to other institutions to get things done.

Flying over Kuznetsky in a car, he met Nozdryov. The first thing Nozdryov said was that he had already sold both the chain and the watch. And, indeed, on him there was neither watch nor chain. But Nozdryov was not in despair. He said how lucky he had been with a lottery, in which he had won a half-pound of vegetable oil, a glass from a lamp, and soles for children's shoes, but then he lost his luck and in addition he, goddammit, put into the lottery his own 600 million. He said how he had proposed to the Foreign Trade Ministry to export a consignment of authentic Caucasian daggers. Which he exported. And he would have made a jillion of money, if not for those English bastards that saw the inscription *Blacksmith Saveliy Siberian* on the daggers and rejected them all. He dragged Chichikov to his room and poured him an amazing cognac, allegedly received from France, which, however, smelled like moonshine in all its force. And finally, he out-lied himself to such an extent that he claimed that he had been given 1,800 feet of textile, a blue car with gold trim, and the rights for commercial space in a building with columns.

When Nozdryov's son-in-law Mizhuev expressed doubt, Nozdryov simply called him an asshole.

In a word, he annoyed Chichikov to the point that he didn't know how to get the hell out.

Yet the stories of Nozdryov led him to think of getting into the foreign trade himself.

IV

So he did. And again he filled in a form and began to act, and showed himself in all his glory. Wearing two-layered sheepskins, he drove sheep across the border, and under the sheepskins he carried Belgian lace. He also drove diamonds: in wheels, shafts, ears, and God knows where else.

And very soon 500 billion of capital appeared in his hands.

But he did not stop, and submitted paperwork to a certain institution stating that he wishes to rent some company and, painted in remarkable colors the benefits the state would receive as the result of this enterprise.

At the institution, they simply unzipped their mouths – the benefits, indeed, were colossal. They asked him to identify the enterprise. Certainly. On Tver Boulevard, just opposite the monastery, across the street, it is called Pampush on Tverbul. They sent an inquiry to the authorities: Is there such a thing. Response: There is and it is known throughout Moscow. Excellent.

— Give us technical estimates.

Chichikov's estimates are already in his pocket.

The lease is approved.

Then Chichikov, without wasting time, flew to another institution:

— May I get a loan?

— Provide a statement in three copies with appropriate signatures and seals.

Two hours hadn't passed, when he presented the statement. In accordance with the instructions. Seals as numerous as the stars in the sky. With signatures prominent.

Director: Mr. Disrespect-Trough, Secretary: Mr. Jug Mug, Chair of the Tariff Commission: Ms. Elizabeth Sparrow.

— All right. Here is the loan approval statement.

The cashier almost choked, glancing at the total.

Chichikov signed, and drove away with the banknotes in three cabs.

And then to another institution:

— A business loan please.

— Show us the product.

— Ok, do me a favor. Let me see the appraiser.

— Give him the appraiser.

Capital! And the appraiser is a friend: the scatterbrain Emelyan.

Chichikov took him for a drive. Brought him over to a random basement along the way and showed him around. Emelyan saw that the number of goods was incalculable.

— Hmmm... And all of this is yours?

— All is mine.

— Well, — said Emelyan, — in that case I congratulate you. You are not just a millionaire, but a trillionaire!

Nozdryov, who had tagged along, poured even more fuel on the fire:

— Do you see, — he said, — a car entering the gate with boots inside? The boots are also his.

And then he got excited, dragged Emelyan into the street and showed him around.

— You see the shops? So these are all his shops. Everything that is on this side of the street. It's all his. What's on the other side, it's his too. You see the trams? His. Streetlamps? His. See? See?

And he spins him around in all directions.

So Emelyan cried out:

— I believe! I see... Just leave my soul in peace.

They went back to the institution.

The institution asks:

— So?

Emelyan just waved his hand:

— It, he says, is indescribable!

— Well, if it is indescribable. Give him N +1 billion.

V

From that point on, the career of Chichikov took on a head-spinning form. The things that he did were inconceivable. He founded a trust for the manufacture of iron from sawdust and for this purpose also received a loan. He became a shareholder in a huge co-operative and fed all of Moscow sausage made from the most rancid trimmings of rancid meat. Landowner Korobochka having heard that nowadays everything is 'permitted' in Moscow, wanted to buy real estate: Chichikov formed a company with Mr. Zamuhryshkin and Mr. Comforting and sold her the arena facing the University. He grabbed the contract for the electrification of the city, a project that will lead nowhere in three years, and having established contact with the former mayor, put up some kind of fence, put up survey stakes so that it looked like the layout of the plan, and as for the money allocated for electrification, he wrote that it had been stolen from him by the gangs of Captain Kopeikin. In a word, he performed miracles.

And shortly thereafter, a rumor buzzed throughout Moscow that Chichikov was a trillionaire. Institutions began to scramble to recruit him as their specialist. Chichikov took over a 5 billion ruble five-room apartment, Chichikov dined and supped at The Empire.

VI

But suddenly came the collapse.

Chichikov was ruined by Nozdryov, as correctly predicted by Gogol, and finished off by Korobochka. Without any wish to do a nasty trick to him, but just from being drunk, Nozdryov ran off at the mouth about the sawdust, and the fact that Chichikov rented a non-existent company, and capped it off by saying that Chichikov was a crook and that he ought to be shot.

The public thought about it, and then, like a spark, rumors took wing.

And then stupid Korobochka elbowed her way into an institution to ask when she would be able to open a bakery in the Manege. They swore to her in vain that the Manege is a public building and that it is neither permitted to buy it nor to open anything there. The silly woman understood nothing.

And the rumors about Chichikov became worse and worse. They started wondering what kind of bird this Chichikov was, and where he came from. Rumors appeared, one more sinister and monstrous than the other.

Anxiety moved into hearts. Telephones rang, meetings commenced. The Building Commission went to the Supervisory Commission, the Supervisory Commission to the housing division, the housing division to the People's Commission of Healthcare (NARKOMZDRAV), NARKOMZDRAV to the Directorate of Custom Fabrication (GLAVKUSTPROM), GLAVKUSTPROM to the People's Commission for Enlightenment (NARKOMPROS), NARKOMPROS to the Proletarian Cultural Division, and so on and so forth.

They rushed to Nozdryov. This was, of course, absurd. They knew that Nozdryov was a liar, that one should not believe a single word of his. But they summoned Nozdryov and he responded to all of the points.

He testified that Chichikov indeed rented a non-existent company, but that he, Nozdryov, did not see a reason not to take it, since everyone was taking. To the question as to whether Chichikov was a spy for the Whites, he responded that he was a spy, and that recently they even wanted to shoot him, but for some reason he was not shot. To the question as to whether Chichikov produced counterfeit bills, he said that he did, and even told an anecdote about the extraordinary dexterity of

Chichikov: how, having learned that the government wanted to issue new banknotes, Chichikov had rented an apartment in Maria Grove and from there released counterfeit bills for 18 billion, two days earlier than the real ones, and when the truth transpired and the apartment was raided and sealed, Chichikov in one night mixed the fake with the real ones, so that the devil himself could not distinguish which banknotes were counterfeit and which were real. To the question as to whether Chichikov exchanged his billions for diamonds so as to flee the country, Nozdryov replied that it was true, and that he took it upon himself to help and participate in this enterprise, and if not for him, nothing would have worked.

After the stories of Nozdryov, everyone was seized by utter dismay. They saw no possible way to find out what Chichikov is, no way. And who knows what would have happened if it had not been for one guy amongst them. It's true, that he, like all the others, did not even leaf through Gogol, but he did possess a small dose of common sense.

He exclaimed:

— Do you know what this Chichikov is?

And when everyone in unison thundered:

— What?

He pronounced, in a sepulchral voice:

— A swindler.

VII

Then it dawned on everyone. They dashed to search for the questionnaire. No questionnaire. In the incoming? Not there. In the files? No. They went to the registrar.

— How should I know? Ask Ivan Grigorich.

— Where?

— It's none of my business. Ask the secretary, etc., etc.

Then suddenly, unexpectedly, in a wastebasket, there it was.

They started to read and were stupefied.

Name: Pavel. Middle Name: Ivanovich. Last Name: Chichi-kov. Occupation: Gogol's character. What did you do before the Revolution? Bought dead souls wholesale. Attitude towards the draft? Neither this nor that, nor God knows what. To which party do you belong? Compassionate (to whom is *unknown*). Were you ever on trial? [a wavy line]. Address? Turn into the yard, on the third floor, to the right, ask the information desk for staff-officer Podtochina, she knows.

Personal signature: An ink blob!

They finished reading and were petrified.

They called instructor Bobchinsky:

— Drive your ass over to Tver Boulevard to the rented-by-him property and to the yard where his goods were. There may still be something there!

Bobchinsky returns. Wide-eyed.

— An emergency!

— So?

— No, there is no business there. He gave the address of Pushkin's monument. And the goods are not his, but belong to the American Relief Administration.

And everyone howled:

— Holy Saints! What a goose! And we gave him billions! It turns out that now we have to catch him!

And they started to hunt.

VIII

A finger pressed a button:

— Courier!

A door opened and Petrushka appeared. He had left Chichi-kov long ago and entered the institution as a courier.

— Take the package immediately and get going immediately.

Petrushka said:

— Yes, sir.

He took the package immediately, got going immediately, and

immediately lost it.

They called to the garage for Selifan:

— Get the wheels. Now!

— I'll be right there.

Selifan snaps to it, covers the motor with a pair of heavy pants, pulls on his jacket, hops onto the seat, whistles, hums, and flies off.

What kind of a Russian does not like to go fast?

Selifan also liked it, and for this reason at the entrance to Lubyanka he had to choose between a trolley car and the glass window of a shop. In a split second, Selifan chose the latter, veered from the trolley car and, like a whirlwind, screaming "Help!" entered the shop through the window.

Even Tentetnikov, who was in charge of all the Selifans and Petrushkas, lost his temper:

Fire their asses!

They were fired. Sent to the Labor Exchange. From there, they sent Plushkin's Proshka to replace Petrushka, and in place of Selifan, they sent Gregory Go-Never-Get-There.

In the meantime, the business boiled over even more!

— The loan approval statement!

— Certainly.

— Ask Mr. Disrespect-Trough to appear.

It appeared it was impossible to ask. Two months ago, Mr. Disrespect was purged from the Party, and he had purged himself from Moscow immediately after this, because there was absolutely nothing for him to do.

— Mr. Jug Mug!

He left for the middle of nowhere to advise provincial offices.

They turned to Elizabeth Sparrow. There is no such person! It is true that there is an Elizabeth the typist, but she is not a Sparrow. There is also an assistant to a vice-junior clerk of a vice-director of a junior department named Sparrow, but he is not an Elizabeth!

They pressured the typist:

— You?!

— What are you talking about! Why me? The name 'Elizabeth' is spelled here with a 'z' but mine is spelled with an 's'...

And she bursts into tears. They left her alone.

Meanwhile, while they were fiddling around with Mr. Sparrow, the lawyer Samosvistov tipped off Chichikov on the sly that a flutter had started regarding the case and, of course, Chichikov's trail went cold.

In vain had they a car to the address: turning right, of course, no property was found, there was only an abandoned and dilapidated public diner. And then Fetinya the maid came out and said that no soul was around.

Truth be told, turning left, they found the information desk, but sitting there was not Podtochina the officer's wife, but someone named Podstega Sidorovna and, as a matter of fact, she herself was unaware not only of Chichikov's address, but of her own.

IX

Then despair attacked everyone. The case had become so entangled that even the devil would not find anything to his taste in it. The non-existent rent mixed with the sawdust, the Belgian lace with electrification, and Korobochka's purchase with diamonds. Nozdryov got his foot stuck in the case. The sympathetic scatterbrain Emelyan and the nonpartisan thief Anton turned out to be implicated in the case as well, and some kind of Panama Canal was opened with the rations of Sobakevich. And the ball started rolling!

Samosvistov worked tirelessly and mixed into this hodgepodge some trips regarding trunks and a case of fraudulent invoices for travel expenses (this case alone implicated close to 50,000 persons) and so on and so forth. In a word, only the devil knows what started to happen. And those who had billions discharged from under their noses and those who were supposed to find them, thrashed about in terror. In front of them there was only one immutable fact:

There were billions and they had disappeared.

Finally someone's Uncle Mitya stood up and said:

— Let's face it, brothers... Clearly we can't avoid appointing an investigation commission.

X

And here (what can't one see in a dream!), I myself appear *deus ex machina* and say:

— Entrust it to me.

They, in amazement:

— And you... That... can you make heads or tails of it?

I:

— Do not worry.

They hesitated. Then the red ink:

— Authorized.

Then I began (in my life I haven't had a more pleasant dream!).

From every direction, 35 thousand motorcycle cops flew to me:

— Do you need anything?

And I say to them:

— I need nothing. Do not distract yourself from your work. I can manage myself. Singlehandedly.

I filled my lungs with air and shouted so that the windows shook:

— Get Lyapkin-Tyapkin on the line!

— Unable to connect... The phone is broken.

— A..ha! Broken! The cord is broken? So that it does not dangle in vain, hang yourself on it!

Goodness gracious! What have I started here!

— Excuse me, sir... What do you, sir... This very... Hehe... Just a minute... Hey! Repairmen! The cord! They will get it fixed in a moment.

They fixed it in two shakes and handed it to me.

And I zoomed ahead:

— Tyapkin? Sh..shithead! Lyapkin? Go after him, the rascal! Give me the lists! What?! They aren't ready? Get them ready in five minutes, or you yourself will appear in the lists of the dead! Eh, who is this? Manilov's wife was the registrar? Drag her out by the scruff of her neck! Ulinka Betrissheva, the typist? Scruff of the neck! Sobakevich? Go after him! Does the scoundrel Mirzofeykin work for you? Mr. Schuller Comforting? Go after him! And whoever appointed him, go after him too! And him! And him! And that one! Fetignya, get out! Send Poet Tryapich-kin, Selifan, and Petrushka to the precinct for booking! Nozdryov, to the dungeon... Right this minute! This second! Who signed this statement? Go after that rascal! Fish him up from the bottom of the sea!

A thunderclap reverberates around Hell...

— Lo and behold! The devil has landed! Where did they find him?

I:

— Bring me Chichikov!

— Imp.. Imp.. Impossible to locate him... He esssscaped.

— So, he esssscaped? Marvelous! So you will sit in his place.

— Have mercy...

— Shut up!

— Just a moment... This very... Wait a second. Searching, sir.

And they found him in two shakelets!

And, in vain, Chichikov sprawled at my feet, tore at his hair and jacket, and swore that he had a disabled mother.

— Mother? — I growled, — Mother?.. Where are the billions? Where is the public money? Thief! Cut up this bastard! He has diamonds in his belly!

They opened him up. There they were.

— That's all of them?

— All, sir.

— Tie a stone to his neck and into a hole in the ice!

And all became quiet and clean.

And I'm on the phone:

— Clean.

And they say:

— Thank you. Ask what you want.

So I danced around the telephone. And I nearly sent all the elusive fantasies that had long tormented me through the telephone handset:

"Trousers... a pound of sugar... a lamp with 25 candles..."

But suddenly I remembered that a decent writer should be selfless, I wilted and muttered into the phone:

— Nothing, except for the works of Gogol in a binding, the works that I recently sold at a flea market.

And... Bang! On my desk is the gilt-edged Gogol!

I was so glad to see Nikolai Vasilyevich, who had comforted me on a gloomy sleepless night more than once, that I roared:

— Hurray!

And...

Epilogue

...Of course, I woke up. And there was nothing: no Chichikov, no Nozdryov, and most importantly, no Gogol...

— E-heh-heh, — I thought to myself and began to dress, and the humdrum of daily life was again parading before me.

Translators' note

1. *Dead Souls* is a novel by Nikolay Vasilyevich Gogol (1809–1852). The main character, Chichikov, travels throughout Russia acquiring ownership of serfs who are already dead so that he may qualify for a higher civil rank and its attendant benefits. In "The Escapades of Chichikov," Bulgakov brings Gogol's characters to 1920's Moscow, where they quickly find themselves right at home.

Gogol was Bulgakov's favorite author. Bulgakov's works are often referred to as *Gogolian*. In his masterpiece, *The Master and Margarita*, Bulgakov transports Satan and his retinue to Moscow. Bulgakov's third wife, Yelena Sergeevna, united the two authors in death by obtaining a large burial stone from Gogol's grave and placing it on Mikhail Afanasevich's grave. Gogol's grave is also located in the *Novodevichi* cemetery, the most famous necropolis in Moscow.

If you google *Gogol*, you will learn that Gogol is considered the father of Russian realism. He wrote about con artists, cheats, crooks, bullies, chiselers, misers, the complacent, the cruel, the sentimental, the stupid, and the self-absorbed. His writing exposed the dogs at the heart of the corrupt Russian empire, a service for which the reward was, in his case, exile.

2. A *britchka* is a horse-drawn carriage.

3. *Lyubyanka* was a notorious prison in Moscow. It also served as the headquarters of the *Checka*, the secret police.

A translation of "The Escapades of Chichikov" by L.D. Kesich can also be found in the book *Great Soviet Short Stories*, edited by F.D. Reeve, Dell Publishing, New York, 1962, p 59.

Pavel Chichikov. Artist, P.M. Boklevsky, 1892. The original is in the Museum of Literature, Moscow.

The newspaper "Nakanune" (On The Eve), Berlin, December 31, 1922

A Cup of Life (Чаша жизни)

A funny Moscow story with a sad end

Truly, before God, I tell you, citizen, I am lost because of the cursed Pal Vasilich... he seduced me with a cup of life, and then he betrayed, the scoundrel!..

This is how it was. I'm sitting, you know, peaceful and quiet at home, occupied with a calculation. But, of course, it isn't just 'a calculation.' In reality, my salary is 210. Fifty remains in my pocket. So one calculates: ten days until the first. What does it come to? It comes to five per day. Correct. Can one manage? It is possible, if you are calculating about it. Splendid. But then the door opens and Pal Vasilich enters. I tell you, a fur coat on him isn't just any fur coat, and a hat on him isn't just any hat. I think, what a bastard! Red-faced, and I sense that he smells like port wine. Creeping behind him is someone, also well dressed.

Pal Vasilich immediately introduces him:

— Allow me to introduce, — he says, — one of ours, also from the Trust. And he slaps the table with his hat and shouts:

— I'm burned out, my friends! Work's been eating me alive! I want to relax, spend the evening in your company! I beg you, friends, let's drink from the cup of life! Let's go! Let's go!

So, how much money do I have? I render the account: 50. But I am a gentleman, I am not used to mooching off of others. And what can you do on 50 rubles? And these are my last!

I reply:

— Money I have n...

He looks at me just so.

— You swine, — he screams, — insulting a friend?

Well, I think, if that's the case... And so, off we went.

And as soon as we went off, the wonders began! A janitor is chipping ice from the sidewalk. And Pal Vasilich flew up to him, grabbed the ice scraper from his hands, and he himself began to chip.

While doing this, he shouts:

— I am an intellectual proletarian! I do not despise work!

And through one of the galoshes of a comrade passerby: snip! He cut it. The janitor dashed to Pal Vasilich and pulled the scraper from his hands.

And Pal Vasilich roared:

— Comrades! Help! I am, a responsible proletarian, being beaten!

Of course, there is a scene. A crowd gathered. I see that things are bad. The guy from the Trust and I snatched him up under the arms and into the first doorway. The door sign read: ...*Supply of Wine*. The comrade is behind us, with the galosha in his hand.

— May I have money for my galosha?

And what do you think? Pal Vasilich unzips his wallet and as I looked into it I was horrified! Nothing but hundreds. A wad four fingers thick. Oh my God, I think. And Pal Vasilich peels off two banknotes and says to the comrade with disdain:

— Pppulease, c-comrade.

With that, he began to laugh through his nose, like an actor:

— A-ha-ha.

That guy, of course, scrammed. Those galoshes at today's prices wouldn't fetch more than 50. Well, tomorrow, I think, he will buy a pair worth 60.

Marvelous. We sat down and it began. Moscow port wine, y'know? A man doesn't get drunk on it, just loses all power of comprehension. I remember we ate crawfish and suddenly found ourselves in Passion Square. In Passion Square, Pal Vasilich hugged some lady and kissed her three times: on the right cheek, on the left, and again on the right. I remember we were laughing, but the lady was left in a daze. Pushkin standing, looking at lady, and lady at Pushkin.

And then, the street vendors swooped in with bouquets, and

Pal Vasilich bought a bunch and crushed them under his feet.

And I heard a muffled voice from a throat:

— May I offer you a rrr-ide?

We got in. The cabman turns to us and asks:

— Where to, your Excellency, your order?

Pal Vasilich! His Excellency! Look at this bastard, I think!

And Pal Vasilich flings open his fur coat and replies:

— Wherever you wish!

He turned the wheel, and we flew like a whirlwind. And after five minutes, a stop on Neglinny Lane. And then he grunted with the horn three times like a pig:

— Oin... Oink... Oink.

And what do you think! To this very 'oink' come valets! They jumped out of a door and grabbed us under our arms. And the maître d'hôtel, like some kind of Count:

— Ta-ble.

Violins:

Under the hot sky of Argentina.

And some man in a hat and a coat fully half covered by snow dances among the tables. Here Pal Vasilich has already turned not red, but some form of blotchiness, and he thundered:

— Away with these port wines! I want champagne to drink! Waiters scattered, and the maitre d'hôtel bowed:

— I can recommend a brand...

And the corks started flying around us like butterflies.

Pal Vasilich embraced me and shouted:

— I love you! Enough of this rotting in your *Centrosoyuz* co-operative. I appoint you to our Trust. We are now laying off, which means there are openings. At the Trust, I am czar and god!

And his trusty friend croaked: "Right, you are!" And from the excitement a glass went to the floor and into smithereens.

You won't believe what happened next with Pal Vasilich!

— What, — he screams, — you want to show the breadth of your soul? Smashed a glass and you are happy? Hah hah-ha. Get a load of this!!

And with those words, a stemmed vase went to the floor... BANG! And the friend of the Trust... another glass! And Pal Vasilich... a condiment set! And the one from the Trust... another glass!

I regained consciousness only when they presented the check. And then I saw through the mist: 1 billion 912 million. Yes-s.

I remember, Pal Vasilich wet the wad of banknotes and... wshhht... peels off five hundreds and says to me:

— Friend! Take this loan! You are vegetating in your *Centrosoyuz*! Take 500! When you join us in the Trust, then you will have your own!

Citizens, I could not resist. I took the 500 from this scoundrel. Judge for yourself: he would blow this money on booze anyway, the rascal. There is easy money in their trusts. And then, can you believe it, as I took this accursed 500, something suddenly seized my heart.

And I turn mechanically and saw, through the mist, sitting in the corner, some man. And standing in front of him, a bottle of seltzer. He is looking at the ceiling, but it seems to me that he is looking at me. As if, y'know, he has invisible eyes, an extra pair on his cheeks.

And somehow, I suddenly became nauseated, I cannot express it to you!

— *Hop, tsa, dritsa, hop, tsa, tsa!*

And we cake walked to the door. And waiters waving napkins rushed to the front!

Then the smell of fresh air in my face. I also remember the cabman grunting again, and perhaps I rode standing. Where to isn't known. I completely lost my memory...

And I woke up at home! Half past two.

And, my God, I can't lift my head! I remembered with difficulty what happened yesterday and, as the first order of business,

I checked my pocket. Here they are: the five hundred! Well, I think, swell! And although my head is coming apart, I lie there and dream how I will work at the Trust. I convalesced, drank tea, and my head felt a little better. And early in the evening, I fell asleep.

And then in the middle of the night, the doorbell rings...

And I think, probably, it is my aunt arriving from Saratov.

And through the door, barefoot, I ask:

— Auntie, is that you?

And from behind the door, the voice of a stranger:

— Yes. Open it.

I opened it, and froze...

— May I be permitted... — I say, and my voice is gone, — to know what it is about?..

Ah, the scoundrel! What do you think happened? During the investigator's interrogation Pal Vasilich (he was seized this morning) revealed:

— I gave 500 of it to citizen so and so.

Which means me!

I wanted to shout: It is not the case!

And, you know, I looked at him, the one with a briefcase, in the eyes... And I remembered! Oh! Heavens, seltzer! The eyes that were on his cheeks are now on his forehead!

I froze... I don't remember now how I pulled out the 500... Then, cold-bloodedly, he says to the other:

— Attach him to the case.

And to me:

— Be so good as to get dressed.

Oh my God! Oh my God! And as we were approaching, I saw, through my tears, a bulb burning above a sign *Commandant's Office*. Here I dared to ask:

— What is it that this bastard did that I should lose my freedom because of him?

And he says through his teeth, sneeringly:

— Oh, nothing of importance. And it doesn't concern you.

And what exactly doesn't concern me? The next thing I know, he is indicted on almost seven counts... giving bribes, taking them, negligent storage, and, most importantly, embezzlement! Here's how the 'nothing of importance' turns out! It is he, it turns out, the most scurrilous of all scoundrels, living his last evening, drinking the cup of life! So... in short, they let me out after two weeks. I rushed to my office in the department. I knew in my heart that someone new, in a field jacket, with a part in his hair, would be sitting at my desk. He said:

— Layoffs... And besides, with everything that had happened... It's also awkward...

And he turned his back and picked up the phone.

I was numb... received severance pay... 105 for two weeks, and left.

And so, since then, I endlessly wander... and wander, without a lunch break. And if there is one more week like this, I think I'll kill myself.

DEVELOPMENT OF TRANSPORT. ONE OF THE MOST IMPORTANT TASKS FOR FULFILLMENT OF THE FIVE-YEAR PLAN. Artist: G. G. Klutsis (1929)

1923

The newspaper "Golos rabotnika prosveshcheniya" (The Voice of an Employee of the Educational System), № 4, Moscow, March 15, 1923

KNP and KP (Каэнпе и капе)

A big room. The secretary and the commission had arranged themselves at a table with a pile of applications. In the hallway, behind the door, a crowd of school workers waits their turn. They summon name number one. The door opens, showing for a moment several anxious faces, and a teacher enters. She worked these years in a province, just recently has come to Moscow. Dressed poorly and provincially: men's style boots on her feet. Just at the doorway, she sighs heavily.

— Sit down, please.

— Mer... ci, — says the teacher in a broken voice, and sits on the edge of a chair. They look over her cover letter and application.

— With what did you engage the children there?

— Field trips... — says the examinee quietly.

— So, describe then, what did you do on the field trips?

A pause. The teacher moves her fingers, then says, between blanching and blushing:

— Well... we studied a flower...

— Describe how you studied it.

Pause.

— So, you studied... Why? For what purpose?

The teacher after a heavy sigh:

— Beau-ty...

— What kind of beauty?

— The flower... it's beautiful... I told the children how beautiful the flower is...

— You believe that children develop an understanding of the beauty of a flower from your stories?

Silence and grieving are in the eyes of the candidate. Sweat appears in small beads on her upper lip.

— What material did you read on the topic of the field trip?

Silence.

— Enough, — says the chairman, with a sigh.

The candidate exits, having sighed deeply and noisily.

— K-N-P, — says the chairman, — bad. (KNP means 'Kandidate Not Pass.')

The next wishes to be employed at an orphanage.

— What are the goals of an orphanage?

— I would try to develop the children, we would occupy them with...

— Hold on a second. What are the goals of an orphanage in general?

—– I would try...

— The goals of an orphanage, what are they?

— I would...

— Well, okay. What would you do with the children?

— I would... er… introduce them to the new contemporary social movements... I would...

— Speak more simply, be honest. Which contemporary social movements are we talking about... What would you do with the children? Simply. Maybe it would be 1,000 times better than all these figments and movements.

— We would arrange holiday parties… I would...

— Hmmn... What meaning do you attach to holidays in the life of children?

— They are eager... field trips... The 1st of May...

— What meaning do you attach to holidays?

— I would...

— Enough.

A German woman. Speaks with an accent.

— Do you resort to Russian language in your lessons?

— I try... to avoid... the ear of the baby accustoms...

— Tell us in German, how do you teach?

— *Ja... das ist sehr schön*, — and the German woman glibly describes her methodology.

— Enough.

The German lady politely bids them farewell, says:

— *Danke schön. Auf Wiedersehen!*

K-P. Good. (KP means 'Kandidate Pass.')

A mature teacher from Samara. With experience.

— What composition of students was there at your school?

— Russian, German... and *Khokhols.*[1]

— Excuse me, — reproachfully says the chairman, — why do you call them that? It would be unpleasant if they started to call us *Katsaps!*[2] 'Ukrainians,' and not *Khokhols.*

— What kind of Ukrainians are they... — indifferently protests the teacher, — Ukrainians are more in the Ukraine. And ours are trans-Volgans... so... *Khokhols.* They also speak incorrectly...

— Hmmm... all right. You taught Russian language? What books did you use?

— What kind of books could we get? Soldiers were stationed there at the beginning of the Revolution. They smoked all the books.

— Hmm... so what did you do?

— Field trips.

— Field trips, according to a plan?

— Oh, yes.

— Where did you take the children?

— To the bone-grinding mill. To excavations.

Several more questions. She responds coherently. She has a knack for the job, apparently. Has read something. Enough.

The next ones go. People of all sorts. Here's one, desires non-academic work; his specialty is rhythm programs, gymnastics, and singing. A teacher of German language. An elementary school teacher. A candidate for the post of director of the neuropsychiatric clinic. A schoolmaster of a boarding school.

Here is one in a black coat wearing a shawl on her head. Wishes to direct an orphanage.

— What literature have you read?

— "Readings on Upbringing" by Baltalon, "Worker's School" by Sinitsky.

— Any others?

Silence.

— What is your view regarding the work of the director of an orphanage?

— I sympathize with the new social movement.

— In what way?

Silence.

— What will you do with the children?

— Holidays... the 1st of May...

— What kind of explanation will you give the children on the 1st of May?

— To whom? The children?

— Well, yes. To the children.

Silence.

— What do we celebrate on the 8th of March?

Silence.

— Have you heard of the International Day of the Female Proletarian?

Silence.

— Do you ever read newspapers?

— Hmm... no... I don't get to the newspapers much.

— Enough. K-N-P.

The next one. Also aims for the orphanage.

— What will you do with the children?

— Holidays... 1st of May.

— Hmm... well, besides holidays. For example, what if it is necessary with the children on a religious question to spe...

— I am against all religions! — cheerfully responds the candidate.

— Hmm... well, that's good. But what if is necessary with the children...

— Religion is the jimson weed of the people! — confidently responds the teacher.

— Well, yes. But what if it is necessary with the children...

— Yes, the church is separated from the state!

— Well, yes. But what if it is necessary to speak with the children about a question of religion. Suppose, for example, the children hear church bells ringing. They get interested by it. What discussion would you conduct with them?

Silence.

— What's your take on the Comprehensive Method of Teaching?

— I somehow have not heard about it...

— Hmm. Enough.

A young teacher from the outback, from the city of Surozh. Came here to study in the Medical Pedagogical College. He has no means. Wants to become a schoolteacher.

— How will you combine college with teaching? It will harm the college and the school.

— What can one do about it? — he sighs, — many are doing it. It will be necessary to sacrifice part of the lectures. It is hard.

And it is, indeed, apparently hard. He is wearing an old sheepskin coat. An oily shirt.

The commission begins to ask questions. He coherently describes the arrangement of field trips.

— Why do you want to arrange excursions in the springtime?

— In springtime nature is reborn. We will observe the blooming of flowers.

— What will be the first flower you will encounter? The earliest?

— Sleep-grass.

More questions. He responds thoughtfully. To the most intricate questions, he honestly says:

— This, I myself have not grasped.

The commission confers and gives him a probationary period.

Behold a highly qualified one. From the most advanced courses for women. She will be graduating from the Petrovsky

Academy. She wants to work in the № 2 Suburban School with Agricultural Specialization. Approved. K-P.

Behold an already elderly teacher. In his hands, a cap with a faded velvet band. He taught French and Russian in the provinces in Morshansk in a secondary school. Wrote in the newspapers. Here is his poem "To the Learning Youth." A hymn.

— Translate your hymn to French.

— *A la jeunesse etudiante...* — the teacher begins, — ... *nous esperons...*

Stumbles a little.

— Your pronunciation is poor. But, as regards the Russian language, tell us what you did?

— I must say... — the teacher, having coughed, continues, — the studies were heavily affected by the absence of heat... There wasn't firewood. It was cold. But, nevertheless, we did something.

He describes how he analyzed the work of Gorky and Chekhov concerning the theme 'on public service.'

The commission confers, pronounces him worthy to occupy the position of a teacher of the Russian language.

More come. More unskilled masses. They read little. Know little. Indolent, lacking initiative.

But here is one. She wants the orphanage. Responds briskly. There is skill, wit. She stumbles on one point only. The commission asks which poems she will give to the children in the first grade.

— This one: Tyutchev:

> *Russia is a thing of which*
> *The intellect cannot conceive.*
> *Hers is no common yardstick.*
> *You measure her uniquely:*
> *In Russia you can only believe!*

— You will give them this?

The teacher wavers...

— This one! Hmmn...

— How would you explain the phrase: "In Russia you can only believe?"

She sighs. Wavers.

— How would you yourself explain it to them?

She goes silent.

— Well, how would you interpret it?

— Uh... I don't know, — confesses the teacher.

Behind the door there are fewer people. The pile of applications diminishes. The last ones pass through.

A young man bombs it, hadn't read anything. Puffing. Silent. K-N-P.

A young schoolteacher from the provinces. She hadn't read anything. No knowledge. Blushes. Ringlets stuck to her forehead.

Bad. K-N-P.

— That's it, — says the secretary. The commission rises and disperses. Through the corridors cheerfully leave those who answered successfully, and the unfortunates, scenting a negative response.

The classroom empties. Then empties the corridor.

Translators' notes

1. Russians call Ukrainians, pejoratively, *Khokhols*.

2. Ukrainians call Russians, equally pejoratively, *Katsaps*.

The Russian-language newspaper "Nakanune" (On The Eve), Berlin, July 29, 1923

Moonshine Lake (Самогонное озеро)

At 10 p.m., before Easter Sunday, our accursed hallway became quiet. In the blissful silence, the burning thought was born in me that my dream had been realized and that the bimbo Pavlovna, who trades in cigarettes, had died. I decided this because the cries of her tortured son Shurik did not carry from Pavlovna's room. I smiled voluptuously, sat down in the torn armchair, and unfurled Mark Twain's volume. Oh this blissful moment, this bright hour!

…Then, at 10:15, in the corridor, a rooster thrice crowed. A rooster is nothing special. Indeed, a suckling pig lived in Pavlovna's room for half a year. In general, Moscow is not Berlin, for one thing, but in the second place, you will in no way astonish a man who has lived for one-and-a-half years in the corridor of № 50.

It wasn't the fact of the unexpected appearance of a rooster that frightened me, but rather the circumstance that the rooster sang at 10 p.m. A rooster is not a nightingale and, even in the prewar times, it sang at dawn.

— Did these villains really get a rooster drunk? — I asked my poor wife, after pulling myself away from Twain.

But she did not have time to answer. Following the entrance flourish, an unbroken howling began from the rooster. Then a male voice began to wail. And howl! It was an uninterrupted bass howl in C-sharp, of soulful suffering and desperation, an agonal, painful howl.

All the doors started drumming, footsteps thundered. I dropped Twain and sprang for the corridor. In the corridor, under the lamp, within a tight circle of amazed inhabitants of the famous corridor, stood a citizen unknown to me. His legs were spread as wide as the letter W, he rocked, and without shutting his mouth, emanated the most frenzied howl, which frightened me. In the corridor, I caught how the inarticulate long note gave way to the intoned recitative:

— Such a one, — hoarsely choked and howled the unknown citizen, being doused by large tears, — Christ is risen! Very well you act! So you will belong to no one!!! A-a-a-a-a!!

And with these words, he tore bundles of feathers from the tail of the rooster, which thrashed in his hands.

One glance was sufficient to ascertain that the rooster was completely sober. But on the face of the rooster was written inhuman suffering. Its eyes were popping out from the orbits, it clapped its wings, and thrashed out from the tenacious hands of the unknown citizen. Pavlovna, Shurka, the chauffeur, Annushka, Annushka's Misha, Duskin's husband, and both Duskas stood in a circle in perfect silence, motionless, as if nailed to the floor. On this occasion, I do not blame them. They even lost the gift of speech. They saw, as did I, the scene of the peeling of a live rooster for the first time.

The *kvartkhoz¹* of apartment № 50, Vasily Ivanovich, crookedly and desperately smiled. Grasping the rooster first by the elusive wing, then by the legs, he tried to pull it from the unknown citizen.

— Ivan Gavrilovich! Be God fearing! — he yelled, sobering up before my eyes. — No one is taking your rooster away, be it thrice cursed! Do not torment a bird on the eve of Easter Sunday! Ivan Gavrilovich, come to your senses!

I was the first to come to my senses and with inspired voltage knocked the rooster out from the hands of the citizen. The rooster shot up, struck heavily against the lamp, then descended, and disappeared behind a turn to where Pavlovna's pantry is. And the citizen instantly calmed down.

The case was extraordinary, if you please, but only because it ended successfully for me. The *kvartkhoz* was not saying to me that if I don't like this apartment I could look for a mansion for myself. Pavlovna was not saying to me that I burn a lamp until 5 a.m., occupying myself "with who knows what kind of business," and that I, in general, needlessly intrude here, where she lives. She has the right to beat Shurka because it is her Shurka. And let me bring forth for myself "my own Shurkas" and eat them with porridge. (My "Pavlovna, if you hit Shurka on the head again, I will file a lawsuit on you and you will be imprisoned for a year for the torture of a child" didn't help). Pavlovna threatened that she will file a claim to the administration so that they would evict me. "Really, if someone is not pleased, let him go there, where the educated people are."

In a word, nothing happened this time. All the inhabitants of the most famous apartment in Moscow dispersed into the sepulchral silence. The *kvartkhoz* and Caterina Ivanovna led the unknown citizen by the underarms to the stairs. The red stranger walked trembling and rocking, silently bulging his doomed and ebbing eyes. He resembled a man poisoned with henbane. Pavlovna and Shurka caught the exhausted rooster under the tub and also took it away.

Caterina Ivanovna, upon her return, narrated:

— My son of a bitch (read: the *kvartkhoz*, the husband of Caterina Ivanovna) went for groceries like a good husband. He bought a fifth from Sidorovna. He invited Gavrilych, let's go, he says, and try a little. People are usually decent, but they, forgive me my sin Lord, lapped up their fill before the priest in the church rang the morning bell. I have no idea what happened to Gavrilych. They finished the bottle and my husband said to him: why are you, Gavrilych, going with the rooster to the bathroom. Give him to me, I will hold him. But then suddenly, he gets mad. And, he says, you, he says, want to appropriate my rooster? And he began to howl. Lord only knows what on earth he was imagining!

At 2 a.m., the *kvartkhoz*, after breaking the fast, broke all the windows, thrashed his wife, and explained his action by the fact that she ate up his life. I was at that time with my wife at Morning Prayer and the scandal proceeded without my participation.

The population of the apartment trembled and summoned the chairman of the administration. The chairman of the administration appeared immediately. With blazing eyes, red as a flag, he looked at the bruised Caterina Ivanovna, and said:

— I am surprised at you, Vasily Ivanych. You are the head of a household and are unable to cope with some bimbo.

This was the first time in the life of our chairman when he was not delighted with his own words. It fell to him personally, to the chauffeur, and to Duskin's husband to disarm Vasily Ivanych. In fact, he himself got his hand cut (Vasily Ivanych, after the words of the chairman, had armed himself with a kitchen knife in order to cut Caterina Ivanovna: "Now I will show her"). The chairman, having locked Caterina Ivanovna in the pantry of Pavlovna, convinced Ivanych, that Caterina Ivanovna had run away, and Vasily Ivanych fell asleep with the words:

— OK, tomorrow I will slaughter her. She will not escape my hands.

The chairman left with the words:

— That Sidorovna's moonshine is one helluva evil beast, that home-brew.

At 3 a.m., Ivan Sidorych showed up. Publicly I declare: if I were a man, and not a rag, I would, of course, throw Ivan Sidorych out from my room. But I fear him. After the chairman, he is the most powerful person in the administration. Maybe he won't succeed in evicting us (or maybe he will, the devil only knows!), but he can poison my existence at will. For me this is the most terrible thing. If someone poisons my existence, I will not be able to write feuilletons, and if I do not write feuilletons, then a financial crash will occur.

— Herro… Mr. Djourn-a-lisht, said Ivan Sidorych, rocking like a blade of grass in the wind. — I came to see you.

— Nice to see you.

—I'm here about the eshperanto…

— ?

— I would like to write a note... an article... I desire to open a shociety... Sho write thus: "Ivan Sidorych, experantist, deshires, pleashe"...

And suddenly Sidorych started speaking with me in Esperanto (by the way, an amazingly repulsive language).

I do not know what the esperantist read in my eyes, only that he suddenly crumpled, the strange dock-tailed words, resembling a crossbreed of Latin-Russian words, began to drop and Ivan Sidorych moved into an easily understood language.

— Actually, exshcuse me... I will come tomorrow.

— You are welcome anytime! — I affectionately answered, escorting Ivan Sidorych to the door (he, for some reason, wants to leave through the wall).

— He cannot be expelled, can he? — asked my wife, upon his departure.

— No, honey, it is impossible.

In the morning, at 9 a.m., the holiday began with a performance by Vasily Ivanovich on the accordion (Caterina Ivanovna danced), and the speech of the into-smithereens-drunk Annushka's Misha, addressed to me. Misha, on his own behalf, and on behalf of citizens unknown to me, expressed to me his respect.

At 10 a.m., the junior yard-keeper arrived (slightly drunk), at 10:20 the elder (dead drunk), at 10:25 the stoker (in a terrible state). He kept silent and silently left. He lost the five million I paid him right there in the hallway.

At noon, Sidorovna impudently underfilled a fifth for Vasily Ivanovich by three fingers who then, bringing along the emptied fifth, headed to a place where things are investigated, and stated:

— They are selling moonshine. I want them arrested.

— Are you sure? — they asked him darkly, where things are investigated. — According to our information, there is no moonshine on your block.

— None? — bitterly smiled Vasily Ivanovich. — Your words are very remarkable.

— There is none indeed. And how is it that you appear sober, if you really have moonshine? You'd better go and sleep it off. You will file a complaint tomorrow about those who have moonshine.

— OK... understood, — said Vasily Ivanych, smiling dazedly. — So it means there is no regulation of them? It's OK to under fill you? As regards to my sobriety, smell the fifth!

The fifth proved to be "with the clearly expressed smell of fusel oils."

— Lead the way! — they then said to Vasily Ivanovich. And he brought them there.

When Vasily Ivanovich awoke, he said to Caterina Ivanovna:

— Run off to Sidorovna's for a fifth.

— Wake up, damned soul, — answered Caterina Ivanovna, — Sidorovna's was shut down.

— What? But how did they get wind of it? — Vasily Ivanovich said with surprise.

I rejoiced, but not for long. A half-hour later, Caterina Ivanovna appeared with a full fifth. It turned out that a fresh source started flowing at Makeich, two houses from Sidorovna.

At 7 p.m., I pulled Natasha away from the hands of her husband, the baker Volodya. ("Do not dare to beat!!," "My wife" and so forth).

At 8 p.m., when Matlot burst out dashing and Annushka began to dance, my wife arose from the sofa and said:

— I can't take any more of this. Do what you want, but we must get out of here.

— Honey, — I answered in desperation. — What can I do? I am not able to get a room. It costs 20 billion, and I make four. Until I complete the novel, we cannot hope for anything. Be patient.

— It's not about me, — answered my wife. — But you will never finish the novel. Never. Life is hopeless. I will take morphine.

With these words, I felt that I had become iron. I answered

and my voice was full of metal:

— You will not take morphine because I will not permit you to do that. And I will finish the novel and, I dare to assure you, it will be such a novel that heaven will become hot.

Then, I helped my wife to dress, secured the door with lock and key, and asked the first Dusya (she drinks nothing but port wine), to make sure that nobody breaks the lock, and I drove my wife away for three days of holiday, to Nikitskaya, to her sister's.

EPILOGUE

I have a program. Over the course of two months, I shall undertake to effect a desiccation of Moscow, if not completely, then by 90 percent.

Terms and conditions: I will run the show. I will personally select the staff of candleholders from students. They must receive a very high stipend (400 gold rubles. The deal is authorized). 100 hires. For me, an apartment with three rooms with a kitchen and a lump sum payment of 1,000 gold rubles. A pension to my wife in the event that they kill me. Unrestricted authority. By my order, they will be taken without delay. A trial within 24 hours, with no possible change in fine.

I will carry out a massacre of all the Siderovs and Makeiches and a reflectively just massacre of The Corner Standers, Flowers of Georgia, and Tamara's Lock.

Moscow will become like the Sahara, and there will be only light red and white wines in the oases under the electric signs that read *Business open until 12 midnight*.

Translators' notes

One of the many reasons for loving this feuilleton is its Russian title, *Samogonnoe ozero*, which is an allusion to the ballet *Lebedinoe ozero* (*Swan Lake*) by Tchaikovsky.

1. *Kvartkhoz* is an abbreviation for *glava kvartirnogo khozyastva*, the manager of a communal apartment.

Chanson d'Été (Шансон д'этэ)

A summer song (from Fr. *chanson d'été*)

A RAINY INTRODUCTION

The summer of 1923 in Moscow was very rainy. One ought to decipher the word 'very' here. It doesn't mean that it rained often, say, every other day, or even every day. No, it rained three times a day and there were days when it did not stop at all. On top of that, about three times a week it rained at night. Downpours began unexpectedly. Hour-and-a-half-long thick downpours with green lightning and hail that attained the size of pigeon eggs.

At the end of the flood, when the first blue tufts had just appeared in the sky, unusual voyages were taking place on the streets of Moscow. For a price of 5 million, they were crossing in cabs and drays from one sidewalk to another. On top of that, one could see men riding on one another, and women going on foot with legs naked to the permissible limits, and beyond those limits.

During rare intermissions, when the sky over Moscow resembled whipped cream, Muscovites said:

— Well, thank God the weather is settling itself down. It hasn't rained for half an hour...

Several blue–gray barrels rode onto Tverskaya Street and Theater Square, each drawn by a horse driven by a man in overalls (canvas coat and helmet of the same canvas). Water plopped in tablespoon dollops, through frequent holes in a horizontal pipe placed behind the barrel, leaving a damp track four-feet in width behind the riding-at-a-snail's-pace barrel.

Sitting at the window of a tram, I penciled a count in a notebook: To water Theater Square, one would need simultaneously

90 such working barrels, assuming they ride at a full gallop.

The sky, in mockery of the sprinkling barrel, responded with sinister cannon peals, with oblique machine-gun hail that smashed windows, and with rivers of water that flooded basements. On Neglinny Lane, two women drowned because an underground pipe broke and exploded the pavement. Fire teams worked siphoning water from Café Riche. Cabdrivers' nags were going mad from the whipping hail. This was in June and July. After that, the crude barrel cart disappeared, and the rain assumed normal form.

But if the barrel cart appears again at Theater Square to tease the heavens, the responsibility for the death of Moscow will indeed rest on it.

MULTICOLORED MUSHROOMS

The rainfall summoned up an interesting mushroom sprout in Moscow. The first to appear, at all the street crossings, were the red-capped ones. These were policemen in a new uniform. On them, caps with red bands, black on top with green braid, tunics, tabs in the same green, and breeches. With whistles, badges, and traffic wands resting in their cases, they make an appearance so gallant that the eye pleasantly rests on them. The police bosses are positively brilliant.

Roaring, howling, quacking cars numbering three and a half thousand are running around Moscow, and at all the crossings, the sculpted red-capped figures on green legs circle, euro–coquettishly.

Trams in Moscow have a composed appearance: no one is hanging on the footboards, and no one, not a single man in Moscow, jumps on or leaps off while the tram is in motion. The Moscow Council attained the tram ideal in some five or six days, through the brilliant and simple establishment of a 50-ruble fine, payable at the scene of the crime. But, over the course of these six days, near the trams and inside the trams, there was a sizeable commotion. The red-capped ones, with citation books, popped up exactly as if from underground, and politely fined the dumb-struck Russians.

The most obstreperous paid, not 50, but 500, and not at the place of the jump, but at the police station.

MAY I HAVE A LIGHT?

The success of the tram fine had quite unexpected consequences. Exactly a week ago, at Lubyanka Square, I approached a citizen at a tram stop, and asked him for a light. Instead of extending me a cigarette, the citizen rushed to escape from me. Deciding that he was crazy, I moved further along Theater Avenue and received three more refusals.

At the words: "May I have a light?" citizens paled and hid cigarettes behind their backs. I lit up behind a column at the Alexandrov passageway next to the Myur department store. Notably, the one giving me a light looked around, like a wolf. I learned from him that a decree had come out to fine for lighting up on the street. The basis: idlers delay Soviet workers who are hurrying to work.

Frankly, I must confess that I was among those who agreed. It all ended after several days with a note in *Izvestia*, in which Muscovites were called 'Philistines.' But the melancholic tone of the article clearly showed that the author himself, duly manifesting his civil duty, never lit up.

Never-seen-before mushrooms, with black caps, sprouted after the red mushrooms. These are youngsters, of male and female genders, wearing caps exactly like those of boy–receptionists in foreign cinematographic films. The black-capped ones have bands on their arms and trays with cigarettes on their stomachs. On the cap is a gold inscription: *Mosselprom.*[1] And so, Mosselprom went into a final and decisive battle with the illegal street trade. A wonderful idea, all the more so because the black caps, it turns out, are unemployed students. But the point is that students love reading books. Therefore, very often on the stomach was a tray, and on the tray, *Historical Materialism* by Bukharin. *Historical Materialism*, no doubt, is an interesting book, but business has its own whims and laws. It demands that a man spin, yell, harass, and remind one of his existence. The public looks at the black caps favorably, but is sometimes afraid to ask about goods from a man with a book because to harass a boy who's busy reading with a demand for matches is impudent. Perhaps he is preparing for an exam?

I would write on these trays, in gold:

Book Now, and Business Later[2]

Me, personally, I like the white mushroom best of all. This is a multistory apartment house on Novinsky Boulevard, which sprouted in place of unfinished, abandoned-during-the-war red brick walls.

To build, to build, to build! We must go to bed with this thought. With it we must rise. Our salvation is in construction, our way out, success. At an exhibition park, pavilions have already sprouted,[3] railway lines branch, and from transportation parks sometimes exit brilliant lacquered tram cars (probably, a major repair), but we need housing even more.

SUMMER RESIDENTS, MAY THE DEVIL TAKE THEM

And so, it started this year. They moved in clouds along all the rail lines that diverge from Moscow and sat on the necks of the villagers. The villagers welcomed them like Biblical locusts, but fat locusts; and, for each hour of their sitting, stripped from them as much as possible. All March long, the Ellie Mays and Jethros[4] used credit to purchase dairy cows, material for pants, scythes, and dishware in anticipation.

The Ivan Ivanoviches and Maria Ivannas took with them kerosene lamps, *Keys to Happiness*,[5] blankets, and scrofulous children. They settled into wooden chicken coops and howled from mosquitoes. A week later, it turned out they were malarial mosquitoes. The summer residents drank real dairy milk, which was diluted 50 percent with water; and quinine, for which the village pharmacies took three times more than in Moscow. Male parasites with rotten boats perched on all the rivulets. Female parasites were at the outposts with ice cream, beer, cigarettes, and dirty cherries. In the verdure, caressing the eyes, grew the beautiful inscription:

Game of Lotto at Khyazma Starting at 5 p.m.

And everywhere: *Restaurant.*

At rivulets and ponds, motors jabbered until dawn. Flocks of bearded vultures in blue caftans hung out at the outposts and stripped off more for 1/6 mile than they take for one mile in Moscow.

For meat, for apples, for firewood, for kerosene, for blue milk... double!

— Our beach, sir, is extraordinary... You will be satisfied. On Sundays, what a scandal. Stark naked, in their birthday suits, they lie all along the river. Only behold: a single rain drop and they're gone. (To himself.) What kind of people are these, forgive me Lord! During the day, they lie naked along the river; at night, devils carry them into the woods!

The villagers rose at 3 a.m. to work; the vacationers at this time went to bed. During the day the villagers milked cows, mowed, harvested, cleaned, and pounded with axes; the vacationers languished in wooden cells, read *To Atlantis* by Benois, hung out in the rain in a melancholy quest of beer, invited vacationing doctors to treat them for malaria, and, in the mornings, in installments, yawning, agonizing, standing, rushed in vacationer railcars to Moscow.

In the end, the rain overpowered them, and they began to desert in battalion strength: to Moscow, the Hermitage, and the Aquarium. After five or six days they all will return. There's no escape from them!

THE FINAL CHORD

The rain, can you imagine, started again.
We will leave for the shore,
There, waves will kiss our feet.

Translators' notes

1. Bulgakov is playing with the proverb, *Delu vremya, a potekhe chas,* which translates as 'business now, fun later.'

2. *Mosselprom* is an abbreviation for *Moskovskaya assotsiatsiya predpriyaty selsko-promishlennoy produktsii,* the Moscow Association of State Enterprises Processing Agro-industrial Products.

3. Bulgakov is referring to permanent exhibition space supported by the government, whose purpose was to showcase and promote industrial development. This idea was most fully realized under Stalin and resulted in the creation of multiple *VDNHs, Vystavka dostizheniy narodnogo khozyastva,* (Exhibition of the Achievements of the National Economy), which were parks in major cities containing pavilions devoted to each major industry. The pavilions contained exhibitions of machinery and manufactured products.

4. For readability, we replaced the stereotypical first names of male and female villagers—Egor and Akulina—with rural American equivalents. In the next paragraph, Ivan Ivanovich and Maria Ivanna are simply common Russian names, like Smith or Jones.

5. *Keys to Happiness* is a series of five best-selling books (1909–1913) by the Russian author Anastasia Aleksandrovna Verbitskaya, each of which sold in excess of 40,000 copies. The subject of the series was the sexual liberation of women.

Beware of Counterfeits! (Остерегайтесь подделок!)

> We rely only upon our former allies, the French, and in particular, upon Monsieur Poincaré...
>
> *(From the so-called 'manifesto' of Russian workers, printed in "The New Time")*

— They don't believe me, the bastards! — said Mikhail Suvorin. — They say that Russian workers won't be able to pronounce the name *Poincaré*. I'm about to lose my cool. If this manifesto isn't persuasive, then I don't know what else to do!

— Here's what I think, — said Rennikov, — let's send a delegation of Russian workers to *Die Rote Fahne*.[1] Coco Shakhovsky promised me that he would find experienced actors, who played in "The Fruits of Enlightenment." These guys will pull it off... it will be delicious...

— Well, all right, — said Suvorin wearily.

***

The editor of *Die Rote Fahne* looked at the delegates sternly and asked: "Comrades, where did you learn German so well? It's just amazing!"

— It's from the prisoners of war, — quickly retorted the head of the delegation, the unmarried farmer, Varsonofy Pumpkin. — During the War, we had a lot of them in our villages.

— They are good people, the German captives! — underscored Stepan Drafty, the worker from Petrograd, — indeed they are of a hostile nationality and of different customs, but we have come together... Just as the saying goes: *les extrémités se touchent*[2]...

— You probably learned French from the captives as well? — the editor asked ironically.

The delegates fumbled. From embarrassment, Stepan Drafty took out his monocle from somewhere in his jacket and placed it to his eye. But he changed his mind upon hearing the derisive whispers of the others and hastened to hide it back.

— So you say *Poincaré* is the most popular name among Russian workers? — continued asking the editor of *Rote Fahne*.

— There's no question about it! — firmly said Ostap Steppenwolf, by consensus the Bashkirian nomad. — I am a worker, so I know. My uncle, thank God, owned two factories...

— In Bashkortostan? — was the malignant editor-question.

— Actually, — muttered the embarrassed delegate, — he's not exactly my biological uncle. In Bashkortostan, we call neighbors uncles. An uncle is a he-neighbor and an aunt is a she-neighbor.

— And a grandma? — was the point-blank editor-question.

— A grandma is... when she is from another village... — mumbled the Bashkirian.

— Mussolini's also a very popular name among Russian workers, — hurriedly started the head of the delegation, Varsonofy Pumpkin, so as to change the subject. — We have a shepherd in our village, a lovely old man, who converses about him so openly: *Ecce,* — he says!

— A classical observation! — said the editor laughing. — Your shepherd is an educated old man. Probably a philologist?

— A lawyer, — readily picked up Soviet deputy Anna Cheboksarov, the textile worker from Ivanovo–Voznesensky, — he was directly in line for the Senate, but now...

***

— Bastards! Scoundrels! — grumbled Mikhail Suvorin. — Look at you! You staged "The Fruits of Enlightenment"... You yourselves should be staged instead of "The Fruits of Enlightenment!" Put all of you in a row and punch, in the mug, in the mug, in the mug...

— We're not guilty of anything, — sullenly objected Varsonofy Pumpkin, aka Coco Shakhovsky. — It was bad luck, nothing more! Everything was going fine, but as soon as Madame Kuskova started speaking, the whole thing went to ashes! He, the rascal, recognized her voice. "I," he says, "once heard you giving a lecture. Excuse me," he says, "but you will not deceive me!"

— Scoundrels! — hissed Suvorin. — And regarding Rennikov, I will...

But Rennikov was not around. He, Rennikov that is, knew that, in the event of failure, it is dangerous to appear near Suvorin. His hand was heavy and the letterpress on his desk was even heavier...

Ol-Wright

Translators' notes

1. The German newspaper *Die Rote Fahne (The Red Flag)* was established in Berlin on November 9, 1918 by Karl Liebknecht and Rosa Luxemburg. It became the central publication of the Communist Party of Germany (January 1, 1919). During the Nazi regime, from 1933 to 1942, underground groups distributed it illegally.

2. The French expression *les extrémités se touchent* means the extremes touch one another.

The newspaper "Nakanune" (On The Eve), Berlin, October 17, 1923

A Restless Trip (Беспокойная поездка)

The monolog of a CEO (not a fairy tale, but a true story)
Dedicated to the Head of the Central Railroad

Malbrouck s'en va en guerre![1]
From a folk song

— Well, as a matter of fact, it happened like this. In the evening, after tea, I set off with my colleagues from Novorossiysk Station, according to schedule. Just before departure, someone comes up to me and says:[2]

— Well, — he says, — here's the story: our turntable is under repair. I have no idea how we are going to turn you.

We began thinking. Finally, I say: in that case, have them turn us in Tikhoretskaya. Okay. If it is to be in Tikhoretskaya, then it must be in Tikhoretskaya. We sat down, whistled, and departed. Well, we arrive in Tikhoretskaya. Just imagine: on time. I look at my watch and am surprised: to the minute! Here, I say, cool. And, of course, I've spoken too soon. As if Satan himself had landed on their turntable. They turned and turned, maybe they turned for an hour and a half. I feel that I am getting dizzy. "Will it be soon?" I yell. "Just a moment," they respond. Well, they turned and began to assemble a train. I looked out the window: a positive picture, valiant work. They run around, whistle, and wave with flags. Fine fellows, I say, the boys at this Tikhoretskaya are eager beavers. But, of course, I spoke too soon. Just before the departure, some guy comes up to me and says:

— It's impossible to move...

— What?! — I shout. — Why?..

— Yes, — he says, — in a moment, we will start aborting a few cars from the train. They are inoperative.

— Then abort them, quick! — I shout. — Why the devil did

you assemble them in the first place?..

No answer. He coyly smirked and left. Again, they started whistling, waving, and running. Finally they aborted the sick cars. We were delayed by two and a half hours because of this procedure.

Finally, we set out. Thank God, I say, now we are rolling. Well, I spoke too soon, of course!

Our train put on such speed that, can you imagine, when I lost my pince-nez through the window, the conductor jumped from the train, picked it up and, at a trot, caught the train. I shouted then: What are you, joking, or what? At such a speed, how can I determine the condition of the tracks and the rail-cars?.. Get me to the speed limit for freight trains on this track in 24 seconds! Well, as you may imagine, I yelled at them in such a way that I was not happy in the end! They did put on the speed, but what then started boggles the mind! We thundered and rolled. Five minutes later, I hear a shout: "Stop, stop! Stop, for Christ's sake!" They are pulling a rope, waving a flag. I was scared to death. Well, I think, we are screwed! I yell, "What's the matter?" The answer: the axle-bearings are burning. I lost my temper. I shout, "What a mess!" On what basis are they burning? "Stop! Abort! Detach!"

Marvelous. At the first station they detached a car. And we set out again.

Well, wouldn't you know, we haven't galloped three steps, when again there is a rumpus. The axle-bearings in two cars have caught on fire! Aborted these two. In the next section, two more caught on fire. Five stations later, I looked out the window and was horrified. When I set out, the train had been long, like the Paris meridian, and now it had become short, like a pig's tail. Holy Saints, I think, in this manner, after another 50 miles, I will lose the entire train. And what if suddenly, I think, it starts burn-ing in my car, then at some station they will detach me to the devil! But I'm expected in Rostov. I summon the person in charge and say: "Look, you should be kind of... lighter. To hell with your speed limit. Go, as decent people go, not with a speed that makes your eyes pop."

Excellent. We set out, and I head for the observation car to look at the scenery. And what do you think I see? Some two pinheads are sitting on the bumpers in front of my very eyes. I lean out the window and ask:

— Wh-what is this?.. What are you doing there?

And they, can you imagine, respond, so impudently:

— The same as you. Going to Rostov.

— How? — I scream. — On the bumpers?.. So, it means, you're rabbits.[3]

— It is clear, — they respond, — that we aren't tigers.

— How is it possible, — I shout, — rabbits... On the bumpers?.. On my railcar?.. On the staff?.. On the staff-only railcar? Pop off of there like corks!

— Yeah, right, — they answer, — pop off! You pop off, if you're sick of life. You pop off right here while moving, you break both arms and legs!

What is there to be done? Hmmm?.. I yell: "Send a signal! Sto-o-p the train!.. Remove these rabbits!"

It wasn't meant to be. There is no signal, as it turns out. There's no direct connection with the locomotive.

We started yelling through the window to the engineer:

— Hey! My good man! He-ey! What's your name? Be a pal, slow down! — It wasn't meant to be. He doesn't hear!

What would you do while these two are sitting on the bumpers, giggling?

— What? — they say, — did you have us removed? Bite me!

You see what insolence this is? In addition to the violation of the rules, more importantly, I cannot see a damn thing in the observation windows. Two grinning mugs are sticking out and obstruct the whole landscape. I see that there is nothing I can do about them, so I start to negotiate.

— Listen, — I say, — here are 50 rubles for each of you, just get off.

They refused. Give us, they say, five hundred each! What should I do?

And here, can you imagine, just then, to my good fortune: an incline. The train, understandably, stopped. Can't make it. You bet I was happy. I shout, "Seize them, these slaves of God! Show them what it means to ride on the bumpers!" Well, of course, the conductors flew down, seized them, put them into a railcar, and we got back underway. Splendid. I had just cuddled up to the window when the train stopped! What now? — I yell. It turns out that it is again because of those accursed rabbits. It is impossible to restrain them! They burst from the hands and, game over! We made a council of war here, and in the end decided to release them to the pigs. And that's what we did. We released them five miles from the station. They were grateful, said thank you, we were aiming for this very station anyhow, and the five miles we will go on foot...

We rolled on. After ten minutes: Stop! What?! A rabbit! Well, I could not take it any longer and started crying. What, I say, did I do to deserve this disaster? Will I ever make it to Rostov or not? As I am saying this, tears pour down like a stream. I am crying, the conductors are weeping, and the rabbit could not stand it and also started sobbing. And all this disgusted me such that I wished my eyes didn't see it! I threw up my hands, drew the curtains and went to bed. I arrived in Rostov and was treated for a nervous breakdown. That's the story, that's how trips can be!

Translators' notes

1. *Malbrouck prepares himself for war!* is from the French folk song "Marlborough Left for the War."

2. Direct speech was set inconsistently in this piece. Sometimes with en dashes (—), sometimes with quotes, and still other times as indirect speech (i.e., *He said that the food was good*, instead of *He said, "The food was good."*)

3. 'Rabbit' (*zayats*) is slang for a person who is trying to beat the fare on a train or other public transportation.

The newspaper "Gudok," Moscow, November 1, 1923

The Secrets of the Harem (Тайны мадридского двора)

Mr. Gloomy, a clerk in the 2nd Reconstruction Organization, sat in a room illuminated by a kerosene lamp and said to his guest, the clerk Petukhov:

— You have it good, you devil! You live in Kiev. You're surrounded by all kinds of antiquities: shrines, monasteries, theaters, and cabarets... and here, in this lice-infested Polotsk, there's nothing but mud and pigs. Is it true that you have the whatchamacallits… that they're renovating the dome?

— They're lying, — responded Petukhov's bass, — I went out to look, at the hay market. The dome looks like the dome. The women dreamed it all up.

— Too bad! — sighed Gloomy. — The churches are disintegrating and God doesn't care… Take the Spassky Monastery... falling completely to pieces. They aren't any rubles in heaven, that's the main problem.

Gloomy sighed, stirred the muddy tea with a spoon, and continued:

— Incidentally, about the rubles. There aren't any, there aren't any, and then it happens, bang! They rain down upon your head. We, for example, had an amazing incident with these rubles. In May, we applied for four million two hundred and one thousand and change, for 2,700 workers, and the Center says yes and gives us four million seven hundred thirty thousand for, in actual fact, 817 men.

— You're a liar! — shouted Petukhov.

— I'll show you 'liar!' — answered Gloomy. — May I drop dead on this very spot!

— So it turns out there's a surplus?

— Naturally. But then, if you follow me, the problem is how to hide this money entirely in the expenses without a carry over.

— How is it possible? — marveled Petukhov. Gloomy looked around, listened around, and whispered conspiratorially:

— In the manner of our chief of the mechanical workshops. He has, if you follow me, the following practice: He writes an order for five times more equipment than is needed and shoves it all into the expenses! He's already been told: "Watch out, you could get your head handed to you." "Yeah, right," he says, "my head. Their arms are too short. I have a legitimate excuse: There's no place to store it." A capable fellow!

— Won't he go to jail? — asked Petukhov excitedly.

— Of course, he will go to jail. Mark my words. And he'll go to jail because of the workshops. No matter what he does, the workshops will give him away. He saws firewood by hand because the power saw is out of commission, and a 30-horsepower motor powers the only fan for four blacksmith furnaces!

Petukhov laughed and choked.

— Be quiet! — whispered Gloomy, — That's nothing. We had fun here with rivets not long ago (Gloomy giggled) – "For what," he says, "do we purchase rivets, when we have our own workshop? I will," he says, "blast rivets out to all of Russia!" Well, he blasted them out... 308 pounds of them. Remarkably beautiful: crooked, with thick bucktails, and overly-fired. One hundred twenty eight pounds went back into the furnace, and the rest sit in the warehouse to this day.

— Wow, that's something! — gasped Petukhov.

— That's nothing! — perked up Gloomy, — listen to what's happening with our audit. Your hair will stand on end. We have an RKK[1] in the mechanical workshop, and we have toolmaker Belyavsky, — croaked Gloomy, — who's a member of the RKK. So he, can you imagine, he grabs all the orders for himself. He prices them himself, executes them himself, and receives all the money.

Engineer Geyneman, with a goal of simplifying all manner of formalities concerning the accounting function, established a new practice. One day I look and see: Invoice № 91 for piece-work performed by pieceworker Mikhail Blacksmith and his comrades for the sum of 42,475 rubles, cash. Paid by chief craftsman so-and-so, received by Blacksmith. And that's it!

— Wait, — interrupted Petukhov, — maybe he didn't have any comrades?

— That's my point!

— How is it possible?

— You are a naïve fellow, — sighed Gloomy, — he, this Geyneman guy, has staffed the entire office with his relatives. The boss is Geyneman; the leader of the work is his in-law Markov; the technician is his sister Emma Markov; the clerk is his own daughter Geyneman; the timekeeper is his nephew Geyneman; the typist is Shulman, the niece of his own wife!

— Doesn't Geyneman have grandchildren? — asked the dumbfounded Petukhov.

— No grandchildren, unfortunately.

Petukhov sipped his tea and asked:

— Excuse me, my friend, where is the RKI[2] looking?

Gloomy whistled and whispered:

— Lunatic! The RKI! Our RKI is Timofey Yakutovich. A capital fellow, he's your guy. Give him anything, he'll sign it.

— Good-natured, huh? — asked Petukhov.

— Hell yes, he's good-natured. It's rumored (Gloomy bent to the outspread ear of Petukhov), that he received ten cartloads of firewood from the supplies for the bridges over the West Dvina River, 4 ½ pounds of flour and 100 feet of textile. If we gave you textiles, you would be good-natured!

— The secrets of the harem! — exclaimed Petukhov admiringly.

— Secrets, indeed, — agreed Gloomy, — only, if you follow me, an outright unpleasantness came to us already because of these secrets. One beautiful day, two kooks arrived at our place. Nondescript appearing, frayed trousers, and they say: "Your books, please." Well, we handed them over. And then the fun began. According to us, if the accounting is a year behind, it's a trifle! According to them, it's a crime. According to us, it's not necessary to certify and seal the cash books; but according to them, it is necessary! According to us, it's efficient to cut bolts manually; but according to them, it is necessary to do it mechanically! Rivets for a bridge truss, according to us, must be produced by hand, and according to them, it is criminal! So we did not come to an agreement. They left, but we haven't had any peace since then. These very visitors won't cook something up, will they? So we walk around with sour pusses.

— Hmmm, yeah, it is a nuisance... — agreed Petukhov.

They both fell silent. The green lampshade stained the faces with a green color and both clerks resembled mysterious gnomes. The lamp droned ominously.

The conversation was eavesdropped by G.P. Ukhov.[3]

Translators' notes

A bit about *Gudok*: In 1923, Bulgakov took a job as a corrector at *Gudok (The Whistle)*, the official trade newspaper for railroad workers. His responsibilities included sorting out letters received from worker–correspondents, putting them into a form for publication, and giggling with the typists. He quickly became a staff feuilletonist.

Bulgakov wrote about his work at *Gudok* in the story "To a Secret Friend:"

"...Here let me tell you another secret: the writing of a sketch of seventy-five or a hundred lines took me, including time out for smoking and whistling, from eighteen to twenty-two minutes. Retyping it, including giggling with the typist, took eight minutes. In a word, half an hour and the deed was done. I signed it, usually with a pseudonym but occasionally with my own name, and took it to Julius (aka July), or the other assistant editor, who had the odd name of Navzikat...

Navzikat would begin by turning around the feuilleton in his hands, and first of all, looked in it for some criminal idea directed towards the Soviet regime. When he was convinced that there is no obvious harm in it, he would begin giving advice and correcting the feuilleton.

In those moments, I was anxious, smoked, and had a desire to hit him with an ashtray on the head.

Having spoiled the feuilleton to the best of his ability, Navzikat wrote on it: 'To the press,' and the work day for me was over."

1. *RKK* is an abbreviation for *Rayonnaya kontrolnaya komissiya*, the Regional Control Commission, which is a regional subdivision within the Soviet hierarchy responsible for financial accounting.

2. *RKI* is an abbreviation for *Raboche–krestyanskaya inspektsiya*, the Worker–Peasant Inspector's Office, whose function is to audit places of work to ensure compliance with labor regulations.

3. The penname *Ukhov* is derived from *ukho* (the ear).

The magazine "Drezina" (Railway Handcar), № 13, Petrograd, November 1923

Arithmetic (Арифметика)

— It has begun! — wheezed a breathless general, having run up to the 6th floor to the 'keeper of the Russian throne,' Cyril.

Cyril turned pale, let the pump for a primus stove that he was pumping fall from his hands, and whispered:

— Already?

The breathless general immediately caught his breath.

— Forgive me, Your Highness, — he reported, — Your Highness did not understand me correctly. Not the pogroms, but the restoration, Sir!

Cyril came to his senses in a flash.

— It's not... it's not possible!

— I give you my word.

— In Russia?

— For now, Your Highness, only in Germany. The Crown Prince Wilhelm has arrived. He has returned. Stresemann expressed himself bluntly regarding this matter: I will not permit, he said, a single German to remain abroad...

— And so?

— And so, Your Highness... We see it like this: Germany today, Russia tomorrow. After all, sir, it's like an epidemic. A revolution is an epidemic. And a restoration is an epidemic. It needs only to begin.

In the evening, when they visited Cyril to find out when His Highness intended to leave, Frau Kuskova and Herr Milyukov witnessed a strange scene.

Cyril and the general were sitting on a floor covered with scraps of paper, and they were feverishly multiplying numbers on the margins of some kind of a book. From the number of zeros, one's eyes would blink.

— Get out! — screamed Cyril in response to their respectful

questions. — You know what it means to get out?

— But, the Crown Prince...

— Why are you poking me in the eyes with your Crown Prince! The Crown Prince... The Crown Prince has it good. The Crown Prince draws his salary in guldens. What does he care? A limo ride costs him 10 guldens. A tip to the chauffeur is 5 guldens. A hindquarter of ham is 3 guldens... But me, I draw mine in marks!

— But, Your Highness...

— I myself am aware that I am *The Highness...* Look at this: the journey for one person costs six quintillion, 781 quadrillion, 835 trillion... and small change. In the case of four persons...

— For simplification, Your Highness, omit three zeros...

— Hold on a second about the three zeros... Do we need to make some sandwiches? Assume a half billion for sandwiches. Forty-eight billion, 172 million rubles, 460 thousand, 382... Okay. We need to bring cigarettes...

— Your Highness pleased to start smoking young... Heh-heh...

— This is no time for joking! Assuming ten cigarettes, that's four billion, 221 million, 400...

— Put down a round number: one quadrillion! — said Milyukov, and took off his coat. — Allow me, Your Highness, I'll have it in a second. Through double-entry bookkeeping...

— In the German newspapers, — Milyukov reported to the group of friends of the Russian monarchy, — they wrote that the attempt by the great Prince Cyril to return to Russia amounted to nothing. This is, first of all, factually incorrect... I myself took part in the preparations for the journey of His Highness, and can attest that the designated trip came to three sextillion, fifty-five quintillion, three hundred and twenty one trillion, seventy-eight billion, one hundred sixty-seven million, two hundred fifty-one thousand, and eight hundred twenty-four zeros...

But we, at *Drezina,* hold a different opinion regarding all of this. All these astronomical quantities of zeros, we, with regard to the restorational potential of Cyril, undertake to reduce in one stroke:

— To two zeros.

This will be meaningful, and, above all, beneficial.

Ol-Wright.

Translators' note

A bit of historical background: Cyril and the general represent the Russian aristocracy, who had fled Russia during the Revolution, but hoped for the restoration of the Tsarist regime. German Crown Prince Wilhelm fled to Holland after WWI.

The mark is German currency and the gulden, Dutch. There was massive hyperinflation in Germany and the Soviet Union after WWI and the Russian Revolution. The price of a loaf of bread in Berlin increased from 0.63 marks in 1918 to 250 marks in January 1923. By July, the price was 3465 marks and in November, 201,000 million. At the height of the inflation, one US dollar was worth 4 trillion German marks. One of the firms printing bank notes submitted an invoice for the work to the Reichsbank for 32,776,899,763,734,490,417.05 (~33 quintillion) marks. [*The Penniless Billionaires* by Max Shapiro. New York Times Book Co., 1980, page 203]

In Russia, the purchasing power of 1,000,000 rubles in 1914 had dropped to 0.00002 rubles by March 1924. [*Planning for Economic Growth in the Soviet Union 1918-1936* by E. Zaleski, translated by M.C. MacAndrews and G.W. Nutter. University of Caroline Press, 1971]

A 25,000-ruble note, 1923

The newspaper "Gudok," Moscow, December 12, 1923

Stairway to Heaven (Лестница в рай)

(From nature)

> A stairway leading to the library at the Moscow–
> Belarus Station (1ˢᵗ Meshanski St.) is completely en-
> veloped in ice. In the pitch dark, workers fall and die.
>
> *A worker–correspondent*

The worker Kosin fell successfully. With a thunderclap, he arrived to the ground floor from the first, then spun around in the plaza, and slid headfirst out onto the street. Following behind him arrived his hat, and behind the hat, the book *War and Peace*, the creation of Leo Tolstoy. The book slid out, bound side up like a hunchback, and came to rest next to Kosin.

— Are you all right? — asked those waiting their turns below.

— Trousers got ripped, — Kosin replied dully, — good trousers, my wife got them in Sukharevka. — And he felt a stunning starburst fanning out on his thigh.

And then he picked up the work of Tolstoy, put on his hat, and, limping, left for home.

Balchugov risked going second.

— I will plough through you, I will surmount you, — he muttered, clutching to his chest a collection of compositions by Gogol in one volume, — I once climbed in the Carpathians, in 1915, didn't utter a single complaint. Wounded twice... On my back a sack, in my arms a rifle, on my feet boots, but here with Gogol, even with Gogol, I cannot break through. I want to borrow *The ABCs of Communism*.[1] I... you son of a bitch!.. I (he was lost in impenetrable darkness)... may you and your library never again see the light of day!..

He made an attempt to grab for invisible handrails, but they slid abruptly from his grasp. Then Gogol slipped away from him and in a flash, he was on the street.

— Oy! — squeaked Balchugov, feeling that an evil spirit had torn him from the ice-covered steps and dragged him to somewhere in the abyss.

— Hel… — he began, and didn't finish.

An icy bump under his feet insidiously pushed Balchugov to somewhere where an iron bolt met him. Balchugov was the loser, and the bolt found its target directly in his teeth.

— Help… — gasped Balchugov, falling headfirst.

— Me!! — he finished, already sitting in the snow.

— Try using snow… — advised those waiting their turn, seeing how Balchugov spit beautifully red blood.

— Not with shnow, — replied Balchugov lispingly (his cheek is blowing up in front of your eyes), — but with a club to the head of thish very librarian and the leadership too… may they… shlide shnout-firsht down shish shtaircashe…

He fumbled in the snow with his hands and gathered up the scattered pages of *Taras Bulba*. Then he got up, spit red on the snow, and left for home.

— Eschanged a book, — he mumbled, holding his cheek, — Damn, did I ever eschange a book. — He reeled…

The darkness swallowed him.

— Shall we ascend, Mitya? — timidly asked someone awaiting his turn. — It would be nice to read a newspaper.

— May they go to the pig dogs, the sons of bitches, — replied Mitya, — you can kill yourself, but I just got married. I have a wife. She'll be left a widow. Let's go home!

The darkness ate them as well.

F. S-ov.

Translators' note

1. *The ABCs of Communism: A Popular Explanation of the Program of the Russian Communist Party,* by Bukharin and Preobrazhensky, was published in Oct. 1919. Its authors described it as a textbook for a first course in Communism, but also indicated their intention that it be readable by every worker and peasant on his own. By 1923, more than one million copies had been printed. By 1930, the book had been translated into 38 languages.

1924

The newspaper "Gudok," Moscow, January 1, 1924

A Drastic Remedy (Сильнодействующее средство)

A Play in One Act

> If C. Voytenko does not get paid, *Gudok* will send the play to the Little Theater in Moscow, where it will be staged.[1]

Characters:

CLAUDIA VOYTENKO: a teacher of indefinite age. Wearing a fur coat and hat, some papers in her hands.

CHIEF, CRIMEAN CULTURAL DEPARTMENT: middle aged, cute. Dressed in an orange jacket and pants of the same color.

COURIER IN THE CULTURAL DEPARTMENT: 50-years old.

The stage is set as the office of the chief of the Crimean Cultural Department. It is smoky, cramped, and nasty. One door. At the front of the stage is a table with a phone and an inkwell. Above the table are three posters: *If You Come to a Busy Person, You Will Perish*; *Business Before Pleasure*; and *Handshakes Have Been Canceled Once and for All*. The chief faces the audience. The courier sits in a chair near the door. It is noon.

***

COURIER. Hack-hack-hack... (coughs).

A pause.

The door opens and Voytenko enters.

COURIER. Where do you think you are going? Where? Who are you looking for?

VOYTENKO. I need to talk to him (points a finger at the chief).

COURIER. He's busy, it's not possible.

VOYTENKO (shyly). Well, I'll wait.

COURIER. Sit there, just don't make any noise (Voytenko sits down in the chair. A pause.)

VOYTENKO (in a whisper). What is he busy with? No one is here.

COURIER. I don't know. Maybe he's thinking... This and that... (a pause).

VOYTENKO. My dear, I need to catch a train. I'm going to be late. Perhaps you could tell him...

COURIER. Well, all right. I'll report it to him (approaches the table and coughs. A pause. Coughs).

CHIEF (awakens). Go away, Afanasiy, you're getting on my nerves (contemplates).

COURIER (returns). So, you see... I told you so… so, be off with you.

VOYTENKO (becomes worried). I need to go to Yevpatoria, I'm going to be late (she approaches the table, coughing).

CHIEF (confusedly). Are you ever leaving, Afanasiy? (raises his eyes). Pardon me! Are you here for me?

VOYTENKO. Excuse me. Yes, for you...

CHIEF. With whom do I have the honor of speaking?

VOYTENKO (curtsies). Allow me to introduce myself: a school teacher in the Illiteracy Liquidation Program at the Yevpatoria Station of the Southern Railroad, Claudia Voytenko, née Manko.

CHIEF. Oh, well. What do you need, née Manko?.

VOYTENKO (nervously). You see, I have yet to receive my pay for August of this year.

CHIEF. Hmm... That's a shocker! You probably didn't send in your timesheets.

VOYTENKO (wearily). What do you mean, 'did not send!' I sent them (fiddles with some papers). The time sheets were sent, as I told the representative of the Professional Union of the Yevpatoria Station… twenty times.

CHIEF. Hmm... Af-fanasiy.

COURIER. What is your pleasure?

CHIEF. Get busy and find out where the time sheets for née Manko are!

A pause. The courier returns.

COURIER. There is no née... (coughs)

CHIEF. So, you see!

VOYTENKO. Excuse me, what is there for me to see? (getting nervous). It is you who must see! If you lost it...

CHIEF. Excuse me... I request you to be careful. You are not in Yevpatoria.

VOYTENKO (starts to cry). Since... August... of this... I've been running around... going around ... and around...

CHIEF (taken aback). I request you not to cry in a public office.

COURIER. They fill the entire room with tears, and wiping it up falls on me... The only thing I know is how to run around with a rag (mumbles to himself).

VOYTENKO (crying).

CHIEF. I request you to calm yourself down!

VOYTENKO (weeping).

CHIEF. Bring me different timesheets!

VOYTENKO (through boisterous sobs). I will file a complaint about you with the *KK*.[2]

CHIEF (offended). Pul-leaze. It doesn't matter if it's the *KK* or the *RKK*.[3] You won't scare me!

VOYTENKO. I will write to *Gudok*!! About how you...

CHIEF (pale as death). My apologies... Heh-heh, why would you do that? Er... in haste? Afanasiy, a glass of water for née Manko. Sit down, please. Heh-heh, you are a ball of fire! Just a second. Hmm! Hmm! *Gudok*!... Afanasiy! Run over to Maria Ivanovna. Tell her that there should be a time sheet. Go to the bottom of the sea to find it. Heh-heh. You know, the volume of paperwork kills us, one's head spins.

VOYTENKO (drying up, wipes her eyes with her handkerchief).

COURIER (enters). Found it (extends the document).

CHIEF (triumphantly). Well, you see, it's been found. And you were crying... *Gudok*! Right here and right now, we will write you an authorization... Signed with a quill pen and done... Issue her the money.

VOYTENKO (completely dried up). And I had lost all hope!

CHIEF. How could you! How could you! One ought never to lose hope! Here, with the authorization, go straight, then to the right, then to the right again, then left, then give it to them...

VOYTENKO (shining). I thank you, I thank you!

CHIEF. Oh, please, it is my duty! As for *Gudok*, you know, what's the point?.. To make a big deal out of facts, to what end? Af-fanasiy! Escort her! (Smiling nicely).

Mikhail B.

Translators' notes

1. Bulgakov's ideas for the *Gudok* feuilletons often came from letters written to *Gudok* by railroad workers. He used excerpts from these letters as epigrams.

2. *KK* is an abbreviation for *Komitet kultury*, The Cultural Committee, which was the central authority over all regional and local cultural departments. The functions of a cultural department were liquidation of illiteracy, curriculum design for schools at all levels, and organization of extra-curricular and social activities.

3. *RKK* is an abbreviation for *Rayonnaya kontrolnaya komissiya*, a Regional Control Commission, which was a regional subdivision within the Soviet hierarchy responsible for financial accounting.

The Performance at Little Roosters (Спектакль в петушках)

I

THE MAN WHO HATED THEATER

He wore a warm, fur-trimmed woolen jacket, trousers, and boots. Ordinary mustache, beard, average nose. A distinguishing characteristic of this man, however, was that the man hated theater.

His hatred fed every day and, in the end, grew into an evil fury, which gobbled up the man without a trace. He started to cough in a strange manner, and a spotted rosiness appeared on his cheeks.

A theater stood nearby, within two steps, at the Little Roosters Station, where the man served in the capacity of stationmaster (I say 'served' because, perhaps, he has already been killed by now).

II

AN OMINOUS PAPER

One day, the man received a mysterious paper and buried his nose in it. Having read it, he became crimson from joy. His eyes shone like stars.

— Okay... okay... all right, — he muttered, — all right... I've got you fenced in. I'll get you fenced in! I'll get you so fenced in... — Here he gathered air into an exhausted chest and shouted: — Hey, you!!

And, workers appeared before the man. No one knows what kind of instructions he gave to the honest working people (they are not to blame, I repeat this one thousand times). It is known that, come evening, driven fence posts appeared around the theater, like candles. Many saw these posts, but no one paid particular attention to the posts insofar as suspicion was unable to enter into anyone's heads about the man's infernal plan.

— Our stationmaster has thought up some kind of nonsense again, — a few said, and went on their way.

III

THE BARBED WIRE ARRIVED

Unfortunately, no one saw how it appeared, because they all were properly at work.

Honest workers dragged enormous rolls of barbed wire, unwound them, and then tightly strung the wire on posts around the entire theater. You think it was somehow done hurriedly? Shoddily? You are mistaken. This was heavy-duty wire, the trench warfare kind, which was capable of busting up the best armored divisions. Only a single entrance remained, and this entrance was of width six feet...

IV

THE PERFORMANCE AT LITTLE ROOSTERS

And so, dear citizens, a performance was scheduled for the evening. Everyone knew about the performance, but no one knew about the barbed wire surrounding the performance.

And at sunset, smiling railroaders from all corners, with their families, flowed to the theater.

A howl rose up above Little Roosters! Moaning and gnashing of teeth!! The finest and most durable fabric, purchased on credit, ripped like cigarette paper. One touch of the accursed barrier was enough to turn trousers to shreds.

The railway mob, to the last man, fell upon the barbed-wire fence and left on it skirts, sweaters, scraps of coats, and fat pieces of wool from the linings. The lacerated mob climbed to the theater, dropping drips of blood and screaming at the stationmaster such words as are forbidden to be printed in a newspaper...

— ...!!

— ...!!!

V
FIRE!!

Speaking hypothetically: Could a fire happen in Little Rooster Theater? Respond immediately: Yes or no?

— Yes. No theater is secure from that.

— Well, imagine what will happen in a theater that is wrapped tightly with barbed wire all around? That's my point.

TELEGRAM TO STATIONMASTER
AT LITTLE ROOSTERS:

Remove the wire, goddamit.

Mikh B.

The newspaper "Gudok," Moscow, January 20, 1924

How He Lost His Mind (Как он сошел с ума)

I.

The door opened into an isolation room and a doctor entered, accompanied by a nurse and two guards. From a tumbled bed, over which shone the sign: *Director of the Chaadaevskaya School on Syzranka Street*, Violent, a man in underwear, rose to meet them, flashing with his eyes:

— *From Seville to Grena-a-d!! My best to you, you scumbags!!. In the quiet darkness of nights! Serenades, you bastards, are heard! The clash of swords is heard!..*

— OK... 'Serenades.' Allow me to take your pulse, — said the doctor politely, and extended his hand. Meanwhile, he was blinking to the assistant with his left eye, and with the right one to the guards.

The white man shook and howled:

— Rascal!!. Confess: Are you PD[1] sixty-eight?

— No, you are mistaken, — the doctor responded, — I am a doctor. How is your temperature?.. OK... stick out your tongue.

Instead of a tongue, the white man showed the doctor a scary hairy middle finger,[2] and struck up a squat–kick dance and sang:

— *There's a terrible noise in the Schneerson home...*

— Potassium bromide, — said the doctor, — a tablespoon...

— Bromide?! — howled the white man. — Did you see the windows without glass, you scoundrel? Did you see the zero?.. What properties does the zero have, did you see it, I ask you, you whistler in a white robe?!!

— Morphine subcutaneously, — the doctor whispered cordially to the assistant.

— Morphine? — squalled the man, — morphine?! Beat him, Christian brethren, PD sixty-eight!.

He took a swing and hit the doctor in the ear so horribly and accurately that the pince-nez jumped off of his nose.

— Get him, brothers, — sniveled the doctor, wiping blood from under his nose with a handkerchief, — put a straightjacket on him...

The guards, puffing, ganged up on the white man.

— Help!! — a cry echoed under the arches of the Kanatchikovo Dacha.[3] — Help! Sixty-eighpp!!

II.

In the doctor's office, two months later, a sad emaciated man sat in a coat with a shabby collar and kneaded a hat in his hands. His belongings, tied into a knot, were lying at his feet.

— As for the rampage, — said the man with a sigh, — I am asking for forgiveness. Do not hold it against me. Please understand that I was not myself.

— Nonsense, my dear, — said the doctor, — it happens here often. Here, take this syrup, one tablespoon every two hours. And, of course, avoid stress.

— Thanks for the syrup, — the man responded with a sigh, — but as for stress... It's impossible for me to avoid stress. I have that kind of a job, with stress, — he sighed heavily.

— What's the matter, my dear? — sympathized the doctor. — Tell me.

The sad man grunted and related:

— Winter, you understand, it's cold... Our Chaadaev School is without windows, the heating system is out of order, same with the lighting. And the students, you know, a carload of them. Well, what's to be done? I began to write to our PD 68 for Syzranka. I wrote once, no answer whatsoever. The second time I wrote, he sent a response: what's the matter... sure... needs to be done, etc. I was delighted. But a significant amount of time goes by, but nothing to be seen for it. Meanwhile, the students at the school are disappearing. Well, sir, me again to PD 68. He responds to me: How could that be, it should absolutely be done. Me again to him. He to me. Me to him. He... No, I think. This will never work. I then wrote to PT,[4] so and so, do me a favor, put together a memo. What do you think happened? Silence. I then gave up on PD 68, began to attack PT. Me to him. He in response: I sent a copy of your esteemed letter to P.[5] I write to him again. And he to P again. Me to him. And he to P... P.. phooey... to him again. He to P. Me, him, him, me. What am I supposed to do? He goes silent. What kind of punishment is this, I think? Huh? And then my bad mood began. No appetite. Flickering in my eyes. Weird stuff. Once I walked out of the school and saw my deceased grandmother walking. Yes, she was walking, and in her hands she had a pretzel shaped like a sixty-eight. I said to her: Grandma, you're dead? And she said: Go away, you fool! I went to see our doctor. He looked at me, and said: You need to drink bromide. You are not supposed to see grandmas.

I became possessed and began to write to Lord knows whom: I wrote six times to the Cultural Department of the Railroad: no response. Then I wrote four times to the management of the railroad, whatever for, the devil only knows! They did not respond. I wrote again. What began at this point is inconceivable to the human mind. A telegram arrives: Do not expend any operating funds on social–cultural needs.[6] At night, my grandmother: "What are you lying there for, like a log? Write to N. He is a good man." Be off, I say, you witch. You died, now shut up! I threw a candlestick at her, but it hit the mirror. Yet in the morning, I could not resist, and wrote to N. Then, a telegram arrives: Make the necessary repairs. I, of course, write to P. A telegram from P: Make the most necessary repairs. *Voila!* The most necessary. I write a letter to the Cultural Department of the Railroad: Yeah, I write, do you get it? Make the repairs! And from there, a telegram arrives: "Do not disburse pre-tax school funds." Heavenly Father! I go outside and see Peter the Great, standing there, with his fist pointing at me. I blacked out, pulled out a knife, and went after him. Well, then, of course, I was seized and brought to you...

The man suddenly went quiet... bugged out his eyes and started to get up. The doctor turned pale and recoiled.

— Qua... qua!. — squeaked the man. — Sixty-eight! Where's the repair? Huh? Beat him! Aaa-aaaaa!

— Guards... Help! — screamed the doctor.

The windows thunderously shot out from the office.

— Too early to discharge him, — said the doctor to the rushing-in white robes, — to Room 6, and a straightjacket.

Em.

Translators' notes

1. *PD* is the official railroad abbreviation for *Putevoy dispetcher*, a train dispatcher.

2. Showing your thumb protruding between the index and middle fingers is an emphatic way of declining a request. It means 'you will get nothing from me!'

3. Kanatchikovo Dacha is a psychiatric hospital in the south of Moscow, built in the 19th century. This hospital resembles the clinic of Professor Stravinsky in Bulgakov's *Master and Margarita*.

4. *PT* is the official railroad abbreviation for *Nachal'nik puti*, the manager of a rail line.

5. *P* is the official railroad abbreviation for *Slujba puti*, the central office of a railroad (multiple rail lines).

6. 'Social–cultural needs' *(kultnuzhdy)* had a specific sense in Soviet times, referring to the use of funds for the material stimulation of workers and support of children in order to stimulate procreation.

The newspaper "Gudok," Moscow, January 27, 1924

The Hours of Life and Death (Часы жизни и смерти)

(From nature)

> There is a coffin with Lenin's body in the Hall of Columns of the House of Trade Unions. Around the clock, day and night, enormous crowds of people in the square flow into the Hall of Columns. They come in rows, in endless ribbons, which disappear into the surrounding streets and lanes.
>
> This is workers' Moscow, coming to bow unto the ashes of the great Lenin.

The arrow of a fiery clock trembled and stopped at five. Then it steadily went on, because the clock never stops. As always, since the 5 p.m. dusk began falling on Moscow. The frost was bitter. A squadron began to enter the square, heading towards the white house.

— Hey, hey-hey-ey there, get off the tram tracks, off the tram tracks!

The traffic director at the intersection, wearing a boyar's coat and a silver mustache, with obligatory wand in hand, was spinning himself around. Groaning trams ploughed through the crowd. Automobiles lit up their headlights and howled.

— Hey, watch out!

The squadron entered to the sound of snow crunching under foot. Helmets were tightly fastened and the horses were dressed in frost. The headlights and windows of trams spun around in the freezing smoke. At the tram tracks, a black line of people instantly grew out of the ground. People were running, running in different directions, but upon seeing the horsemen, they realized that they would soon be let in. One, two, three... one hundred, one thousand!..

— Get off the tracks!

— Tram! Watch out! A car on the tracks, watch out!

— Maintain order, comrades, order. Hey, where are you going?

— Brothers, for Christ's sake, let me into the line to say goodbye. To say goodbye!

— It's too late, my auntie! Aunti-i-i! Where are you gooooeing?

— Get in line! Get in line!

— Good heavens, the tail is going all the way down Dmitrovka Street!

— Where am I supposed to go, me, my poor soul? Drop through the earth, or what?

The woman's coat jumped and paced around, and the giant police horses continued to press. Where should the poor old lady go? Drop through the earth, old lady... The red-capped policemen and horses dancing. A snake with a tail of a thousand segment walks quietly toward the Church of St. Paraskeva, but it's moving, and moving! Ah, we'll get in quickly!

— My dears, don't let anyone cut the line!

— Maintain order, citizens.

— We are all going to die...

— What are you saying? Think with your brain before you speak. Suppose that you're dead, for example, what's the difference. What's the difference, tell me, citizen?

— Don't insult him!

— I am not insulting, I want to make him think. A great man died, so shut up. Be quiet for a moment, contemplate in your head what has happened.

— Where are you going? Hey! Hey! Hey! Hey!

— Squadron, halt!

The crowd is moving nearer, nearer, nearer... Crunch, crunch. Stop. Crunch... Crunch... Stop... The door. My dear brothers, the river's flowing!

— Three at a time, comrades.

— Up! Up-p-p-p! Up the stairs!

— The lights, the lights, so many!

Stone guards stand along the walls. Walls of white, on the walls are bushy chandeliers. Originating from the tram tracks of Okhotny Row, the river flows, trampling the red carpet.

— Quiet, you. Shhh...

— Have they removed their hats, are they coming? No, not them, not them. This is not 'them,' brothers, this is a river of a million flowing.

Snow is falling on the carpet.

And in the sea of white light, the river flows.

* *
*

In a coffin, on a red pedestal, lies a man. He is golden, with a waxy yellowness, and the bulges on the forehead of his bald head are pronounced. He is quiet, but his face is wise, important, and calm. He is dead. He is dressed in a gray jacket. On the gray there is a dab of red, The Order of the Red Banner. The wall banners in the white hall are checker-boarded: black, red, black, red. At the center of a tapestry of a gigantic Order — a rosette glowing in bushes of fire — on the pedestal, doomed to the eternal silence of death, lies the man.

Just as his words once moved the immortal helmets of his guard to word and deed, so now has his silence killed the guard, and the river of those processing for the last goodbye.

The guard is quiet, having set its rifles to parade rest, and the river quietly flows.

Everything is clear. In Moscow, they will be walking to this coffin through the bitter frost for four days, and then, through the centuries, down distant caravan routes of the world's yellow deserts, where once, at the very birth of humanity, above his cradle, moved the perpetual star.

* * *

The river flows and flows. The white hall, red carpet, chandeliers. The red army men stand, watch sternly.

— Lisa, do not cry. Do not cry... Lisa...

— Water, give her water!

— Let the nurse in, comrades!

The frost. The frost. Cover yourselves up, cover yourselves up, brothers. Outside is bitter frost.

— Brothers. How do I get in?!

— Not here!

— Citizens, please keep order!

— Exit only. Exit only.

— My dear comrade, but a million are waiting on Dmitrievka Street! I can't wait, I'll freeze to death. Let me in? Huh?

— I can't, — get in the line!

The lights from a car hit with light explosions. They hit the face, then go out.

— Hey! Hey-hey! Watch out! Watch out! A car will run over you. Watch out!

The fiery clock glows.

M.B.

Special edition of the newspaper *Gudok,* Jan. 23, 1924, two days after Lenin's death. The headline reads:

"VLADIMIR ILYICH LENIN

PASSED AWAY,

but the steel rows of workers and peasants still alive under the leadership of the COMMUNIST PARTY,

LOYAL TO THE TESTAMENT OF ILYICH,

will wipe the Kingdom of Exploitation and Oppression from the face of the earth and

ERECT THE BANNER OF COMMUNISM OVER THE WORLD."

The newspaper "Gudok," Moscow, March 15, 1924

The Electrical Lecture (Электрическая лекция)

> Science nourishes the young, and consoles the old.
> Science shortens our lives, which even without it are short.

The bell rang in the hallway of the Ryazan Construction College of Communications. A classroom filled with students, red, steamed, their heavy breaths whistling.

The door opened and to the pulpit ascended an esteemed professor of electrical engineering, who was also the boss of a workshop.

— Shh, silence, — said the electrical professor, sternly glancing at the ruddy faces of his listeners, — why such looks? So revolting?

— We swabbed out the fan for the blacksmith's furnace! — a hundred voices bellowed in unison.

— Aha, but why don't I see Kolesaev?

— Kolesaev died yesterday... — replied a chorus *basso profundo*, like at the opera.

— Over-swab-bed! — echoed a choir of tenors.

—Ummn. Well, may his be the Kingdom of Heaven. Since he's dead, there's nothing more that can be done. It's not in my power to resurrect him. Right?

— Rrrr-ight! — thundered the choir.

— Do not howl in savage voices, — suggested the scientist. — On what topic did we leave off last time?

— What is electricity?.. — answered the class.

— Correct. Well, well, let's proceed further. Take your notebooks and write down my words...

Notebooks rustled, like leaves in the forest, and 100 pencils started scribbling on paper.

— Before I say what electricity is, — sang out from the pulpit, — I... er... I will speak about steam. In essence, what is steam? Any fool has seen a teapot on the stove... Have you seen it?

— Seen it!.. — like a hurricane replied the students.

— Don't scream... Well, now, therefore... It seems from the outside, a trivial thing, every woman is able to boil water, but in fact, it is not so... Far from it, I tell you, my dears, it is not so... Can a woman start up a locomotive? I ask you?

No, dears, a woman cannot start up a locomotive. First, it is not a woman's business, and thirdly, the teapot is nonsense, and in the locomotive, the steam is of quite a different sort. There, the steam is under pressure, that's why under the aforementioned pressure, exiting from the boiler, it rushes to the wheels and pushes them into perpetual motion, the so-called *perpetuum mobile*.

— What is 'perpetuum?' — asked Kuryakovsky, a student.

— Do not interrupt. I'll explain. Perpetuum is such a thing... it is, dear brothers... *Ooh la la!* In the morning, for example, you got on a train at the Bryansk Railway Station in Moscow, it whistled, and rolled, and, behold, after 24 hours you see that you are in Kiev, in a very different Soviet republic, the so-called Ukrainian, and all of this because of the concentration of steam in the boiler that passes through the levers to the wheels of the so-called piston, according to the Law of Eternal Perpetuum, discovered by the famous steam scientist Von Step in the 18th century B.C. when he looked at a teapot on a very ordinary stove in England, the city of London...

— But they told us in mechanics class yesterday that no stoves existed before the birth of Christ? — squeaked a voice.

—And England did not exist! — blurted another voice.

— And no Christmas!.

—Ho-ho-ho! Ho! — the class thundered...

— S-silence! — grumbled the teacher. — Haryuzin, leave the class! Instigator! Get out!

— Get out! Haryuzin! — howled the class.

Haryuzin, pouring out stormy sobs, stood up, and said:

— Excuse me, comrade teacher, I won't do it again.

— Get out! — unflinchingly repeated the professor. — I'll

report you to the board, and you'll fly out of here in 24 hours!

— In perpetuum you'll fly off, hurrah! — affirmed the excited class.

Then Haryuzin fell into despair and defiance.

— Either way, I forfeit my head, — he swashbuckingly snapped, — so I'll tell you it like it is! I've waited too long!

— Fire away, Haryuzin! — replied the chorus, taking the side of the tormented.

— You yourself do not know a damn thing, — snivelled Haryuzin, addressing the professor, — neither about perpetuum, nor about electrical engineering, nor about steam... You grind out nonsense!..

— O-ho-ho! — sang the interested class.

— Me?.. How can you say that?.. I don't know? — gaped the professor in amazement, turning crimson. — You will answer to me for these words! You, Haryuzin, will weep!

— I do not fear anyone but God himself! — answered Haryuzin, enraptured. — I have nothing to lose but my chains! Beat me? You can beat me! You can drink my blood for the mother truth!

— Take that! Come on, Haryuzin! — thundered the class. — Suffer for the truth!

— And I will suffer, — intoned Haryuzin, — you only mess with our heads! Feeding us nonsense! You yourself couldn't install a motor in a fan!

— That's right, — raged the class in excitement, — tortured us with your gig! There was no Christmas. And Von Step did not exist! You yourself, old devil, don't know anything!

— This is... a rebellion... — wheezed the professor, — a conspiracy! I will!!.. Yes, you will!!..

— Beat him! — the class disintegrated amidst the tumult.

A bell rang in the hallway, and the professor rushed out, and the brigand's whistle of a one-hundred-voiced class whistled after him.

Mikhail B.

Translators' note:

The students in this story are adults who were required to attend night classes as part of Lenin's massive campaign of Collective Enlightenment (aka Liquidation of Illiteracy).

The newspaper "Gudok," Moscow, March 23, 1924

Shopping Center on Wheels (Торговый дом на колесах)

The typically quiet station 'Small Smithereens' of the Nth Soviet Railroad buzzed like an anthill into which a boy had poked a stick. Railroad workers gathered in small groups near a huge question mark on a white poster. Under the question mark was printed:

IT IS COMING!

— Who's coming?! — groaned the railroaders, crawling over one another.

— A cooperative store–railcar! — answered the poster.

— Ho-ho, cool! — whooped the railroaders. The next day it arrived. It was a long freight car, covered with slogans, signs, and appeals:

Exclusive to our shopping center!
Sonyas, Mashas and Natashas, rush to our store!
Railroader!
Why be sucked dry at the privately owned store of the spider.
When you're able to come to us?!

— He-he, cool! — admired the transport workers. — The spider's our Mitrofan Ivanovich.

The station spider Mitrofan Ivanovich stared gloomily out of his little store.

Cooperativization of transportation, through normalization, standardization and stock control, will be the salvation of soil restoration, electrification and mechanization.

This slogan most of all pleased the switchmen.

— It's impossible to understand a damn word of it, — said the red-bearded Gusev, — but clearly it's a smart thing.

Anyone who can prove with a document that he is a member gets a discount of 83.5%, — read the poster, — *all non-members get the same thing!*

Pandemonium ensued at the cashier of the mutual-aid organization. The transportation workers stood at the end of a queue and borrowed paper money and gold coins.

And at noon, the plastered-with-people cooperative store started doing business.

Three clerks twisted about, a cashier screamed: "No change," and the station people pressed the assault.

— Three pounds of sausage, please, we've been craving for sausage. Spider Mitrofan Ivanovich offers putrefying ones.

— No sausage-s. We ran out. In place of sausages, I can offer you marinated lobsters.

— Lapsters? How much are they?

— Three fifty, sir.

— Three what?

— Everybody knows, rubles.

— Per jar?!

— Per jar.

— How about a discount? I am a member...

— I see, sir. Three fifty is the discounted price, otherwise they are six twenty.

— And why do they stink?

— They're imported.

— Please don't shove!

— We currently don't have any belts available, instead I can offer you 'Duplex' patented pants-holders from London with 'Fire' automatic buttons. Seven rubles 25 kopeks.[1] Those that buy a dozen at a time receive an additional discount of 15%. Excuse me, citizen. You should put it around your waist.

— Good gracious, it snapped!

— Pay the cashier 7 rubles 25 kopeks.

— There is no chintz, mademoiselle. We have curtain fabric from Lyon, with a print of large bouquets. It is indispensible for upholstery.

— Hee-hee. We don't have any furniture.

— It's a pity. I can offer you 'Comfort' folding chairs for picnics...

— And, madam, what would you like?

— I am not *madam*, — said the flabbergasted Gusev, stroking his beard.

— Pardon me, how may I help you?

— I would like some chintz for my woman as a gift.

— A thousand pardons, we are out of chintz. As a gift to your honorable wife I can offer you a silk Parisian whalebone corset.

— And where are the sleeves?

— Excuse me, it is not supposed to have sleeves. If you want sleeves, get her pajamas. There is no substitute for this item on sea voyages.

— We don't travel by sea. Give me the corset. It's a solid thing.

— Don't worry, it's bullet proof. What number size does your wife wear?

— I, a simpleton, haven't numbered her, — replied Gusev shyly, — we are known for mediocrity here...

— Pardon me, then let's eyeball it. Is it possible to wrap an arm around her?

Gusev thought.

— Not at all. Two arms could, if the arms are long enough...

— Hmm. This is a significant size. Your wife needs to go on a diet. We can offer you size number 130, specifically for the obese.

— OK, — agreed the accommodating Gusev.

— Eleven rubles 27 kopeks... What else?

Besides that, Gusev bought a 'Jockey Club' shaving mirror,

which reflected a man magnified on one side, and on the other side, reduced. He asked for soap, but instead they offered Russian Swiss cheese. Gusev declined due to lack of funds and, fortifying himself with moonshine at Mitrofan Ivanovich's, appeared before his wife.

— Show me, what you bought, drunkard? — Gusev's wife asked.

— You see, Masha, the selection at the store was all imported, nothing, dammit, — explained Gusev, opening the package, — they say, you are obese, number 130...

— Oh, the swine! (The wife threw up her hands.) Did they measure me, or what? And you are a fine one. Such words about your own wife!

She glanced in the mirror and gasped. A giant physiognomy was looking out from the round glass, with drooping cheeks and hair, as thick as rope.

The wife turned the mirror to the other side and saw herself with a head as small as an inkwell.

— That's me? № 130? — asked the wife, turning purple.

— You're obese, Ma... — Gusev squeaked, sat down, but didn't manage to shield himself. His wife wielded the corset and hit him on his ear so hard that the silk burst and the whalebone pierced his eye.

Two minutes later, Gusev, legs wide apart, was sitting in front of his house, looking with his swollen eye at the rear of a train, carrying away the cooperative store.

Gusev threatened it with his fist.

He got up and took himself to Mitrofan Ivanovich's.

Translators' note

1. A kopek is 1/100th of a ruble, and plays the same role as the American penny does to the dollar.

The newspaper "Gudok," Moscow, March 29, 1924

Enlightenment with Bloodshed (Просвещение с кровопролитием)

Dedicated to the Principal of the Railroad School at the Agryz Station of the Moscow–Kazan Railroad

> Promulgate enlightenment, but without bloodshed if possible!
> *M.E. Saltykov-Schedrin*

Someone's boots tumbled noisily down the stairs, and the school janitor, the godly old woman Fetinya, didn't manage to protect herself! Vanka's head bounced up from the stairs and hit the godly old woman in the back. The old woman dropped to the floor and water flooded from the buckets.

— May you turn to stone! — exclaimed the old woman. — have you gone mad, damn fool?!

— Anyone would go mad here, — responded Vanka, panting, — I barely escaped! Get up, old woman…

— Why don't you get up yourself?

— Do you hear that?

A roar carried from the school, as if a tiger had revolted:

— Bring this scoundrel before me!!! Bring him to me, and I will cut him up like a Cornish hen!!! Aiiieee!!

— He means you?

— Uh-huh, — replied Vanka, wiping off the sweat, — I didn't wipe off the blackboard in classroom № 2.

— Bring me Vanka, the custodian, dead or alive! — the school building thundered. — And I will make hamburger out of him!!

— Vanka! Vanka!! Vanka!! To the principal's office!! — the pupils' voices shrieked.

— Like hell I'll go! — croaked Vanka, and shot across the playground. In the blink of an eye, he, carrying himself up the stairs to a hayloft, disappeared into a dormer.

The building fell silent for a moment, but then a thunderous and predatory basso again howled:

— Bring me the teacher of geography!! Ee -ee!!!

— Gee! Gee-gee!! An echo rumbled in the building.

— The geography teacher flunked... — squeaked a soprano in the hallway excitedly.

The geography teacher, as white as death, rushed into the physics–geography classroom and froze.

— What the heck is this? — the principal asked him in such a voice that the legs of the unfortunate researcher of the globe gave way.

— A map of the *RuSovFedRuSovFedsovfedsovfed...* — the geography teacher responded with jumping lips.

— B-be silent!! — the principal fired back, and started stomping his feet. — Be silent when the principal is speaking to you!.. This is a map?.. This is a map, I ask you?! Wha-why isn't it on an easel?! Why is the Volga River somehow crooked?! Why is Leningrad not Petrograd! On what basis is the Black Sea blue?! Why did your snake drop dead yesterday?! Who, I ask you, poured ink into the aquarium?!

— It was the student Fisukhin, — said the dead teacher, selling out Fisukhin, — he got the snake drunk on opiate drops.

The windowpanes quivered from the roar:

— A-hah-hah!! Fisukhin!! Get me Fisukhin and I will lynch him!!

— Fisu-u-u-u-khin!! — the building moaned.

— Brothers, don't give me up, — wept Fisukhin, sitting fully clothed in the bathroom, — brothers, I won't come out, even if you break down the door...

— Come out, Fisukhin! What can you do?.. Come on out! It's better that you alone die, than all of us, — the students begged him.

— Is he here?!! — rumbled near the stall.

— He's here, — the students moaned, — he barricaded

himself in.

— Aha! Aha!.. Barricaded himself... Break it down!.. The doors!! Bring me a pry bar!! Call the janitors!! Get Fisukhin out of the stall!!!

In the building, the terrifying blows of axes rained down like hail, and in response, the thin shriek of Fisukhin sailed up.

M. Ol-Wright

The newspaper "Nakanune" (On the Eve), Berlin, April 6, 1924

The Golden Documents (Золотые документы)

From my collection

PREFACE OF THE COLLECTOR

When you portray the Soviet way of life, comrade–writers of the Russian land, and especially those from abroad, you should never lie. So as to never lie, it is best to use original documents. Of such documents (e.g., letters of worker–correspondents from the Soviet provinces), thanks to the courtesy of my associates, I have accumulated as many as 200 items. Here I quote several of them in full, preserving with exactitude the style.

I

A FIRE CAPTAIN BY THE NAME OF FIRE

I humbly ask you, comrade–writer, to portray a prettier picture of our fire captain named fire (last name in small letters. – *M. Bulgakov*).

At the N. Baltic Soviet Station, we had a fire captain Fire, an endearing citizen. Such a fire, such a famous fire, a first-water Hercules, our fire captain courageous.

As a first duty, the fire captain swooped down upon every temporary iron heating stove in absolutely every lodging place and blew every one of them to pieces, so that our railroad workers — comrades, citizens, brothers, and sisters — went south for the winter, like whales.

Wearing his helmet, Fire swooped down upon our club like a knight from the Middle Ages, and, wanting to wipe it from the face of the earth, he shouted that the club was unfireproof. Our local committee stood up to him, went to war with Fire, led a seven-meeting battle with the destroyer of our way of life: seven meetings, no less than Perekop.[1]   In the battle of the club, the local committee chased Fire into a vial; but, on the library front, Fire, with torches, completely extinguished the 'ideals of the stove.' That is why Comrade Bukharin,[2] along with his *ABCs*, and Leo Tolstoy were covered with ice, and the population of the library has disappeared for now and forever. Amen. Amen. Get enlightened wherever you can!

But still, that was not enough for the citizen–fire captain to prove his fealty to the October Revolution! When the anniversary of the Revolution came, he annunciated with trumpet sounds in the firehouse entrance that he will make her a gift. And then he dismantled the fire truck down to the last screw. And now there's no one to put it together, and, because of fire, we will all burn in fire without further discussion. Now that's an anniversary present!

Best of all, the fire captain skimmed from our mutual-assistance fund. He took a ten-ruble gold piece and left, and it is unknown in which direction! They said that Fire was observed, apparently, steering a course for suburban train station X. We congratulate you, suburban brothers, you're gonna get it! We had a fiery life for exactly two months, and then came the total frosty silence of the North Pole. May he rest in peace, but let him still return the 10-ruble piece to its place under lock and key in our fireproof safe of mutual assistance.

Don't publish my family name, just put 'Ivan Magnit' as my byline, and make him sound much nastier.

N.B: Dearest Magnit, of writing more nastily about your fire captain than you yourself, I am not capable.

II

CROCODILE IVANOVICH

At our factory, by the grace of our illustrious dimwit factory manager Gavryushkin, an unbelievable story transpired. On the 13th and 14th of the month, two proletarian she-workers, the wives of Firemen Ivan Morozov and Semyon Voldyrev, gave birth. And then our factory committee proposed to arrange a

Soviet baptism for the infants in order to wrest them from the hands of priests and reactionary heresy obscurantism, naming them with the revolutionary name, 'October.'

At the appointed hour, the hall of our club 'Komintern' was filled with jubilant she-workers and he-workers. And then, suddenly, Gavryushkin, well-known for his fallow mind, but ostensibly sympathetic, seized the floor out of turn and loudly proposed for Morozov's male child, the name:

— Crocodile.

And at that instant, the indicated innocent, in the arms of the weeping mothers, died.

A benighted elderly contingent of women raised a superstitious cry, and the second mother rushed to the village priest, who then, naturally, pouncing on ignorance, christened the innocent with malevolent glee, 'Vladimir.'

Our factory woman-doctor Syringe-Shukhova explained over the outcries of the assembly that the infant had died from an overwhelming intestinal disease, irrespective of what they had named him, and that he had already been sick with a fever of 39 degrees. But the backward women destroyed everything, and threatened Gavryushkin with his life. Not to mention that they spread rumors through all the villages, or the propaganda of the crafty priest, and that no one got christened after that.

And for my penname, use 'Conscious.'

N.B: *Crocodile* is a humorous Moscow magazine, well known to workers, even in remote provinces.

III

STAYING ABREAST

The petition of an innkeeper, addressed to
the Nth district's Executive Committee

...I request approval, under current law, for permission to open a beerhouse–teahouse on the square Karl Liebknecht under the name 'Red Alyosha-sha.'

N.B: Whether it was permitted is not known to me.

IV

MASSACRE OF ST. BARTHOLOMEW

Thanks to our PEZE! Our workers attended a show! About 200 people left, leaving behind blood stained skirts, and some pants too. Our PEZE received an order to fence off the theater from the rail yard's bums. And so overnight he erected poles, and in a day of work encircled the entire theater with barbed wire, leaving a single two-foot crawlway in the door. The denizens of the station knew, but the villagers didn't, so from all directions they came, with children and family members, and they impaled themselves, like a regiment on a moonless night. All clothing was ripped apart with dreadful screams, and hands, and faces, and valuable cotton coats as well. It was a nightmare, and in point of fact the theatrical show didn't take place, and then it was proposed to kill this PEZE.

N.B: PEZE – stationmaster (railway vernacular).

Translators' notes

1. Perekop was a battleground during the Russian Civil War

2. Bukharin, who co-authored *The ABCs of Communism,* was as influential in Communist Russia as was Leo Tolstoy in Czarist Russia.

The magazine "Zanoza" (The Splinter), № 9, Moscow, April 9, 1924

Square-feet on Wheels (Площадь на колесах)

The diary of the genius citizen Polosukhin

November 21st

Ugh, I tell you – this city of Moscow. No apartments. To my dismay, none! I sent my wife a telegram to wait a bit, do not depart. I slept three nights at Karabuev's place, in a bathtub. Comfortably, only it dripped. And two nights at Schuevskiy's, on a gas stove. They said in Yelabuga that a stove is a comfortable thing. What the devil! Some kind of screws stinging at me, and the cook is unhappy.

November 23rd

I have no strength whatsoever. I paid my fines, in exchange got a few coins for the tram, and set forth on the 'A' line. Rode it for six circuits; the conductress accosts me: "Where are you going, citizen?" "I am going to the devil's mother," I say. In fact, where am I going? Nowhere. At half-past midnight, I went to the park. I spent the night in the park. Beastly cold.

November 24th

I took some sandwiches and went. In the tram, it is warm from accumulated breathing. The conductors and I toasted and snacked on the Arbat. They took pity.

November 27th

He sticks to me like glue: why am I on a tram with a primus stove? I say that such a legal paragraph does not exist. There is a paragraph against singing, so I am not singing. I lubricated him with tea and he unglued.

December 2nd

A fivesome of us are spending the night. We are cute. We spread out blankets, as if in first class.

December 7th

The Purtsman family settled in. We curtained off one half for ladies and non-smoking. We puttied the window frames. No need to pay for electricity. In the morning, we acted accordingly: when the conductress came, we bought all her tickets. At first, she was horrified, but then recovered. So we rode on. At the stops, the conductress shouted: "The tram is full!" A controller crawled in. Also became horrified. I said, "Excuse me, there isn't any violation here. We've paid." And so we rode on. He ate breakfast with us near the Church of the Savior. We drank coffee on the Arbat and then went to the Monastery of the Passion of the Christ.

December 8th

My wife arrives with the children. Purtsman moved into № 27. "I," he says, "like this route better." He settled in on a grand scale. Carpets, beds, paintings by famous artists. We were simpler. I put in a stove for the driver, a lovely lad. He turned out to be like family. He teaches Petya to drive. I put in another stove in the car, a third on the rear platform for the conductress. She is cute, one of ours. I installed a cooker set. We ride on. May God bless everyone with such an apartment!

December 11th

Good heavens! What an example I've set. We arrived today to Pushkin. I got out at the square to wash my face, and I see Schuevsky in № 6 turning from Tverskaya!.. It turns out he was crowded out of an apartment. He shouts, "I don't give a damn. I moved." The № 6 is convenient for him. He works on Myasnitskaya Street.

December 12th

What is being done in Moscow is mind-boggling. There's cacophony at the tram stops. I read about myself in the newspaper today as we were going to Pure Ponds. They called me a man of genius. We set up a rest room. Simple, but good. We bored a hole in the floor. And even without a restroom, things are great. If you wish to relieve yourself – please, at the Arbat, or if you wish – at the Passion Monastery.

December 20th

We are planning a Christmas party. We have become cramped. I aim to move to № 4, a double. Yes, there are no apartments. My picture appeared in the American newspapers.

December 21st

All hell breaks loose! That's Christmas for you! The Central Housing Committee appeared. Gasped. "And we," they say, "dug through all of Moscow looking for living space. And it is right here…"

They are kicking everyone out. The institutions step on the gas. They set a three-day deadline. A police department will be stationed in my tram. Into Purtsman's goes the Lunacharsky Elementary School.

December 23rd

I am leaving to go back to Yelabuga…

M. Ol-Wright.

Ratspeak (Крысиный разговор)

Rats aren't able to speak, you say? Well, it depends!

An entire gang gathered in the half-ruined *TPO*[1] building of the Skobelev Station of the Central-Asian Line, and started chattering!

— Mama, why are you wearing such a sour puss?

— I pigged out on facial powder, damn it! It's making me nauseous, the powder.

— Why did you do it?

— Well, I thought it was flour. Y'know… it's white, powdery… so we thought it was semolina. We started gobbling it up… Ugh, disgusting! It smelled like violets and wasn't filling, and on top of it all, diarrhea for three days.

— That's nothing, — squeaked a weasely little one, — well, just yesterday, my uncle began to gorge on the coat of the TPO director and he swallowed a button. The button got stuck in his throat, wouldn't go up or down! Then he died, before repenting. May he rest in peace.

— I myself love leather hats best of all, — said a solid young rat man, — they're healthy, zero risk. Gorge yourself on leather, and you're full for two days.

— And where do they keep these hats?

— Well, at the moment, it's like this: you crawl through the hole in the main wall, then hang a right, pass by the upholstered furniture… the bottom line, they're where the aprons are.

— Why are you confusing him? The main wall collapsed yesterday. And a rat's sister-in-law got her paw stuck. That's when they were crawling in to gobble up the director.

— Tasty?

— Well, what can I say… average. But the main thing is that he had already rotted.

— Rotten is bad for you!

— That's nothing! His assistant had turned completely green and the rat pack from the tracks came in and gobbled up his feet together with the boots. With gusto!

— We must throw the rat track-pack out by the scruff of the neck. How dare they! He's our assistant, they should run around in their own places.

— What are folks gathering about? — a young man in tails landed on the fly.

— You see, they locked up the *TPO* warehouses with the stock intact and cast us adrift, and here, y'know all the aprons and the hats, and everything! And now we are free.

— And what are they saying about the director?

— Well, they're saying that both the director and the assistant were forgotten there in the warehouse, and the wall collapsed and buried them.

Mikhail B.

Translators' note

1. *TPO* is an abbreviation for *Tovarno-prihodyasshee otdeleniye,* a government store that sold goods to railroad workers on credit.

A Wedding with Party Secretaries (Свадьба с секретарями)

A genuine letter from worker–correspondent Pushman

Forgive, dear comrade editors, that my letter does not have a metropolitan character, but a provincial one. However, if Gudok, the famous muckraker of everybody, did not exist on earth, then my story–report would perish in the abyss of obscurity thanks to the existence of our wall newspaper,[1] the editorial board of which includes a person I have described below (see number one). He is not such a fool as to publish a full-size, revealing, correspondence about himself!

No, not a fool at all, and in particular, with respect to moonshine.

Well, in our God-protected Lgov II, I was walking in the company of Young Communists, and the politically unaffiliated, and we were talking about raising productivity in the republic when our ears were struck by the sound of a brass band pumping out the march "On the Hills of Manchuria" onto all of Lgov II. Looking around, we found that the band originated from railroader Kharchenko, who has an apartment nearby. Immediately, we established the fact that there was a wedding on an anti-religious basis in the home of the aforementioned Kharchenko. Being interested in anti-religious marriage, we nuzzled up to the illuminated windows and discerned, through an abyss of politically unaffiliated young people, these dissolute faces of old men:

1) The secretary of a cell of the Workers' Communist Party, Comrade Polyakov

2) The former secretary of a cell of the Young Communists

Moreover, on both faces, the former as well as the latter, was written desire.

Astounded, we started to wait to see what it meant, and in

that regard, Senya, a Young Communist, said:

— I know that Polyakov wormed his way in there specifically for the wedding. Just wait, you guys, any second now he will make a speech, and you will all gasp at how amazingly eloquent he is.

And we stayed, glued to the windows, like raisin clusters.

And the host, Kharchenko, handed P. and the former secretary huge goblets of moonshine, triggering riotous laughter in the politically unaffiliated masses enjoying the wedding from outside the windows, and various words, like:

— Look at our secretaries. They, it turns out, were waiting for moonshine, like buzzards for carrion.

And then I, burning with shame, heard the anti-religious speech of P., the content of which I immediately entered into my notebook, word for word:

— To the health of the newly-weds! Hooray!

And then, after a second glass of moonshine:

— Kiss! Kiss!

After that, to the accompaniment of thunderous laughter, everyone got drunk.

I simply blush…

Pushman.
Letter copied by Mikhail.

Translators' note

1. A wall newspaper is a one-page newspaper, typically printed by a local public organization, which was distributed by posting it on walls in offices, factories, and public places.

The newspaper "Gudok," Moscow, May 16, 1924

A Talking Dog (Говорящая собака)

> Everyone has his own style of cultural work.
> *A Russian proverb*

The same thing always happens with trains: one goes and goes, only to arrive at some godforsaken place where there isn't a damn thing but forests and cultural workers.

One of these trains dropped by a certain station of the Murmansk Railroad and spit out a certain man. The man had been at the station exactly as long as the train – 3 minutes – then departed, but the consequences of his visit were uncountable. The man managed to dart around the station and paste up two posters: the first on a red wall near a bell, and the other on the door of a sour building bearing the plaque:

RAILROAD CLUB

The posters precipitated Babylonian pandemonium in the station. People crawled over the shoulders of one another.

Stop, passerby! Hurry to see!
One time only, then they go to Paris! With official approval.
The famous cowboy and fakir
John Pierce
with his world famous attractions, such as: he will perform a dance with a boiling samovar on his head, barefoot he will walk on broken glass and lay his face in it.
In addition, at the request of the distinguished audience, a person will be eaten alive, and other sessions of ventriloquism.
For the finale, there will be shown a clairvoyant talking dog

or

the miracle of the 20th century
Respectfully, John Pierce, white magician.

Approved: The Chairman of the Board of the Club.

* * *

Three days later, the club, which usually accommodated eight, admitted 400, of whom 350 were not club members.

Even the surrounding peasantry came, and their wedge-shaped beards watched from the peanut gallery. The club roared and laughed. The roar flew up and down. A rumor fluttered like a bird that the chairman of the Local Committee was to be eaten alive.

The telegraphist Vasya seated himself at the piano, and to the sound of "Motherland Nostalgia," the cowboy and magician John Pierce presented himself before the public.

John Pierce turned out to be a frail man in a beige leotard with sequins. He came on to the stage and blew the audience a kiss. The audience responded with applause and howls:

— Let's go!

John Pierce drew back, smiled, and just then the blushing sister-in-law of the chairman of the club carried a boiling pot-bellied samovar on to the stage. In the first row, the chairman flushed with pride.

— Your samovar, Fedosey Petrovich? — whispered the adoring public.

— Mine, — said Fedosey.

John Pierce took the samovar by the handles, planted it on a serving tray, and then placed the entire construction on his head.

— Maestro, a tango if you please, — he said in a pressured voice.

Maestro Vasya pushed on the accelerator pedal and a tango began to hop on the keys of the broken piano.

John Pierce, kicking up his skinny legs, pranced around the stage. His face turned crimson from the strain. The samovar clattered with its legs on the tray and spat.

— Encore! — roared the delighted club.

Then Pierce showed further miracles. Baring his feet, he walked on broken glass brought from the station, and lay face down in it. Then there was an intermission.

* * *

— Eat a person alive! — howled the theater.

Pierce placed his hand over his heart and invited:

— May I have a volunteer?

The theater froze.

— Petya, go up there, — offered someone's voice from a box seat.

— What a wise guy, — they answered from the same place, — go up there yourself.

— So there are no volunteers? — asked Pierce, smiling a bloodthirsty grin.

— Give us our money back! — burst a voice from the gallery.

— Due to the lack of volunteers to be eaten, this part is canceled, — announced Pierce.

— Give us the dog! — they thundered from the orchestra.

* * *

The clairvoyant dog turned out to be a very ordinary dog, from a breed of mongrels. John Pierce stopped in front of her, and again said:

— I invite to the stage volunteers who wish to talk with the dog.

The chairman of the club, breathing heavily with the drunken beer, climbed on to the stage and stopped beside the dog.

— I invite you to ask questions.

The chairman thought, became pale, and asked in the sepulchral silence:

— What time is it, doggie?

— A quarter to nine, — said the dog, sticking out her tongue.

— May God save us, — yelled someone in the gallery.

The peasants, crossing themselves and trampling one another, instantly cleared the gallery and went home.

— Listen, — said the chairman to John Pierce, — here's the deal my good man: tell me, how much do you want for the dog?

— This dog is not for sale, for goodness sake, comrade, — replied Pierce, — this dog is learned and clairvoyant.

— Do you want 20 in gold? — said the chairman going into overdrive.

John Pierce refused.

— Thirty, — said the chairman, and reached into his pocket.

John Pierce hesitated.

— Doggie, do you want to work for me? — asked the chairman.

— I do, — replied the dog, and coughed.

— Fifty! — barked the chairman.

John Pierce sighed, and said:

— OK, take her.

* * *

John Pierce, drunk with beer, was carried away by the next scheduled train. It also carried away the chairman's 50 golden ones.

The next evening, the club again accommodated 300 people.

The dog was standing on the stage, smiling pensively.

The chairman stood before her and asked:

— Well, how do you like it here at our station of the Murmansk Railroad, my dear Milord?

But Milord remained completely silent.

The chairman paled.

— What's the matter, — he asked, — what, did you become mute or something?

But the dog didn't want to answer this either.

— She doesn't speak with fools, — said a provoking voice in the gallery. And everyone burst out laughing.

* * *

Exactly one week later, a train shook a man out at the station. This man did not put up any posters, but, clutching a briefcase under his arm, took himself directly to the club, and asked for the chairman.

— Is it you who has the talking dog? — the owner of the briefcase asked the chairman of the club.

— It is us, — said the chairman, turning purple, — only it has turned out to be a fake dog. It doesn't say anything. We had a con man here. He spoke for her from his stomach. My money disappeared...

— Yea-ah, — said the briefcase pensively, — and I brought a document for you, comrade, that you're resigning as the club chairman.

— Why? — gasped the stunned chairman.

— It's because you, instead of occupying yourself with cultural work, arranged some kind of buffoonery at the club.

The chairman's head drooped, and he took the paper.

M. Ol-Wright.

Did They Post It or Not? (Повесили его или нет)

> Do you know what red tape is?
> No, you do not know.

A MEMORANDUM BY KOPOSOP AND KOGOCOX

It started with a typist pounding on a crummy typewriter and crummy paper the below-following:

"To Yuzovo Station, PC-17, DS, MS, and SHT:[1]

The Local Committee of Yuzovo Station asks you to concern yourselves urgently to request and to post in all on-premise workshops, depots, offices, etc. the General Collective Contract, the Code of Labor Laws, the new Local Contract and the Internal Code of Conduct for their wide and daily review by workers and employees under your direction; moreover, be warned that after some time the Labor Protection Unit of the Local Committee will conduct an inspection of the actual implementation, and, on administrative persons who have not fulfilled these presented-before-the Union requirements, complaints will be filed."[2]

Voila! Complaints will be filed.

Speaking of complaints, by the way: Why is it that everyone among us believes it's his duty to sign illegibly? After all, comrades, you aren't ministers! There are two signatures on the memo. The upper one wouldn't be discernable at all if the typist hadn't repeated it: *Nechaev.* And the lower one can be read in two ways. If one assumes that it is written in Latin letters, it becomes *Kogocox,* but if one assumes Russian, then *Koposop.*

However, it isn't important. What's pleasant is that there is a legible ink stamp on the memo: *Workers of the World, Unite!*

It was the 18th of October 1923.

A SNIDE QUESTION

"To the DS of Yuzovo:

Where are those copies of the 1922 Code of Labor Laws and the Internal Code of Conduct that were sent to you by the head office of the railroad? They have already been posted in the administrative offices of the station. The new Collective Contract has still not been sent out to us. It was announced in *Gudok* № 1022."

(We will set the signatures just as they were written, we can't do anything about it.)

From the Director of the Second Division of the Utilization Service. *A. Pulplu.*

GIVE US THE CONTRACT!

"To DN-2:

Because of the attitude of the Yuzovo Local Committee, I request that you send me three copies of the General Collective Contract, the Code of Labor laws, the new Local Contract, and the Internal Code of Conduct.

Head of the Yuzovo Station, *Kozakil.*
November 21, 1923."

GIVE IT TO US, I SAY!

"To DN-2, Re: № 18999:

The Local Committee requires one copy for the merchandise cashier, the ticket cashier, the clerical office, and the technical office, but I have received only one copy. For this reason, I request three more copies,"— desperately wrote the head of the Yuzovo Station, and, from fear, transformed his signature from *Kozakil* to *Kozelkov.*

And it's already been a month, the 19th of November 1923.

SUPPORT ARRIVES

"To DS:

I am petitioning for the satisfaction of the request of the DS of Yuzovo."

Signed: A. Purlis (the former Pulplu).

And countersigned by the former Keshevlent and current Konvoy.

MIRACLES, COMRADES!

"To Railroad Station Yuzovo:

According to interpretation of document № 396444 of December 4th of this year, the railroad received from the Center only 60 copies in total of the Collective Contract, the implication of which is that more cannot be sent and it is recommended to contact the leaders of nearby local committees with a petition."

A PATRON? NOPE...

Who could so disappoint Kozakil, the poor head of the station? Can you imagine, it was the very Pulplu who petitioned for him. For variety, he signed it A. Pulit...

It was already two days before Christmas, the 23rd of December.

WHAT SHOULD KOZAKIL DO NOW?

There remained nothing more for him to do, but to turn again to the Local Committee.

So he turned to them.

"To the Local Committee of Yuzovo, Re: № 807:

...Applying for... №." etcetera. "I request you send... that quantity which you deem necessary," etcetera.

December 24th, Christmas Eve.

DID THEY SEND THEM?

It is unknown.

The Local Committee wrote on New Year's...

It is required to post them, "but the clerical department is in charge of the necessary quantity of supplies."

Kozakil was busted! There was no way forward.

***

With that, the correspondence breaks off. Amongst all this correspondence is a note by an unknown person:

"To the editor of the newspaper *Gudok*. Together with this, the local cultural needs committee sends you the material (January 9, 1924)."

Merci.

When all was said and done, did they post the Collective Contract after all?

Maybe they posted it. And now it is hanging and smiling with its uncountable paragraphs.

— They did post me, hot damn!

Or maybe they didn't post it.

More likely, they didn't.

Because in the fat bundle of correspondence there are several documents in which there is a howling that milk is not supplied. But it is clearly stated in the Collective Contract that milk should be supplied.

That's how things are...

M. Ol-Wright read the documents

Translators' notes

1. *PC* is an abbreviation for Director of Railroad Service; *DS*, Director of the Station; *MS*, Mechanical Service, and *SHT*, senior telegraph operator. *DN* is an abbreviation for *Direktsiya jeleznodorojnikh perevozok*, the Directorate of the Rail Line, which is the head office of a rail line.

2. This paragraph is a masterpiece of bureaucratese.

The newspaper "Gudok," Moscow, June 8, 1924

The Sahara (Пустыня Сахара)

A horrible dying by thirst in one act and eight scenes

Scene 1

The crowded train 'Maxim' approaches Station Waterless. From a half-mile away, the passengers are heard to be singing, in hoarse beastly voices, something to the tune of "Varyag." From a quarter mile, it is possible to make out the words:

Farewell, friends! We will not return.
Our last hour is coming.
Throat cracked and eyes are burned
Bloody mist is veiling.
Glimpses of fields and ravines...
We will give up our souls for a water drop
For a drop of life-giving moisture!

Scene 2

The train is approaching the station. The passengers, delirious from joy, pour out onto the platform. They leap onto the bandstand and shake pots and teapots. A choir to the "Kamarinskaya" tune:

Enough, brothers, enough of anger,
Nice on a hot day to get drunk,
On-li-fe-giv-ing water,
On icy spring water!

Clattering dishes, they run around the platform and search for a barrel of water. No barrel. They run to the station. No water at the station either. Confusion begins in the crowd:

— Aggh!

— What to do now?

— It seems there isn't any water!

A suspicious young man, coming out from a corner:

You have no understanding, city swell!
Behind the station is a well!
You only have to go out the door...

— Ah! A well! What are you talking about?

— A well, my brothers, a well!

— Let's go!

— Here it is, the well.

— Where, where is it?

— Right here!

— Huh? Dammit, it's a pit latrine!

The crowd rushes back to the station.

The DS[1] strolls along the platform, fanning himself with a handkerchief.

The crowd presses:

— Why isn't there water at the station?

— Water? At the station? I swear to God, you're lunatics! Our employees fetch water from a nearby village, half a mile away. Go to their apartments, go and get drunk there.

The crowd runs from the station to a nearby street.

Scene 3

A dormitory for employees. In front of the entrance, house-wives are standing with yokes over their shoulders. Crystal clear, cold water sparkles in buckets. A choir of the housewives:

A young la-dy went for wa-ter,
For ic-y-co-ld wa-ter.
At very noontime, in the hot heat,
In the hot noon, oy-oy-oy.
Oy!

Aggh, the wa-ter, you, the water.
Our fer-ocious do-om.
We'll be getting a hernia soon -
From the half-mile walk with water

— Oy! What's that?

A bareheaded woman is running from the station. Waving her arms:

— Homeowners! Go home! Lock the doors! The passengers are coming for water. They've become rabid! The beasts!

Everyone hides in the house. The door locks click.

Scene 4

The crowd with empty teapots and kettles approaches the house. Weary faces, eyes burning with a feverish brilliance. They knock on the door:

— Housewives! Help us! Sisters, take pity!

— We are dying! Give us a sip of water!

From all of the windows simultaneously protrude fat middle fingers, and an invisible choir of housewives sings:

In vain, Vanka, you walk,
In vain, you strike your legs.
You won't get a damn thing,
Go home with nothing, shmuck!

In tears, the crowd looks at the sticking-out-of-the-windows middle fingers.

The PC[1] passes with a fishing net in his hands. The PC isn't at all surprised by this scene. The PC even sympathizes with the poor people:

— Go, — he says, — poor people, turn right at the corner. The station's swimming pool is there. Filled with water. Go get drunk there.

Scene 5

The station's swimming pool. A stench. The water is heavily seasoned with oil. In the stinking mixture swim five dead cats, six crows, and a rat. Gigantic malarial mosquitoes swarm around.

The roar of the approaching mob, to the tune "She Was Tired to Death."

Where is it, where is it, where is it,
Our salvation swimming pool?
We are tired, we are worn out,
We are being tor-men-ted!

They approach closer... Still closer... Closer... Closer... Aggh, no! Lower the curtain! To the next scene!

Scene 6

The station's back yard.

A water barrel stands with the inscription: *Bottled Water.*

The PC, MC[1], and VC[1] are fishing tadpoles out from the barrel with nets: Who scoops the most?

Then they release the tadpoles back into the tank, and the game starts again.

They are so engaged that the crowd of the thirsty catches them at this exciting game.

— Hey, that's what they are playing here?!

— Monsters, bloodsuckers, where's the water?

— Why isn't the barrel in its place? Why are there tadpoles in it, tell us!

The PC calmly waits for the storm of indignation to abate. With true, honest eyes, he looks into the eyes of the weary people:

— Comrades! These tadpoles... They are not ordinary. They are bred for scientific purposes.

— For scientific purposes? Oh, you Herods! And the dead cats in the swimming pool, they too are for scientific purposes?

— Comrades! Don't worry about it! May God strike me dead, we are not guilty on the count of the cats! You know these cats... they're... suiciders. By God I swear, in front of my own eyes, a tenth cat commits suicide. And for this reason, they need this accursed pool!

— Why are you lying with your little shameless eyes!

— Why are you messing with people's heads!

— In the Russian language we are asking you: why wasn't the water in the swimming pool changed? Why weren't the dead cats fished out?

— We tried, comrades! By God, I swear, we tried. There just wasn't any way to remove them. They clutched with their claws to the water... I mean, to the fuel oil, and there is nothing one could do about them. We pulled, pulled and left it alone...

— You left it alone? That's what you call it, 'left it alone!'

— I wish you left yourselves alone in there instead of those cats!

— Well, tell us, you Herods, where can we find water!

— Comrades, do not worry! Honestly, the water is two steps from you. At the pump house. Across the tracks, to the left.

The embittered crowd makes its way to the pump house. The ears of the PC, MC, and VC begin to burn, and they wonder: "Who is it, so to speak, that is remembering us so tenaciously?"

Scene 7

In the foreground is a water pump. It looks grim, preoccupied...

The half-dead people approach it, timidly stretching out pots and kettles.

— Water pump! Mother! Nurse!

— Have pity on us miserable folks!

— Give us water!

— A droplet!

— A sip!

The crowd fell silent in horror. The water pump suddenly shuddered, and they could distinctly hear her stone, sepulchral voice:

Man is annoying, and stupid...
Each and every one comes with requests...
I myself languish with thirst -
Fricking nay! May cholera get you in your... umbilical chord!

A suspicious sound thunders, then the water pump starts to spew out foul-smelling clumps of mold and various junk.

The crowd bursts into a storm of threats to the PC, MC, and VC. At this moment, at the station, the third call for the train is heard.

Scene 8

The workers' train 'Maxim' departs from Station Waterless.

Cries, dying groans, and curses carry from the cars.

The PC, MC, and VC listen to the curses and shake their heads reproachfully. They say with their demeanors:

— My God! What did we do? And it's like this every day!

And after that, aloud:

— People are impatient these days! Rowdy people! And us, we are martyrs!

A bloodcurdling scream erupts from the last car of the train:

— Water! Wa-t-er-r-r!

EPILOGUE

If the reader, having read the above, says "fiction," we must, with regrets, disappoint him. Everything written is essentially the naked, unvarnished truth. Our worker–correspondents gathered it piecemeal at the following stations: 1. *Red Beach*, Western Railroad (worker–correspondent № 291); 2. *Kamenskaya*, Southeastern Railroad (Polyakov); 3. *Alyaty*, Transcaucasian Railroad (worker–correspondent № 255); 4. *Pachelma*, Syzr.–Vyazemsk Railroad ('Grimy'); 5. *Batraky*, M.–Kazansky Railroad (worker–correspondent № 694); 6. *Gomel*, Western Railroad ('Sting'); 7. *Hundredth Mile*, Moscow-Kazan Railroad Barracks (worker–correspondent № 694).

Naturally, those howling at the indicated stations aren't always the passengers. More often than not, they concede this honor to the workers in the repair shops, depots, barracks, and switch posts.

Naturally, cats don't commit suicide everywhere (there aren't swimming pools at every station).

We don't dispute that all of these stations are very different from one another. But their essence is one: each of them is a piece of the arid Sahara, and each is under the threat of epidemic.

For those who have ears with which to hear, let them hear...

M. Mishev

Translators' note

1. *DS, PC, MC,* and *VC* are management positions: *DS* is an abbreviation for Director of the Station; *PC*, Director of the Railroad; *MC*, Director of Mechanical Services; and *VC*, Director of the Railcar Depot.

The Story of Makar Devushkin (Рассказ Макара Девушкина)

Our life, although not cosmopolitan, is nevertheless an interesting, crossroads life. An incredible quantity of events happen here, and one is more astonishing than the other.

TROUSERS AND ELECTIONS

There was, for example, an event of the following type: Fitilev, our secretary of the local committee, purchased for himself new woolen trousers with stripes. For a world-class city such as, for example, Moscow, such a thing would be nothing surprising. Everyone there has pants with stripes, but in our suburbs it is a novelty!

Naturally, it would be gratifying for everyone to gaze upon Fitilev's trousers. But Fitilev was a particular man; he didn't advertise the trousers until the right moment. And then a notice of a distinguished general meeting completely and unexpectedly unfolded before each and every member of our station. And in the notice stood such questions as the report of the vice chairman of the professional union, the report of the UDR[1] and, in a concluding chord, the report of the Local Committee with their re-election, which was the crux of the matter.

On top of that, everyone was saying that our famous Fitilev, the secretary, will speak at the official meeting, wearing the new purchase. So, the hall filled to an unbearable degree of stuffiness and, indeed, Fitilev appeared in creases, and the trousers looked like the cast iron ones on the statue of the poet Pushkin in Moscow, they were so well-sown.

So far, so good. Exactly at six o'clock, the chairman stood up and declared the meeting open, and our magnificent vice chairman of the professional union entered, coughed, and cut open the meeting with a speech. He started to report about the Railroad Congress, and he reported from six to nine, but until 21:00 in the new style, drinking half a pitcher of water in total from the first row. What happened in the hall, I am unable to express, except that suddenly the entire first row fell asleep, and then the second, like on a field of battle. In vain, the chairman rang the gong and appealed to social consciousness. What kind of consciousness does a person have if he is asleep?

But then a storm broke out on the face of the repair worker Vasya Danilov, disturbing the flow of the meeting's professional life. Vasya rose from his row and started crying as if he had lost the companion of his life, his wife. Addressing the speaker in a thunderous voice, he said:

— If you don't shut your trap, I will kill myself! I can't bear to hear any more about your facts after an eight-hour workday.

And a commotion erupted in the rows of the united workers,[2] and they expelled Vasya from the meeting until he calmed down.

Vasya, crying all the way to the exit, left. But not before enticing many by saying:

— I'm going, dear comrades, to the beer hall because without beer I won't be able to take the second speech.

And a few exited with him. In the confusion on a matter of quorum, the chairman liquidated the first speaker, and produced a second. The second spoke about the direction of the work until 23:00, more than two hours about assorted statistics. There was no brand of trousers that could help in any way: Fitilev placed his face on his white hands, pretending to be listening, but actually falling asleep. The young ladies, who had been feasting their eyes on the beauty of Fitilev, all exited because, although Fitilev was a bachelor, they couldn't take it either.

And finally, around midnight, it all ended, and best of all, Fitilev stunned everyone by resurrecting himself at the conclusion of the speech.

Fitilev stood up at the podium, squinted his eyes, and declared:

— In the name of the Russian Communist Party of the Bolsheviks...

The entire hall awakened because they thought that he would announce a radio message of international importance, and he continued:

— ...in the name of the party cell of our station, and in the name of the committee, I propose the list of candidates for the Local Committee. And so, comrades, please no deletions or substitutions. I will not allow it, comrades, because I will conduct this as I was instructed.

A refortified Vasya Danilov returned for the re-election along with his companions, intending to lead a healthy workers' criticism of the candidates, and he even opened his mouth.

— What a cranberry, — yelled Vasya, and, without further criticism, voted with his hand.

And after him, they all voted.

But when they had dispersed, a worm ate at my heart, and I couldn't stand it. I asked Nazar Nazarich, our party representative, a cultivated man:

— Is it true what he said, that in the name of the Russian Communist... your tongue cannot say a word?

And then he says:

— Nothing of the sort!.. It's a pity that I was in my sickbed. Otherwise, I would have explained. Outrageous! He is Gogol's Khlestakov in striped pants.[3] It isn't healthy business, but heinous bureaucratic red-tapism!

And he went on and on.

So that's how it is. Unorthodox meetings such as this do happen in our backwater life.

The story is recorded by Mikhail B.

Translators' notes

1. *UDR* is an abbreviation of *Upravleniye dokumentatsii i raspredeleniya gonorara,* the Director of Documents and Benefits.

2. *Splochennye ryady,* which we translated as 'rows of the united workers,' evokes an image of workers standing or marching in rows, holding hands, with arms half-raised or crossed in front of them.

3. *Khlestakov*—a poser, liar, and swindler—was the principle character in Gogol's play, *The Inspector.*

The newspaper "Gudok," Moscow, June 15, 1924

The Invisible Boots (Сапоги невидимки)

A story

> And may I ask you, with what do you grease your boots, lard or tar?
>
> *From Gogol*

> Drown in a swamp, brother! I don't grease them with anything because I don't have them!
>
> *From me*

IN A DREAM

A splendid dream came to Petr Khikin, a railroad-car coupler at the Kiev-Freight Station. It was as if an unknown citizen, wearing a golden chain on his stomach, appeared to Khikin in the flesh, and said:

— You, Khikin, they say, are experiencing a footwear crisis.

— What kind of a crisis? — replied Khikin. — It's just that these boots went to the devil. There's nothing to go out in.

— Ay, yay, yay, — the unknown said, smiling, — what a scandal. Such a handsome guy like you, and suddenly unable to go out. It's not for you to sit the entire day at home. What's more, your work might suffer from this imprisonment. Am I right?

— Your judgment is correct, — agreed the hibernating barefooted Khikin, — and it isn't possible for me to sit at home. Because my wife gnaws at me.

— A witch? — asked the stranger.

— A perfect witch, — confessed Khikin.

— Well, here's the deal, Khikin. You know who I am?

— How would I know? — snored Khikin in his dream.

— I'm a wizard, Khikin, that's the deal. And for your virtues, I bestow upon you, boots.

— My humble thanks, — Khikin whistled in his sleep.

— Only, my friend, keep in mind that these boots are not ordinary, but magical. Invisible boots.

— No way!

— Way!

The dreamy haze parted and in front of Khikin appeared boots of amazing beauty. And Khikin immediately grabbed them, pulled them on, and wheezing and lip-smacking in his sleep, went to his lawfully-wedded wife Mariya.

A three-legged kerosene lamp spewed a black stench, which the coupler swallowed, then went haphazardly sideways, and turned into a nightmare.

The face of the lawful Mariya surfaced, and her voice asked:

— What are you doing? Why are you running around in underpants, you caveman?

— Just look, Manyusha, at the boots that a wizard gave me, — squeaked Khikin softly.

— A wizard! — shouted the wife. — Oh my Lord, you drank to the point of wizard-visioning. You're barefoot like an insect, you alcoholic wretch. Look at yourself in a puddle!

— You will answer to me, Manya, for this word, — uttered Khikin in a quivering voice, offended by 'insect,' — your head must understand: the boots are invisible.

— Invisible!? Woe unto me. Good people, look at the father of a huge family! He's progressed to delirium tremens.

And the children began to wail from above the fireplace and a burning hell began in the coupler's family.

Khikin rushed in his sleep from Kiev-Freight to Khreschatyk, a busy street, and perished.

It seemed as if a crowd of citizens in patent leather shoes followed Khikin, and hallooed and howled at him:

— Hallooo... looo.. Loo-loo! Look, citizens, at the coupler! He guzzled away his boots. Hooray! Beat him, the son of a bitch!

And policemen whistled. And one of them jumped to

Khikin, saluted, and reprimanded:

— Shame on you, Citizen Khikin. I request that you get off the main street and not spoil the scenery.

— Get away from me, bullfinch! — Khikin roared in his sleep. — What are you, blind? The boots are invisible.

— Aha, invisible? — asked the policeman. — Then please, Monsieur Khikin, accompany me to the station, where we will show you who's invisible.

And he whistled like a nightingale.

And as a result of this whistle, Khikin woke up in a sweat.

And there was nothing: no wizard, no boots.

AWAKE

Khikin went into the terminal, and saw a remarkable advertisement:

A WORKER'S LOAN
WON'T MAKE YOU GROAN
OTPO[1] offers its esteemed customers unlimited credit. And, on credit, everything is cheap and good.

— My dream is coming true! — Khikin brightened up, and headed into the shop.

The indescribable was happening in the shop. They pressed like a wall. They demanded boots. Khikin also demanded, received the demanded, tried them on, and only asked:

— And why are boots at your place three rubles more expensive than at the market?

— But just look at them, sir, what kind of boots these are, — said a clerk, smiling like an angel, — connoisseur boots. Exactly what boots should be! Made from our own material.

Khikin put on the connoisseur boots, and headed towards the execution of his responsibilities: to connect rail cars. And during the responsibilities, a connoisseur rain thundered, exactly like rain should be, and after five minutes Khikin was without boots.

Khikin got mad. Khikin removed the connoisseur residues from his feet, and showed up barefoot at the *TPO*.

— From your own material? — he asked the representative menacingly.

— Yes, — brazenly and casually replied the representative.

— But look here, they're made of cardboard!

— Did I promise you boots of iron for 15 rubles?

At this point, Khikin flushed, waved the muddy boots, and said to the representative such words as cannot be printed here.

Because they were unprintable words.

M.B.

Translators' note:

1. *OTPO* is an abbreviation for *Otdelenie transportnogo potrebitelskogo obshestva,* a government division that operated stores that sold goods to railroad workers on credit. People called the stores *TPOs*.

The newspaper "Gudok," Moscow, June 18, 1924

Skull Hunters (Охотники за черепами)

> The head of security for the Moscow M.–B. Station of the Belarus Railroad, Citizen Linko, issued a security order that requires each security worker to apprehend four evildoers. In the event of failure, the violators of the order will be fired.

— Well, my loyal supporters, — said the director of transportation security of the Moscow–Belarus Station, nicknamed for his bravery Antip QuickToCatch, — report what incidents happened over night.

The loyal supporters strummed rusty weapons and shyly turned sour. Speaking first was the well-known brave one, the assistant to QuickToCatch:

— Well, nothing happened…

— What? — grumbled Antip. — Again nothing? The fifth night with nothing! Wh-why aren't there any evildoers?

— They're saying that social consciousness has triumphed, — added the assistant in an apologetic tone.

— Hmmn, — Antip whined ominously, — triumphed! The boxcars with merchandise are intact? No devil stole the being-repaired series W locomotive? And nobody made an attempt on the life and wallet of the director of the glorious Moscow–Belarus Station? What's going on? What do I have to do, snatch them myself, the devils?!

The supporters went morosely silent.

— This, my brothers, is impossible, — Antip continued to whine. — It means that you burden the earth for naught. How dare you scoff down Belarusian–Baltic bread? This will all end with you being thrown out of the service by the neck and me along with you. Such a huge station and nothing is happening! And if the head office asks: How many evildoers, Antip, did you apprehend in the last month? What will I show them? Bupkis?

Do you think that they will pat me on the head for bupkis?

— There aren't any, — sang the assistant morosely, — where would we get them? You can't give birth to them!

— Give birth, overriding the laws of nature! — howled Antip. — Search! Look! If a man is going along the tracks, you instantly approach him. What kind of ideas are in your head? Do not see that he has the sanctimonious mug and eyes of a pedagogue. Maybe the only thing he is dreaming about is picking the lock of a boxcar. In a word, this is how it is: In the Soviet State, each beetle fulfills a quota, and you should fulfill yours! So you should present four evildoers to me every month. I ask you, how is it possible that we are without incidents?

— In fact, there was an incident the other night, — croaked one of the transportation warriors, — Foreman Shukin's dog almost ripped Khlobuev's trousers when we were crawling under a boxcar.

— See, — screamed the leader. — See! And he says "nothing!" And what about wild animals on the Belarusian territory that has been entrusted to us? Isn't that an incident? Apprehend and kill! Shoot on sight!

— Who, the foreman or the dog?

— Think with your brains! The dog. Put the foreman against the wall. Show him the regulation about infestation of the station with rapacious animals. In a word, forward march!..

***

Foreman Shukin had a lucky star; therefore, the bullet slipped between his knees.

— What the hell is going on, have you lost your minds, accursed fools?! — screamed the stunned Shukin. — Why are you firing on a godly dog?

— Beat him! Seize him. Bayonet him! Oh, he ran away, the bugger. And you, 'Beard,' show us the document that says who you are.

— But you know me, — hissed Shukin, turning green, —

Khlobuev, you'll drink yourself to death. Look me in the face...

— There is nothing for me to see in your face. Your face is sufficiently well known to me. Show me your ID.

— Slither away from me, you purple devil.

— Ah-ha. Slither away? Enough. Bikin, take him. Let him prove that he has reason to be on the tracks.

— Hel-p!!

— Scream, scream as much as you like...

— Hel!..

— I dare you to scream again...

— Qua... qua...

— I'll show you how to quack.

***

The second to flunk was Lamtsa-Dritser, a member of the Association of Defense Attorneys, who had just returned on the weekenders' train from the Rotten Roots suburban station and had decided to take a short cut across the tracks.

— It's a flagrant violation! — cried the criminal, being escorted by Antip's troops, — I will lodge a complaint to the Small Soviet People's Committee, and if it isn't possible, then to the big one!

— Go straight to the big one, — wheezed the brave ones, — the Soviet People's Committee doesn't protect bandits.

— I'm a bandit?! — blazed Dritser, then extinguished like a candle.

— C'mon, there are alistocrats[1] with brief-cases who pick pockets too.

***

...The third was the mother-in-law of the head of the station, carrying a basket.

— Our native fathers! Dear sons! Where are you dragging me?!

***

...and the fourth was the entire team of seasonal workers in full: with shovels, picks, and hard crusts of black bread. The team's elder, looking like the Patriarch,[2] struck blind by the shining weaponry of Antip's guards, kneeled and murmured:

— Take it, my brothers, everything: the shovels, the shirts. Take our pants, only let these Christian souls go, so they can repent.

***

It isn't known how Antip's quest would have ended if the all-seeing leadership hadn't sent him a telegram:

"To Antip.

Antip! You are authorized to catch evildoers; but, if there aren't any, give thanks to fate and don't invent them!

Our vision is precisely that there won't be any evildoers. Shame on you, Antip! Your loving management."

Antip received the telegram, burst into tears, and ended his quest. And because of that, peace and quiet settled over the territory of Belarus.

M.B.

Translators' notes

1. The character does not know how to pronounce the word 'aristocrat.'

2. The Patriarch is the senior religious leader of the Russian Orthodox Church. He wears a long beard.

The newspaper "Gudok," Moscow, June 27, 1924

The Adventures of a Dead Man (Приключения покойника)

— Cough please, — said a doctor of the 6th district M.–K. of the National Railroad.

The patient complied with this straightforward request.

— Not into my eyes, man! You've spit all over my eyes. Breathe.

The patient began to breathe, and it seemed to the doctor as if a phonograph had begun to play in the clinic.

— Aha! — exclaimed the doctor. — Impressive! What is your temperature?

— One hundred fifty degrees, — said the patient, coughing onto the doctor's coat.

— Well, it can't be 150, — mused the doctor, — here's the deal, friend, you have nothing special, just fulminant tuberculosis.

— Fancy that! So does it mean I'll die?

— We all will die, — evasively answered the doctor. — Listen, angel, I will write you a note, and you will go to Moscow for a special X-ray picture.

— Will it help?

— How shall I put it, — replied the servant of medicine, — for some it helps a lot. And with a picture, y'know, it's somehow more pleasant.

— It's true, — the patient agreed, — you will be dying, you will look at the picture. Consolation. Then your widow will hang the picture in the living room to entertain the guests: "Here is a picture of my deceased railroader, may his be the Kingdom of Heaven!" And the guests are pleased.

— It's wonderful that you are not losing your spirits. Take the note and stomp over to the director of the Zernovo–Kochubeevsky fueling branch. He will write you a ticket to Moscow.

— My humble thanks.

The patient spit out a full spittoon in farewell and stomped over to the director. But he did not quite stomp over to the director because a secretary blocked his way.

— What do you want?

— I have the *Fulminant.*

— Sheesh! Dumbhead! What do you think, that you need to go to the director of the sanatorium, in his office? You, my dear, stomp over to the doctor.

— I was there. Here's a note from the doctor for the ticket.

— You're not entitled to a ticket.

— But what about the picture? You will you take it?

— I'm not your photographer. And do not cough on my papers.

— Without the picture, the doctor said, it's not right.

— Well, so be it, crawl over to the boss.

— Hi! Hu ... ukh! .. Aggh, hack, khakh!

— Cough into your hand! What? A ticket? You're not entitled. You have worked for only two months. Wait one more month.

— I will die without the picture.

— Go to the park. They'll take it there.

— Not that kind of picture. That's the dilemma.

— Go and discuss it with the accountant.

— Hi!

— Stand further away from me. What's up?

— A ticket. For a picture.

— Earhead! Do you think I have a cash register, huh? Go to the secretary.

— Hi! ... ugh. Hukh. Harrumph!..

— You've been to me already. You haven't spat enough already? Go to the director.

— Hello ... huk.... ukhrrr ...

— What, are you kidding? Courier, wipe off my trousers. Go to the doctor!

— Hi!.. They won't give it to me!

— What can I do, my pigeon? Go to the director.

— I will not go... I'll die... Uhhrrrr...

— I will give you some drops. Don't fall on the floor. Nurse, pick him up.

TWO WEEKS LATER

— Holy Spirit protect us! You died, didn't you?

— Apparently.

— So why have you turned up here? You, may yours be the Kingdom of Heaven, go straight to the cemetery!

— Without a picture, it's not permitted.

— How inconvenient! Stand further away, a strong spirit is emanating from you.

— There's nothing special about my smell. It's hot, that's the main reason.

— You should drink beer.

— They don't give it to the dead.

— Well, go visit the boss.

— Hell-o...

— Assistants! Help! Oh my dears, my dears!

— Are you really trying to squeeze the casket into the office, you accursed corpse?

— Speak, speak quickly! Just do not you look at me, for Christ's sake.

— I want a ticket to Moscow... for the picture...

— Write it for him! Write it! A first-class seat in the international car. Just to get him out of my sight, otherwise my heart will burst.

— What shall I write?

— Write: From Zernovo to Moscow, Mr. Skeleton so and so.

— And what about the casket?

— The casket goes in the baggage car!

— It's ready, take it.

— My humble thanks. Allow me to shake your hand.

— No, no, handshakes have been canceled!

— Leave, my dear, I beg you, leave quickly! Assistant, please see off Comrade Dead!

The newspaper "Gudok," Moscow, July 17, 1924

Meeting in the Presence of a Member (Заседание в присутсвии члена)

The news spread around the New Bakhmutovka Station in two seconds flat: there will be a meeting, not just any kind of meeting, but one in the presence of a member of the Avdeyevka Local Committee of the Professional Union of Railroaders. And at the appointed hour, the hall of the club was filled with the proletarian faces of the members of the professional union. The member was showing himself off at a table on the stage, arousing general attention and affection.

It began normally: they elected a chairman and he, swaying like grass in the wind, said confusedly:

— Hmm... Well, now, it seems, we need a secretary...

— Right! — confirmed muscular voices in the hall, — Vasya Guzin!

— So be it, Vasya, — said the chairman, and addressed the member: — They want Vasya, is it OK?

— Be it as it may, — said the member, — let them have him. I have nothing against Vasya.

— So, by the majority of votes, it is Vasya... — started the chairman.

— Comrades, — Vasya's voice rang out, — I humbly beg you to allow me to decline, on the strength of the reason that I have insufficient literacy because I have just finished the illiteracy liquidation program.

— Vasya, don't be a wimp! — thundered the hall, — Really, Vasya, can't you scribble five times or so with a pen for the common good?

Amid a thunder of applause, Vasya took his seat at the table.

— The first question standing before us is on what basis did they start pushing dear Comrades Dziuba, Dusheba, and Samiska out of the workplace without any knowledge of the trade unions,

— declared the chairman. — I invite you to express your opinions.

The hall immediately expressed outrage with a boisterous growl.

— Shhhh, — said the chairman, — one person at a time.

But two stood up at once and, interrupting one another, expressed:

— It's all the foreman's fault!

— PD-9, may he have neither roof nor floor!

— He said that he's your trade union representative for six months, but I am the foreman forever!

— Craftily done! — the hall thundered.

— Read Clause № 1...

— That's right! — someone shouted.

— It was because of № 10 that they fired them!

— How is it 'right?'

— Quiet down! — howled the chairman, perishing in a wave of public outrage, — who votes 'yes?' I am voting. I request that you raise your hands! Vasya, write it down.

A forest of hands went up and, just as quickly, as if toppled, went down.

Vasya inked the pen and wrote:

"Read Clause № 1, heard the case for № 10 the abstained 6 people incorrectly abbreviated PD-9 Fedorenko."

Then he thought a little, and added:

"Clarification is confirmed for № 8 Gavrikov and Filonov."

— What did I vote for?

— Let's start over!

— Explain, chairman, what are we raising our hands for?

— OK, let's start over again, — said the chairman, turning pale.

— How could it be, — someone started speaking, — the unloading of the soil took place on a holiday... Overtime and, instead of relaxation, we got bupkis?

— This foreman should be drowned in the cistern!

— Murder is not acceptable! — shouted the chairman, busting a gut.

— He's negligent.

— A troublemaker!

— Kerosene was delivered, but we haven't seen it with our own eyes.

— And we were stuck on a sidetrack for three months without any water.

— And where is the trade union representative?

— The foreman said that he had been caught with a bribe: five pounds of potatoes!

— Who had caught whom!

— Qui-et down! — shouted the chairman, wiping sweat from his face, — Vasya, write.

Pale Vasya began to scribble:

"Gave a hearing: Received kerosene and other objects PD-9 nearby did not refuse."

"It was resolved: Didn't receive kerosene unacceptable presented PD-9 approximately Fedorenkov."

— He should be kicked out of the union!

— Who?

— We mowed cattails at the pump station for eight days, but he stayed in the office…

— Exploitraition[1] of labor!..

— Your guys are hot-tempered, — said the bewildered member to the chairman, — that's the trouble!

— What am I supposed to do now? — the chairman asked.

— You should vote, — the member advised, — maybe then, they will shut up.

— I vote, comrades! — the chairman whined.

— For whom? — thundered the hall.

— That's obvious. To get the hell out!

— Who?

— Who votes 'yes,' raise your hands!

— On the contrary: send him off to the pigs!

— Whom?

— Foreman Fedorenkov!

— Yeah!

— Who wants him to be expelled?.. One, two, three... Vasya, write...

"Expel by 15 votes," — Vasya wrote.

— Hooray! We threw him out, — triumphed the hall.

— We worked hard and cleaned up the union!

— Now what? — the chairman asked the member.

— Close the meeting, — he responded, — may they rest in peace.

— I declare the meeting closed! — the chairman shouted with relief.

— That's right, — replied the Bakhmutovsky people, — it's time for soup.

And with a roar the hall emptied. Vasya thought, and wrote: "The meeting was closed in 7:00."

— Well done, Vasya, — said the chairman, and buried the minutes.

Note from *Gudok*:

This feuilleton is based on a copy of the minutes of the union members meeting at Station N. Bakhmutovka on June 19. The minutes are utter nonsense.

It is absolutely unclear how a meeting could proceed in such a manner in the presence of a member of the Avdeyevka Local Committee of the Professional Union of Railroaders.

Translators' note

1. The word is misspelled intentionally in the Russian original.

The newspaper "Gudok," Moscow, July 24, 1924

CentralPoliticalSermon[1] (Главполитбогослужение)

> The Executive Committee of the city of Konotop, in ac-
> cordance with the agreement of July 23, 1922 with the
> community of church members in the village at
> Bakhmach Station, transferred a building for their per-
> manent use for religious worship. It is built on a strip of
> the railroad, adjacent to a building that belongs to the
> Western Railroad, and where the railroad school operates.
> …The windows of the church look out at the school.
>
> *From legal correspondence*

In the end, Father Deacon of Bakhmach Church, whose
windows look out at a school, could not take it. He sozzled himself up on the very morning of Saint Paraskeva's Friday[2] and,
drunk as an umbrella, arrived at the altar for the execution of his
official duties.

— Father Deacon! — gasped the abbot, — what's with you?..
Take a look at yourself in the mirror: You don't look like yourself!

— Father Abbot, I can't take it any longer! — howled Father
Deacon, — they torture me, the accursed fools. No kind of
nerves could possibly st... st... stand it. What kind of service is
it, when right nearby into your head they buzz this alphabet? —
Deacon sobbed and large tears, like peas, slid along his nose. —
Can you believe that yesterday, after an overnight service, I open
the Book of Devotions and before my eyes in flaming letters
jumped out: *Religion is the opium of the people.* Pshaw! The Devil's
work. This is... hic... up... where does this lead?.. And you
yourself won't notice how you will start to believe in the Cam...
com... mun...nist party. There was a deacon, and now there is
no deacon! Where is he, the good people will ask, our dear deacon? Well, the deacon is, he's in hell, in the flames of hygiene.

— In the flames of *Gehenna,*[3] — corrected Father Abbot.

— Six of one, half a dozen of the other, — said Father Deacon desperately, awkwardly getting into his robe, — I'm haunted by the devil!

— You drink a lot, —hinted the abbot carefully, — this is why he seems to appear before you.

— Oh that's what you call it, 'seems to appear?' — angrily asked the deacon.

— *Labor will be master of the world!!* — stretched out through the open windows of the neighboring building.

— Uuuh, — sighed the abbot, who opened the curtain and roared, — Bless me, Lord!

— *A Proletarian has nothing to lose but his eyes.*

— Always, now and forever, — agreed Father Abbot, making the sign of the cross on himself.

— Amen! — responded the choir.

The lesson in politvocab ended with a powerful singing of *The International* and the ektene:[4] *We will destroy the whole world of violence to the base!* And then:

— Peace be to all! — sang the abbot benignly.

— They have pestered all life out of me! — sobbed the teacher of politvocab, handing over the class to the teacher of the mother tongue, — I say one word, they say ten in return!

— I will overrun them, — boasted the Russian teacher, and ordered, — Read, Klyukin, a fable!

Klyukin stepped forward, fixed his belt, and recited:

All summer long
The Dragonfly had sung,
And then she looked—the summer is all gone.

— As she gave birth to our Father!! — thundered the choir. The entire class thundered in response, and the congregation spluttered with laughter. The top student, Klyukin, started crying in the class, and at the altar, Father Abbot started crying.

— To hell with them, — said the teacher, giggling dazedly, — enough, Klyukin, sit down, A+.

Father Abbot stepped up to the ambon[2] and saddened the congregation with the message:

— Father Deacon has suddenly taken ill and because of this, he is unable to conduct the service.

The suddenly-taken-ill Father Deacon lay inside the sanctuary and mumbled in delirium:

— Oh Lord… to the all-powerful Lord of ours… they tortured me, the damned!

— Be god-fearing, — hissed Father Abbot, — if someone hears, we'll be in trouble.

— Who cares… — mumbled the deacon, — I have nothing to lose… hic…up… except for my eyes.

— Amen! — sang the choir.

Note by *Gudok*:   The editor's office has received materials showing that the case about the co-existence of the school and the church has been dragging on for two years. A request to all appropriate institutions: Announce when this unbearable co-existence will come to an end.

M.B.

Translators' notes:

1. Bulgakov invented the Russian title, *Glavpolitbogoslujenie,* from *Glavnoe politicheskoe prosveshenie* and *bogoslujenie. Bogoslujenie* is a sermon. *Glavnoe politicheskoe prosveshenie,* Central Political Enlightenment, was the central coordinating center of Lenin's program to educate and indoctrinate the masses.

2. Saint Paraskeva is the patron saint of crops and livestock. She was prosecuted by the Romans during their purge against Christianity and beheaded in the third century. Although her day is celebrated in October, she is also the personification of Good Friday, the day of crucifixion.

3. *Gehenna* is a Greek word used in the New Testament and often translated as 'Hell.'

4. *Ektene* is a penitential litany.

5. *Abon* is an elevation in the floor in front of the sanctuary section of an altar.

The newspaper "Gudok," Moscow, August 1, 1924

How the School Collapsed into the Underworld (Как школа провалилась в преисподнюю)

Makar Devushkin's transportation story

— That's nothing! — exclaimed Devushkin, the popular Moscow–Belarus–Baltic railroad worker who was sitting in a circle of his friends at a pub, — but at our Nemchinovsky Station we had an incident, a real curiosity!

Devushkin tapped a silver 20-kopek coin on the marble table. A member of the Professional Union of Local Foodstuff Workers, wearing a white apron, hustled toward the sound. Upon his face played a kind-hearted professional smile.

— My good man, give us another two doubles, — requested Makar Devushkin.

— More than one double at a time isn't permitted, — replied the national-foodstuff seller with regret.

— My friend! — exclaimed Makar, — does it really matter what is permitted? You should somehow put it together, — and at that, Makar again tapped with the 20-kopek coin.

The national-foodstuff seller sighed, looked askance at a sign on the wall:

Accepting of Tips is Unworthy of a Member of a Trade Union.

He sighed again, flit off somewhere, and presented two doubles.

— That's the spirit! — exclaimed Makar, took a pull at the mug, and began:

— Do you know the dacha of former citizen Senet?

— We've never heard of it, — his friends replied.

— An amazing dacha. With all the inconveniences. So, consequently, they seized this dacha for an elementary school. The main thing is the location was nice: a small woods, this and that, naturally, an outhouse… is there. In a word, a perfectly serviceable dacha for 90 schoolchildren. But here's the thing, there's no water supply! That's the problem.

— One can dig a well.

— Exactly, it's a simple matter. But, everything happened because of that damned well, and the dacha disappeared, went to the pig–dogs. This well was under the very porch, and so last year a sorrowful event took place: the log house caved in… So, then the head of the school blew the whistle to all the institutions in our apparatus. Back and forth… He writes to the Emergency Director (ED): such and such must be repaired. The ED sends material, workers. Specialists in well drilling were driven in. So, it goes without saying that they chopped out a new log house in two shakes. Placed it at the top, and what was left for them, my brothers, was to put on the finishing touches, mere trifles, a piece of cake.

But in fact, it didn't happen. Instead of taking and finishing the work there and then, they left it unfinished until spring. Marvelous.

In the spring, as the ground began to thaw, everything slid into the well, and the well is 40 meters deep! The earth slid down into the well, then the entire new log house. And basically everything else fell in… My friends, a deep pit appeared, more than six-meters wide, under the very wall of the school.

The school foundation thought and thought, then cracked, and crawled along, following the log house to the well. It went from bad to worse: kraaaaKK! The wall cracked. From inside the school, everything, naturally, went up hill and down dale. Two more days passed, and fare thee well, the entire school motored into the well. The good people come and see an outhouse for 90 persons with a sign on the door, *Elementary School,* and nothing else. A bald place!

And that's how our enlightenment came to a halt at the Nemchinovsky Station of the Moscow–Belarus–Baltic Railroad… I drink to your health, comrades!

From the words of Makar Devushkin, recorded by Mikhail B.

The newspaper "Gudok," Moscow, August 9, 1924

Interrogation without Prejudice (Допрос с беспристрастием)

> The Polish newspapers are trying to prove that the rebel attack on Stolbtsy was led by Red Army men.
>
> *(From the newspapers)*

The rebels, surrounded on all sides, tried to defend themselves in vain. The Polish police ganged up, steamrolled over, and then began investigations and reprisals.

— You! Beat him! Go to the left. Rip off the son of a bitch's head. Grab him. Aha! We've got the ringleader! Hip, hip, hurray! Confess, cockroach, what is your last name?

— My last name? — asked the insurgent, strangled by nimble hands. — My last nnn... release my throat... name... Khrr... Khryssky...

— You're lying!

— Khryssky.

— Lying! Lying!

— Don't hit an unarmed man, — poured out the rebel, — I am telling you, Khryssky.

— Confess, you devil, are you with the Red Army?

— I'm a local... don't hit me, I cannot talk... from around nearby Stolbtsy...

— You're ly-y-ing! You are from Minsk!

— Nothing of the sort... don't hit me in the stomach...

— From Minsk, dog's blood!

— I hope you're kidding, sirs... I might as well say I'm from Hell...

— Aha, he started talking, he started talking! I'll have you talking.

— Oh... of course, I'll start talking after you... you've stuck a fist in my mouth.

— I'll kill you!!! How many are there of your Red Army

men?

— But I wasn't one... There weren't any.

— Weren't any?! Weren't any?! Weren't any?!

— There were... there wer...

— Write it down, Mr. Ensign: The ringleader of the gang confessed that Red Army men from Minsk participated in the attack. How many of you were there?

— Thwak, thwak, thwak!

— Ugh... th... th...

— Thirty?

— Write down "three hundred." Or better yet, for a round number: 3,000.

— Was Budyonny involved? You're silent, you scoundrel?!

— Hit him on the head, with a cannon rod. He'll start talking right away.

— Ux... b... y...

— Well, look here, he was involved. Write down that according to the testimony of the insurgents, Budyonny himself led the attack. Aha?! But maybe Trotsky himself led it? None other than Trotsky. Something smells strongly like Trotsky. Respond!!

— ...

— He doesn't answer, the scoundrel.

— Try with the cannon...

— I tried, it doesn't help.

— Scum! He died in vain. Well, OK, take him away. Bring in the next one!

***

A telegram in the Polish newspaper:

"According to the testimony of members of the insurgency, the attack on Stolbtsy was led by large Red Army brigades from Minsk under the direct command of Budyonny. There are reasons to believe that the plan of attack was worked out by Trotsky himself, who arrived in Minsk by airplane."

Em.

The newspaper "Gudok," Moscow, August 12, 1924

On What Basis Did the Foreman Get Married?! (На каком основании десятник женился?!)

(Everyday life)

...You are asking why I'm depressed? How could I not be depressed, dear citizen, if I am unjustly offended on a work-related basis? I fell in love, comrade, and, having fallen in love, proposed to my subject with hand and heart, and received an acceptance, as a result of which I was in seventh heaven. Having purchased everything that one ought to have for a wedding, I managed to get married to my subject, not spending a single second of work time on the wedding, and between two jobs we slipped directly into the honeymoon month, ready to drink fully from the cup of life.

But nothing of the sort was to be! I bump into the head of operations for wheel inspection of the Slavutsky Railway Branch, Citizen Loginov (I work as a foreman), and he asks in a bossy tone, jingling the chain of his watch:

— How dared you, highly respected man, marry without my consent?

Even my tongue failed me. Excuse me. Am I a serf, or what? It's none of his business! It would be a big deal if I spent work time on the marriage or, say, got drunk with friends, disgracing our Professional Union. But I quietly and peacefully joined in marriage as any individual on Earth has a right to do. But a thought torments me: What if it comes into the head of my wife to bestow progeny upon me in the amount of one child. Should I run to Loginov? "May I have your permission..." What if it's a baptism ceremony? What if it's a dead mother-in-law? Does she have the right without Loginov?

No, citizen, you will get depressed with such a boss.

From the words of the foreman written by Mikhail B.

The newspaper "Gudok," Moscow, August 17, 1924

A Beer Story (Пивной рассказ)

> For four months, the supply train of the Kiev TPO[1] sold only beer.
>
> *From the letter of a correspondent*

At a station, they waited impatiently for the supply train, and their waiting paid off. It arrived, and the railroaders dashed for it as one.

— At last, deliverance...

The first thing that threw itself at the eyes of the inhabitants of the station was a slogan on the side of the train:

Do Not Express Yourself in Swear Words.

And beneath it another:

Non-sober Individuals Will not be Served.

— Marvelous! — exclaimed the railroaders. — Look at what the sloganmaniacs are doing now. In the old days, they all, as it happened, wrote: *Strengthen Cooperation...* or, how does it go: *Soviet Cooperation Saves the* whatchamacallit... *Situation* or something... Or something more scholarly... And nowadays, it's simple.

— That means they were strengthened!

— And it means don't express yourself using swear words.

— The smell of beer, my brothers, I can't figure out where it's coming from?

— The smell comes from Yeremkin. He and his boss just killed a six-pack.

The door of the car opened and a man with a cooperative appearance looked out.

— Don't push the door, citizens, — he asked, and from his words such a pleasant scent hit the air that Yeremkin, instead of asking: "Do you have any boots?" asked:

— Do you have Caspian roach fish?

— Of course, epicurean, — the cooperative one joyfully answered.

— I would like cotton chintz.

— Chintz, I'm sorry, we don't have it.

— Perhaps you have gingham?

— Gingham, I'm sorry, we don't have it.

— Calico?

— No calico, sorry.

— Well what fabric do you have?

— Velvety beer, black.

— Ah-ha! May I have a six-pack?

— How much are boots?

— Boots, unfortunately, we don't have... What?.. Kerosene? We don't carry it. And we don't carry gasoline. Instead of gasoline, I am able to offer you, auntie, 'Stenkya Razin' or 'Red Bavaria.'

— For what do I need your 'Razin.' I need something for the primus stove.

— We don't carry anything for primuses.

— What the hell is wrong with you, you spotted devils!

— I ask you, grandma, not to express yourself in swear words.

— I wish that this bottle would land on the head of your cooperative. Here you wait for goods, and they bring swill...

— Beer if you will, two mugs.

— Do you have any peas?

— Give me a beer!

— A beer!

— A beer!

— A beer!

— A beer!

— A beer!

***

In the evening, when the station had sunk in beer up to the onion domes, a single sober correspondent sat, and under the light of the moon (there wasn't anything to pour into the lamp), wrote to *Gudok*:

"On behalf of the workers of our station M.-K. Voronezh Railroad and implicitly in the name of the rail branch, I request *Gudok* to demand from the sleeping Division № 5 of Professional Union Workers of the Railroad and the leadership of the cooperative to come to this rail branch with groceries. Otherwise, as a form of protest, we are exiting from voluntary membership in the cooperative."

The fat moon sat on top of the sky, and it seemed as if she had also got drunk, and got stuck in the middle of a wink[2]...

Mikhail B.

Translators' notes

1. *OTPO* is an abbreviation for *Otdelenie transportnogo potrebitelskogo obshestva,* a government division that operated stores that sold goods to railroad workers on credit. People called the stores *TPOs.*

2. The Russian verb *podmigivat',* when used in the present tense as it is here, means either to wink repetitively or to get stuck in the middle of a wink.

The newspaper "Bakinskiy rabochiy" (The Baku Worker), Moscow, August 18, 1924

The Funhouse Mirror (Кривое зеркало)

Three Dungeons

1

For 30 kopeks. A torture with syphilis. A cramped compartment in the bowels of the establishment. Outside, a sign: *Barber.* Inside: *Master Barbers are Guaranteed by the Enterprise and Tips They Do Not Accept. Accepting of Tips is Unworthy of a Member of a Trade Union.*

The guaranteeing enterprise comprises fly-specked mirrors, jars with wisps of cotton wool, atomizers, and a clumsy bald apparition with an unshaven face and husky voice that vividly attests to a completely new case of syphilis.

The apparition begins the conversation:

— What do you want? To be shaved?

— Yes.

— Sit down!

From behind a cotton curtain, the sound of a razor stropping on a belt, and still other sounds extremely suggestive of quiet spittings on this belt. I think, "Maybe, to my good fortune, he doesn't have syphilis. Maybe he just caught a cold?"

— Krrch... the razor scrapes...

— Well? What did it scrape...

Krrch... krrch... krrch…

— Ah, what the devil, are you cutting my ear?

— You had a pimple and I popped it.

— Do you have iodine?

— No iodine, I'll compress it with a stone. Shave your neck?

— No need.

— Need cologne?

— No need.

— Need powder?

— No need.

— What about the hair?

— Do nothing, please, with the hair. How much do I owe?

— Thirty kopeks.

— Goodbye.

No response.

For 20 days of self-shaving, every morning and evening, he approaches the mirror, pulls at his cheek, looks. Anxiously he awaits the syphilis. He curbsides doctor acquaintances and says:

— What's up? Nice weather. And, y'know, I took a shave in our Union's barber shop... Hehe... you will excuse me for disturbing you. Does syphilis present like this?

— Hmmn... it's just a bruise.

— *Merci.* You must excuse me... I am, you know, a neurasthenic.

— He simply tore up your entire mug.

— Hee-hee. Yes, he's a terrible scoundrel.

On the 21st day of shaving, he calms down, begins to gain weight.

2

For 1 ruble. Torture with eau de cologne. Four mirrors, eight electric lamps. Powder, atomizers, green cologne. Two spittoons. At the door, a pregnant woman in a white frock with a clothes brush in hand. On the first page of the magazine *Ogonyok*, the chairman of the Union, Kamenev, in green. Occasionally, Kamenev is temporarily replaced by Budyonny or by workers rejecting coins at the Mint.

— Uh... Is the wait long?

— Please... Five minutes, no longer... Eh, what do you need?

— A shave, please.

— Eugene! An order. You haven't travelled outside of Moscow?

— Mnnn... no.

— Does a razor frighten you?

— Uh... no, it's OK.

— We haven't seen you in a long time for some reason. We thought you were at the country house.

— No, can't afford a country house. No money.

— Heh-heh. A fact of general significance. You've been shaving yourself?

— No, somewhere else, some turdball shaved me...

— Hee-hee. So I see... Freshen up your face?

— Well, OK...

Slap... slapp... grrr...

— Uh, oh! Your eau de cologne is caustic!

— It got in the eyes. God forbid it gets in the eye! Will you have powder on the entire face?..

— How much do I owe?

— Eighty-five kopeks... Zhenya, clean up... Krrch krrch...

(I think, "Ten or fifteen kopeks more for her? The devil take it all. Fifteen, make it an even ruble.")

— Goodbye!

— (Chorus) Goodbye!

3

For 3 rubles, 50 kopeks. Torture with luxury. Nine mirrors. Marble pier-glass tables piled up with cut-glass flacons. Imported Koken barber chairs in crimson. Countless mirrored lights. At the door, a gold-braided chevron[1] with a worn-out snoot.

— Your hat, if you please...

("I've been trapped, therefore, he gets twenty kopeks?..")

("A shave - 30 kopeks.")

("A haircut - 50 kopeks.")

("Well it's still bearable... should the scoundrel offer to wash my hair, I will say that I am going to the banya. Get out of here before it's too late? I will be fleeced of two rubles, perhaps...")

— Who's next? You? After you... Shall we wash your hair with shampoo or hair soap?

("The devil take him!")

— I... to the banya... um... just a moment, perhaps... sh... shampoo...

— Boy! For a shampoo!

Electric dryer with hot air, a white towel. In the mirror a Bedouin. Hmm... how much can a washing cost?.. Hmm... price schedules are not visible...

— You have tender skin... a hot compress is required. For a hot compress!

Would you like pomade?

("Lord, how much does pomade cost?")

A brush goes along his eyebrows.

— After yooo.

— How much do I owe?

— Three rubles, esteemed sir.

— Hmm...

— Pay the cashier, please. Get three of the ruble. — On the way to the cashier, a haunting white apparition. What does the apparition want? A half-ruble to the apparition, she does not deserve to be a member of a trade union! You can see it in her eyes. And this 20-kopek coin. Damned gold-braided chevron. It used to be a five-ruble piece. It became about 1 ruble, 30 ko-peks. Get the hell out of here! For good!

Translators' note

1. A non-commissioned officer

How to Fight with *Gudok*, or The Art of Responding to Comments (Как бороться с Гудком или искусство отвечать на заметки)

A short guide for administrators

CORRESPONDENCE ABOUT GRIME

How should one respond when they write that it is very dirty at some railroad station?

One ought to respond like the public-health doctor of the first region of the Moscow–Kazan Railroad responded:

"The concept of grime is subjective, and, although due to the many deficiencies of a yet unfinished railroad station it is not possible to attest to its actual cleanliness, it is still far from the point of griminess, in my opinion."

At *Gudok,* when they received this response, two employees were immediately so seized by paralysis that they will no longer be able to write a thing.

Those remaining among the living convened a general meeting to resolve the following questions:

1. At what precise point does 'subjective' griminess end, and does railroad-station griminess, from spittle resembling a double gold coin, from cigarette butts, and from all kinds of slush, begin?

2. To what elevation it is necessary to begrime the railroad station so that the sanitary doctor will attest that 'the point of griminess,' in his opinion, is 'at hand:'
   a. To the ankles
   b. To the knees
   c. Or to the waist?

They didn't resolve these questions. The only hope lies with the public health doctor, that he will inform us.

2,000 TEETH

It was written in *Gudok* that they did not provide artificial teeth to railroad worker Kuznetsov, notwithstanding the decree of the Teeth Commission.

What would one write in response to such a thing?

The Health Service of the Moscow–Kazan Line responded:

"It is resolved to insert artificial teeth into Kuznetsov in the second round."

Rejoice, Kuznetsov! You will have teeth. Wai... wait, Kuznetsov, wait... Weep, Kuznetsov! Look what's written further along: "Additionally, the Health Service considers it necessary to communicate that prosthetic work is limited to 500 teeth, given the demand for 2,000 teeth by the 1st of August."

PEROGIES WITH NOTHING

They write, for example, that some kind of work on the railroad isn't occurring, red tape, this and that, in general, an unpleasant commentary.

The administration of the Orlov–Viterbsky Service ably responded to this commentary:

"Although as of this moment we have received credit for this work, but seeing as to how money is not provided, in reality it isn't possible to do anything at this time."

Indeed, there is no way to trump such a response.

Credit without money is the same as perogies with nothing.

You know what, Orlov–Viterbsky? Try to get money with credit.

CUPS ON A LEASH

One correspondent concerned himself with the question of why there aren't any cups for water at Lyblino–Dacha.

A response arrived: "Thirty-three will be there any day now." As Anton Pavlovich Chekhov once said:

"The domestic-materials department did not have a supply of cups with chains, and it is forbidden to leave cups unchained."

Get chains, my brothers!

"RS (Railroad Station) Lyblino received three cups with chains."

Hip, hip, hooray! Drink to your health.

M.

The newspaper "Gudok," Moscow, August 20, 1924

How While Exterminating Drunkenness the Chairman Exterminated the Transportation Workers (Как истребляя пьянство, председатель транспортников истребил)

A tearful tale

A snap was heard from a room with a sign on the door: *Do Not Enter Without a Report.*

It was the chairman of the Divisional Committee of the Professional Union of the Railroad hitting himself on the head about the evils of drunkenness.

— You should understand, — he said, spinning the secretary by his jacket button, — that all of our misfortunes come from drunkenness. It destroys our collective discipline, threatens transportation; it undermines our cultural-enlightening work at its root and destroys the body! Am I right?

— Absolutely right, — confirmed the secretary, and added: — You are so wise, Amos Fedorovich, it is even unpleasant!

— See, you get it. Therefore, before us lies the problem of how to exterminate this hydra of drunkenness.

— It's a difficult business, — exclaimed the secretary, — how does one exterminate the damn thing?

— We must, my friend! Don't worry. I will rip our transport workers from the clutches of drunkenness and vice, no matter what the cost to me! I will think something up.

— You will conquer it, —said the secretary sycophantically, — you are a clever one.

— That's exactly what I'm talking about.

And, planting himself down to think, the chairman thought for some 16 hours, and then he thought up an amazing thing.

***

A few days later, a notice appeared in all the rathskellers, beer halls, and similar liquid establishments:

Owners, Be Aware that Transportation Workers Are Not Creditable. So Do Not Give Them Anything.

The results were, indeed, unexpected.

***

— Hello.

— Hello, — replied the owner glumly.

— Why are you wearing such a sour puss? Well anyway, give us two double shots.

— We don't have double shot.

— How can that be? Are you nuts?

— I am in no way nuts. Show me your money.

— Are you kidding or what? I get a paycheck tomorrow. I will pay you back.

— No. Maybe you won't get paid.

— Have you lost your mind?.. I won't get paid?! What's with you, don't you know me?

— I know you well. You are not creditable.

— And what if I give you a boxing around the ears for those words…

— Leave my ears in peace. Read the notice…

The transportation worker read it and froze…

***

— A bottle of beer!

— And who exactly are you?

— Phew! Don't you recognize me? The assistant to the head of the station?

— Then, there isn't any beer.

— How can that be? Hey, what's that in the crate?

— It's castor oil.

— So why are you lying? Those two guys got sloshed on your castor oil, and are singing songs.

— They aren't like you.

— What are they?

— They are creditable. Woodworkers.

— Ah, you are a viper! How do you have the right to offend us, the transportation workers?..

— Read the notice.

***

— Hello, Abram. I brought the fabric. My friend, tailor my pants for me.

— Money first.

— What money? Your place has a sign hanging: *To Members of the Union We Extend Wide Credit.*

— Not to members like you. To transportation workers, we extend bupkis.

— Wha...t the???

— Look... your chairman hung a notice in the bars...

***

— Manka! Run to the store, get kerosene for the... Well, what?

— Hee-hee. They won't give it to me.

— How can they not give it to you?

— They say: To the transportation workers, they say, we won't give. They, they say, aren't creditable...

***

— Fedos Petrovich, give me a fifth. I will pay you back Saturday.

— I won't give...

— On what basis do you deny your best friend?

— You are not creditable.

***

After two weeks, a howling of transportation workers had arisen throughout the entire territory of the Division of the Commissariat of the Workers' Union. And we don't know how it all would have ended, if the Directorate of the Division of the Commissariat of the Workers' Union hadn't sent this letter to the Division of the Commissariat of the Workers' Union:

"Dear Amos Fedorovich! Send your notices to the pigs. They don't help counter drunkenness, but only bedevil life.
Signature"

Rattled was Amos Fedorovich, and the notices he removed.
M.B.

The Comrade Director and the Masses, or Swinehood in a Professional Setting (Сотрудник с массой или свинство по профессиональной линии)

(A story–photograph)

Dunka flew in like a storm.

— Comrade Opishkov-e-e, — howled Dunka, prowling with her eyes. — Where is he? Comra...

A basso cough rang out from the porch, and Comrade Opishkov, tying the waist string of his long underwear, appeared before Dunka.

— Why are you yelling like crazy? — he asked, yawning.

— They're calling you, — explained Dunka, — hurry up, they're waiting!

— Who's waiting? — anxiously inquired Opishkov.

— The meeting... the people have assembled, more than the eye can behold!..

Comrade Opishkov spat from the porch.

— Foo, damn it! I thought that... Tell them I'll be there right away.

— Will you have some tea? — his spouse inquired.

— No time for tea, — murmured Opishkov, donning his trousers, — the masses await, screw them... I've had it up to here with these masses (Opishkov hand chopped up to his neck). What the hell do these masses need? — Opishkov's voice resembled distant thunder, or a cart on an embankment... — The masses... I don't have time. They must have nothing better to do...

Opishkov buttoned up his fly.

— Will you be home anytime soon? — asked the wife.

— Very, — responded Opishkov, knocking with his boots on the floor, — I won't dawdle there... with these masses...

And he disappeared.

Upon the appearance of Comrade Opishkov, a stir and clamor flew up in the hall accommodating the masses of railroaders of the Third Line, First Division:

— He's here... He's here... the train dispatcher... look...

The chairman of the meeting stood to meet Opishkov, and smiled warmly.

— Very nice to see you, — he said.

— Brrr... brr... brrrah... — roared Opishkov's bass in reply. — What is it?

— What do you mean 'What is it?' — responded the chairman respectfully. — Your report... Hee-heee.

— Ra-port? — said Opishkov in amazement. — A report to whom?

— What do you mean 'to whom?' To them, — and the chairman gestured in the direction of the sweating masses, piled up in rows.

— Vrrr... let's go... gu... gu... — the masses stirred and blew their noses.

A sour expression spread across Opishkov's entire face, and it even drooped onto his jacket.

— I don't get it, — he said, curling his lip, — What's this report for? Uh... I report to the track director every day, so why on earth also to these?..

The chairman blushed and the masses quivered. In the last rows, heads raised up...

— Well, not exactly, — murmured the chairman, — it's one thing to report to the track director, but this, pardon the expression, is another thing, which you must do...

— Grr... grr... — grumbled Opishkov, and sat in a chair. — Well, all right.

In the hall they blew their noses for the last time.

— Qui-et! — said the chairman.

Hmmn, — began Opishkov, — Well, that is... What is there to say?.. Well, 1.8 miles of acceleration track was laid.

The room was silent like a coffin.

— Well, — continued Opishkov, — a thousand railroad ties were replaced.

Silence.

— Well, — continued Opishkov, — we weeded the grass.

(Silence).

— Well, — continued Opishkov, — the rail bed was, whatchamacallit, raised.

A thin voice broke the silence:

— Look how difficult it is for him to report. Eyewatering!

Again there was silence.

— So? — timidly asked the chairman.

— What do you mean 'So?' — asked Opishkov, noticeably irritated.

— How much did it cost, and in general, I beg your pardon, how long did it take, as they say, and so on... and so forth...

— I didn't have enough time to prepare this, — Opishkov responded in a voice from the underworld.

— Then, I beg your pardon, it was necessary to warn us... because we did indeed ask for it, begging your pardon.

The Opishkovian patience snapped and his face became the same color as the cap of the stationmaster.

— I, — yelled Opishkov, — do not report to you!..

(Deathly silence in the hall.)

— Well, the hell with all of you!.. I'm fed up with you and no longer desire to speak with you. — Opishkov puffed up and, having covered himself up with a cap, stood up and walked out.

Deathly silence reigned for three minutes. Then it exploded.

— Sourpuss, — someone squealed.

— He reported!

— We offended Opishkov...

— Look at what a pigsty he's created!

— What does it mean, is he spitting on us?

The chairman sat as if someone had spat upon him and rang the bell. And some worker–correspondent's voice arched over the rumbling and the ringing:

— I am going to write to *Gudok* about him! They'll fix his wagon!! So that he doesn't spit on the masses!!

Em.

The newspaper "Gudok," Moscow, September 3, 1924

Three Kopeks (Три Копейки)

The senior switchman of the Orekhovo Station presented himself to receive his pay.

The payer clicked his abacus and said the following to him:

— Your pay: You are owed 25 rubles 80 kopeks (click!). Deduction to the *TPO*[1]: 12 rubles 50 kopeks (click!). Deduction to *Gudok*: 65 kopeks (click!). To a Moscow seamstress: 12 rubles 50 kopeks. To the school: 12 kopeks. The total owed to you on hand... (click! click!) T-h-r-e-e-k-o-p-e-k-s. Here you go.

The switchman reeled but didn't fall because a tail grew behind him.

— What do you want? — asked the switchman, turning around.

— I'm the *MOPR*,[2] — said the first.

— I'm a Friend of the Children, — said the second.

— I'm the cashier of the Mutual Aid Society, — the third.

— I'm the Professional Union, — the fourth.

— I'm the Society of Friends of Chemical Protection and Industry,[3] — the fifth.

— I'm the Voluntary Fleet, — the sixth.

— OK, — said the switchman. — Here, my brothers, are three kopeks. Take them and divide them as you wish. And then he saw yet another one.

— What do you want? — asked the switchman curtly.

— For the banner fund, — said the respondent curtly.

The switchman took off his clothes and said:

— Only you'll have to sew it yourself; and give the boots to your wife.

And then, yet another.

— For the statue! — said yet another.

The naked switchman thought a bit, then said:

— Take me, my brothers, instead of the statue. Put me on

the windowsill.

— It's impossible, — they responded to him, — you don't bear any resemblance...

— Well then, do whatever you like, — answered the switchman and left.

— Where are you going naked? — they asked him.

— To the express train, — replied the switchman.

— Where are you going to go like that?

— I am not going anywhere, — replied the switchman, — I will sit there until next month. Maybe then they will begin to deduct like humans. As ordained by the law.

Translators' notes

1. *TPO* is an abbreviation for *Tovarno-prihodyasshee otdeleniye,* a government controlled store that sold goods to the railroad workers on credit.

2. *MOPR* is an abbreviation for *Mezhdunarodnaya organizatsiya pomosshi bortsam revolyutsii,* the International Aid Organization for Fighters of the Revolution

3. The Society of Friends of Chemical Protection and Industry (*Obsshestvo druzey khimicheskoy oborony i promyshlennosti*) was formed in 1924 at the initiative of different professional, scientific, and military organizations as a propaganda tool for proliferating among the people the means for protection against poisonous chemicals and the means for application of chemistry in agriculture and national defense.

The magazine "Smekhach" (The Laugher), № 16, Leningrad, September 10, 1924

The Egyptian Mummy (Египетская мумия)

The story of a trade unionist

I arrived in Leningrad, on a business trip, with the chairman of our local committee.

After we rushed through the business, the chairman says to me:

— You know what, Vasya? Let's go to the People's House.

— And what, I ask, did I forget there?

— You are a piece of work, — responds the chairman of our local committee to me, — in the People's House you will receive wholesome entertainment and you will rest, according to the 98th Article of the Labor Code (the chairman knows all the articles by heart, for which he is even considered a miracle of nature).

Okay. So we went. We paid the money, as required, and began to apply the 98th Article. For the first duty, we resorted to the wheel of fortune. An ordinary huge wheel, with a stick in the middle. Notably, the wheel for some unknown reason begins to spin at an incredible speed, sending each member of the Union, whoever chooses to sit on it, to the devil. A very fun thing depending on how you fly off. I popped out extremely comically, flying over some young lady, and tore my pants. And the chairman creatively sprained his leg with an awful scream of horror, and broke one man's mahogany cane. And as he was flying, everyone was dropping to the floor in that our chairman of the Local Committee is a man of enormous weight. In short, when he landed I thought that it would be necessary to choose a new chairman. But the chairman stood up, vigorous like the Statue of Liberty, and, conversely, the man with the recently deceased cane coughed up blood.

Then we headed for the enchanted room, with revolving ceiling and walls. Here the bottles of beer 'New Bavaria,' drunk with the chairman in the buffet, popped out of me. I have never been sick like I was in this damn room. The chairman survived.

But after we left the room, I said to him:

— My friend, I disavow your article. Damn them, these entertainments № 98!

And he said:

— Since we have come here and paid money, you still must see the famous Egyptian mummy.

And we entered the room. A young man appeared in the blue light and declared:

— Now, citizens, you will see a phenomenon of unspeakable quality: a genuine Egyptian mummy, brought here 2,500 years ago. This mummy prophesizes about the past, present, and future; and answers questions and gives advice in difficult situations, and, confidentially, to pregnant women.

Everyone gasped with delight and horror, and, indeed, imagine, a mummy appears in the form of a woman's head and around her are Egyptian writings. I froze in astonishment at the fact that the mummy was totally young, not only for a 2,500-year-old, but even for a 100-year-old.

The young man politely invited:

— Ask questions. Easy ones.

And then the chairman came out and asked:

— In what language should we ask? I do not know Egyptian.

The young man, without embarrassment, replied:

— Ask in Russian.

The chairman cleared his throat, and asked:

— But tell me, dear mummy, what did you do before the February Revolution?

And here the mummy went pale and said:

— I attended courses.

— OK. Tell me, dear mummy, were you on trial under the Soviets, and if not, why not?

The mummy blinked and said nothing.

The young man shouted:

— What's wrong with you, comrade, does paying 15 kopeks entitle you to torment a mummy?

But the chairman had begun his slam-bang:

— And, dear mummy, what is your stand on conscription?

The mummy starts crying. Says:

— I was a sister of mercy.

— And what would you do if you saw Communists in a church? And who is Comrade Stuchka?[1] And where does Karl Marx live now?

The young man saw that the mummy was washed out, and shouts out regarding Marx:

— He died!

But the chairman barked:

— No, he lives in the hearts of the proletariat!

And then the light went out and the mummy, sobbing, disappeared into the underworld, and the crowd roared to the chairman:

— Hurray! Thanks for spotting the counterfeit mummy.

The crowd wanted to throw him up in the air. But the chairman declined the honor of a throw up in the air and we left the People's House, and behind us went a crowd of roaring proletarians.

Translators' note

1. Peter Ivanovich Stuchka was a well known Communist Party member, lawyer, and revolutionary. Before the Revolution, he was a member of the editorial board of the newspaper *Pravda*. After the Revolution, in 1917, Stuchka was appointed to lead the People's Commissariat of Justice.

The newspaper "Gudok," Moscow, September 17, 1924

Chopin's Overture (Увертюра Шопена)

An unpleasant story (based on the material of a worker–
correspondent)

— What scoundrel has spread rumors that our club doesn't
serve a purpose? — exclaimed the boss of the club.

— Our enemies are saying this, — replied Board Member
Kolotushkin.

— The swine, the swine, — observed the boss, shaking his
head. — Look here, if you will: Income from paid perform-
ances: 248 rubles 89 kopeks. Expenditures: 140 rubles 89 kopeks. The rest, it means, is clear profit: 108 rubles. And I
wouldn't be a boss if I didn't use them...

Here the door opened and the boss of the mobile theater entered.

— Hi, — he said. — My brothers, I got myself into a mess. I
don't have any money. I am lost! I will shoot myself!..

— Don't do it, — said the boss in horror, — the fatherland
needs your life. How much do you need?

— Ten rubles, or I will poison myself with potassium cya-
nide.

— Here, — said the gracious boss, — just don't kill yourself.
And write me a promissory note.

The theater boss sat and wrote:

"I request from you ten rubles until my next visit to Sebej."

And the boss wrote: "Disburse."

— You saved my life! — cried the theater man, and disappeared.

Whereupon Citizen Balabolin entered, and asked:

— Won't you lend me a rope from the curtains, my friends,
for a half an hour?

— For what? — asked the amazed club members.

— I am going to hang myself. I owe a debt of honor but have nothing to pay it with.

— Write!

Balabolin wrote: "I ask for two days..."

He received approval from Kolotushkin, and five rubles disappeared.

Pidorin entered and wrote:

"Until receipt of pay..."

He received 30 rubles and disappeared.

Elistratov entered with a note from Pidorin, and wrote:

"A credit against my pay..."

And having received 20 rubles, he disappeared.

Then the piano tuner entered, and said:

— They probably played on your piano with their feet or walking sticks. It rattles like a bitch.

— Are you serious? — said the club members in horror. — Repair it quickly!

— It will cost 55 rubles, — said the craftsman.

They wrote a work order and appended to the end:

"Upon completion of the repair, the piano tuner is obliged to play Chopin's Overture and to drink a shot for the road."

The piano tuner hadn't managed to finish playing Chopin and to finish drinking the shot when the door opened and several men suddenly piled in:

— There's nothing left, — cried the boss, and waved his hand, — it's cleaned out!

— But we don't need it, — a sepulchral voice responded, and added: — we are the Audit Commission.

Silence fell.

— What are these? — asked the commission.

— Promissory notes, — answered the boss, and started to cry.

— And who is that?

— The piano tuner, — answered the boss, weeping.

— What is he doing?

— He's playing an overture, — sobbed the boss.

— Enough, — said the commission, — the overture is over; now begins the opera.

— Wh-which one? — squeaked the boss.

— *Clubmembers–Hooligans*, — answered the commission, — words by *Mosselprom*,[1] music by Korneev and Gorshanin.

And amidst the loud club-members' sobs, the commission sat down to write a report.

Em.

Translators' note

1. *Mosselprom* is an abbreviation for *Moskovskaya assotsiatsiya predpriyaty selsko-promishlennoy produktsii*, the Moscow Association of State Enterprises Processing Agro-industrial Products.

The newspaper "Gudok," Moscow, September 24, 1924

The Lullaby of a Station Master (Колыбель начальника станции)

Sleep, my beautiful son,
Rockaby by
The clear moon quietly shines
In a lullaby of yours.

Lermontov

Sleep, my little one,
Sleep, my dick,
Your mother left for Paris...

From a composition by Sasha Black,
the men's room scribe

— I declare the general meeting of the workers and assistants of the Shelkhov Station of the Kazakhstan Railroad open! — excitedly announced the chairman of the meeting, looking around a hall filled primarily by workers of the rail service. — On the agenda before us stands a report about a week of the War of 1914. I yield the floor to Comrade DS. If you please, Comrade DS. DS!

However, Comrade DS didn't please.

— And where is he? — asked the chairman.

— He's home, — responded someone's voice.

— We have to send for him....

Absolutely, send for him! — thundered the hall. — He's an interesting man. He will speak about the war. And everyone will listen!

The one sent returned without Comrade DS, but in his place there was a letter.

The chairman solemnly opened it, and read:

"In response to your invitation of such and such a date, I convey that I am unable to present myself at the meeting.

The reason: I went to bed..."

The president froze with the letter in hand, and in the hall someone remarked:

— He 'ffshilly responded!

— We wish you good night!

— What kind of night is it, when it is five o'clock in the afternoon? — thought the chairman. He looked at the ceiling, then at his boots, then somewhere through the window, and announced sadly:

— I declare the meeting adjourned.

And from the hall they added:

— The lullaby of the stationmaster is the funeral of the general meeting.

And they quietly fanned out to their homes. Amen!

Mikhail B.

The newspaper "Gudok," Moscow, September 25, 1924

No More (Не свыше)

At the Biryulevo Station of the Ryazano–Uralskaya Railroad, the workers decided not to allow the sale of wine and beer in the cooperative, where a shortage of necessary groceries was in evidence.

A worker–correspondent

— I don't want it!

— Hold on a 'sec, check it out! What an ashberry! A kick to it. When you drink this invention you will not know where you are, in the station or in heaven!

— But I don't want it. I have no desire.

(A pause).

— Do you have cooking oil?

— Nope. There's a shortage.

— Then you know what... weigh out some granulated sugar for me.

— Next week we will have it…

— Is there flour?

— We'll get it the day after tomorrow.

— So, what do you have now, you devils?

— Be careful. To you, it's a cooperative. There aren't any devils. And, look, we received a shipment of wines. Such wines that will make you gasp. From the governmental cellars in the Azerbaijan Republic. From autonomous vineyards in the Sparrow Mountains in Moscow. Nothing better! Sherry, port, Madeira, Alicante, Chablis like Bordeaux, Muskat, Porto-Franco, Porto-Rico... № 14...

— Why are you tempting me, you fascist!

— I am not tempting you. I'm telling you for your own good. Try the autonomous port. The other day, the assistant to the boss bought three bottles, like a handcar wreck, it was.

— Why do you torture me?

— Reds, table wines of different strengths. Dry whites, Tsinandali, Napareuli, Mukuzani, Oreanda!..

— Stop it!

— Ay-Danil!

— Well, I'd better run along now. God be with you.

— Wait! Riesling, Russian vodka, orange vodka, March beer, zubrovka, Abraham, porter.

— OK, give, give it to me... The hell with you. You defeated me. Give me two bottles of mountain ashberry...

— A stein of beer, to go?

— Wrap it up, a pestilence on you.

***

Eh, eh! But this firewood is all asp!
Eh, it won't burn without kerosene!..
Dunka is crying near the stairs!
Lantsa-dritsa! Tsa, tsa!!!

— What a wonderful man... Where the devil did you get so sozzled?

— I... ...ashb... ashbry.. brry...bryy. At the coop... cooperative...

***

— Citizens, I appeal to you directly. I'm at the end of my rope. I weep, but I still drink!.. Mukuzan... The only solution is to close down the hornet's nest!..

— Close down the hornet's!..

— A hornet's nest with bottles. There's no sugar, so why is there Moscow Malaga instead? Let me ask you a question: Why, instead of offering sunflower oil, do they offer Tsinandali for no more than 1 ruble 60 kopeks per bottle?

— Exactly!!.

— End it!

— It shouldn't be allowed at all!

— I'm for it!

— Comrade Secretary, sign it in the name of the Revolution...[1]

Translators' note

1. It was customary in the USSR to end official documents with the phrase "In the name of the Revolution" — even the minutes of meetings.

A Story About Podjilkin and Grain (Рассказ про Поджилкина и крупу)

A citizen appeared at a transport section, went to the office, sat in an upholstered chair, pulled a pack of 'Tais' cigarettes out of his pocket, then a ring of keys, and placed all of them into the other pocket.

Next, he took out a handkerchief and began weeping into it.

— I request that you not weep in a government office, young man, — sternly said the one sitting at a table to him, — weeping is cancelled.

But the citizen increased his weeping.

— Did you have a death in the family? Perhaps your mother? Then you ought to go to the Funeral Department of the Insurance Cashier and weep to them as much as your heart desires. But don't spoil our carpet, y-young man!

— I'm not a young man, — through sobbing declared the guest. — I am, on the contrary, Podjilkin, the chairman of the Primary Railroad Cooperative.

— De-lighted to meet you, — said the transport section worker, — why are you crying?

— I am crying because of grain, — replied Podjilkin, quieting down, — in the name of all that is holy, give me the grain!

— What does it mean... give me? — widely grinned the transport section head, — take all that you want! The Central Union just now offered us three railcars of buckwheat grain. Oh you, weeping, weeperer... a pitiful weeper!

— For how much? — asked Podjilkin, becoming jolly.

— For two rubles, 20 kopeks.

Podjilkin thought about it deeply.

— Gee, — he murmured, — what an opportunity! Y'know what, hold the grain for me a bit... I'll just be a minute.

And then he hastened out.

— Weirdo, — they said in his wake. — One minute he howls like a jackal, the next he runs off.

Podjilkin rushed directly to the Commission for Price Regulation of the *MCPO*.[1]

— Where is the commission *M-C-P-O*?

— Here's the door. Do not knock people off their feet. You'll make it.

— My brothers, here's the deal... the grain turned up here... buckwheat... For 2 rubles 20 kopeks. But you set the mandatory price at 2 rubles 20 kopeks for retail sale in a cooperative.

— So what? It's set. What of it?

— So, let me sell it for a little more. Otherwise, how will I cover transit, the staff, etc.

— Look at you, so cunning. It's forbidden.

— Why?

— Because it's forbidden.

— What am I supposed to do?

— Hmmn... Nip on over to Varvarka, to the People's Commission of Interior Trade.

Podjilkin flew there by tram № 6. Landed.

— Look... buckwheat... I'm afraid to miss out... two twenty, you understand... and the set retail price... you understand... is also two twenty... You understand...

— So what?

— Give me permission to mark it up.

— Look at you, a juggler! It's forbidden.

— Why?

— Because because.

— What am I supposed to do? — asked Podjilkin, and reached into his pocket.

— Don't even think about it. See the poster over there, *You Are Requested Not to Cry*.

— How is it possible not to cry?..

— Go to the *M-C-P-O*.

Podjilkin went back on № 4.

— You again?

— Well, they sent me to you...

— A bunch of geniuses. Go back...

— Back?

— Precisely.

Podjilkin left. Stood a bit, then spit on the ground. And a policeman approached him

— Three rubles.

— What for?

— Don't spit, except in the garbage can.

Podjilkin paid three rubles and went back to his cooperative. He took a poster board and drew on it:

There Is No Grain!

The workers approached the poster and cursed Podjilkin, and nearby a private trader sold grain for four rubles. That's all, folks.

Translators' note

1. *MCPO* is an abbreviation for *Moskovskiy soyuz potrebitel'skikh obshestv,* the Moscow Union of Consumer Societies. MCPO was created in 1899 to control the prices of consumer goods in Moscow. In the late 1920s, *MCPO* became *Centrsoyuz,* the central regulatory agency for consumer cooperatives in the Soviet Union.

Librarian–Bartender (Библифетчик)

> In one of the rail yards, the librarian in the reading car is at the same time the bartender in its Lenin section[1]…
>
> *From the letter of a worker–correspondent*

— Welcome! There's an empty table. I'll clear it in a second. Do you want a book or a beer?

— Vasya, the librarian–bartender is asking what we want… A book or a beer?

— For me… a… ni… nutebook and a sandwich.

— We don't carry notebooks…

— Oh, you… *votre maman*…

— Vulgar words to please not express.[2]

— I am express… ex…presssing… a protest!

— C'mon dear, give us a half liter.

— *The ABCs*, the work of Comrade Bukharin,[3] do you have it?

— It's absolutely fresh. We just received it. Gerasim Ivanovich! Bukharin, one portion! And a half-liter of lager!

— Carp and caviar?

— You want carp?

— We need something to read.

— What would you like to order?

— Well, if I may, Gogol.

— You want to take it home? It's not permitted. We don't deliver take-out books. Eat here, read here.

— I ordered schnitzel. How much longer will I have to wait for it?!

— Just a second. I'm swamped. They ran to the cellar to get *Erfrut Programme*.[4]

—To your health!

— Hooray! We've been here since morning. We are reading

to your health!

— That's why I see that you are lit to the gills, what did you sozzle yourselves on?

— Critic Belinsky.

— A toast to the critic!

— A toast to the health of our chairman of the Lenin section! If I may have two samples of Martovka?

— No! Eh! Can I get some ham here? And for my kid something of the Communist youth kind for his development.

— I can offer you a history of the movement.

— OK, give me the movement. Let the kid read it.

— Of all the writers, I adore Trekhgorn most.

— A famous man. His mug is printed on every wall and every bottle.

— Our Gerasim Ivanovich flitters around like an eagle.

— A do-gooder! He waits on everyone, he satisfies everyone.

— An angel!

— Gerasim Ivanovich, from the group of readers, we send our "Hurray."

— I have no time, brothers… Drin… I mean read, for your health.

— *You will die! They will bu…r…ry you as if you never existed on earth.*

— *You will disappear… you won't be resurrected… to the joy… to the joy of your friends!*

— *Pour… pour!..* [5]

Translators' notes

1. Every library had a section containing books, posters, banners, photographs, and propaganda material about Lenin's life and teachings.

2. Some characters are uneducated and make grammatical mistakes.

3. Bulgakov plays with the verb *bukhat'*, which means to get shit-faced drunk, and the last name *Bukharin*, an authors of the *ABCs of Communism*.

4. *Erfrut Programme* was a book about a Marxist program.

5. The drinkers sing these closing lines.

Concerning the Naked Case (По голому делу)

A letter

"Everything was peaceful, everything was very good, but then suddenly a rumor started at our respected Gudermes Station of the C. K. Railroad that, allegedly, at 6 p.m., on train № 12 from Moscow, would arrive all the naked members of the 'Down with Shame' Society.

The interest turned out to be of extreme magnitude, including from women, who said:

— It's disgusting!

But nevertheless, everyone came to look.

And others said:

— We will beat them up!

In short, all of Gudermes more or less came out to the train.

Well, it turned out to be a disappointment because the train came dressed to the t's, except for the stoker, and even he was only undressed to the waist. And we had already seen the stoker naked because for him soot is like overalls.

In summary, everyone went home laughing.

But here's what's interesting to us: what's the deal with this society, and how should we understand their conduct when in Moscow?"

Letter of Comrade Beer.
Rewritten by M. Bulgakov.

Bulgakov's response:

"Comrade Beer! Notify the dwellers of Gudermes that the behavior of the nudists must be understood as silly conduct.

Indeed, in Moscow, two nudists got on a tram, but they only got as far as the nearest police department.

And now this 'society' will be liquidated for two reasons: First, police can't stand nudists, and second, frost is coming.

Therefore do not wait for anyone: The nudists will not come."

The newspaper "Gudok," Moscow, October 16, 1924

The Swallowed Train (Проглоченный поезд)

The story of a worker

If some administrator is zealous and energetic, then he can create such a stinkmess that there is no kind of scoop with which one can clean it up.

Suspecting nothing, we came to our Murom workshops and noticed on the walls an announcement, which reads as follows:

Announcement

By order of the management of the railroad, because of the huge costs of the upkeep of the worker's train Murom–Selivanova along the Murom Lower Railroad, the running of the latter will soon be abolished and therefore it is offered to all employees, artisans, and workers, riding on the workers' train on the Murom Lower Railroad, who will remain in service after the cancellation of the working train, i.e., who will commute every day to an apartment in the village on foot or find an apartment in the city on their own, as the provision of flats from the road, having no such flats, is not possible, to sign up on the list of his shop master.

Those who will have to resign from the workshops with the termination of the workers' train plying Murom–Selivanova should also sign up.

By order of TM Murom Likhonin

September 17, 1924
True copy: Secretary (Signature).

What transpired after that, no story can tell, and no pen can describe. Each, looking into the distance of his life, saw the future: either to spend the nights in the open air, or immediately make tracks and leave the service.

The announcement stunned the workers to the point that many hurled their hats to the ground.

I personally, looking at our sooty buildings, felt despair and sorrow, and am now writing to all who are listening in the entire republic:

— On what basis does the Kazan sub line operate an allegedly workers' train every holiday, populated by wives, servants and, in general, all the elements from Murom, almost to the Novashino Station, and, moreover, each and every one slips through the train door for free?

And why does the Kursk Railroad, like some kind of beast of prey, burn fuel without remorse and drive the crew aimlessly, sending a train from Murom to Selivanova, where they detach the locomotive and head back to Murom, and at night again, this locomotive is hurtling to Selivanova to get the rest of the working train, and finally in the morning it rides from Selivanova, driving workers to work! About this no one says a word, but the administration swallowed our workers' train with extraordinary ease!

I write and await protection from the newspaper *Gudok.*

The story of the worker was recorded by
worker–correspondent № 68 and M.

The newspaper "Gudok," Moscow, October 19, 1924

Wall Against Wall (Стенка на стенку)

> On a religious holiday, in the village of Poplevin, in the region of Ryazhsk Station, a traditional fistfight among the peasants occurred. A medic from the Ryazhsk Emergency Room, who had just filed an application for admission to the Party, participated in this fight.
>
> *A worker–correspondent*

PART I. IN A PASTURE

In an unknown village, on the Day of the Patron Saint Sergey, a war cry rumbled.

— Brothers! Prepare thyselves! Brothers, do not fail us!

A known-to-the-entire-population man, by the name of Goat Wattle,[1] an instigator and fool, screamed in a commanding voice:

— Wait, brothers! Not everyone is here. Some are still at the sermon.

— That's right! — agreed the feisty population.

In the church, they hurriedly rang the bell and the father pastor with a quick hand murmured the words of release. With that, the final chord of the choir stretched out like a sigh and the male population gushed towards the pasture.

— Hurray, hurray!..

Uncle Wattle's head flashed in the stampede, and his words reached out:

— Stop! Wait…

It quieted down.

And Wattle delivered the introductory speech:

— Don't squeeze copper five-cent coins from 1924 in your palms as a weapon. Don't beat our dear opponents below the lungs, so that we don't exterminate the population. Don't stomp anyone on the ground; he is not a pile of grain. God be with us!

— Hurray! — a knightly cry rang out.

And then the male population divided into two ranks. They walked away from each other in different directions and then, with a cry of "Hurray," started moving towards one another.

— Don't fail us, Prokudin! — the left rank howled. — Smash them, the sons of bitches. To our leader!!!

— Smash them! Smash, smash! — spread through the reserves.

The ranks came together and poor Wattle was the first victim of strongman Prokudin. Even though they were beating Prokudin from all sides, he managed to get to Wattle's chin, and also hit him so hard on the spot on which he usually sat at general assemblies of the Rural Union that Wattle immediately flew out from the line. His head was thrust forward and his legs were in the air, and six double-grivel coins popped out from Wattle's pocket; from his mouth, two crown teeth; from his eyes, flashes; and from his nose, dark blood.

— Brothers! — howled the right rank. — Are we really ready to concede?

The blood of Wattle made an appeal to heaven, and revenge was delivered.

The walls collided and the fists started drumming, like a chain drag scraping a manure pit. The second to be thrust from the ranks was Vasya Klyukin, and Vasya rode along the ground with his face, scraping both the former and the latter. He landed next to Wattle, and said only these words:

— Give my boots to my widow…

Ptakhin flew out next, sleeveless, and with a ripped-to-shreds seat of the pants. He turned around, hit someone on the back of the head, but then he himself was immediately knocked on the side of the head for a two-mile loop, after which he barked:

— I surrender! I see a white light…

And he dropped to the horizontal position.

In the neighborhood, dogs howled nervously, and women-onlookers quietly began to whimper.

And then, the local medic, Vasily Ivanich Talalykin, glowing in holiday spirit, presented himself in starched collar, tie, and rubber boots. When he got close to the seething battle, his little eyes narrowed. He stomped in place; then, with an uncertain hand, pulled off his tie, then, more assertively, went down the buttons of his jacket, took it off in one move, and, emitting a victorious cry, ripped into the battle. The right rank had received a reinforcement. Like an eagle, the servant of medicine threw himself to crippling his patients. But they returned the favor. Something broke, and the medic rolled out like an empty jar of zinc oxide, sowing drops of blood on the green grass.

PART II. HE WAS KICKED OUT

Two days later, the medic Vasily Ivanich Talalykin appeared before the Local Committee of city R. He wore a leather coat with an emblem portraying the Leader, and he had so much social consciousness on his face that it was nauseating to look at. On top of the social consciousness, and under the medic's right eye, was placed a multicolored bruise, and his left cheekbone was somewhat wider than the right one. Glowing, with his eyes clearly saying that the medic had mastered, in-depth, the entire political vocabulary, he greeted everyone with words full of dignity:

— Greetings, comrades.

To this, they responded with sepulchral silence.

And the secretary of the Local Committee, having gone silent, said these words to the medic:

— Shall we go to my office for a minute, citizen?

At the word 'citizen,' Talalykin squirmed.

The door closed, and the secretary, placing his hands into his pants' pockets, said the following:

— Here is your application for admission to the Party.

— Yes, of course, of course, — replied Talalykin, sensing misfortune and covering the black eye with his palm.

— Did you injure yourself? — asked the secretary with suspicious gentleness.

— Ummn... er... injur, — relied Talalykin. — Of course... on the door jam. Um...yeah... the application. I have already been knocking on the door of our dear Party for a year, under the banner of which, — suddenly Talalykin started to sing in a soprano voice, — *I am striving with every fiber of my being. Remembering the great teachings of our lead...*

— Enough of that, — interrupted the secretary in an unpleasant voice, — enough. You won't find your way under the banner!

— But why? — asked Talalykin, deadening.

In place of a response the secretary pointed a finger to the colorful shiner.

Talalykin said nothing. He hung his head and retreated from the Local Committee.

Once and forever.

Translators' note

1. In the original Russian, this character's name is *Kozi Zob,* which is what you call the two protuberances on a goat's neck.

The newspaper "Gudok," Moscow, October 21, 1924

A New Means of Book Distribution (Новый способ распространения книги)

> Booksplit (a book co-op) in Kharkov sold, for wrapping paper, 182 pounds 6 ounces of books published by the People's Commissariat for distribution in rural areas.
>
> Additionally, for 4 rubles per pound, shopkeepers were selling publications of the Ukrainian Writers Union *The Plow*.
>
> *A worker–correspondent*

At a book distributor there was not a single buyer, and the salesmen were standing sadly behind the counters. The bell rang, and a citizen appeared with a red beard in the shape of a fan. He said:

— Hi...

— How may I be of service? — delightedly asked a salesman.

— We would like Citizen Lermontov's work, — said the citizen, hiccupping softly.

— Would you like the complete works?

The citizen thought, and replied:

— Complete. About fifteen to twenty pounds.

The salesman's hair stood on end.

— Excuse me, but the one we have weighs in total about five pounds, no more.

— We know, — answered the citizen, — we buy it on a regular basis. Please wrap up fifty copies for us. Have your boys carry them out. I have a van waiting outside.

The salesmen sprinted up the wooden stairs and from the furthest reaches of the shelves respectfully reported:

— Unfortunately, only five copies remain.

— What a pity, — bemoaned the customer, — well, at least give me the five. And then, my dear fellow, scare up *World History* for me.

— How many copies? — excitedly asked the clerk.

— Well, weigh out fifty...

— Copies?

— Pounds.

All the salesmen crawled out from the book nooks, and the director himself offered the buyer a chair. The salesmen ran up and down stairs, like sailors going aloft.

— Vasya! Shelf number 15. Throw down *World History*, all that there are. Would you like the ones with bindings? Hard covered, embossed with gold...

— We can't use them, — replied the buyer. — To us the bindings mean nothing. To us, the most important thing is that the paper is of low quality.

The salesmen were stunned again.

— If you really want low quality, — one of them woke up finally, — then I can offer you the works of Pushkin and the publications of the People's Commissariat.

— We can't use Pushkin, — said the citizen, — it has pictures and the pictures are stiff. But wrap up five pounds of the People's Commissariat as a sample.

Not long after, the shelves had emptied, and the director himself politely issued the buyer an invoice. The boys, grunting, carried packages of books to the street. The buyer paid with rustling white ten-ruble notes, and said:

— Until the next enjoyable meeting.

— Would you permit me to ask, — politely asked the director, — you are probably a representative of a major distributor?

— Major, — responded the buyer with dignity, — we sell herring. Our compliments to you.

And he bowed in parting.

The magazine "Paprika," № 21, Leningrad, October 21, 1924

Three Orders of Swinehood (Три вида свинства)

> "In our densely populated houses there are no rules and order of coexistence."
>
> *(From the newspapers)*

1. DELIRIUM TREMENS

Five times the son of a bitch Grishka slid down along the handrail on his stomach, from the fifth floor to 'Red Bavaria,' and returned with two bottles. In addition, it is well known that the Boldins, wife and husband, returned from work accompanied by one and a half bottles of premium Nezhin, a dogberry-flavored brandy made by *Gosspirt*;[1] and a tender green bottle of Russian vodka and two port wines bottled in Moscow, also produced by *Gosspirt*.

— The Boldins were just paid, — said Duska, and locked the door to her room.

The *kvartkhoz*, the baker, Volodya, and mamasha Pavlovna also locked themselves in.

So, they locked themselves in at 11 o'clock. But at exactly midnight, they unlocked themselves, when the first glass shattered in the Boldins' room. The second glass to shatter was that of the door. Then, in the corridor, one after another, appeared a pistol, the spouse of Boldin, and then the husband himself in a completely torn shirt.

Not everyone can scream "Help" as ably as did Boldin's wife. Consequently, every window of apartment № 50 flashed light simultaneously, like fireworks for the czar. It was impossible to aim well after the 're-bottling of the port wine,' so the hurled pistol, having just missed the head of the *kvartkhoz* by a hair, killed Duska's mirror. There remained only a walnut frame. Just then, a thunderous word went off for the first time, like a siren:

— Police!

— Police, — echoed the ghosts in sleeping gowns.

No, it wasn't the voice of Felia Litvin[1] and an orchestra of a 100 slicing the air of a theatre with terrible cries of *Aida*. It was Vasily Boldin slicing his screaming wife.

— Police! Police!

2. BOUND BY LEGAL MARRIAGE

When a handsome young man with a handlebar mustache headed down the corridor, these rapturous words fluttered out in unison:

— Ah, what a man! Oh, wow, Pavlovna's Tan'ka! Has a bachelor on the leash!

Bashful Tan'ka–the-typist's *Ah-what-a-man* went directly to room № 2 and said these words to mamashka Pavlovna:

— I'm not some kind of dandy dude, mamashka. A no-party man. I'm not the one who would play with an innocent girl and then kick her out. And you, mamasha, we will cherish. You will go to the church, I myself will help you with your business.

The stern Pavlovna teetered, and then sent the bastard Shurka sliding down along the handrail to Mosselprom to get granulated sugar for moonshine.

Ah-what-a-man was married in the church of St. Matthew, the one on Sadovaya St., and they saw the lubricated-with-vegetable-oil head of *Ah-what-a-man* next to the crowned-with-fleur-d'orange head of Tanya.

And a month later, *Ah-what-a-man* said to mamasha Pavlovna:

— And when will you breathe your last, dear mama, with your funeral observance? I can't breathe because of you.

Pavlovna stood up slowly and her eyes became like an old snake's:

— I breathe my last? You yourself will breathe your last, son. Thief. Parasitized me and Tan'ka. Mary, Mother of God, please strike him, the devil, with thunder!

But thunder did not strike *Ah-what-a-man*. He stood up slowly from the tea table, and spoke thusly:

— And who is this 'thief?' Please tell me, mamasha? Am I the thief? — he asked, and his voice fell to a whisper. — I am the thief, — he hissed already quite near, and his reptilian eyes dimmed.

— Help! — replied Pavlovna, and loudly and easily flew out the repetition: — Help!

— Police! Police! Police!

3. NAME DAY

On the Day of the Saints of Faith, Hope, and Love and their mother Sophia (we celebrate their day on Sept. 17th, but in the Soviet style on the 30th) an Italian accordion struck up in apartment № 50, and the entire huge building started shaking. And at half past one in the morning, the famous dancer Pafnutich decided to show how he, once upon a time, did "The Fish." He did it, and plaster weighing six and a half pounds fell from the ceiling in the downstairs apartment of Dr. Fortochker. The doctor survived only thanks to the circumstance that at the time he was in an adjoining room.

Fortochker returned, saw a huge sedimentary layer and a white cloud in the very place where once was his desk, and screamed:

— Police! Police! Police!

Mikhail Bulgakov
A writer with a wife, childless,
non-drinker, looking for a room with a quiet family.

Translators' note

1. *Gosspirt* is an abbreviation for *Upravleniye gosudarstvennoy spirtovoy promyshlennosti*, the government wine and spirit monopoly.

2. Felia V. Litvin (1861-1936) was a famous Russian singer whose vocal range covered two and a half octaves, from lower G to upper D.

A Notice from the Emperor (Повестка с государем императором)

The worker Vlas Vlasovich Vlasov received a notification about a money transfer from the Ascension Postal Division. Vlas unfolded it and started to read aloud, because it was easier this way for Vlas:

— As-cen-sion p-o po-st st-al. Postal. Di-vi – Division no-ti. Notifies. Katerina, listen, it is notifying us. It seems that my brother sent us money. That a transfer of 15 rubles is credited in your name on the day indicated herein... in the name of his Em-per-per-or...

Vlas choked:

— His Majesty...

Vlas fearfully looked around, and continued to read in a whisper:

— Czar?! What the heck? The En-pe-ror Ni-ko-lay Alexan-drovich.

Spaced-out Vlas went silent, then he himself added:

— *Kravavava*, — although this word was not in the notice, — Issuance of monies occurs daily, with the exception of twe-twenty holidays and the birthday of Her... Imperial Majesty the Sovereign Empress Alexandra Feodorovna. Wow! — exclaimed Vlas. — That's one helluva notice. Listen, Katya, the notice was sent by the Imperial Emperor!

— You are imagining everything, — replied Katerina.

— There is nothing special about your Emperor, — ruffled Vlas, — that I would be imagining him. Anyway, you, as an illit-erate person, are not led anywhere by evidence.

— Well then go to the literates, — answered the tender spouse.

Vlas went to the literates at the Ascension Division, received 15 rubles, and then thrust his head in a hole covered with netting, and asked:

— For what reason did you print "Imperial Majesty" on the notice? It is very curious to know, comrade.

The comrade in the image of a woman with a short screwed hairdo on her head and turquoise on her index finger answered as follows:

— Don't hold up the line, I have no time for you. They're old forms, czarist issue.

— That's a fine kettle of fish, — Vlas buzzed into the hole, — in Soviet times, such a screw up...

— He cut to the head of the queue! — they howled from the tail. — Every one of us needs to pick up...

And they pulled Vlas from the window by his pants. All the way home Vlas twisted his head and whispered:

— 'Czar The Emperor.' Extremely nasty words!

Having arrived home, he armed himself with a stump of a chemical pencil and the old spine of a baggage tag, onto which he wrote a letter to *Gudok*:

"Naaah, it wouldn't hurt to remove the remnants of the obsolete regime, printed on the back side of notification letters, which oppress and irritate the working class.

Vlas."

The War Between Water and Iron (Война воды с железом)

Part 1

HOW DID IT START?

These are not sailors, but assailers! I swear. We have noticed that whenever our railroad man must travel somewhere by water, they give him a seat either in the stern, or on a hatch, or in the cargo hold, and the transport worker rides like a piglet.

Our bosses have long tolerated this abuse of the individuals of the railroad transport, but finally their patience ran out.

One boss summoned another boss of a lower rank, and said to him the following:

— Are they bullying us, or what?

— Exactly.

— They probably think that transport workers are some kind of donkeys that can travel in cargo holds?

— I guess so, sir.

— I will show them gue-guess! With me, they will ride... Write, Alexey, on paper.

— Yes, sir.

And this piece of paper was received:

"From Saratov. To all DS, DN, DF, MF, CM, CD, C, and D.[1] Given that the management of the sea transport provides transportation for railroaders in the aforementioned places, with the receipt of this paper, it is proposed that the sea transport workers riding on one-way tickets will be provided seats only in heated freight cars, and will not be allowed in third-class cars." The signatures follow.

Part 2

THE FRATERNAL WELCOME

A sailor appeared at the designated railroad place to get a ticket.

— What do you want? — asked the railroad face, and gazed glumly at the anchors on the buttons.

— I would like a ticket to Tambov, — replied the sailor.

The railway face predatorily rejoiced.

— Oh, you want a ticket? Pleased to meet you! Please have a seat. Perhaps you wish to visit relatives? You must miss them... Heh, heh. Courier, a glass of tea for the citizen–sailor. Well, how are things going in the Pacific Ocean, everything all right?

— Thank you very much, — said the descendant of Christopher Columbus, — we sail mainly to Samara. I'd like to go by high-speed train, if possible...

— Of course, of course, absolutely! However, I have an order here concerning you, sea wolves, to give you seats in boxcars only, but for such a lovely representative of your element, I can make an exception. I would imagine that on your battlewagons you're used to chief cabins and such, hee-hee. By the way, my mother-in-law recently went to Samara, so they gave her, this God's little old lady, a seat on the bags in the cargo hold. And so, like that, the lady rotted all the way to Samara.

— We were not the cause.

— Well, of course, of course. Here we go, please. A wonderful little spot. You can sit, smoke, it's spacious and private. Courier, see Mr. Admiral off!

The sailor read the resolution, lurched, his eyes boggled, and he said:

— A big *merci!*

Upon it was written:

"Give him a seat in the toilet in second class all the way to Tambov."

Part 3

DRAMA IN THE CAR

A coattail with towels and toothbrushes stood in the aisle of the sleeping car of the high-speed train, disheveled and angry.

— I do not understand, — muttered the distinguished citizen, shifting from foot to foot. — Some punk crawled in at the very Saratov and hasn't come out!

— It's impudence! — shouted a lady to the coattail. — I have been waiting for half an hour.

— We, madam, have been waiting for three hours already, — said a sad voice in the front, — and hear only silence. We've run out of patience...

— I think he committed suicide, — worried someone's voice. — Such things happen. We should break down the door.

— Conductor! Conductor!

— Hang on, wait a minute, be quiet...

The tail fell silent. And a muffled singing reached through the clicking of the wheels:

On the sea, on the wave...
Here today, then away²...

— sang a nice muffled *basso.*

The tail immediately shouted:

— This is unheard of impudence! He's singing, apparently!

— Conductor!!

The tail broke down and started up a terrible banging on the lacquered door. It opened, and in the smoke-filled narrow space appeared a cute man with anchors and a cigarette.

— What do you want? — he asked embarrassedly.

— 'What do I want?' How can you ask me 'what'?!

— How can he be asking 'what'?!

— Are you going to sit there long? — venomously asked the distinguished one, waving a towel.

— Until Tambov, — confusedly replied the passenger.

— He's insane! — screamed women's voices from behind.

— Get the hell out!

The passenger flushed, and stammered in confusion:

— I cannot get the hell out, I would be glad to. They will fine me. My ticket is for here.

— Conductor, conductor, conductor...

EPILOGUE

They were recording the incident in Atkarsk and, at the next table, smiling ironically, a worker–correspondent of *Gudok* wrote a report for *Gudok,* and ended it with the words:

"When will it ever end, this fratricidal war between water and iron?"

Translators' notes

1. The abbreviations *DS, DN, DF, MF, CM, CD, C,* and *D* designate officials of different ranks in the railroad hierarchy.

2. A sailors' song

The newspaper "Gudok," Moscow, November 11, 1924

A Worker–Correspondent's Story about Extraneous People (Рассказ рабкора про лишних людей)

As the fateful hour of five approached, the workers flocked to the Bakhmachi barracks to hear the chairman of the Local Committee give an account of his work.

At exactly 8:15, in a ringing voice, the president invited them to take their seats, and then the chairman of the Local Committee entered and, without fear, freely and smoothly, like a nightingale, began his report:

— In September, we have 406 employees, among them only six are not union members, in total 400 are members of the union. They are all subscribers to *Gudok*. Four hundred times one issue of *Gudok*, in total, is 400 *Gudoks*. The assignment has been fulfilled by 100%, in total, one hundred. A flute band has been equipped; in fact, a part of the money has been paid for it…

— In total? — they asked from the last row.

— In total, we must find the remaining money, so as to settle with them, — responded the chairman and continued:

— The wall banner does not come out on time, from time to time, because of the printing machine.

— What's wrong with it? — they asked.

— It doesn't exist, — explained the chairman, and continued:

— And the position of Commissar of Paperwork of Bakhmachi Station is completely extraneous and we must eliminate it. Just like the position of the fire chief.

— May I have the floor? — someone suddenly cried out and, craning their necks, everyone saw that the commissar of Paperwork had cried out.

— Here, I give you the floor, — said the president.

The commissar of paperwork came out before the audience and, at that moment, everyone saw that he was nervous.

— It is I who is extraneous? — the commissar of Paperwork

asked, and continued, — Many thanks to you for such an expression on my behalf. *Merci*, I sit for 24 hours, digging into my reports... and for this I am extraneous? I work, like some kind of a dog, the chairman of the Local Committee doesn't notice any of it, and then he claims that I am extraneous! I have, possibly, written one million different papers! I am extraneous?..

— Exactly... extraneous... — rumbled the meeting.

— Totally extraneous! — confirmed the chairman.

— It's not true. I am not extraneous! — cried the commissar of Paperwork.

— Well, I deny you the floor, — said the chairman.

— I am not extraneous! — irritably screamed the commissar of Paperwork. Then the chairman summoned the bell ringer to himself, after which the commissar of Paperwork calmed down.

— May I have the floor, — a voice rang out, and everyone saw the fire chief. — Am I also extraneous? — he asked.

— Yes, — the chairman replied firmly to him.

— May I be permitted to know on what basis you decided the question of my elimination? — asked the fire chief.

— On the basis of social consciousness and the defense of economic frugality, — firmly replied the chairman to him and raised his gaze to the portrait of Lenin.

—Aha, — the fire chief replied, and he did not raise any kind of uproar. He is a courageous man, thanks to the fires.

After this, the chairman spoke about the Mutual Assistance Fund; that in it there was more than 1,000 rubles, but it was a pittance, because all of this money was still in their pockets, and the meeting came to an end. And that's all of it, all of our Bakhmachian business.

The letter of the worker–correspondent was copied by:

M. Bulgakov

The newspaper "Gudok," November 15, 1924

Under the Influence (Под мухой)

(A scene from nature)

They were unveiling the 'Red Section' at Station N. At the appointed hour, the benches filled with railroaders. The red armbands of the workers flashed friendlily. The chairman stood up, and announced solemnly:

— On the occasion of the unveiling of the Section, the floor is given to speaker ShotGlassov. If you please, ShotGlassov, to the stage.

ShotGlassov carried himself in a strange manner. He teetered, ripped himself out from the thicket of bodies that was standing near the stage, climbed up to the table; and while he was doing that, everyone saw that his tie was behind his left ear. Then he smiled, then he became serious and stared at the electric lamp on the ceiling with such an expression, as if he was seeing it for the first time. All the while he puffed, as if in extreme heat.

— Begin, ShotGlassov, — said the chairman in a surprised voice.

ShotGlassov began to hiccup. He covered his mouth with the flap of his hand and hiccupped quietly. Then he briefly hiccupped five times and with that, the air smelled like beer.

— Seems like the bar opened, — whispered someone in the front row.

— Your speech, ShotGlassov, — said the frightened chairman.

— Deeer citizens, — said ShotGlassov in a wild voice. He thought, and added, — And also citizens... of the femin... ine department.

Then he laughed, and from this, the air smelled like onions. On the benches they could not help laughing in response.

ShotGlassov became gloomy and looked at the water pitcher with reproach. The chairman anxiously rang the bell and asked:

— Are you not feeling well, ShotGlassov?

— I'm always shwell, — said ShotGlassov, raising his hand like a young pioneer.[1] The audience laughed.

— Please continue, — said the chairman, becoming pale.

— Corn... I have nothing to corntinue, — started Shot-Glassov in a hoarse voice, — and without a corntinuation it is very... good. Hic! However... If you insist... then I'll say... I will say it all! — he suddenly shouted with a threat. — As a matter of fact, what is the occasion of the general assembly? I ask you? Who is laughing? I ask them to leave! Citizen Chairman, you your own duuuu...ties...

A roar flew through the ranks and everybody began to stand up. The chairman clasped his hands.

— ShotGlassov! — he exclaimed in horror, — are you indeed drunk?

— As a fiddler! — someone shouted.

— Me? — asked ShotGlassov in amazement. He thought, lowered his head, and said, — Yes, I'm drunk. But in fact I didn't use your money to get drunk...

— Remove him!

The chairman, red and confused, gently took ShotGlassov by his arm.

— Keep your hands off of China! — shouted ShotGlassov indignantly. The secretary rushed to help the chairman and they began to lead ShotGlassov out.

— Such Chinese should be thrown out of the union! — someone shouted.

The assembly stormily discussed the incident.

After five minutes, everyone calmed down. The embarrassed chairman appeared on the stage and announced:

— The floor is given to the next speaker.

Translators' note

1. The *Young Pioneers* resembled Boy Scouts and Girl Scouts, but participation was the second step towards membership in the Communist Party.

The newspaper "Gudok," Moscow, November 16, 1924

The Demise of Shurka the Commissioned (Гибель Шурки-уполномоченного)

(The literal account of a worker–correspondent)

Shurka N is our assistant to the head of the station. Do you know him? Well who doesn't know this illustrious figure of the twentieth century!

When they asked Shurka whether his father was a man of machines, he replied that his dad had been a station watchman.

For this reason, in the 12th year of his young life, Shurka started along a transportation career, and, after ten years of service he rose to the high title of Professional Commissioner.

Then, at the peak of his career, with this very title, he fell.

They had asked him:

— Shurka, what will you do in the capacity of commissioner?

And he said:

— I will initiate, brothers, an energetic bond with the village.[1]

And he initiated the bond with the village. He started to travel to the village and drank moonshine in it. The moonshine in the village is very good, from bread.

And then, who knows how or from where, he gets himself a revolver. He walks around the village drunk, brandishing the revolver. And he so accustomed himself to the moonshine during the bonding that he started to drink 17 bottles a day.

His elderly mother followed him around crying, but Shurka kept drinking and drinking. And then, lo and behold, he started to retain the money of the workers, which he received from the insurance cashier on power of attorney.

After more or less time, they began to complain to the Union, where, on one beautiful day, they reviewed Shurka's case and booted him out of the commissioner's position. And so now, instead of bonding, you have estrangement! There the story ends.

A worker–correspondent

Please publish this story of mine and Shurka's mother will be very happy, because, to this day, he is still drinking. And a few days ago they conducted a search of his place, but they didn't find the revolver for some reason. He must have misplaced it somewhere...

The letter of the worker–correspondent, copied by
M. Bulgakov

Note by Bulgakov:

My dear Shurka! Look at what kind of a story we published about you. Sitting here in Moscow, being far away from you and not knowing your address, I will give you this published advice: Reform yourself before it's too late, otherwise you will be unseated from that lower office to which you have been transferred.

Translators' note

1. During this period, the Soviets encouraged officials to bond with rural provinces and village to advance the Party and its programs. See also the translators' note on page 306.

The newspaper "Gudok," Moscow, November 19, 1924

The Sounds of Heavenly Polka (Звуки польки неземной)

> No, really... after every ball it's as if I've committed some kind of a sin. And I don't want to remember it.
>
> *From Gogol*

Strike up the music the band has begun
Bum, bum, bum, bum - the sounds of heav'nly polka!!!

— Whis... — Wh-whistled a flute.

— I hear, I hear, — they sang at the bar.

— Bum, bum, bum, bum, — boomed the horns in the orchestra.

The sounds of heav'nly polka!!!

The building of the Lgovsk People's House was shaking. Light bulbs flashed in the fog, and completely green ladies and sweaty purple gentlemen swirled like a tornado. The wind swept up cigarette butts, and husks from sunflower seeds crunched under foot, like lice.

Pick up an angel and join in the fun!!

— Angel my dear, — a telegraphist in a frenzy whispered to a young lady, flying her to heaven.

— Polka! *A gauche*, Madame! — howled the conductor, swirling someone else's wife. — The gentlemen are abducting the ladies!

He was dripping and spraying. His collar drooped.

In the hall, as on the Sabbath, deviltry was scurrying about.

— Watch the toe, the corn, you devils! — muttered a nondancer, making his way to the bar.

— Musicians! Play № 5! — a man shouted from the bar in a sinking voice, looking like the drowned.

— Vasya, — lamented a second one, clutching the sides of a jacket, — Vasya! I do not notice any proletarians! Where did the proletarians go?

— Why on earth do you need proletarians? Musicians, pump on that polka!

— Proletarians were hanging out near the wall and disappeared...

— Where?

— There... over there...

— They pasted over them, our darlings! Glued. Look, they pasted a poster over them: Pur... pur... *Purchase Streamers and Unite...*

— How sad I am! I am suffering...

— Ah, ooh, how I am suffering! — the telegraphist, drunk on perfume, howled in a whisper. — My soul is yearning for you!

I want a polka... to dance it with you!!

— Gentlemen step into the ladies, and vice versa! *A droite!* — roared the conductor.

A cloud floated in the bar.

— One round, citizens, — invited a barman with a lacquered face, pouring a mysterious pink liquid into glasses, — To the health of the library! Ivan Stepanovich, I beg you, support this rock of science!

— I'm not big on lemonade...

— Are you crazy, who said it was lemonade?! Take a sip before you speak.

— Oh-ho-ho... Moonshine!

— That's what I'm talking about!

— And may I request a little glass?

— To the health of the prize-winning, most-handsome-at-the-ball Ferapont Ivanovich Shukin!

— What a lucky guy. He won a box of powder for his beauty!

— I protest. Mr. Crookednose was unfairly rewarded.

— Tone it down. From such words, y'know.

— Do not quarrel, citizens!

Shiny faces, with frozen eyes resembling perch, laid siege to the bar. Ash-gray smoke belched in big puffs. Double vision set in.

— May I have a light?

— Sure...

— Why are you offering me three matches?

— My good man, you're seeing things!

— From which one may I get a light?

— Take aim at the middle one, should be about right.

The hall roared. Ceilings and floors were collapsing. The old walls were shaking. In the windows, the glass clattered.

— Jing... jing... ding... ding!

— Bum, bum, bum, bum! — barked the horns.

The sounds of heav'nly polka!!!

Translators' note

1. Bulgakov probably used the words from a popular polka, but we could not find the music, so we do not know what sound it evoked in the mind of the readers of that period. Therefore, we used "The Pennsylvania Polka," which is well known from the film "Groundhog Day" and happens to match the meter of Bulgakov's polka. We only changed words in the first and third stanzas, otherwise the words are those used by Bulgakov.

The newspaper "Gudok," Moscow, November 27, 1924

The Banana and Sidaraf (Банан и Сидараф)

> — What form of government is there in Turkey?
> — Er... er... Turkish!
> *"The Public Service Exam"*
> *a short story by A. P. Chekhov*

I

This business happened last year. Fifteen people from one of the stations of the Southeastern Railroad completed the two-month course at an illiteracy liquidation school and then presented themselves at the exam.

— Ok, let's begin, — said the chief examiner and, pointing a finger to a newspaper, added, — what is written here?

A questionee sniffed with his nose, prowled briskly with his eyes through the big familiar letters underlined in a thick line, admired a picture of the artist Axelrod, and responded cunningly and joyfully:

— *Gudok*!

— Very good, — responded the examiner joyfully and, pointing to the beginning of an article published in a middle font, cunningly squinted his eyes, and asked:

— And this?

Two words appeared printed clearly in a middle font on the examinee's face: "It's harder..."

Sweat appeared on his forehead, and he began:

— B-a-ba, n-a-na. It's banana!

— Er.. No, it's not banana, — rued the examiner, — it's Baghdad. Well, anyway, after two months we cannot expect anything better. Grade: C! Send in the next one. Can you write?

— How shall I put it, — the second replied glibly, — I can do it on a form, but without a form I can't.

— What do you mean 'on a form?'

— The pay form, the last name.

— Uh-huh... OK. A good fit. Next! Mmm... hmm... What is *MOPR*?[1]

The questionee hesitated.

— Tell me, my friend, do not be afraid. Well...

— *MOPR*?.. Hmm... it's the chairman.

The examiners turned green.

— The chairman of what?

— I forget, — the questionee responded.

The chief examiner was seized by paralysis, so the following questions were posed by the second examiner:

— What about Lunacharsky?

The examinee looked at the ceiling, and said:

— Luna... char... sky? Ha... That's the one in Moscow...

— What is he doing there?

— God only knows, — simple-mindedly replied the examinee.

— OK, you can go, my dear, — muttered the examiner in horror, — I give you a B minus.

II

A year passed. And the graduates have forgotten everything they learned. About Lunacharsky, about the banana, about Baghdad, and they have even forgotten how to write their last names on forms. They remembered only one word *Gudok*, and that is because everyone, even the illiterate, was familiar with the masthead and the big headline letters rolling into the Local Committee from Moscow every day.

III

Once a trade union representative and a worker–correspondent struck up a conversation regarding this topic. The worker–correspondent was horrified.

— It's, in fact, horrible, comrade, — he said, — Is it possible to educate people in this way? This is a travesty! Some guy was mumbling some nonsense in the exam, on the form is written the word: 'Sidaraf' and 'cow' is spelled with a 'u' and he was still given a certificate that he is literate!

The trade union representative was at a loss, and became sad.

— You may be right... But what is there to be done?

— What do you mean, 'what is there to be done?' — flared up the worker–correspondent, — they must be retrained!

— But what can you possibly do in two months? — asked the trade union representative.

— Then not in two, but in four, or six, or as long as is needed. You cannot just graduate people and fool them saying that they are literate when they are actually as illiterate as they were before! Am I not speaking the truth?

— It's true, — tearfully said the trade union representative, and hung his head. He had nothing to refute it with.

M.

Translators' note

1. *MOPR* abbreviates *Mejdunarodnaya organizatsiya pomoshi bortsam revolutsii,* the International Aid Organization for Fighters of the Revolution.

The newspaper "Gudok," Moscow, December 2, 1924

A Lucky Man (Счастливчик)

> I won! I won!
> There's a lucky man...
> He always wins.
>
> *A song*

In the evening, at Station N, there was a knock on the door of the apartment of railroader Karnaukhov. Karnaukhov's wife, slipping on a downy shawl, went to open it.

— Who's there?

— It's me, darling Dashenka, — the gentle voice of Karnaukhov himself answered from behind the door through the sobbing of the rain, and then suddenly neighed like a horse.

— You got drunk, you tyrant? — said Dasha, rattling the lock.

A trickle of light sputtered into bare bulbs and the confused and completely sober face of Karnaukhov appeared in a shroud of rain and, next to him, out from the darkness, came the muzzle of a horse with a cataract in its eye. The wife recoiled.

— Come on, come on, Savrasochka, — said Karnaukhov in a beseeching voice, pulling the horse by the bit. Thundering with hooves, the horse climbed onto the porch and, from there, into the mudroom.

— And you?! — began Dasha, but stopped with an open mouth.

— Whoa!.. Dashenka, don't be angry... Git... git... g, you bitch, — gingerly spoke Karnaukhov, — she's nothing, a gentle horse. She'll stay in the mudroom!..

Just then Dasha recovered her senses:

— What do you mean, 'in the mudroom?' A mare in the mudroom? Yes, you have indeed gone crazy!

— Dashenka, it's not possible to keep her in the yard. And we don't have a barn. She's a fragile creature. The rain will get her wet; the horse will perish.

— May you perish along with her! — bellowed Dashenka. — Why did you bring such a vile creature onto my head? Just look, she's lame.

— And blind, Dashenka, — added Karnaukhov, — you see, she has a cataract like a pancake.

— Are you kidding? — roared Dasha. — How much did you pay for her? And what the hell do you need a horse for, you loser!..

— A half ruble, Dashenka. Fifty kopeks in total.

— A half ruble? I could have bought two pounds of sugar...

— Dashenka, trust me, I was aiming for ladies shoes. I was thinking of a present for your birthday.

— What shoes, you alcoholic?

— I'm not an alcoholic, Dashenka... There was a lottery. I wanted to escape it, but the boss of the rail yard nabbed me. Hello, he says, Karnaukhov, I am raffling, he says, Karnaukhov, some interesting lottery tickets: take a ticket. I say: I don't want to. But he responds in such a voice: Ah, you don't want to! Well, as you wish... I've long noted that you, Karnaukhov, don't like me. Well, okay... I see that you won't take them, too bad. Well, I say, may I have a ticket? And he assures me: You have, he says, a lucky nature, you will for sure win either ladies shoes size 36 or a music box that plays 19 songs. They started to draw tickets, no winners, and then, bang, to me, № 98, the mare! The audience was laughing. I wanted to run away, but the boss of the rail yard says: No, stop! It's against the rules. You won, so cart it away. But where will I put it? I tried to give it away, but no one took it, the audience laughed.

— Get out! — roared Dashenka. — Get out together with the mare, and may your soul never again smell home!

— Dash...

— Get out! — repeated Dashenka, and threw the door open wide.

— But... whoa!.. Dashenka, listen... Come on, come on,

bitch...

The mare rumbled with her hooves. The bulbs glistened one last time on the sheets of rain. And then a curtain of fog swallowed the lucky man and his winnings.

Through the murmur of the rain dully carried:

— C'mon, git-along, git... Why don't you just die already?

The newspaper "Gudok" (The Whistle), Moscow, December 4, 1924

The Life of a Dog (Собачья жизнь)

Dear Comrade Editor!

Publish my humble story about a Japanese dog–gift.

While checking tickets on Train № 1, Chita–Moscow, I chanced to discover the remarkable presence of a dog on the train.

In particular, an Austrian she-citizen, the wife of the Austrian consul located in Japan, was riding in the international car from Shanghai to Vienna. She was holding two berths: one bunk in train car № 10 for herself, and another in № 9 for the dog.

It fell to me to fine the Austrian she-citizen a small sum for not possessing a ticket for the dog. The Austrian she-citizen paid me the money.

But I was very interested in what kind of dog went first class, and allowing as to how I didn't speak any language other than Russian, I had to turn to a translator.

— Tell me, — I said, — on what business is this dog?

The translator spoke a little with the she-citizen in a foreign language, and responded:

— The dog is special, being transported by the she-citizen as a present to the Austrian Minister of Foreign Affairs. She paid 1,000 gold rubles for the dog in Japan.

— And ask, — I say, — why the hell the Minister of Foreign Affairs needs such an expensive dog.

He replied:

— As it turns out, the Austrian minister has a Japanese male dog, and, as it turns out, she is taking the she-dog to him.

— Aha, — I say.

And I started to add up the cost of the fiancée–dog: 1,000 rubles gold in Japan and a first class international ticket from Chita to Moscow of 187 rubles, 34 kopeks. And also other tickets. Additionally, what is it that the dog eats? As it turns out, they feed her, for a first course, bullion made from birds; for a second course, porridge; and for a third course, imported chocolates.

— Why, — I ask, — imported?

As it turns out, the dog proclaimed that she won't lap up Russian chocolate! The dog was extremely interesting to me. She has a silk blanket, a silk pillow, and on top of it, there are quite a few dresses, also of silk.

— And what about boots, — I ask, — does she wear them?

— No, — says the translator after an exchange in the foreign language, — it turns out she goes barefoot.

—And what if she, — I say, — catches a cold from the mud? And the translator responds to me:

— You silly man, would she really walk in the mud? She goes about by automobile.

— Like, — I say, — a small dog's automobile?

— No, — he says, — in a regular automobile. Her owner drives her in the aforementioned car.

So, I understood everything, thanked the translator. I say: "Goodbye." The dog in no way acknowledges me.

And the translator says: "She doesn't like the proletariat."

***

Please, Comrade Editor, print my true story about the ministerial dog so that all workers in our transportation industry can read it.

Railroader.
A letter of a railroader copied,
without changing anything,
Mikhail Bulgakov.

The newspaper "Gudok," Moscow, December 10, 1924

The Desired Paymaster (Желанный платило)

> The American cockatoo
> Sings on the fly.
>
> *A scientific communication*

At dawn, in the fog of Murmansk, the whistle of a locomotive howled across from the barracks at mile 226. Thereupon began a commotion in the home of a railroad worker. The railroader jumped out of a warm bed and, stomping with slippers on the floor, howled like a madman:

— Where are my underpants?! Marya, where are my underpants?.. Oy, my pay! Marya... My underpants... They will depart!!

— Lord, give us strength! — yelped Marya, jumping around the shack.

A child screamed in a cradle.

— Light the lamp! — the railroader groaned. — Oh, Maryushka, light it. My underpants have fallen through the earth!!

— Here they are, here they are, aggh, you accursed fool. They fell down behind the bench. Oh, heavens, it's whistling... Breadwinner, at least put on your pants! Put on your pants, you'll catch a cold.

— It's whistling! — like a madman the railroader screamed, pulling on the striped underpants. — It's whistling, damn it, oh, hurry up!!

— Your pants...

— To the devil's mother with them...

The door squeaked and the railroader fell out. He flew two hundred yards in the autumn mist and made it. The pay train stood opposite the barracks, howling like a wolf...

— What's with you, brother, in such a state of disarray? — asked the paymaster benignly. — Why are you wandering around naked?

— Ha-aha-aha-aha! Ha-aha-aha! — breathed the railroader like a dog on a hot day. — No time to worr... worry about appearances... Sal ... aha-aha-aha... sala... Salary, give me, hurry...

— Yes, we must hurry, we are about to get under way, — said the paymaster. And he began to count. — Here's ten... fifteen, sixteen...

— Oh, crap! — exclaimed the railroader in horror. — We're under way, damn it!

— It's all right, you can ride 'till the 240th mile, — comforted the paymaster, — and get out there.

— Get out! — mocked the railroader. — It's easy for you to say, but how am I going to get back?

— Well, you will make a proménaje, — reassured the paymaster, — although surely it will be cold in such lightweight décolletage.

At the 240th mile, the railroader gripped the bills in his fist, threw himself out of the train, and shot back to the 226th mile.

Having come flying home, he collapsed on a bench and began to moan:

— My finger is frozen, damn it; may the devil take it along with the pay. Marya, bring me some tea!

— At least put on some pants...

— Wait a second. No time for pants. Seventeen, eighteen... forty kopeks. Wait a second, wait a second... The loan payment... May the devil rip you to shreds! They made a mistake! It's not enough! What a disaster, I swear!

Exactly two weeks later, the railroader announced to his wife:

— Marya, lay the pants out next to me on the bench. Wake me up as soon as you hear the whistle. I'll kill you on the spot if you don't wake me up.

They slept uneasily, but there was no whistle. The pay train went by without a whistle, heading towards the 220th mile.

The railroader stood near the window and, jabbing at it with his fist, swore on his mother, and the pay train, and the paymaster, and the one who sent it, and the fog, and the 226th mile.

He announced to his wife:

— Well, if it comes back, I will get it. He will pay me!

He waited until the 23rd. Five days. And after five days, the pay train went by in the opposite direction without the slightest whistle or stop. The railroader turned red, took out a pencil stub, and wrote a letter to *Gudok*.

"Our desired paymaster haughtily and nobly flashed by on a high-speed train. It only remains for us to stare into the distance, spreading our eyeballs across the landscape to the horizon, and await the eternal attainment of our own stupefaction.

Deliver us from evil!"

The newspaper "Gudok," Moscow, December 24, 1924

"The Government Inspector" with a Knockout Punch
(«Ревизор» с вышибанием)

A new production

> In our club, a board member grabbed a club member by the collar and threw him out into the foyer.
>
> *A letter of a worker–correspondent from one of the stations of the Donetsk Railroad*

Characters:

The mayor
Strawberry — a trustee of charitable institutions
Lyapkin-Tyapkin — a judge
Khlopov — superintendent of educational institutions
A board member of the club
A member of the club (Goryushkin)
The prompter
Audience
Voices

***

The stage represents a club at Station N of the Donetsk Railroads. The curtain is closed.

***

AUDIENCE: It's time. It's time for the show!.. (Stomping of feet, the lights dim, from behind the stage are heard the muffled voices of the ticketless fighting a ticket taker. The curtain opens. On the illuminated stage is a room in the house of the mayor).

VOICE (from the balcony): Si-lence!

MAYOR: I invited you, ladies and gentlemen...

PROMPTER (in a hoarse whisper from the prompt box): In order to inform you of the most unpleasant news.

MAYOR: In order to inform you of the most unpleasant news: a government inspector is coming to visit!

LYAPKIN-TYAPKIN: A government inspector?

STRAWBERRY: A government inspector?

PROMPTER: Mur-mur-mur...

MAYOR: The government inspector from St. Petersburg, incognito, and even worse, with a secret mission.

LYAPKIN-TYAPKIN: Cripes almighty!

STRAWBERRY: We didn't have a care in the world, and now this!

KHLOPOV: Good Lord, and in addition with a secret mission.

MAYOR: Seems like I had a premonition of it... (There's a terrible racket behind the stage. The door swings open on to the stage and a club member flies in. He is wearing a jacket with a torn collar. His hair is disheveled.)

CLUB MEMBER: You have no right to shove me around! I am a club member. (Confusion on the stage).

AUDIENCE: Aggh!

PROMPTER (hissing like a snake): Spit yourself off the stage. Have you gone mad?

MAYOR (stupefied): What's with you, comrade, have you lost your mind?

AUDIENCE: He-he-he-he...

MAYOR (wants to go on with his part): Today, I dreamed all night... Get off the stage for Christ's sake, I beg you... Two unusual rats of some kind... Go out through the door, through the door, I'm telling you... The son of a bitch ruined the play...

STRAWBERRY (in a whisper): The door is to the left... You're going through the scenic backdrop, bastard.

The club member rushes back and forth across the stage, finding no way out.

AUDIENCE (gradually getting amused): Bravo, Goryushkin!

Bravo, nice jacket!

MAYOR (at a loss): I'm telling you, I've never seen such... What a scoundrel!

PROMPTER (growls): They were black, unnaturally big... Go to the devil's mother!.. Move away from the prompt box at least...

AUDIENCE: Ha-ha-ha-ha-ha...

MAYOR: I will read you a letter... Here is what he wrote. (Behind the stage there is noise and a voice of a board member: "Where is that bastard?" The door opens, and the board member appears on the stage. He is wearing a suit and a red tie).

BOARD MEMBER (menacingly): You're here, wretch?

AUDIENCE (enthusiastically): Bravo, Khvataev!.. (A shrill whistle from the gallery.) Beat him up!!!

CLUB MEMBER: You do not have the right. I'm a member!

BOARD MEMBER: I'll show you 'a member.' I'll teach you to crawl in without a ticket!!!

STRAWBERRY: Comrade Khvataev! You may not apply physical force during the Soviet era.

MAYOR: I am ending the play. (Removes his sideburns and wig).

VOICE (from the gallery, with admiration): Van'ka, he's young, look! (Whistle).

BOARD MEMBER (in ecstatic rage): I'll show you!!! (He grabs the club member by the collar, swings him like a rag, and throws him into the audience).

CLUB MEMBER: Help!!! (With a dull shriek he falls into the orchestra).

MAYOR: Pakhom, close the curtain!

STRAWBERRY: The curtain! The curtain!

AUDIENCE: Police!!! Police!!!

The curtain closes.

1925

The newspaper "Gudok," Moscow, January 5, 1925

The Healer (Целитель)

On December 12th, a repair worker of the Vereytsovskaya branch of the Western Railroad, Comrade Bayashko, being diseased in his legs and knowing that medic-citizen K arrived from Uborki to see his neighbor, asked to be examined as well, but the medic did not examine Comrade Bayashko, but said that his legs needed to be amputated, and left without rendering any help.

Minus

He entered, tied the straps of his white gown, and shouted:

— One at a time!

The first turn fell to a citizen with a cane. He jumped like a sparrow, having tucked one leg up.

— So, brother, got you down, huh?

— Father Medic! — sang the citizen.

— Pull down your pants. Geez!

— Father, don't scare me!

— Why would I want to frighten you? We're not assigned here for that. We're assigned here to treat you sons of bitches of the transport service. Gangrene of the knee joint with a lesion of the central nervous system.

— Father!!

— For forty years I've been a father. Put on your pants.

— Father, what's going to happen to my leg?

— Nothing special. Next! It will putrefy up to the knee, and drop anchor!!

— Fath...

— Why are you croaking 'Father, father.' What kind of a father am I to you? I'll prescribe drops for you. Come back when the leg falls off. I'll write you a certificate. Social Insurance will pay you for the leg. It will be even more advantageous for you. And you, what do you want?

— I can't see, handsome man, I can't see anything. In the evening, I can't find the doors.

— Do not, by the way, cross yourself, granny. Can't you see you're not in church. You, Grandma, have trachoma. With cataracts of the first degree, according to Article A.

— A handsome man you are!

— For forty years I've been handsome. When your eyes drain, you'll know!

— Handsome!!

— I'll prescribe drops for you. Come back when you can't see a damn thing. I'll write you a paper. Social Insurance will pay you in rubles for each eye. Don't cry in here, granny, you'll cry in the Social Insurance office. And you, what do you want?

— Sonny boy's mug is sloughing off, Citizen Medic.

— Uh huh. OK. Bring him here. Don't howl. It's time to get you married, and you're crying. Uh oh...

— Citizen Medic. Do not torment a mother's heart!

— I am not touching your heart. Your heart will stay with you. Your offspring has cancer of the cheek.

— My Lord, what will happen next?

— Hmmn... It is known that with perforation of the cheek that the whole side of the face will go. He will suffer for one month, and then curtains. Come back then, I'll write you a paper. And you, what do you want?

— I cannot climb stairs. I'm out of breath.

— You have a fifth valve defect.

— What does that mean?

— A hole in the heart.

— Neat!

— Hard to beat.

— Do I have time to write a will?

— If you run.

— *Merci*, I will sprint.

— Sprint! All the best. Next! No one else? So be it. I did it, so let's call it a day.[1]

Translators' note

1. *Otzvonil, i s kolokolny doloy* means "I rang the bell, and left the bell tower."

The newspaper "Gudok," Moscow, January 7, 1925

The Pharmacy (Аптека)

The NKPC Pharmacy on Basmany St. is open only on workdays, and is closed on holidays. And what if someone gets ill, what is there to do?

From the letter of a worker–correspondent

It's snowing. On the corner is a pharmacy...

— *Love wears out a man...*[1] — in a pleasant voice sang a man in grey, standing in front of a porch. In the windows on the sides of the porch are two orbs: red and blue; and a painting depicting a bottle of mineral water.

A very pale citizen in a black coat tumbled from around the corner, threw himself onto the porch, and bumped into a hanging padlock.

— Don't beat on it, — the grey coat said to him, — it's locked.

— How could it be locked? Oy, my dear fellow, — said the black one paling, — I beg you. Oy, it's stabbing. I tell you, stabbing. On the left side.

— Is it your stomach? — he asked sympathetically.

— My stomach... My dear fellow, — murmured the citizen in anguish, — here's my prescription... For five drops, oy, opium... Three times a day!!! Oy, I will die... It's stabbing again... For drops... five... A jar of hot water... I implore you, comrade!!!

— Why are you imploring me? I'm just the watchman. There is no benefit in imploring me.

— O-ow-ow-ow-ow... — suddenly screamed the citizen, widely and resonantly opening his mouth. Passersby recoiled from him. — Oooh, it eased off, — the citizen added, suddenly calming down, and he wiped sweat from his forehead. — In accordance with what law is it closed?

— What day is it today?

— Sun... Sunday. Oy, my dear fellows, Sunday, little Sunday, my dears.

— Tomorrow, on Monday, come back... You know what, no, don't come back tomorrow... it's a holiday... Come back after New Year's.

— I will die in the old one, oh-oh-oh, o-o-o!

— Go to another pharmacy, what else can you do!

— Where is there another one around here?

— I don't know, my good man, ask a policeman.

The black one flew off the steps, twisted like a screw, yelped soulfully several times, and flew crookedly through the streets to a policeman.

— My stomach hurts, comrade policeman, — he cried, flourishing the prescription, — I implore you...

The policeman removed a cigarette from his mouth and, waving his arm, began to explain to the citizen where to run to...

He hovered there for about another five seconds and vanished.

M.B.

Translators' note

1. The two quoted lines are from a song. The man sings the first to himself, and the second out loud.

The newspaper "Gudok," Moscow, January 9, 1925

An Enchanted Place (Заколдованное место)

> At the Bobrinsky Station of the South–Western Railroad there is a cooperative kiosk. Everyone who ever got sent to work there is accused of embezzlement after two months and goes to trial.
>
> *From the letter of a worker–correspondent*

1

Citizen Taldykin sat in a circle of acquaintances and listened. Citizen Taldykin's face glowed; the acquaintances were clinking glasses with Taldykin.

— We congratulate you, Taldykin. Prove yourself in the position of the boss of the kiosk.

2

After two months, Citizen Taldykin sat on the bench for the accused and, quietly weeping, listened to the speech of a member of the Union of Defense Attorneys, who was standing behind him with thumbs resting in the armholes of his vest.

— Comrade Judges! — whined the member of the union. — Before speaking about whether my defendant embezzled 840 rubles, 15 kopeks in gold, let's ask ourselves the question: Did these 840 rubles, 15 kopeks in gold exist on earth at all? A careful examination of monthly ledger № 15 shows that this money did not exist. One asks how then did Citizen Taldykin embezzle it? He didn't spend anything; in fact, it is clear to every sober-minded person that one cannot embezzle something that doesn't exist! On the other hand, monthly ledger № 16 shows that 840 rubles, 15 kopeks in gold existed, but if this is so, they are on hand, it means that there wasn't any embezzlement!..

The judges, completely bewildered, listened to the defender, and sweat dripped from them.

And from Taldykin, tears.

3

The judge stood up and read:

— "... but taking into account... a suspended sentence of three years."

Tears dried up on the face of Taldykin.

4

The members of the management of the Merchandise-Producing Division sat, and discussed:

— What a swine, this Taldykin! We need to appoint someone else.

It seems that Bandage will have to work at the kiosk. Bandage: Take the appointment.

5

Citizen Bandage sat on the bench of the accused and listened to the defender.

And the defender sang:

— I contend that, firstly, these 950 rubles, 23 kopeks do not exist at all; in the second place, I will prove that my defendant, Bandage, didn't take them; and, in the third place, that he returned them in the entirety!

— "...taking into account, — solemnly said the judge, and nodded his head in the direction of Bandage, — treat it as suspended."

6

At the Merchandise-Producing Division:

— To the devil with this Bandage, appoint Peach.

7

Peach stood up and, pressing his hat to his stomach, said his last words:

— I won't ever do it again, Citizen Judges...

8

After Peach, sat Noisemaker, after Noisemaker, Goatmilker.

9

At the Merchandise-Producing Division, they sat down and discussed:

Enough. Designate a special unit of 15 comrades to investigate what's with this infamous kiosk! Whoever sits there for two months ends up in the People's Court! It can't go on like this. No matter who you look at, whether it's a bright individual or a good honest citizen, as soon as he sits down behind the counter he's got mud on his face. Investigation unit, get going!

10

The special investigation unit got ready and got going. The results of the investigation are still unknown to us.

Mikhail B.

A Genius Individual (Гениальная личность)

The secretary of the District Committee, who was present at a general meeting of union members at the Junction Station of the Donetsk Railroads, contrived to prepare in advance not only the resolutions for the meeting, but even to write its minutes. Everyone was struck by the genius of the secretary.

Worker–correspondent Nail

1

The secretary of the District Committee sat in the railway station and gnawed on his pen. Before the secretary laid a big sheet of paper, divided by a vertical line. On the left it said: "Discussed," on the right: "Decided." The secretary excitedly looked at the ceiling, and murmured:

— So, apparently, there's a question about overalls. Am I speaking correctly, comrades? Absolutely correctly! — the secretary responded to himself chorally. — Right! That's why they discussed it and, having discussed it, decided... — the secretary dipped his pen and began to scratch: "To take comprehensive measures for the distribution of overalls without delay, providing overalls by and large to each and everyone." — Do you agree, comrades? Is anyone opposed? — the secretary asked his ink well.

It wasn't opposed to anything, so the secretary wrote on the paper: "Accepted unanimously." And to himself gave praise: — Bravo, Makushkin!

— Now what do we have next? — continued the secretary, — The Mutual Aid Fund. As clear as day. Well, there is no money in the fund, this is as clear as day. And, like the day, it's clear that loans do not get returned on time. So that's why they discussed the fund and resolved: "To cooperate in every way in the development of the Mutual Aid Fund, fully and completely attracting the lower ranks of transport workers into participation in the fund, and equally take measures for the increase of the fund by a socially conscious, timely repayment of loans fully and completely!" Is anyone opposed? — victoriously asked Makushkin.

Neither the cabinet nor the chairs said a word against it, and Makushkin wrote: "Unanimously."

The door opened and a neighbor entered.

— Scram, — Makushkin said to him, — I'm busy... writing a protocol of the meeting.

— Yesterday's? — asked the neighbor.

— Tomorrow's, — answered Makushkin.

The neighbor opened his mouth and, just like that, with an open mouth, left.

2

The hall for the general meeting was packed to capacity and all heads were directed towards the stage, where Comrade Makushkin stood next to a pitcher of water and a bell.

— The first question on the day's agenda, — said the chairman of the meeting, — we have a question about overalls. Who wishes to speak?

— Me, me... me... me... — the hall answered with twenty voices.

— May I be permitted, Comrade? — asked Makushkin in a musical voice.

— I yield the floor to Comrade Makushkin, — said the chairman respectfully.

Having cleared his throat, Makushkin began:

— Comrades, — hooking his fingers under his lapels, — every socially conscious union member knows that overalls are necessary...

— That's right! They didn't distribute the felt boots until June! — thundered the hall.

— I ask that you not interrupt the speaker, — said the chairman.

— Therefore, my dear comrades, we must take comprehensive measures for the distribution of overalls without delay.

— Right! Bravo! — cried the hall. — They sent the canvas pants in January!

— Si-lence!

— I suggest that speakers not speak up so as to not waste time, — said Makushkin, — and immediately proceeded to the discussion of a resolution.

— Does anyone have a resolution? — asked the chairman, straying from protocol.

— I have, — said Makushkin modestly, and instantly read a resolution.

— Is anyone opposed? — said the flabbergasted chairman. The hall immediately and in one voice fell silent.

— Write: "Without a single abstention," — said the stupefied chairman to the secretary of the meeting.

— Do not write it, comrades, I already have it written, — said Makushkin, beaming with his eyes.

The general meeting rose as one man, drinking in Makushkin with their eyes.

— A mover and shaker, — said someone admiringly, — not like our boorish local yokels!

***

When the general meeting ended, the crowd accompanied Makushkin down the street for half a mile, and women took their children into their arms, and said:

— Look, there goes Makushkin. You too someday will be like this man.

The newspaper "Gudok," Moscow, January 17, 1925

A Collection of Putrid Facts (Коллекция гнилых фактов)

(From the letters of worker–correspondents)

Fact 1

A STORY ABOUT HOW A MEDIC DONATED FABRIC TO *MOPR*[1]

This putrid fact, thoroughly infused with alcoholism, happened in our N[th] Club of the Western Railroad, when they organized an evening to support *MOPR*.[1]

The evening proceeded with extreme solemnity, with brisk sales of fabric at an auction for the benefit of *MOPR*.

Then suddenly a shriek rang out, resembling that from a piglet.

All the workers turned their heads as one.

And what did they see?

Our medic from the emergency room.

He was rocking like a pendulum, his face completely red.

Everyone asked himself the question: Where did the medic come from?

And, secondly, was he drunk?

It turned out that he was indeed drunk; but what's most surprising of all is that the club director, chairman of the board, and members of our commissions proved to be drunk as well, which became immediately obvious.

One of the astounded club members stepped forward and declared to the medic:

— You do not look like yourself!

The medic responded insolently:

— None of your business.

Then, everyone understood that the medic got shit-faced, together with the board, allegedly on beer.

But we know what kind of beer it was.

In spite of the intoxication, the medic pushed through the crowd to the stage and, in the blink of an eye, won some fabric at the auction. With that, he declared to everyone:

— And you thought I was drunk! Just to spite you, I'm donating the fabric to *MOPR*!

As soon as the auctioneer announced about his donation, the medic, seeing his fabric being taken away, repented of his deed and, weeping, declared:

— I did it unconsciously, in a state of intoxication. I consider this transaction invalid and demand the return of the fabric.

Amidst public shouts of contempt, they returned the fabric to him, and he left the club.

After that, the chairman of the board fell and bloodied his face, and the director of the club was led out by his fiancée.

That's how the evenings can be here...

It is shameful to write about it!

The letter was copied by
M. Bulgakov

Translators' note

1. *MOPR* abbreviates *Mejdunarodnaya organizatsiya pomoshi bortsam revolutsii*, the International Aid Organization for Fighters of the Revolution.

The newspaper "Gudok," Moscow, February 12, 1925

Love Collateral (Залог любви)

A novel

I

THE MOON SHADOWS

Sounds died out at the station. Even the restless yard engine stopped howling and fell asleep on the track. The moon, smiling, appeared over the forest and poured out a magical greenish light. And then the acacias started giving off a fragrance, hitting one in the head, and an unemployed nightingale whistled... And things similar.

Two shadows huddled in the patterned shade of bushes and a conductor's buttons occasionally shone in the gleam of the moonlight.

— I know you're lying, you bastard, — whispered a woman's voice, — you'll play around and then dump me.

— Marousia, you should be ashamed of yourself, — whispered a hoarse voice, trembling from the offense. — I am, in your opinion, capable of such a lowly deed? I would rather, Manya, put a bullet in my forehead than cheat on a woman!

— Yeah, right, you'll put a bullet in yourself, — murmured the woman's voice nervously. — That will never happen! After you pick the flowers, you'll get on an express train, and your trail will go cold. Better that you get yourself off of me!

"They're kissing, the devils, — wistfully thought the bachelor chief of the station, sitting on a balcony, — kissing under this moon, so to speak, is like kissing under a traffic light."

— We know, — whispered one shadow, pushing away the other shadow, — we've seen your type. You sing and sing, and then I'll be crying with a child, wiping tears from his face with the back of my hands.

— I will not let you cry, Manyusha. I myself will wipe the

tears from this child, if it appears, with the back of my hands. He will not squeak once. Let me kiss you on the neck. I will give the baby forty golden rubles or thirty.

"Phooey, a demonic obsession," — grunted the station chief, and fled the balcony.

— Look, just go away.

— Give me your lips.

— OK... Now get off of me... Cleaved to me, like a demon.

— "Stubborn woman, — thought the shadow, gleaming with buttons. — Well, I will crack you. Oh, shit. A thought flashed through my... Oh, what a brilliant head I have..."

— You know, Marousia, I'll tell you what. If you don't believe my word, I will give you collateral.

— You and your collateral can get lost, stop torturing me!

— No, Marousia, wait. Do you know what I'll leave you, — the shadow whispered, and began to unbutton the jacket. — Oh it's such a collateral... without it, I cannot exist. Anyway I'll come back to you.

— Show me...

For a long time the shadows were whispering, hiding something. Then silence came.

The moon suddenly looked out from behind the pines and in embarrassment wrapped itself in clouds, like a Turkish woman in a veil.

And darkness.

II

THE PLEDGE IN THE HOPE CHEST

It was pouring rain. Marousia sat by the window thinking: "To where has he, the rascal, disappeared? Oh, my heart sensed it. Well, he'll hop and hop around, and then he'll come back. He will not get far without the collateral. My happiness is locked up in a hope chest... Still, it's interesting. Where is he, the seducer of my life?"

III

THE EVIL PLAN

The seducer, at that time, was at a police station.

— What do you want, citizen? — the police commander asked him.

The seducer coughed, and said:

— Um... An unfortunate thing happened to me.

— What's that?

— An indescribable thing. I lost my worker's ID.

— The thing is quite describable. It happens with careless people. Under what circumstances did it happen?

— Ordinary circumstances. Please note the hole in my pocket. I went out for a walk... The moon was shining... I said to her...

— Who is 'her?'

— Phew!.. Slip of the tongue. My bad. I did not say anything, but simply was looking around, and then, oh my Lord, a hole, and my worker's ID was gone!

— Print a notice in a newspaper, then cut it out, and come back here. We will issue you a new one.

— Yes, sir.

IV

THE FATAL LETTER

In *Gudok,* some time later, appeared: "Lost worker's ID number such and such, in the name of so and so. Issued by such and so police department on May 8, 1923."

And some time later, a letter arrived to *Gudok* that struck the editors like a thunderclap:

"Highly-esteemed Comrade Editor! It's all a lie! The ID is not lost, and so and so is lying. He gave it to me as collateral of love. And now he is publishing this in the newspaper!"

EPILOGUE

So and so tore at his hair, and screamed:

— What am I to do now, after such a disgrace?!

A friend stood before him and said:

— I don't know what to tell you. You played a dirty trick on a woman. So, now you should punish yourself!

The newspaper "Gudok," Moscow, February 18, 1925

Deviltry (Чертовщина)

Here, in Kuznetsk, in the auditorium of the Local Committee were scheduled, on the very same evening, at the very same hour: a meeting of the Foodstuffs Committee, a meeting of the production cell, a labor safety meeting, an assembly of worker–correspondents, as well as a meeting of the Pioneers. The movie, "The Daughter of Montezuma," was also shown nearby. The result is impossible to describe.

A worker–correspondent

In a small room, people were sitting close to one another, disheveled and sweaty. Above their heads hung posters for "The Daughter of Montezuma," starring the people's favorite and queen of the screen and "Around the World in 18 Days."

A door opened by a fourth. A hand with a torn cuff weaseled in, then a mad head. And that head started shouting:

— Let me in, comrades! This is an outrage.

— Wiggle in! — they shouted from the room.

— Let me in! — shouted the head, breaking away from invisible pliers behind the door. A scream was heard from behind the door.

— Do not kick with your feet, Comrade Big Butt! You're not at a flea market!

The wall shook and on it bounced the words: "Napoleon's Messenger."

A disheveled individual finally edged into the small room, surmounted the stage, and from there immediately began to intone in a hoarse voice, like a mechanical gramophone:

— Speaking of the price of pork burgers, comrades, I cannot help but note with indignation the fact that while at the private market they cost 32 kopeks, in our Commissary № 17 they are 33.5...

The assembly responded to this with a vicious roar, and from behind the door burst a hysterical cry:

— Hurry up! You've been holding your meeting for too long!

— What are you mumbling about burgers? — shouted an exasperated man pressed up against "The Daughter of a Millionaire."

— I'm not mumbling! — shouted the speaker in response. — I'm reporting!

— What are you reporting about?

— The price of pork, — shouted the speaker.

— Wheel yourself and your damn pork to the devil! Where is our speaker? — they shouted from all sides.

— There's no speaker, he's late, may the devil take him! So, we need to cede this place to them!

The audience surged to an encounter at the doors with the incoming one, which lickety split occupied the seats. Behind another door, a pianist dully started playing a polonaise by Chopin.

The beat-up speaker looked into the new faces and mumbled:

— Speaking of the price of pork burgers, dear comrades, I cannot help but note with indignation the fact that while at the private market pork burgers cost 32 kopeks, in our Commissary № 17, they are 33.5...

A young man in a hat stood up and politely interrupted him:

— You, comrade, have everything confused. "Meat Production" was featured yesterday, but today it is "Blood and Sand."

— And granulated sugar, too! — shouted the orator in despair. — At a time when, at the private market, it is 25.5 kopeks...

— He must have lapped up quite a bit before the film, — screamed the crowd with laughter, and suddenly rushed to the door, and Chopin instantly fell silent.

The doors poured in a new audience.

— Speaking of the price of pork burgers, — the speaker began in despair, — I cannot help but note with indignation the fact that at a time when granulated sugar at the private market is 25.5 kopeks, in our commissary pork is 36 kopeks. The difference, therefore, dear comrades...

— To hell with pork! — screamed the new audience. — One can see that you haven't talked enough in your Foodstuffs Committee!

They pushed the speaker with the burgers off somewhere, and a different one climbed in his place, closed his eyes, and mumbled quickly:

— The question of work clothes is a pivotal question, comrades. How long can we wait for gloves for the repairmen? Do they want them, one wonders, to work in bare hands...

He mumbled for around three minutes and then his eyes were opened by terrible cries:

— Enough! Enough! Enough croaking about gloves. Give us some time to talk!

Some kind of anxious people with pencils in hand sat down, replacing the previous audience. One of them jumped onto the stage, pinned the glove specialist to "The Indian Tomb," and immediately began shouting:

— To make correspondence in the newspapers more relevant, one should follow these rules...

But he didn't have time to explain what kind of rules to follow to make correspondence more relevant, because from behind a door on the left rattled the march "Iron Division," and from the right, also behind doors, a choir of 200 people started singing:

For the vigil from the tent
No one wanted to crawl out!
So we had to by the heels
Pioneers to drag out!!!!!

Then started the very thing, which, according to the correspondent, is impossible to describe. Therefore, we will not describe it.

The newspaper "Gudok," Moscow, February 25, 1925

Mademoiselle Jeana (Мадмазель Жанна)

> We had, at the club at Station Z., a soiree with the
> prophetess and hypnotizer Jeana.
> She divined the thoughts of other people and
> earned 150 rubles for the evening.
>
> *A worker–correspondent*

The hall froze. A lady appeared on stage with anxious painted
eyes, wearing red stockings and a lavender dress. A jaunty hag-
gard-looking character followed behind her, in striped trousers,
with a chrysanthemum in the buttonhole of his jacket. The character cast his eyes to the right and left, bent over, and whispered
in the lady's ear:

— The bald one, in the first row, with the paper collar is the
second assistant to the chief of the station. Recently, he proposed and she declined. Nyurochka. (Loudly to the audience).
Highly esteemed audience. I have the honor to present to you
the famous prophetess and medium Mademoiselle Jeana of Paris
and Sicily. She divines the past, present, and future, as well as
intimate family secrets!

The hall turned white.

— (To Jeana) Put on a mysterious face, you idiot. (To the
audience) However, you shouldn't think that these are some
kinds of magic or miracles. Nothing of the sort, for miracles do
not exist. (To Jeana) I've told you a hundred times to wear an
armlet for the performance. (To the audience) It is based entirely on the laws of nature authorized by the Local Committee
and the Cultural Enlightenment Commission and it comprises
mental telepathy, based on hypnotism, according the teachings of
the Indian fakirs, who are oppressed by British imperialism. (To
Jeana) Under the banner, to the side, the one with a handbag, her
husband is cheating on her at a nearby station. (To the audience)
If someone wishes to know deep family secrets, ask me ques-

tions, and I shall, commanding via hypnosis, put to sleep the famous Jeana... I beg you to be seated, mademoiselle... One at a time, citizens! (To Jeana) One, two, three. And now you are starting to fall asleep! (He makes some kind of hand gestures, as if poking the eyes of Jeana). You are witnessing an amazing example of occultism. (To Jeana) Fall asleep, why are you gawking for a hundred years? (To the audience) And so, she is asleep! I now invite you...

In the dead silence, the assistant to the chief rose up, he flushed red, then paled, and asked in a voice wild from fear:

— What's the most important event in my life? At this very moment.

The character (to Jeana):

— Look at my fingers closely, you idiot.

The character abracadabra'd his index finger around the chrysanthemum, then formed several mysterious characters with the fingers, which signified 'shat-ter-red.'

— Your heart, — spoke Jeana in a sepulchral voice as if in a dream, — has been shattered by a treacherous woman.

The character lowered his eyes in assent. The hall gasped, looking at the unhappy assistant of the chief of the station.

— What's her name? — hoarsely asked the rejected assistant.

— Ann, you, urrr, oh, h... — whirled the character's finger before his jacket's lapel.

— Nyurochka! — said Jeana firmly.

The assistant of the chief of the station stood up, completely white, looked around woefully, dropped his hat and a box of cigarettes, and left.

— Will I get married? — a young lady suddenly shouted out hysterically. — Tell me, dear Mademoiselle Jeana!

The character measured the young lady with an experienced eye, took note of the nose with a pimple, the flaxen hair, and the crooked hip, and gave the signaling middle finger in front of the chrysanthemum.

— No, you will not, — said Jeana.

The hall thundered like a cavalry squadron on a bridge, and the mortified girl shot away.

The woman with the handbag stepped out from the banners and into Jeana's face.

— Drop it, Dashenka, — a hoarse male whisper was heard from behind.

— No, I won't drop it, now I will find out about your monkey business hanky-panky, — replied the owner of the handbag, and said: — Tell me, mademoiselle, does my husband cheat on me?

The character measured the husband, looked into his muddled little eyes, took into account the dense redness of his face, and folded his finger into a hook, which meant, 'yes.'

— He cheats, — said Jeana with a sigh.

— With whom? — asked Dashenka in a sinister little voice.

(What the hell is her name? — thought the character. — God help my memory... yes, yes, yes, the wife of this... Oh, damn it... ahhh, I got it. 'Anna.')

— My dear J...anna, tell us, J... anna, with whom is her husband cheating?

— With Anna, — confidently replied Jeana.

— I knew it! — Dashenka burst out, weeping. — I've long suspected it. The polecat!

And with these words she bashed her husband's clean-shaven right cheek with her handbag.

And the hall erupted in a storm of laughter.

Translators' note

Elements from this feuilleton are seen in Bulgakov's *The Master and Margarita*, Chapter 12 "Black Magic and its Revelation."

Undespairing Teletypists (Неунывающие бодистки)

There is this apparatus called the *teletype*. An extremely convenient thing for telegraphy. You sit, for example, in Kiev, and your girlfriend is at an apparatus in Moscow. And both of you are so bored at work that your eyes start to cross. And the apparatus doesn't have a damn thing to do either. And then you begin to do magic with your fingers on the keys and it results in a very interesting conversation.

Kiev (starts): Click, click... Is that you, Liza?.. Hello, hon...

Moscow (pleasantly surprised): It's really you, Olya!.. Well, tell me what's new.

Kiev (proudly): And I've got… and I've got...

Moscow (with interest): What have you got?

Kiev: A dear hubby, Kolechka!

Moscow: Really?

Kiev: I swear to... But in addition to Kolechka, everyone adores me... And I, as always, I make them lose their heads over me... In the summer, I'm going to the Crimea, to a resort. (Proudly.) Everyone is after me, like hunting wild game...

Moscow (has nothing to trump it with): I, after an illness, gained weight. And by the way, I'm acting in plays. And I gave up whining and mumbling.

Kiev (teasing): My Kolechka is a prima donna... But I am intentionally cool with him (sexually) clack-clack... So that he caresses more passionately... By the way, it's better here, not like at my previous job. (Pause) They love me... Well, how are you, girly, precious... Still the same pure, shy, inside as well as externally? (The apparatus sighs.) Oh, my baby, my husband Kolechka, he is younger than me; moreover, he is Ukrainian... But there is, click-click... Vasya from Leningrad, I adore him to death!

Moscow (click click on the apparatus): You, I thought, (the machine hisses) were just recently enamored of Petya?.. Hee-

hee... Isn't that true? (Ss-sss, like a snake.)

Kiev (indifferently): Well, it was just a mythical love. I was smeared by all kinds of serpents... At that time, my husband was out of town, and those scoundrel–gossips blabbed that I had acted like a bad girl with him... (Pause) So, then he died.

Moscow (after a pause): What else is new?

Kiev: Katya enlisted in the party!

Moscow: No?!!

Kiev: Shura came to see me on her way to Odessa. I thought about going to visit her in the summer, but then I decided that it is better to go to the Crimea, to a resort... Oh yes, do you remember a Kohanyuk, who used to go out with you? He got married. Do you hear me?.. Got married... Hee-hee... Got married!

Moscow (shudders through the apparatus): Grrrr...

Kiev: Well, all my best to you, baby, I'm going to go nighty-night and advise you to do the same.

Moscow: By the way, you don't foresee any downsizing at your place? They won't fire you?

Kiev (amused): Oh no, I have it very solid... Sweet dreams. Click...

NOTE: The material for this feuilleton was taken from tapes, copies of which were sent by a worker–correspondent. On these tapes, the two telephone operators wired 1,230 words of nonsense, some of which are transcribed verbatim in the feuilleton.

The newspaper "Gudok," Moscow, March 10, 1925

When Darkness Falls (С наступлением темноты)

Outrageous things happen during the showing of a movie at our Center of Labor and Enlightenment in Saratov (our railroad workers' club). When the darkness falls, hooligans on the balcony express themselves using various foul words and spit on heads in the orchestra. The movies are grainy. And besides that, the projectionist for some reason sometimes loads them up upside down.

A worker–correspondent

Yakov Ivanovich Strigun and his wife exchanged two hard-earned five-kopek coins for the right to see the wonderful film "The Secret of the Crypt," an American action movie, starring a box-office favorite.

— Sit down, Manechka, — Strigun muttered, making his way with his wife to the 20th row.

Manechka sat down and the lights went out in the hall. Then, from the balcony, someone spat, aiming at Manechka's bonnet, but missed and it landed instead on her lap.

— Don't you dare to spit! Hooligans, — screeched Strigun like a rooster.

— Shut up, asshole, — in a *basso* voice the darkness responded from the balcony.

— I will complain! — shouted Strigun, waving his fists in the dark and obscurely wondering to whom and about whom he would complain.

— If you do not shut up, I will spit on you. I can clearly see your bald spot shining, — threatened the darkness.

Strigun covered himself with his hat and ended the war.

Something blinked on the screen, split in half, and then dark stripes of rain began to fall, and then fiery words jumped out in an unknown-to-us language. In a flash, they disappeared, and an upside down man in a top hat appeared in their place, and ran quickly, like a fly on the ceiling. A house appeared, roof down, and a palm tree grew from somewhere in the ceiling of the theater. Then a car arrived, wheels up, and from it, a portly man poured out, head down, like a sack of oats, and hugged a lady.

Vigorous stomping shook the hall.

— Hey, projectionist, fix it! — screamed the darkness.

Bright light flooded the hall, then it went dark, and a camel appeared on the screen, ass first. A man got off backwards and then hurried off backwards somewhere. They started whistling in the hall.

— The projectionist loaded the film backwards! — they shouted from the balcony.

The screen suddenly burst like a sunspot. Then a louse, the size of a calf, appeared on the screen, to the tune of a quiet waltz.

— This is disgusting, — said Manetchka in horror, — what's this louse doing in the crypt? I don't get it.

The first louse was joined by seven more and they carried a coffin with their twitching legs and dull mugs. A piano was playing a mazurka by Wieniawski. A man lay in the coffin, as similar to Strigun as are two peas in a pod. Manetchka gasped and made the sign of the cross. Strigun went pale.

A fiery headline jumped out:

Here is what awaits you, railroader, if you do not get a haircut and go to the public bath!

— And get a shave! — howled the balcony. — Get the lice off the screen! We saw the film about lice yesterday. Give us "The Secret of the Crypt!"

Music started, a *polechka*. The words *Chaplin got married!* leaped out and disappeared as well. In their place, legs in white spats appeared on the ceiling. Then they all disappeared from the screen. A few moments later some dark spots were sown, and then they also disappeared. A short individual in an even shorter jacket came out, and declared:

— The show is canceled because the projectionist burned out the bulb.

The hall greeted him with a nightingale's whistle, and the

audience, crushing one another, threw itself towards the ticket window.

All around it, a crowd blustered, for a long time, getting its money back.

Mikhail B.

A Series of Fascinating Projects (Ряд изумительных проектов)

THE GIFT FROM LUKICH

It happens sometimes that people have nothing to do, even though they work in the transportion industry. And so, Lukich composed a letter to the editors of *Gudok*:

"I wish to present many things as gifts to you on the 12th of March, the day of the downfall of the monarchy..."

Such a loud introduction got everyone extremely interested. "Lukich came up with some kind of a present," everyone thought. So what is it that he came up with? It turns out that he did not have anything to give as a present. That's why he presented his own project:

"If you want to know everything about a comrade who is writing to you, without reference checks and red tape, it is necessary, in my opinion, in the future, to standardize the ink color for signatures, so as to know who he is, where he is from, and what organization he belongs to. As follows:

> Party member — red,
> Candidate for party membership — green,
> Politically non-affiliated — purple,
> Banished from the party — black."

Well, thank you for the gift!

We extended your list:

> Criminal — indelible pencil,
> Married person — ordinary pencil,
> Bald person — colored pencil.

But, Lukich, joking aside, I respond to you in purple ink:

This is one intolerable nonsense that you came up with.

Also, for some reason, your letter is written in black ink. Consider what kind of conclusion one can draw from it, based on your project.

HOW TO ERADICATE GIRLS ON THE TRANSPORT

A correspondent was born cunning:

"Citizen X, of such and such railroad, a girl, produced a child with Citizen Y and, according to a court ruling, receives from him 20 rubles per month while still working.

I have nothing against punishment of citizens like Y," haughtily writes the author of the project, "but what does the transport industry have to do with it, giving leave for childbirth, absenteeism for breastfeeding, etc?

As a person working in *NOT*[1] and in other industrial commissions, I believe that in the transport industry due to downsizing there should remain only fully-functioning agents, which can include neither virgins, mothers, nor working wives."

Then, the working-at-*NOT* nonsensist writes something that is impossible to understand... Perhaps the sense of it is that girls need to be driven out of the transportation industry.

Girls, do not be afraid. The bold correspondent will not do anything to you.

THE UNENLIGHTENED MACHINE

"A vending machine stands near the entrance to the passenger hall of the Gomel-Passenger Station of the Western Railroad, spitting out tickets for 15 kopeks."

It turns out that this machine is a rascal:

"It issues the same tickets for the royal silver coin, as well as for the Soviet!"

A malignant machine!

The correspondent pitches a project: to place a person near the machine to check the coins!

No, it does not suit us, comrade. Because a machine will not be needed if a person will be standing nearby.

Collected by M.B.

Translators' note

1. *NOT* abbreviates *Nauchnaya organizatsiya truda*, the Scientific Organization of Labor, which structured the work force based on basic and empirical research.

The newspaper "Gudok," Moscow, March 27, 1925

A Holiday with Syphilis (Праздник с сифилисом)

Based on material certified by
The Lak-Tyzhmenskoy Village Council

On Female Workers Day, which we celebrate every year on the 8th of March, the door to the village reading hall[1] in Laka-Tyzhma Village, which stands under the benevolent patronage of the Kazan Railroad, opened, and admitted the local medic (let's call him Ivan Ivanovich).

If it were not for the fact that no socially-conscious citizen may appear drunk on the 8th of March, especially for a report, especially in a reading hall, and if it were not for the fact that the medic, Ivan Ivanovich, as it is well known, does not take alcohol by mouth, one might have sworn that the medic was utterly and totally drunk.

His eyes resembled two sealing-wax plugs from bottles of Russian 80-degree vodka, but the temperature of the medic was no higher than 86 degrees. And the hall was so struck with the smell of alcohol that the chairman of the meeting stopped smoking, and invited Ivan Ivanovich to speak, in the following words:

— The chair invites Ivan Ivanovich to speak on the occasion of the International Day of Women Workers.

Ivan Ivanovich, full of alcoholic self-esteem, conquered the stage via the steps on the third try and delivered the following:

— Before speaking about the International Day, let's say a few words about venereal diseases!

This introduction was a complete success: a sepulchral silence descended and in it an electric light bulb blew out.

— Yes… My dear international female workers, — the medic continued, breathing heavily, — here before me, I see your little faces, 80 units...

— Forty, — said the chairman with surprise, looking at the

attendance sheet.

— Forty, even worse... I mean, better, — continued the speaker, — I'm sorry for you, my dear young ladies and dames... Sorry!.. Ladies ... Statistics show that the lower the population in a particular region under study, the less the venereal disease, and vice versa. And especially with syphilis... With this horrible scourge of the proletariat, not sparing anyone... Do you know what syphilis is?

— Ivan Ivanovich! — exclaimed the chairman.

— Be quite for a minute. Don't interrupt me. Syphilis, — hiccupping in a prolonged manner, the speaker continued, — is a thing that is extremely easy to catch! You sit here and think that perhaps you are entirely protected? (Here the medic ominously laughed...) Hmm!.. Bupkis. Then some girl is walking over there in a red scarf, happy, because of these 8[ths], all sorts of Marches and the like, and then she gets married and, look, one fine day, she will be washing her face... will blow her nose… and kerplop! Her nose is in the sink, and, instead of a nose, please excuse the expression, a hole!

A rumble went through all the rows, and one of the female workers, completely white, exited through the door.

— Ivan Ivanovich! — exclaimed the chairman.

— Excuse me. I was assigned, so I am speaking. Maybe you think that virginity will save you? Ho-ho-ho! So, not many of you are vir...

— Ivan Ivanovich! — exclaimed the chairman.

Two more female workers exited, glancing back at the stage in horror.

— You come here, for example, and, let's say, there is a tank with boiled water... Such and such... It's hot, of course, — the speaker unbuttoned his collar and continued, — now you, of course, go to grab a cup... Above you reads a sign, *Do Not Drink The Tap Water* and similar posters from the Communist International, and a syphilitic was drinking right before you, touching with his lips... Let's say, our chairman, for example...

The chairman howled wordlessly.

Twenty female workers wiped their lips with a handkerchief in disgust, and those who did not have one, with a hem.

— What are you howling about? — the medic asked the chairman.

— I have never been sick with any kind of syphilis!! — shouted the chairman and he became as crimson as a cranberry.

— Silly... I am saying 'for example'... Well, let's suppose that she, — and the medic pointed with his shaking finger to somewhere in the first row, which was already emptied entirely by the rustling skirts.

— When a woman on the 8th of March... reaches sexual, excuse the expression, ripeness, — from the pulpit sang the speaker, who had become increasingly wasted by the stifling atmosphere, — what is she thinking to herself?..

— Pervert! — said a thin voice from the back rows.

— The only thing she dreams about in the moonlit nights is to strive toward her sex partner, — reported the medic, completely bursting at the seams.

Then, in the hall, groaning and grinding of the teeth began. The benches thundered and emptied. One by one, female workers were leaving, many with sobs.

There were only two left: the chairman and the medic.

— Her sexual partner, — the medic murmured, rocking back and forth and looking at the chairman, — my dear female worker, indulges in love and other vices...

— I am not a female worker! — shouted the chairman.

— Excuse me, are you a man? — asked the medic, bulging his eyes through the mist.

— Yes, a man! — shouted the offended chairman.

— Doesn't look like it, — the medic hiccupped.

— You know what, Ivan Ivanovich, you're drunk as a bum, — shouted the chairman, trembling with indignation, — you, excuse me, ruined the entire holiday for me! I'll be complaining about you to the Center, and even higher up.

So, complain, — said the medic, and he sat in a chair and fell asleep.

Mikhail

Translators' note

1. The reading hall, in Soviet times, was an auditorium for public meetings and gatherings.

Sauna Attendant Ivan (Банщица Иван)

> On women's day, Friday, in the sauna at the Esino Station of the Muromsk Line, invariably, there is one and the same attendant, Pal Ivan, in whose presence female visitors must undress using sauna basins instead of fig leafs. Is it really impossible to appoint one of the women working in the Repair Division to the sauna on Fridays!
>
> *A worker–correspondent*

PREFACE

It is so shameful to write about this, that the pen droops.

1. AT THE SAUNA

— Pal Ivan, hey, Pal Ivan!

— What do you want? You have soap and a sponge, don't you?

— Yes I do, only I beg you, get the hell out of here!

— Look here, Ms. Quick, as soon as I'm gone, they will steal the clothes. And who will be responsible? Pal Ivan. On Tuesday, a men's day it was, they snatched the stationmaster's cigarette case. And who was blamed? Me, Pal Ivan!

— Pal Ivan! Well, then at least turn away for a second to let me run by!

— All right, run.

Pal Ivan turned to the steamed-up window of the dressing room, straightened his red, fan-like beard, and murmured:

— Big deal, nothing special. What a weirdo. Is it a pleasure for me, or what? My position is such an obscene one... But duty calls.

A female figure jumped out of a towel and, like Eve in paradise, ran into the steam room.

— Oy, what shamelessness!

The door to the dressing room opened and released a cloud of steam. And a wet, steaming old lady, the aunt of a railroad foreman, emerged from the cloud. The old woman squeezed her bathsponge and sat on a sofa, blinking her eyes with pleasure.

— Enjoy the effects of your steam, — wished a hoarse bass voice above her ear.

— Thank you, dear. Oh my god... What the!.. Lord save me. You're actually a man?!

— Yes, a man. So what?.. Do you need any towels?

— Mother Mary! Get away from me with your towels, you snot! What on earth is happening in our sauna?

— What are you raging about, auntie? I was here when you came in!

— Well, I didn't notice it before! I can't see well, the shameless swine. And now I look, and he has a beard like a broom! Manka, you're shameless, cover yourself with towels!

— It's a torment, not a position, — muttered Pal Ivan, moving away.

— Pal Ivan, get the hell out of here! — shouted the women from one side, covering themselves with basins like shields against an enemy.

Pal Ivan turned to another side, and from there they howled. Pal Ivan threw himself to the third side, from which he was expelled. Pal Ivan spat on the ground, and left the dressing room, saying ominously:

— I don't accept responsibility if something gets stolen.

2. IN A PUB

On Sunday, exhausted by the work week, Pal Ivan sat at the pub, 'The Red Paris,' and said:

— This is a torment, not a position. On Monday, I start the fire; on Tuesday, all sorts of workers wash themselves; on Wednesday, those with small children; on Thursday, just ordinary men. Friday is women's day. Women's day to me is the very poison; that is, I wish my eyes couldn't see it. The sauna fills with women. They yell and scatter their stuff around. And, most importantly, they are offended by me. But how is it my fault? If I have been appointed for this, should I be watching or not? I must! No, there is no nation on earth that is worse than these women. There is one decent woman: the wife of our new worker Koverkotov. A tidy butterfly. She comes, folds everything, arranges it, and says only: "Pal Ivan, go to hell..." One thing is not that good: such a pretty butterfly from the front, but on the back there is a mole, it is so ugly, looks like a bat, you see it and just want to spit...

— Wh-a-a-a-t! What bat are you talking about?.. What are you saying, you red shit?

Pal Ivan paled, turned, and saw worker Koverkotov. Koverkotov's eyes were flashing and his hands were clenched into fists.

— Where exactly did you see that bat? Why are you spreading this filth? Huh?

— What kind of filth, — began Pal Ivan, but didn't manage to finish.

Koverkotov moved very close to him and...

3. IN COURT

— Citizen Koverkotov, you are accused of insulting a worker of the sauna, Citizen Ivan, on March 21st of this year.

— Citizen Judge, he insulted my honor!

— Tell me how you insulted the honor of Citizen Koverkotov?

— I never insulted anything... It's a pure punishment. I ask you, Citizen Judge to dismiss me from the position of sauna attendant. My strength is gone.

***

The judge spoke at length and with passion, placing his hand to his heart, and he ended the matter peacefully.

A few days later, Pal Ivan was released from his presence at the women's sauna on Fridays, and a woman from the repair division was appointed in his place.

With that, bright days again reigned at the station.

The newspaper "Gudok," Moscow, April 15, 1925

On the Benefit of Alcoholism (О пользе алкоголизма)

Union member Mikula showed up drunk to smithereens at the meeting for the reelection of the Local Committee of Station N. The working masses shouted: "This is unacceptable," but a representative of the Education Committee spoke in defense of Mikula, explaining that drunkenness is a social disease and that it is still permissible to elect drunkards to the Local Committee...

Worker–correspondent 2619

PROLOG

— Kick his drunken mug from the meeting to the devil! This is unacceptable! — shouted the working masses.

The chairman alternated between standing and sitting, as if a spring had been placed within him.

— Please welcome to the stage! — he shouted, stretching out his arms, — comrades, be quiet!.. Please welcome... comrades, be quiet!.. Comrades! I beg you to listen to the representative of the Education Committee...

— Down with Mikula! — shouted the masses, — this drunkard should be eradicated!

The representative's face appeared at the table on the stage. A benevolent smile floated on the face of the representative. The masses were still running high, like the ocean, but then calmed.

— Comrades! — exclaimed the representative in a pleasant baritone, — If I were the chairman! And Mikula a wave! And you, Soviet Russia, the masses, the representative would be enraged, when your rage oceanic amasses!

Such a beginning was tremendously flattering to the masses.

— He speaks in verse!

— You are our savior! — an elderly woman burst out with admiration, and began sobbing. After she was escorted to the exit, the representative continued:

— What are you clamoring about, eloquent-voices-of-the-masses?[1]

— We're clamoring about Mikula! — responded the masses.

— Throw him out! It's a disgrace!

— Comrades! It is precisely regarding Mikula that I intend to speak.

— That's right! Bury him alive, the alcoholic!

— The first order of business before us is the question: Is the referred-to Mikula drunk?

— Wha-a-a-t! — shouted the masses.

— Ok, all right, he's drunk, — agreed the representative. — There's no doubt about that, dear comrades. But here before us arises a question of social importance: On what basis did the respected union member Mikula get drunk?

— He's a birthday boy! — responded the masses.

— No, dear comrades, that's not the point. The root of the evil lies much deeper. Our Mikula is drunk because he is... sick.

The masses froze, like stalagmites. The crimson Mikula opened a completely blank eye and looked at the representative in horror.

— Yes indeed, dearest comrades, drunkenness is nothing other than a social disease, similar to tuberculosis, syphilis, plague, cholera and... Before speaking about Mikula, let us consider what drunkenness is, and from where did it originate?.. One fine day, dear comrades, the former great Prince Vladimir, known as the *Red Sun* for his love of alcoholic drinks, said: "Our joy is in drinking!"

— Nicely spun!

— To make it nicer is difficult. Our historians saw the true value of the words of the unforgettable former Prince and started to drink bit by bit, exclaiming: "Drunk and smart: there are two virtues in him!"

— And what happened to the Prince? — asked the masses, who had become interested in the secretary's presentation.

— He died, my dears. He was burned down by vodka, — explained the all-knowing secretary with regret.

— May his be the Kingdom of Heaven! — squeaked a little old lady, — in spite of being Soviet, he's still a saint.

— Do not distribute religious opium at the meeting, my auntie, — requested the secretary, — there are no 'kingdoms of heaven' here for you. Comrades, I shall continue. After that, in bourgeois society, they drank for 900 years without a break, every single one of them, with no quarter given to children or orphans. "Drink, but think," exclaimed Turgenev, the famous poet of the bourgeois period. After that, a series of proverbs of folk humor appeared in defense of alcoholism, such as: "To the drunken, the sea is to the knee," "What the sober man thinks, the drunkard reveals," "Time, not wine, makes a man drunk," "Don't try to sit in a sleigh that isn't yours," and what else did I miss?..

— "Tea is not vodka, you can not drink a lot of it!" — responded the extremely interested masses.

— That's correct, *merci*. "Can one get drunk with half of a bucket?" "She's a hen but she drinks," "If you drink you die, and if you don't drink you die," "Pour me, pour, comrade, a health-bringing goblet!.."

— *God o-o-nly knows what will become of us...* — crooned the drunken Mikula, falling asleep.

— Comrade Afflicted, I request that you not sing during the meeting, — requested the chairman politely. — Go on, Comrade Speaker.

— "Let us pray," — continued the speaker, — "Let us pray, let us pray to the Creator, then we'll pray to the goblet and the cucumber chaser." "Mister policeman, please be kind to me and take me to the police station so I don't end up in the mud," "Do not use foul language or leave tips," "On February twenty ninth I drank a magnum of the accursed wine," "Fresh crawfish every day," "Up step one, up step two"[2]...

— Where are they going! — the chairman barked. Five men, tiptoeing, had suddenly slid out from the rows, and slipped through the door.

— They couldn't withstand the speech, — explained the admiring masses, — you so eloquently persuaded them. They ran to the bar before it closed.

— So! — thundered the speaker, — you see how deeply this social disease has penetrated into us. But do not be ashamed, comrades. For example, Lomonosov, our famous talented figure of the eighteenth century, loved to stand a bottle to the highest degree, but, despite that, he turned out to be a first-class scientist and comrade in whose honor they even erected a monument near the university building on Mokhavaya Street. I could give you more examples, but I don't want to... I am now finishing and we are proceeding to the election...

EPILOGUE

"... after that, the working masses elected the known alcoholic as a member of the Local Committee and, on the following day, he sat at the train platform, already gassed up, and entertained onlookers with anecdotes, telling them that drinking is permissable as long as it is not harmful."

(From the same letter of the worker-correspondent)
Mikhail

Translators' notes

1. The Russian phrase that we translated as 'eloquent-voices-of-the-masses' is *narodnye vitii. Narodnye* is an adjective that refers to 'the people.' *Vitii* an archaic term that refers to orators or eloquent people.

2. "Up step one, up step two" (*cherez tumbu, tumbu raz*) is from a bawdy students' drinking song. Here's a bit more of the song:

And Isaac the Saint from the bell tower
Looks at the students and smiles,
He also would like to go out with us

But because of his age he declines.
Up step one, up step two,
Up step three-four, then stagger...

But temptation was great, and the elder gave up
From his bell tower he's coming down
He is singing the songs, sells the devil his soul
And starts doing it with somebody---
Up step one, up step two,
Up step three-four, then stagger...

The newspaper "Gudok," Moscow, April 28, 1925

How Mr. Flower-Bud Got Married (Как Бутон женился)

> At the directorate of the Southwestern they provide rations only to the married. Bachelors get bupkis. Consequently, it is necessary to marry. In fact, the directorship will play the role of matchmaker.
>
> *Worker–correspondent № 2626*

> And doesn't the gentleman think to marry?
>
> *N.V. Gogol "The Marriage"*

The railroad worker Valentin Arkadevich Flower-Bud-Never-Been-Kissed, a man stubbornly and obstinately single, presented himself to the directorate of the administrative department, and politely bowed to the rationing authorities.

— How can we help you? Look at how you've arranged your tie, and it's polka-dotted!

— Of course, what of it? I've come to make a request for a ration.

— Hmmn. Then get married.

Flower-Bud quivered.

— What is this?

— It's very simple. You are familiar with the Office of Marriage and Wills? Take yourself there and say: "This, y'know, that. I love her more than anything in the world. Give her to me, otherwise I will throw myself into the Dnieper or shoot myself." Whichever you prefer. Well, they will register the marriage. Grab her documents, and her too.

— Whose? — asked the green Flower-Bud.

— Well, let's say Mademoiselle Varya's.

— Which… Varya's?

— Our typist.

— I don't want to, — said Flower-Bud.

— What an odd ball. I want the best for you, I tell you. Come to your senses. The kind of life you will lead! What do you drink in the morning these days?

— Beer, — responded Flower-Bud.

— That's what I thought. And now you will drink chocolate or cocoa!

Flower-Bud was almost ready to throw up.

— Take a look at yourself in the mirror of the Directorate of the Southwestern Railroad. What do you resemble? A necktie like a butterfly and a shirt, a dirty shirt. There is one button missing on your pants. It is indeed bacheloric hideousness! But as soon as you marry, you won't have time to think; there, before you, will be a wife: "Can I get anything for you?" What is your full name?

— Valentin Arkadevich…

— OK, Valyusha, or as it will go, Valyun. And she will say to you: "Would you like this or that, Valyun, would you like, Valyun, a bit of coffee, perhaps." For Valyusha, that. To Valyusha, this… It will drive you nuts!.. What was I saying?.. You will not know whether you are in heaven or the S. W. Railroad!

— She has a false tooth!

— Look idiot, God forgive me. A tooth! Really, is a tooth an arm or a leg? Yeah, as a matter of fact, it's a gold tooth! Look, dumbhead, in the worst case you can drop it at the pawnbroker. In a word, write an application for entering into legal marriage. We will bless you. After a year, invite us to the baptism. We'll drink!

— I don't want to! — screamed Flower-Bud.

— Well, OK, I see you're a stubborn man. You're as stubborn as a mule. As you wish. I request that you do not occupy a busy man.

— My ration, if you please.

— No!

— On what basis?

— It's not allowed.

— Then why was Ptyukin allowed?

— Ptyukin is way ahead of you. He's married!

— Consequently, without rations, shall I breathe my last from hunger? That's what you want?

— As you wish, young man.

— What is this? — mumbled Flower-Bud, changing his expression. — Is it necessary that I either forfeit my life by starvation, or my precious freedom?!

— Do not yell.

— Take me! — screamed Flower-Bud, going into hysterics, — Marry me. Lead me to the Office of Marriage and Wills. Eat me with the oatmeal!! — And he began to rip his shirt apart.

— Courier! Summon Mademoiselle Varya! Comrade Flower-Bud will propose to her with hand and heart.

— What is he wailing about? — inquired the courier.

— He is overcome by joy. The government changed his life.

Mikhail

The newspaper "Gudok," Moscow, April 30, 1925

A Battle with Stamps (Буза с печатями)

— It has become necessary for me to commute from my place of residence, — said Vasily Utkin, the youngest agent of the security service, — apparently it's my fate to write a petition to my superiors.

Vasily Utkin armed himself with an indelible pencil and scribbled in ugly letters the following:

A REQUEST

To the boss of the 2nd Squad of the 3rd District of Freight Security of the North–Western Railroad,

Comrade Boss, I request your approval of a seasonal rail pass for me from Medvedev Station, the place of my work, to Edrovo Station, my place of residence.

Junior Agent of the Freight Security Service
Vasily Utkin.

Vasily Utkin took himself to the Edrovo Village Council, taking with himself the product of his hands, and said to the chairman:

— Certify this little request for me, my good man!

The chairman of the village council wrote in liquid ink on the back of Utkin's product:

The signature in Vasily Utkin's hand is certified by the Edrovo Village Council.

Chairman Vasyachkin.

With that, Vasily Utkin took himself to the District Executive Committee and, upon exiting, had yet another postscript on his document, two lines lower:

The aforementioned and the signature of Chairman Vasyachkin are certified by the District Executive Committee.

> Chairman of the District Executive Committee
> (signature illegible).
>
> Secretary (signature totally illegible).

In addition, there were two stamps on Vasily Utkin's document: one on the upper left, the other on the lower right corner. The seals were very beautiful, round, blue, and in their center was placed a doodle, vaguely resembling a hammer and sickle.

— Where else can I go for certification? — Utkin, Vasily discussed with himself. — Oh well, I suppose I don't need to go to anyone else. Plenty of signatures and a pair of stamps. It's true that the devil himself couldn't make out what's on these stamps, but what the heck.

***

After that, Utkin's difficulties began. In due time, which allows for red tape and bureaucratism, he received his request back from his boss, upon which was written in a beautiful and lively handwriting:

> Due to the unclear and illegible stamps on the request, the request is declined until we receive a document certified with clear stamps.

In due time, which allows for stupefaction, Utkin again crawled with a new request to the Village Council, and from the Village Council to the District Executive Committee. The new request was again certified with signatures and the same stamps.

In due time, which allows for battles and bagpipes, Utkin again received back his request from the authorities with the verdict:

Rejected for unclear stamps.

Utkin again presented himself at the Village Council and the District Executive Committee with a new request, and said:

— Apparently, my friends, your stamps look like they were made by Fedya while he was looking at his own snoot.

They once again put Fedya's works of art on Utkin's request. Utkin sent the request to the higher ups, and in due time the request came back with a verdict that was already quite familiar to Utkin:

Rejected for unclear stamps.

Then Utkin sat down on a chair and let out a howl, like from a toothache.

***

How all this will come to an end is unknown. Citizens, are you really going to torture junior agent of the security service Utkin to death?

Mikhail

The newspaper "Gudok," Moscow, April 30, 1925

An Assembly[1] to the Skull (Смычкой по черепу)

The basis of this feuilleton is a real incident
described by worker-correspondent № 742.

Finally, one of the villages of Chervonny, in the Fastovsky District, the one in the Kievshchina area, lived to see a joy! Sergeyev himself, a representative of the District Executive Committee, who is also deputy chairman of the Local Committee, and head of the Labor Force Protection of the Fastov Station, had arrived to chair an assembly with the village folks.

The news broke on the radio that on such and such day Sergeyev will turn his face to the village!

The villagers, in dense shoals, went into the library-hut. Even the 60-year-old Grandpa Omelko (by profession, a peasant of average means), armed with a crutch, dragged himself to the general meeting.

The hut was packed to the rafters. Grandpa huddled in the corner, pricked up his ear like a trumpet, and prepared himself to embrace the assembly.

The guest on the stage thundered like a nightingale in honeysuckle. The party program tumbled from his mouth in chunks, as if from a man who has been swallowing it for a long time, but did not chew it at all.

The villagers saw an energetic hand under the side of the jacket, and heard the words:

— More attention to the village... Soil improvement... Productivity... Planting campaign... middle and poor peasantry... united efforts... we to you... you to us... seeds... district... this guarantees, comrades... crop loan... People's Commissariat of Soil... price movement... People's Commissariat of Enlightenment... Tractors... co-operation... bonds.

***

Quiet sighs were fluttering in the hut. The report was flowing like a river. The speaker slowly turned sideways and finally completely turned his back to the village. And the first object that caught his eyes in this village, was the huge and wrinkled ear of Grandpa Omelko, like a gramophone trumpet. On the face of the grandfather was a strenuous thought.

Everything ends in the world, and so did the report. A somewhat strained silence came after the applause. Finally, the chairman of the meeting got up and asked:

— Does anyone have any questions for the speaker?

The speaker haughtily looked around: no, he was saying, there is no question in the world that I would be unable to answer!

And then the drama happened. The crutch rattled, Grandpa Omelko stood up and said:

— I ask, comrades, that Comrade Assembler tell his report in simple words, because I did not understand anything.

Having administered such an obscenity, the grandfather sat down. A sepulchral silence descended, and one could see how Sergeyev had become crimson.

His metallic voice rang out:

— What kind of an individual is that one?..

The old man was offended.

— I am not an individual... I am Grandpa Omelko.

Sergeev turned to the chairman:

— Is he a member of the Poor Peasant Committee?

— No, he is not a member, — responded the bewildered chairman.

— Aha! — rapaciously exclaimed Sergeyev. — It means, he is a *kulak*?![1]

The assembly became pale.

— So get him out of here! — suddenly roared Sergeev, and falling into a trance and forgetfulness, turned to the village but not with his face, but with quite the opposite side.

The assembly was petrified. No one extended a hand to the decrepit old man, and who knows how it would have come to an end if Secretary of the Rural Union Ignat had not rescued the speaker. Like a hawk, the secretary swooped down on the old man, calling him a 'grandpa of a bitch,' and dragged him by the collar out of the library-hut.

When you are being dragged from a solemn assembly, it is a no-brainer that you'll be protesting. The old man abutted his feet on the floor and muttered:

— Sixty years I have lived in the world and did not know that I am a *kulak*... also, thank you for your assembly!

— All right, — sweated Ignat, — we will see how you will be speaking again. You will speak up with me. I'll prove what kind of element you are.

Ignat chose the original method of proof. To be precise, having pulled the old man out into the yard, he hit him on the head with something so heavy that the old man felt as if the midday sun had darkened and the stars had appeared in the sky.

It is unknown with what Ignat made his proof to the old man. According to an account of the latter (and he knows better than anyone else), it was made of rubber.

With this, the assembly for Grandpa Omelko was over.

Well, not quite. After the assembly the old man became deaf in one ear.

***

You know what, Comrade Sergeyev? I will allow myself to give you two suggestions (they also apply to Ignat). First, find out how the old man is feeling.

And secondly: an assembly is an assembly, but still you should not spoil the men.

Otherwise instead of the assembly, troubles will come.

For everyone.

And for you in particular.

Translators' notes

1. We translated the Russian *smychka* as 'assembly.' *Smychka* has two meanings, which Bulgakov plays upon in this story. The older meaning is a mechanical part with a linking function, such as a shackle bolt or a link rod in an automobile. *Smychka* was also used by the Soviets to refer to a social meeting whose purpose was to link and bond a rural province or village to the Party and its programs.

2. *Kulak* is an extremely prejudicial name for a rich peasant.

The newspaper "Gudok," Moscow, June 4, 1925

Work Attains 60 Proof (Работа достигает 30 градусов)

The general meeting of the Transport Communal Cell of the Troitsk Station of the Trans-Siberian Railway did not take place on April 20th because several party members celebrated Easter with drinks and wife beating.

When this development came to attention in the following meeting, a member of the cell spoke, and the secretary of the Local Committee issued a statement that it is permissible to drink, but one must have the ability and the know-how.

Worker–correspondent Toothpick

A man sat alone in the meeting room of the Communal Cell of Station X and languished.

— This is extremely strange. The meeting is set for 5 o'clock, and it's now half past eight. The guys are late for some reason.

The door admitted one more.

— Greetings, Petya, — said the incomer. — You represent a quorum? Go ahead. Represent! Vote, Petro!

— I don't get it, — said the first. — Mr. Tin Can isn't here. Mr. Mug isn't here.

— Tin Can isn't coming.

— Why?

— He's drunk.

— It cannot be.

— Mug isn't coming either.

— Why?

— He's drunk.

— OK, and where are the rest?

Silence fell. The entering-one patted himself on the tie.

— Can it really be?

— I won't hide the bitter Russian truth from you, — explained the second, — they're all drunk: Peabody, and Sausage, and Muskat, and Korneevsky, and the graduate student Gor-shanenko. Wrap up the meeting, Petya!

They turned off the lamp and went out into the dark.

***

The holiday celebrations had ended; therefore, the meeting was overflowing.

— Dear comrades! — Petya said from the stage, — I believe that this state of affairs is unacceptable. It is a shame! On Easter Day, I myself personally saw our esteemed Comrade Tin Can, this very Tin Can was carrying his wife...

— On a promenade, I was carrying her, my little bird, — responded Tin Can in an unctuous voice.

— You were carrying her with plenty of originality, Tin Can! — exclaimed Petya with outrage. — Your wife was being carried with her face on the sidewalk, and her ponytail had found itself into your esteemed right hand!

A roar went up among the teetotalers.

— I wanted to take a lock of her hair in remembrance! — Tin Can cried out perplexedly, feeling how his party ID slid in his pocket.

— A lock? — asked Petya venomously, — I've never seen a lock being taken as a remembrance from a woman while she is getting kicked in the back on the street!

— It's a private matter, — Tin Can replied, sagging, clearly feeling the hand of the party director on his ID. A murmur went through the meeting.

— It is a private matter in your opinion? No sir, dear Tin Can, it isn't a private matter! It's swinehood!!

— Please do not insult! — yelled the insolent Tin Can.

— You create a scandal in a public place and in this manner cast a shadow over the entire cell! And you set a bad example for the graduate students and those who are not in the party! Does it mean that when Muskat broke the windows in his apartment and threatened to slaughter his wife, it was a private matter as well? And when I met Mug in his Easter attire; that is, without a right sleeve and with a swollen eye?! And when Gorshanenko cursed out every passerby on the street, it was a private matter?!

— You are undermining us, Comrade Petya, — uncertainly cried out Tin Can. A murmur went through the meeting.

— Comrades. Permit me to say a word, — suddenly Mr. Knowntoeveryone said in a loud voice (may his name be passed down through the generations), — I personally am against having this question placed under discussion. It is not subject to discussion, comrades. Permit me to introduce a point of view. Here many have been debating: Is it permissible to drink? Basically, it's OK to drink, but one must know how to drink!

— That's it. Precisely!! — they screamed as one from the alcoholic right.

The teetotalers responded with a murmur.

— One must drink quietly, — announced Knowntoeveryone.

— Precisely! — screamed the drinkers, having received a sudden refortification.

— You buy, for example, three bottles, — continued Knowntoeveryone, and…

— Appetizers!!

— Sil-ence!!

— Yes, and appetizers…

— Pickled cucumbers are excellent drinking appetizers…

— Sil-ence!..

— You arrive home, — continued Knowntoeveryone, — you pull down the drapes on the window so that spying eyes can't ruin the domestic tranquility, invite your friend, your wife cleans a herring for you, you sit, take off your jacket, you put the vodka under the faucet so that it will chill a little, and then, y'know, no hurry, you pour out a shot…

— Wait, Comrade Knowntoeveryone! — exclaimed the paralyzed Petya, — what exactly are you saying?!

— And you are not disturbing anyone, and no one will scold

you, — continued Knowntoeveryone. — Well, naturally, it is possible that some kind of unreasonableness, so to speak, may come up between you and your wife after the second bottle. But don't be an ass. Don't drag her by the hair onto the street! Who needs that? A broad likes to be beaten at home. And don't beat her on the face, because the next day the babe will go all around the station with bruises and everyone will know. Hit her in hidden places! I bet she won't go around bragging about that.

— Bravo! — cried out Tin Can, Mr. Appetizer & Company. Applause thundered from the vodkern side. Petya stood up and said:

— In all my days, I have never heard a more disturbing speech than yours, Comrade Knowntoeveryone, and, bear in mind that I will inform *Gudok* about it. It is unspeakable insolence!!

— Oh, I am so very afraid of you, — replied Knowntoeveryone, — inform them!

And the end of the story drowns in the outcry of the assembly.

Mikhail B.

The newspaper "Gudok," Moscow, June 27, 1925

The Fruit Orchard (Фруктовый сад)

(A sad story)

> In the Stalingrad Local Committee for Labor Force Reduction they terminated one railroader as "the owner of a garden." In reality, this garden turned out to be five young apple trees.
>
> *From a report*

The Commission met protractedly, thought deeply, and decided strictly. The secretary read a list, the members ruminated cigarettes with their teeth, drank tea endlessly, and listened attentively.

— Ivan Dyrkin, — buzzed the secretary. — Office manager. Married. Union member since 1920. Considered for termination as a private property owner. His house has four...

— Floors? — the chairman asked with interest.

— Corners.

— Well, for us it's all the same: if it's a house, it means, the matter's settled.

— He doesn't really have a house, — a kind member stood up for him, — it isn't really a house, it's just a shack!

— Well, what does it matter if it's a shack, — the secretary said sternly, — 'A home is not judged by its size, but by its pies.' If only Dyrkin Ivan had ever invited at least someone over. He's passionately unfriendly.

— Well, why should we think further? Go ahead. To be terminated. Next.

— Osipchuk Mitrofan. A conductor. For consideration.

— And we have him for what?

— What do you mean, 'for what?' He has nine children, one is hmm... older than the other. He's well heeled with those kids. In five years they will feed him.

— Well, how will he live for five years?

— He'll manage on nine units, don't forget that. It's capital!

— Purge the capital from the Union! Fry him, terminate! — rattled the commission. — Next!

— Next here is another owner. Kromkin, Pavel. A baggage handler.

— What got him noticed?

— He started a fruit orchid all for himself. Pears of a pineapple species, apples, peaches, just pure Africa. He chews them by the pound.

— Wait, — said the chairman, — did you see these peaches for yourself?

— Yeah, that's the thing, he never gave anyone a berry or a pineapple, instead he kept it all for himself.

— Look at him, what a goose! And how does he get it all down? Terminate him, as the greediest private property owner! Let him eat those pineapples outside the iron-willed ranks of the Revolution!

The chairman swallowed some tea with sugar, smoked, and decided:

— Well, give us the next one, quickly; the soup at home will go bad.

Having received the decision, Kromkin, Pavel came home and sat down gloomily on a low stoop.

— They terminated you, didn't they? — guessed a neighbor.

— Yeah, — growled Kromkin. — But the tragedy isn't in that, but the insult, that's the main thing. You are, — they say, — a private property owner. You have a garden, fruits, peaches, and similar things. But in my entire garden, I have exactly three apple trees. And I only planted them last year.

— Why on earth did you plant them? Well, you got what you asked for, — the neighbor shook his head.

— How could I not plant something, — sighed Kromkin, — I couldn't have done otherwise. It was Forest Day. Everyone was told to plant.

He stood up, blew his nose fiercely, looked at his 'garden,' took it by the treetops, pulled it out with the roots, and in a bass voice said:

— Here are your pears! And here are the pineapples! May you be three-times cursed!

And he left to write a complaint.

El-Es

The newspaper "Gudok," Moscow, July 16, 1925

A Man and a Thermometer (Человек с градусником)

At our station, a worker got sick on an emergency repair train. A doctor came to see him, placed a thermometer, then forgot about it, and left on a handcar. And the patient since then remained with the thermometer.

Worker–correspondent 1212

1.

The doctor was completely burnt out. He arrived at the station and saw five people with gastritis. For one, he prescribed a teaspoon of caustic soda three times a day, for another a half teaspoon of soda three times a day, for a third a quarter teaspoon once a day, for the fourth and fifth, for variety, one spoon every other day, the sixth had broken a leg, two suffered from rheumatism, one had constipation, a switchman's wife complained that she saw the dead in her dreams, two didn't get sick pay, and a forewoman–railroader suddenly gave birth...

In short, when it was time to get onto the handcar, the doctor had only one thing on his mind: "It's time for soup, I am so damn tired..."

And then they came running and said that a man got sick on the repair train. The doctor just grunted quietly and hastened to the patient.

— OK. Stick out your tongue, my dear. One mangy tongue! When did you get sick? The 13th? 15th?.. Oh, on the 16th... Good, I mean, bad... How old are you? I mean, I wanted to ask: Do you have a stomach ache? Oh, it doesn't hurt?.. It hurts?.. Does it hurt here?

— Oy-oy...

— Bear with me, bear with me, do not scream. What about here?..

— Agh-aggh...

— Hang on, don't scream.

— The handcar is ready, —a voice was heard from outside.

— I'll be just a moment... Do you have a headache?.. When did you get sick? I mean, I wanted to ask if your lower back hurts?.. Aha! And the knees?.. Show me your knee. At least pull off your boot!

— Last year I had...

— What about this year?.. OK... And what about the next year?.. Phew, damn, I meant to ask about the year before last?.. Do not eat herring! Unbutton your shirt. Take this thermometer. Don't break it, be careful. It's state property.

— The handcar is waiting!

— Just a 'sec, just a 'sec, just a 'sec!.. Let me just write a prescription. You have influenza, uncle. I will prescribe three days off for you. What's your last name? That is, I meant to ask: Are you married? Single? What is your sex?.. Phew, dammit, that is, I meant to ask: Are you insured?

— The handcar is waiting!

— Just a 'sec! Here's the prescription. You should take some medicine. One medicine a day. Do not eat herring! Well, goodbye.

— I thank you from the core of my being!

— Handcar...

— Yes, yes, yes... I'm coming, coming, coming...

2.

Three days later, in the apartment of the doctor.

— Manya, did you see where I put the thermometer?

— On the desk.

— That one's mine. Where is the one that is state property, with the black cap? Dammit, apparently, I've lost it! I've lost it, and only the devil knows where. I'll have to buy a new one.

3.

At the station, five days later, a man sat in a jacket with a bump under his left arm and related:

— A wonderful doctor. I'll be frank, an extraordinary doctor! So fast, like lightning! Flutters, flutters... So, he says, show me your tongue. He poked a finger in my abdomen, my eyes popped out from the pain, he asked about everything, when, and how... From the cash register he issued four and a half rubles.

— So, then, did he cure you? He probably gave you some drops. He has wonderful drops...

— Well, you understand, not with drops. With a thermometer. There you are, he says, a thermometer, carry it, he says, for your health, just do not break it: state property.

— For free?

— They didn't take a single penny for the thermometer. It's paid for by insurance...

— We have it good. They inserted a porcelain tooth in Petyukov, also for free.

— So, did the thermometer help?

— I tell you, it was like the laying on of hands. Before, I couldn't straighten my back. The day after the thermometer, it felt better. Besides that, I had a headache for two weeks: when evening fell, it started in the top of my head, and drilled... But now, with the thermometer, like water off a duck!

— What progress science has attained!

— The only thing is that it's extremely inconvenient at work. But I've already adjusted. I tied it under my armpit with a bandage, so there it sits, the son of a bitch.

— May I borrow it, just to try?

— Look at you, schemer!

Mikhail

The newspaper "Gudok," Moscow, July 18, 1925

Concerning Wife Beating (По поводу битья жен)

A remarkable letter lies before me. Here is an excerpt from it:

"I'm a family man, and thus, I know that the majority of domestic scenes play themselves out on the ground of materialistic insecurity. The wife squeaks: 'Look here, at such and such acquaintances of ours, how they live!..' An argument of this type arouses one to fury. A disaster, if the head of the household has a weak hand and hits her on the back of the neck!..

So, in this case, in my opinion, to a certain degree, it is useful to appeal to the Local Committee, but not with a complaint, but for advice, and not so as to punish the fighter, but so as to remove the cause, which leads to the family quarrels... The Local Committee isn't a judge, but like the union organ whose duties include caring for the well-being of its members, should be able to find means to help those oppressed by anxiety, for example with an endorsement of the tyrant for an occupation that better provides for his existence..."

***

Dear comrade family man! Allow me to draw a picture of the Local Committee after realization of your proposal.

A certain family man presents himself to the Local Committee.

— What do you need?

— I maimed my wife today.

— So-o, with what did you do it to her?

— With a plate from the factory that used to belong to Popov.

— Hey, lunatic! Who fights with plates? Dishware costs money. You should have used a poker. Well, I suppose you broke the plate?

— Naturally. The head too.

— Well, a head is a tenth-order matter. The head will heal, in the worst case. But you, I hope, didn't dispatch your spouse to death?

— It was nothing for her.

— The fact of the matter is that the plate won't heal. You are an uneconomical individual. For what reason did a dispute transpire between you and your wife? What was the subject of your beating?

— Yes... hrrmn... They gave us a paycheck yesterday. Well, naturally, we stopped with the brother-in-law at...

— At a pub?

— Of course. So, we ordered a double... Then another double... After that, yet another double...

— You should count by tens, it will be quicker.

— Hmmn-yes... we drank, consequently... arrived again...

— Home?

— No, to Sidorov's... We drank Madeira at his place.

— So-o... go on...

— Then I was somewhere, but for the life of me I don't recall where... Well, in the morning I show up and this hydra accosts me...

— Excuse me, who is this hydra?

— My wife, obviously. Where, she says, is the salary, drunkard? Word after word... well, I couldn't take it anymore...

— Yes... what can we do with you? What worker's grade do you hold?

— The 9th.

— Well, OK, you are now in the 10th!

— My heartfelt thanks!!.

***

From the 10th, after he broke the arm of his hydra, to the 12th. Then he bit her ear, to the 16th. Then he beat out her eyes with a boot, to the 24th grade. But a higher grade does not exist in his occupation. One wonders if he pulls out her intestines, to where would he go then?

— Give him a personal bonus?

Well no, it will be too rich!

***

There was a man, a stationmaster, he broke three of his wife's ribs, they made him Inspector General of Transportation! Then he beat her nearly to death. But in fact all higher positions are occupied. One wonders, what to confer on him? They have to give him money!

***

No, family man! Your proposal is bad. The beating of wives in general isn't from financial insecurity. They beat from ignorance, from savagery, and from alcoholism, and no kind of promotion will help. Even if you make the fighter the boss of the railroad, he nevertheless will work with his fists.

Other means are necessary for the treatment of family troubles!

Mikhail

The newspaper "Gudok," Moscow, July 24, 1925

The Negro Incident (Негритянское происшествие)

A letter from worker–correspondent Lag

When you read in various newspapers about the beating of Negroes in America, you are not particularly astounded, because it is a phenomenon of life in the civilized countries.

But when an incident happens in our country, you are astounded to the marrow of your bones! In a socialist state, it is forbidden to hit anyone in the face, even if it's the face of Kirillych.

Well, June 19th of this year was a day of ultimate celebration, and of equally ultimate grief for all wives and children. To be precise: It was payday and the café in Station Ryazhsk-1 was packed to capacity with our responsible employees. Among them, honoring the café with his presence, was our responsible cooperative employee, someone named V. This is point one!

Next in the lineup, a member of the Local Committee, he is also a member of the regional bureau of professional unions, also a well-known brawler, also an alcoholic, an extremely famous personality whose last name starts with the letter 'X.' This is point two!

Point three, a former union member, Korelin. Nothing special, a quite pleasant personality that has not glorified itself by outstanding deeds in the republic; primarily he's a mechanic.

And fourthly, there are miscellaneous other personalities.

The bottom line is that they sat at the tables and drank to the maximum load, 420 pounds per axle, and then even more, as a result of which among them the axles and bearings started to burn.

The first to go off the rails was our very cooperative representative, who loudly proclaimed:

— Brothers! It's starting to seem to me that we are not in Ryazhsk Station, but in America, in the City of Chicago!

Why he imagined Chicago to himself, God only knows. The others howled like children abandoned by their mother:

— Then we are toast! Obviously, we won't be able to procure Russian vodka any more!

— You're mistaken, like fish on ice! — our cooperative member announced to them and barked:

— Psst!.. Hey, nigger!

And the waiter Kirillych appeared. In no way is he a Negro. He's an ordinary white man.

— What would you like?

— Bring us a bottle of Russian vodka.

— Coming right up!

And after some time he brings a bottle of Russian vodka, and with it says:

— Money, please...

Here the entire gang boiled over to the last drop:

— What, don't you trust us? Do you know who we are?

And Kirillych goes ahead and responds:

— I know you very well indeed (how could he not know?! It was for that very reason that he asked them for money).

Then our enraged cooperative member V stood up and shouted:

— Oh, so that's how it is?

And with that, he hit Kirillych in the ear with his cooperative–responsible fist so hard that even the passengers in the 1st class section of the café saw stars.

After that a scandal occurred.

How do you look upon such incidents, comrades?

Worker–correspondent Lag

We look upon such incidents extremely negatively, which is why we are publishing your letter.

Mikhail

The newspaper "Gudok," Moscow, August 8, 1925

When the Dead Rise from the Grave (Когда мертвые встают из гробов)

> In our time miracles do not happen!
>
> *Widely accepted*

Nevertheless, an incidence occurred in Kislovodsk that will make your hair stand on end…

But, we will tell you the story in stages.

On June 17, 1925, in the 8th year of the Revolution, Citizen Korabchevsky, a resident of the just-about-to-be-mentioned house, a former armed guard in the Department of Railroad Security, exited onto the porch of house № 46, on Highway St., in the city of Kislovodsk, and started to weep loudly.

Good people assembled and began to ask:

— Korabchevsky, Korabchevsky, why are you, a former armed guard, weeping?

To which he responded:

— How could I, a former armed guard, not weep, if my oldest son Vitaly, my darling son, just now died!

Women began to wail and interrogate him:

— What a misfortune, from what?

— From pneumonia, — said Korabchevsky, smearing tears on his face.

Everyone sympathized with Korabchevsky and left, and the poor father went to register the death of his descendant.

And so the baby died with due ceremony.

The official documentation serves as evidence.

Thus, for example, it was recorded on June 18th of this year, using form № 391, with the stamp of the Executive Committee of the city Kislovodsk:

CERTIFICATION

The Kislovodsk office of the Registry of Births, Marriages, and Deaths attests that Citizen Korabchevsky, Vitaly, 9 months of age, died on June 17th of this year of pneumonia. This document was registered as № 163.

Signatory: Director, Registry of Births, Marriages and Deaths
  Lidovsky.
And the undersigned also attests:
  Ledger Clerk of the Mineral Water Insurance Office.
    (*signature:* hard to read)

There's more to it. Not only did he die, but he was buried. And this is apparent from the testimony of the Kislovodsk Department of Archives of the Registry of Births, Marriages, and Deaths, where it is recorded that a male child Korabchevsky, Vitaly is interred at Community Cemetery.

Period! A better death is hard to imagine.

However…

A few days after the burial of Korabchevsky-the-son, there was a sinister moonlit night over Kislovodsk.

And then, a neighbor of Korabchevsky was strolling along in the most joyous disposition of spirit, whistling, and completely sober, and he saw, standing near Korabchevsky's residence, a strange-looking woman, all in white, face green from the moonlight.

And in her hands was a bundle, and in the bundle there was something small. The neighbor approached, and said:

— Who's there?.. Ah, is it you, Madame Korabchevsky?

And she replied in a sepulchral voice:

— Yes, it's me.

— And what is that in your arms? — asked the neighbor with surprise.

— And this, — replied the woman dully, — is my departed baby, Vitaly.

— How can it be Vitaly? — asked the neighbor, and felt like a shiver went up and down his spine, — didn't you bu-bu-bu-

bury your Vitaly?

— Yes, — replied the woman, — and here he is. He came back.

And at that moment, a moonbeam skimmed across the bundle and the neighbor saw that in the woman's arms was truly Vitaly, and his face had the green tone of deathly corruption.

— Help! — shouted the neighbor, and sprinted down Highway Street. The moon, from behind a cypress, looked like the face of the deceased, and it seemed to the neighbor that cold hands were reaching up to him by the pants.

An hour later, the bravest of the Kislovodskians stood in front of the porch of Korabchevsky's house. And Korabchevsky himself came out, and related the following story to them:

***

The evening before last, I was sitting with the wife and suddenly there was a knock on the window. We looked out and we nearly dropped dead on the spot. There stood Vitaly, in the air, not touching the ground, and he said: "Look, I have returned!"

— God give us strength!! — said someone from the female contingent.

— And then?! — shouted the men.

— And then, nothing, — replied Korabchevsky, — we had to accept him back.

A commotion started in the crowd. All the faces turned green in the moonlight. At that moment, the moon went behind a cloud and hid, in the black of night, the end of this spine-chilling story.

***

Now we too have a commotion, in the editorial office of *Gudok*.

One screams: "Miracle!" Another screams: "I don't understand anything." One says: "It must be investigated!!" In general, it is as if there is nothing left but to forsake work!

Indeed, the incident is sepulchral! The simplest thing would be to assume that Vitaly didn't die at all. But permit me to ask, then, on what basis did the doctor's assistant, Borisov, who lived at № 11 on Nikolaevsky Street, issue an attestation of death. And for what reason did an insurance cashier pay 17 rubles and 10 kopeks for the burial of a living man?!

Perhaps he didn't rise from the dead. Perhaps the neighbor lied. Perhaps a feuilletonist made it all up, about the moon, and the deceased.

Permit me to ask, then, how could he not have risen from the dead, when the representative of the Mineral Water Insurance Office, Vladimir Ivanovich Nikolaev, wrote:

"It has become clear that none of the family members of the aforementioned Comrade Korabchevsky have died and that the latter, having obtained documents, received payment for the burial illegally."

No, spooky things happen in the city of Kislovodsk!

Mikhail

The newspaper "Gudok," Moscow, September 10, 1925

Using Foul Language (Благим матом)

> On the workers' VIP train of the R… Ryaz–Ural Line, the workers play cards every day, the 'Goat' card game. This game became the occupation of the workers, in the process of which there is cursing, to an impossible level.
>
> It's a disgrace!

Worker–correspondent № 3009

A railcar.

Cheap tobacco.

— And I throw a queen!

— And we, your queen by… (one unprintable word)! Thwack!

— Damn you, !@#$ - !#@# - !#%… (three unprintable words).

— Ivan Mikolaich, lead a king on him!

— You throw your own king on the… (one unprintable word)! We have for your king $*% - !#@# - !@#$ (three unprintable words), an ace!

— And we trump a two on him, the old… (one unprintable word) on… (one unprintable word). $#& - !#@# - $*% (three).

P-sssst!

— Brothers, what was that?

— The $*& - !#% - !#@#@#$ (three) lamp blew out. Couldn't stand it.

— How can anyone stand Ivan Mikolayevich's conversation? He speaks as if shooting from a canon.

— That's funny! Right here, brothers, the night before last the wife of the stationmaster came by, and Vaska right at that moment slapped Ivan Mikolayevich's jack with a queen. And he started in. I'll show you, he says! I'd give him, your !@#$ - !#@# mother, he says, I would do your queen, he says, seven times, he says, !@#$ - !#@#@#$, he says. Do her here, he says! I'd do her, he says!! An undiluted fusillade rained down on the station! The poor thing, she leaned against the railcar, unable to move, hands and legs quaking, she herself pale. She dropped her basket. And Ivan Mikolaich trumps it with a three-inch salute. He worked for about eight minutes. He did the parents of this queen, then he took on the jack's aunt, I would do this to the aunt, he says, yeah, I would do her!! After the aunt, he went through the distant relatives, raped the sister-in-law, daughter-in-law, and brother-in-law. Then he went up the ancestors, dishonored someone's great grandmother, then he wagged his tongue through the grandchildren. Finally, in the eighth minute, he slapped the first cousin once removed with a ten of spades and closed the spigot.

She wiped away the sweat, picked up the basket, walked away, and cried.

— Broads can never stand our game!

— Not just broads! Only yesterday, a peasant came by on a horse. Tied it to the hitching post. And at that very moment, Petya was finishing a round of whist and began to express himself. The horse was standing, standing, and then suddenly spat. Then the horse untied itself, and said:

— I'll go, — the horse says, — as far as the eye can see. Because such a disgrace I have never heard in my horse's life.

After that, they were running after the horse in a field for two hours.

— Was that horse of the female gender? (Three unprintable words).

— A filly, naturally.

Mikhail

Translators' note

Two or three !@#$s seems like the best translation of Bulgakov's *trakh-tara-tam, buts-tara-trakh,* and *boots-tam-tararakh.*

Swearing is an important feature of the Russian language. See, for example, *Dermo! The real Russian Tolstoy never used!* by Russian novelist Edward Topol. Penguin, New York, 1997. *Dermo* translates as (one unprintable word).

The newspaper "Gudok," Moscow, September 16, 1925

The Wrong Pants (Не те брюки)

> Haste is only necessary when catching fleas.
>
> *A proverb*

The chairman of the Local Committee of Enginemen and Stokers declared the meeting open at three minutes past 6.

He then announced the agenda for the day, or rather, the evening.

The menu was composed of a single dish: "Analysis of the existing Collective Agreement and the signing of a new one."

— Following the American tradition, let's not waste extra words, — said the chairman. — We will not read the beginning, there's nothing important there. Let's skip the first page and proceed right to the clauses. Thus, Chapter One, clause one, point L, note b: "We need increased commitment of the individual active workers in production, giving them specific instructions..." Here then, that's what this clause is about. Who's for the commitment?

— I am for it!

— Please raise your hands.

— And I'm for it!

— A majority!

And the committee's typewriter started to busy itself. After clause L, they also reviewed clause P. After P was V, after V, W, and the time passed imperceptively.

In the fourth hour of the meeting, an orator stood up and spoke for one hour and fifteen minutes about the change of payment for piecework to Soviet rubles until everybody howled unanimously and begged him to stop!

After that, they reviewed two hundred and nine paragraphs, and made two hundred and nine amendments.

The sixth hour of the meeting was ticking. On a backbench, two fellows spread out a blanket and demanded to be woken at exactly half past eight for tea.

Half an hour later, one of them woke up and barked hoarsely:

— Aksinya, bring me a glass of *kvass* or I'll kill you on the spot!

They explained to him that he was at a meeting and not at home, after which he fell asleep again.

In the seventh hour of the meeting, one of the speakers woke up and said, yawning:

— I do not quite understand. Under Article 1005 it is written that they receive up to 50 percent, but no more than 40 million. How can it be that it says 'million?'

— It's a typo, — said the American chairman, blue from exhaustion, and he looked dully at Article 1005, — read it as 'rubles.'

Dawn was coming. At dawn, someone's bass voice suddenly asked the chairman:

— Give me, old boy, the collective agreement for a moment, for some reason there is nothing I am able to understand here.

He turned it over in his hands, climbed up to the first page, and screamed:

— Ah, the devil take you, — then he added, addressing the chairman, — You, idiot!

— Do you mean me? — wondered the chairman.

— You, — said the bass. — What are you reading?

— The collective agreement.

— What year?

The chairman flushed, read the first page, and said:

— Holy berries! Forgive me, brethren, I've been force-feeding you the 1922 agreement.

Everyone woke up.

— I was mistaken, my dear brothers, — sweetly said the chairman, — excuse me, dear comrades, do not beat me. The room was dark. I, therefore, did not slip my hand into the right pants. I have the one for 1925 in the striped pants.

Mikhail

The newspaper "Gudok," Moscow, September 22, 1925

Father–Martyr (Страдалец-папаша)

1

After they finished work, Vasily was standing and saying with tears in his voice:

— I have a joyful occasion, friends. My wife was delivered of a child, male, for whom the Baby Insurance Office gives me 18 silver rubles. For the dowry, it means. For the baby we need to buy diapers, undershirts, a blanket, so that he is not screaming at night because of the cold, the damned cat. And what's left goes to my wife to improve her health. Let her eat, the martyr mother. You think it is easy to bear a child, dear friends?

— We haven't tried it, — said the friends.

— Then try it, — said Vasily, and he retired to the Insurance Office, bursting into happy tears.

2

— I have a joyful event. A martyr–mother has delivered, — Vasily said, sticking his head into the cashier.

— Sign here, — cashier Vanya Unsociable replied to him. At the same time as Vasily, nice-guy Aksinich received 7 rubles 21 kopeks for influenza.

3

— A joyful event for me, — said Vasily, — my martyr was delivered of a child...

— Let's go to the co-operative, — answered Aksinich, — we need to toast to your baby.

4

— Two bottles of bitter Russian vodka, — said Aksinich in the co-op, — and what else lighter can we get?

— Get cognac, — advised the clerk.

— OK, give us two bottles of cognac. What else is there, of a refreshing nature?..

— Wormwood liquor is good, — advised the clerk.

— OK, also give us two bottles of wormwood.

— Anything else? — asked the clerk.

— OK, then give us one and a half pounds of sausage, and some herring.

5

At night, the light bulb was burning softly. The mother–martyr laid in bed, and said to herself:

— I'd like to know where his father is.

6

Vasily appeared at dawn.

— *And because of Senya, and because of the red bricks I fell in love with the brick factory...* — Vasily led with a gentle voice, standing in the room. He was holding a liter in his hand, and his whole jacket, for some reason, was covered with feathers.

Seeing a family picture, Vasily burst into tears.

— Mommy, my legitimate wife, — Vasily said, weeping with emotion, — just think of what you have suffered, my beautiful half. Is it easy to bear a child, eh? It must be a horror, one could say! — Vasily threw his hat on the floor.

— Where is the dowry money for the baby? — with an icy voice asked the martyr–wife.

Instead of answering, Vasily started weeping bitterly and lay a wallet before the mother–martyr.

In the designated wallet there were 85 kopeks in silver and 9 in copper.

The mother–martyr said something, but what it was, we do not know.

7

After some time, a delegate of the Women's Department issued a statement from her office, signed by many wives. In said statement, was written the following:

"...that the Insurance Office will distribute benefits from the cooperative for childbirth and nutrition for our children, not to our husbands, but to us, their wives.

This way it will be calmer and better, which is why we intercede."

Signed: "Their wives."

I ask you to add me to the signatures of "their wives."

Em.

The newspaper "Gudok," Moscow, September 25, 1925

The Dead Walk (Мертвые ходят)

An infant died, the child of a boilermaker 2nd grade from the Enginemen and Stoker Service of the Severnyi branch. The local medic required that the child be brought to him to certify the death.

Worker–correspondent № 2121

I

A medical clinic. A local medic receives clients. A boilermaker 2nd grade enters. Somber.

— Greetings, Fyodor Naumych, — says the boilermaker in a mournful voice.

— A-a-a. Hello. Take off your jacket.

— OK, — responds the boilermaker in amazement, and begins to unbutton his jacket, — I, you see...

— You'll talk later. Take off your shirt.

— Shall I take off my pants, Fyodor Naumych?

— Pants? No need. What troubles you?

— My daughter died.

— Hmm. Put on the jacket. How can I be of help? May her soul rest in peace. I cannot resurrect her. Medicine hasn't gotten there yet.

— A certification is required. We need to bury her.

— Ah... to certify the death then? Well, bring her here.

—I beg your pardon, Fyodor Naumych. She is deceased. Lying in peace. And you are alive.

— I am alive, but I am the only one. And you, the dead, are in mounds. If I chase after each one of you, my legs will give out. And I have things to do, you see, I am mixing up powders here. Adieu.

— Yes, sir.

II

The boilermaker was carrying a casket with the girl. Two wailing women walk behind the boilermaker.

— Are you bearing towards the priest, my dears?

— To the local medic, comrades. Let us through!

III

A hearse with a coffin stood at the entrance of the clinic. Next to it, an individual in a white cylindrical hat and a purple nose with a lantern in his hand.

— What's this, comrades? Did the medic die?

— Why do you think it's him? The weighmaster's mother gave her soul to the Lord.

— Why did you bring her here then?

— For certification.

— Ah... Fancy that.

IV

— What do you need?

— If it pleases you to see, Fedor Naumych, I have died.

— When?

— Tomorrow, at lunchtime.

— Lunatic! Why did you haul yourself here in advance? Tomorrow, after lunch, they would have brought you here.

— I am, you see, Fyodor Naumych, a bachelor. There isn't anyone to bring me. The neighbors say, "Go," they say, "in advance, Pafnutich, to Fyodor Naumych. Get certified. There won't be any time to muck around with you tomorrow. In any event, you will not last longer than a day."

— Hmm. Well, okay. I'll get you certified for tomorrow.

— Whenever you wish, you know better. As long as the insurance office pays out. There is still much business to do. I need to swing by the priest again. I want to buy some pants. It would be indecent to die in these pants.

— Well, go, go! You are efficient, old man.

— I'm a bachelor, that's the main reason. There is no one to think about me.

— Well, go ahead, go ahead. Send my regards to kingdom come.

— I will pass them on, sir.

Emma B.

The newspaper "Gudok," Moscow, September 30, 1925

Dynamite!!! (Динамит!!!)

> In the spring, they sent us dynamite for the explosion of the ice jams. There remain 18 pounds of it, and now our site does not really know what to do with it. We fear an explosion, and there isn't anyone to send it to. It's a punishment with this dynamite.
>
> *A worker–correspondent*

Official signs were hanging in every visible location in the administration of the railroad service:

Smoking Strictly Prohibited.
Do Not Speak Loudly.
Do Not Stomp with Your Boots.

In addition, a note of a less formal nature was hanging on the front door of the railroad dormitory:

If your kids don't stop their jumping around, I'll tweak their ears to the roots – Ivanov the Seventh.

Along the rails behind the signal light were hanging red signs and banners:

Do Not Whistle.
Speed Limit 0.9 Miles per Hour.

Trains furtively entered the station with a quiet hiss of the brakes, and in the kitchens of the dining cars they extinguished the stoves. Security walked along the train and warned:

— Citizens, extinguish your cigarettes. They have dynamite here at this station.

***

— I'll teach you to cough (he whispers), I'll teach you to

cough.

— But I've caught a bad cold, Sidor Ivanych.

— I'll teach you to catch a cold. You're booming, like into a barrel! If you keep on coughing here, my entire station will take off into the air.

— Sidor Ivanych, this dynamite is a punishment.

— Stop stomping your boots, and there won't be any punishment.

***

— Where do you keep it, Sidor Ivanych? — asked the newcomer.

— In the living room in the apartment. We wrapped it in a wet rag and put it under the sofa.

— Like tobacco, is that so?

— Cutesy tobacco. It's a dog's servitude, not life. I had to send the kids to my aunt. They were delighted, the little angels. Began to jump: "Daddy brought home dynamite, daddy brought dynamite..." I beat them, the striped devils, and sent them for a visit.

— You are on the road to perdition!

— That's exactly what I'm saying. I had to organize a watch. During the day, my wife stands guard with a rifle; in the evening, it's the cook; at night, it's me.

— You should ship it out.

— I tried, sir. Wrapped it myself. Sealed. Brought it to the station, to the baggage compartment. The weigher asks: "What have you got, Sidor Ivanych, in the parcel?" I responded to him: "Nothing, a trifle," I say, "do not worry, it is 18 pounds of dynamite. I am sending it to Omsk." So he, just imagine, fled from the baggage compartment, escaped through a window and ran away. I saw only his heels.

— What a dilemma!

— A torment. I tried to make a present of it to another railroad. I wrote them a note. So and so, it said: "I am sending you, dear neighbor, the Samara–Zlatoust Railroad, 18 pounds of dynamite as a gift. Use it in good health, as you see fit. Your loving branch of the Omsk Railroad."

— Well, what did they say?

Sidor Ivanych fumbled in his pocket and pulled out a telegram:

"To address № 105. Go to the devil. Stop."

Sidor Ivanych sighed and sadly hung his head.

— You know what, Sidor Ivanych, — advised the newcomer, — you should try to make a present of it to the Red Army.

Sidor Ivanych came to life:

— That's an idea. Why has it never occurred to us?

In the evening, at the management of the railway service, they composed a note with the following content:

"Highly esteemed Comrade Frunze, as a token of our love for the Red Army, we are sending you 18 pounds of dynamite. With respect, the branch of the Omsk Railroad."

There was also the postscript: "Only send your own man for it, experienced and with military training, because none of us have agreed to transport it."

There has yet to be a response from Comrade Frunze.

Emma B.

Vsevolod the Unlucky (Горемыка-Всеволод)

The story of one injustice

1. THE BIOGRAPHY OF VSEVOLOD

The stepfather of Vsevolod is a Red Army line officer. Therefore, Vsevolod traveled for five and a half years, from one city of the USSR to another, following his stepfather, depending on where his stepfather was being sent.

However, Vsevolod was as cunning as a fly, and while traveling clung to one or another educational institution.

In this manner, Vsevolod was able to study at Odessa's School for Marine Engineers, then at the School of Maritime Transport in the city of Baku, and even at the exemplary Professional Technical School in Kiev.

Moreover, Vsevolod wasn't the last man in plumbing and mechanical craft (a consequence of three years of experience in school workshops).

Vsevolod was as curious as Lomonosov, and as courageous as Columbus. That's why Vsevolod presented himself to his stepfather, and announced:

— Dear line officer stepfather, I am applying to the Polytechnic School of Communication Routes in the city of Rostov-on-Don.

— Go for it! — the stepfather replied.

2. WHAT HAPPENED

The stepfather's local committee wrote to the education committee about Vsevolod: "Here's the deal. Vsevolod wants to learn." The Education Committee wrote to the Railroad Professional Union, "We want Vsevolod to learn." The Railroad Professional Union wrote to the Polytechnic: "Please be so kind as to accept Vsevolod." The Polytechnic received Vsevolod's documents and lost them all.

That year, Vsevolod did not get into the Polytechnic.

3. THE FOLLOWING YEAR

The made-wise-from-experience Vsevolod sent all the documents, as copies, to the Education Committee in advance. Among those copies, incidentally, was a recommendation for Vsevolod:

"Vsevolod is a good guy, and his stepfather does useful work."

All of this was delivered to and signed for by a responsible employee of the Education Committee.

And the responsible employee of the Education Committee lost all of Vsevolod's documents.

4. VSEVOLOD PERSEVERES

Vsevolod started avoiding the responsible employees of the Education Committee and hid from them in doorways. The responsible one went on vacation, and Vsevolod dove for his deputy, but the deputy had also gone on vacation, and the deputy had an assistant, to whom Vsevolod again presented his documents. The assistant reviewed Vsevolod's documents and, for an unknown reason, returned them back to Vsevolod via the Local Committee. In this manner, Vsevolod's candidacy collapsed.

5. BUPKIS

Vsevolod received the documents from the Education Committee and, along with them, bupkis.

6. THE EDUCATION COMMITTEE SYMPATHIZES

Vsevolod rushed back to the Education Committee with a howl.

— Poor Vsevolod, — said the staffers of the Education Committee, sobbing into Vsevolod's vest, — we understand you and sympathize with you, handsome young man.

And in a sign of sympathy they wrote a note for Vsevolod to the Polytechnic:

"Here's the deal, admit Vsevolod."

7. AN ARITHMETIC PROBLEM

Vsevolod rushed to the Polytechnic with the note.

— Did you study arithmetic, young man? — they asked Vsevolod at the Polytechnic.

— I studied it, — said Vsevolod politely.

— So, solve the following problem: there are N places available at the Polytechnic. And there are N times 3 inquiries for these free places, plus one more inquiry, yours. The question is, will you get into the Polytechnic?

— No, I will not make it, — said Vsevolod, who was very capable in mathematics.

— You may withdraw, young man, — they said to him at the Polytechnic.

And Vsevolod withdrew.

8. CONCLUSION

Unjust things happen in this world.

Emma B.

The newspaper "Gudok," Moscow, October 14, 1925

The Jubilant Station (Ликующий вокзал)

1. THE LITTLE ANNOUNCEMENT

In one Moscow newspaper the following announcement appeared, verbatim:

"News! (on the left side of the announcement). News! (on the left side). News! (on the right). News! (also on the right)."

— Four times on the sides.

— What kind of news? — a citizen became interested.

The news turned out to be of the following sort:

You can get everything at the café at the Alexander Station!
It's cheap and good.
Lunches, meals a la carte, and waiters.
Wine, vodka 80 proof. Cognacs 120 proof.
Liqueurs 120 proof.
An assortment of herb-infused spirits, by the glass and bottle.
Entrance on Tverskaya Street.

— Cool! — exclaimed a citizen, — after such an advertisement, I wish I could see in a dream what is happening at the station right now.

2. THE DREAM

The station roared like a factory. At the entrances stood rental cars, roadsters with cotton seats, taxis, and cabs.

Not enough seats in the café. That's why tables were placed in baggage claim, the telegraph office, and in the office of the assistant chief of the station. A cloud hung in the air from the steamed sturgeon.

Two hundred waiters hovered, flapping napkins, and from the telegraph office came the howl of violins. There, 15 couples danced the foxtrot.

A sign covered the ticket window:

The train to Smolensk will not depart, but there is fresh crab.

And on the hat of the stationmaster a red crab was painted, along with the golden braid.

At the post office, a poster preened:

To hell with letters, we have pancakes today.

The chief of the station, in a white cap and apron, sat in his former office and talked on the telephone:

— Eight orders of sterlet Kolchik. Salad Olivier, six orders!

The door slammed every minute, waiters flew in, threw brass stamps, and cried out:

— Sturgeon à l'Americain! Five orders! Eight bottles of purified vodka, seven units of brandy!

Screams reached out from the ladies' restroom. Someone was being hit by a bottle of 'Napareuli' and someone's voice squeaked:

— I'll show you not to harass another man's ladies! This is not a bar, it's the main Alexander Station!

— Scht!.. man! Five shots of wormwood!

— I'm bringing it. Just a minute!

A citizen with a suitcase tumbled into the station and was stunned.

— What's happening? — he timidly asked the assistant to the chief of the station, who was towering over the middle of the hall wearing the evening attire of a maitre d'hôtel.

— We're lost, citizen! —the maitre d'hôtel replied to him. — All Moscow rushed to us after that damn advertisement. We had to drop everything. You can see for yourself, it's like *Maslyanit-sya*[1] in the old days in the former 'Yar' restaurant.

— But I have to get to Vitebsk!

— What am I supposed to do about Vitebsk! We have beer stored on the Vitebsk tracks. They're smothered with beer. Go home, citizen. Perhaps you can depart from some other station, where it's dry...

3. THE CONCLUSION

This, of course, is just a dream, but still.
Alexander's Train Station, restrain your 60-proof barman!

Emma B.

Translators' note

1. *Maslyanitsa* is a holiday with pagan roots. It celebrates the end of winter with activities that include building large snow structures, climbing greased poles, staging mock battles (*buza*), eating thin pancakes called *blini,* singing, and burning a scarecrow that symbolizes winter. Bulgakov uses the pre-reform (1918) spelling of *Maslyanitsa* instead of *Maslenitsa.*

The newspaper "Gudok," Moscow, October 16, 1925

The Sentimental Aquarius (Сентиментальный водолей)

The basis of the feuilleton is an actual document written at a station, the Voronezh Freight Line Southeast, and communicated to us by

worker–correspondent № 1011.

The stationmaster of a freight line, Ivan Ivanovich, entered his office, carefully removed his overshoes, put them in a corner, and sat down at his desk.

His eye noticed an official paper on the table. The stationmaster opened it, read it, and immediately began to sob with joy.

— They noticed the stationmaster... They remembered... — he muttered.

He rang the bell.

— Call my assistant, Sidor Sidorych, — he said to a courier.

— Sidor Sidorych, go to Ivan Ivanovich, — said the courier to the assistant.

— Why? — asked the assistant.

— He's crying, — said the courier.

— What the hell is he crying about?

— How should I know?

— May the devil take him, — buzzed the assistant, taking himself into an office down the hall, — with him, there isn't a moment of peace. He laughs, then he cries, then he writes papers. He tortures me with these papers, the bastard.

— What is your pleasure, Ivan Ivanovich? — he asked sweetly, entering the office.

— My dear man, — said the stationmaster through a veil of rain, — I have a sudden and unexpected joy. — With that, water poured from the stationmaster in three streams. — I received a new appointment. Not for naught, it means, have I served the socialist fatherland for the benefit of... Church and Country...

Ugh, what am I saying! In short, I was appointed. I am leaving you...

"Thank you, Lord, Queen of Heaven, and all the Saints, you have heard my prayers," thought the assistant, "the Lord has rewarded my forbearance. My Siberian penal servitude has ended." Then he said aloud:

— No, what are you saying! Oh, what a disaster! How will we live without you? Oh, oh, oh, oh, ah, ah, aha, ah! — "I need to start crying, the devil take me, but I do not know how. I haven't cried since I was fourteen years old, oh, what the hell." — He pulled out his handkerchief, covered his dry eyes, and, at the end, he did manage to burst into sobs in a somewhat unnatural voice, reminiscent of a wolf howling.

— Call the couriers so I can say goodbye, — said the entirely soaked birthday boy.

— So, Ivan Ivanovich is leaving us, — announced the assistant in an artificially trembling voice and, poking the courier with a finger in the side, he added quietly: "Sob!"

And the courier, out of politeness, started sobbing.

After five minutes, out of the same politeness, the whole office of the stationmaster was sobbing.

Having sobbed as much as was required, the office calmed down and returned to its work. But the incident didn't end with that.

— You know what, Sidor Sidorych, — said the slightly dried-out stationmaster, — you know I can't say goodbye to everyone. I have to leave today, you know. How may I part on good terms with my dear colleagues: my dear little office managers, my dear little telegraph operators, my dear little typists, and my dear little accountants?

"Oh my god, he will start bursting into sobs again, what kind of curse is that," thought the assistant. But the stationmaster did not burst into sobs, but thought up a most magnificent plan.

— I will say goodbye to them in written form. They will remember me, my dear comrades, because of the hard struggle of our work in building our dear republic...

And then he sat down and wrote the following piece of art:

"Comrades!

Having received an appointment and not being able to say goodbye to all of you personally, I am resorting to a written farewell.

Fellow workers and employees, having worked together with you for over a year in the front-line, grassroots-driven, practical, detail-oriented, low-paid, but difficult work of the station, I should observe that which has been observed in our Soviet press a few times before me, in particular: It is only through the joint friendly work with the broad masses of workers that a manager is able to improve his economy; that is, in particular, but in general, the working class must rebuild the entire Soviet economy on the new, proletarian principles of ours; i.e., the sooner it will restore its economy, the sooner it will improve its personal well-being and through this heroic unflagging industriousness of workers..." and etc. and etc.

An hour passed and the stationmaster was still writing:

"...Leaving you (here the paper is smudged with tears), let me, comrades, hope that in the future, you workers and employees, as one, will by all means support your authority before the management administration, and, not only your own, but also that of the administration of the station, through the means of an honest attitude to your instructed duties, remembering that to find the single right way of business in the work of the station in order to achieve further improvements in the staff and a cheaper cost of our crude production; i.e., carriage of passenger-miles and freight-miles, we must all be together as one, and thus achieve the removal of obstacles to the proper service of the broad working masses and including, consequently, ourselves individually, and furthermore, to prove his own unshakable devotion to the interests of the working class of the USSR... "

Having written this entire heavy load of nonsense, the stationmaster, sensing that he had a fog in his own head, added out loud:

— It seems that it's screwed together well. What else could I put down for my dear little rascals so that they would remember me? Oh well, it's good enough.

"I wish you, comrades, all the best. Goodbye. With comradely greetings, Ivan Ivanovich," added the stationmaster. Instead of a stamp, he dripped tears on the paper and added to the top of the document:

"I request each of the addressees to announce this to their colleagues in their divisions."

After that, he put on his overshoes, hat, and scarf, picked up his suitcase, and left for the new place of work.

And for three days after this, across all the divisions, there was howling and gnashing of teeth, this time real, not feigned. The managers of the divisions rounded up their staffs and read to them the stationmaster's essay out loud.

— Let him be damned, — said the staff in unfeigned voices, but in a whisper. — It's not possible to understand a single word and why the hell he wrote it, nobody knows. Well, thank the Lord that he left, and pray that he never comes back.

Emma B.

The newspaper "Gudok," Moscow, December 19, 1925

A Mangy Type (Паршивый тип)

If one is to believe a statistic recently compiled by some citizen (I did read it myself), which claims that for every one thousand people there are two geniuses and two idiots, then one must acknowledge that the machinist Bubblehead was undoubtedly one of the two geniuses. This genius Bubblehead showed up at his house and said to his wife:

— So, Mariya, my livelihood resources have dried up in general and completely.

— You are boozing it all away, you scoundrel, — replied Mariya. — How are we going to feed our faces now?

— Don't worry, darling wife, — solemnly replied Bubblehead, — we'll feed our faces!

With these words, Bubblehead bit his lower lip with his upper teeth in such a way that blood streamed from it. The genius vampire then began to lick and swallow the blood until he had sucked it all in, like a tick.

The mechanic then covered his head with a hat, licked off his lips, and took himself to the hospital, to the office of Doctor Powderman.

***

— What brings you here, my dear man? — Powderman asked Bubblehead.

— I am dy...ing, Citizen Doctor, — responded Bubblehead, holding on to the door jamb.

— Really? — marveled the doctor. — You look fantastic.

— Fan...tas...tic? God will judge you for such words, — responded Bubblehead in a dying voice and began to droop to one side, like a flower stem.

— What exactly are you feeling?

— In the... morning... today... I started to throw up blood...

Well, I think to myself, farewell... Bubble...head... Until we pleasantly meet in the other world... Thou shalt be in Paradise, Bubblehead... Farewell, I say, Mariya, my wife... Remember Bubblehead kindly!

— Blood? — incredulously asked the doctor, and grabbed Bubblehead by the stomach. — Blood? Hmm... Blood, you say? Does it hurt here?

— Oy! — Bubblehead responded, and rolled his eyes. — Will I have time... to write a will?

— Comrade Phenacetin, — Powderman shouted to his assistant, — bring me a gastric tube, we will do a gastric analysis.

***

— What is this deviltry! — muttered the perplexed Powderman, staring into the tube. — Blood! By God it's blood. First time I've seen this. Given his excellent appearance...

— Farewell, beautiful world, — said Bubblehead, lying on a couch, — Never again will I stand before the machine, never will I participate in meetings, never again will I introduce a resolution...

— Don't despair, my dear man, — consoled the compassionate Powderman.

— What kind of disease is it, poisonous? — asked the dying Bubblehead.

— You have a benign gastric ulcer. But it's nothing, one can recover. Firstly, you will stay in bed, and secondly, I'll give you powders.

— There's no point to it, Doctor, — spoke Bubblehead, — do not expend your honorable medications on a dying machinist, they will be of service to the living... Don't bother with Bubblehead, he's already halfway to the grave...

"The guy is worrying himself to death!" thought the sympathetic Powderman, and prepared a sedative for Bubblehead.

***

For the round gastric ulcer, Bubblehead earned 18 rubles 79 kopeks, an exemption from work, and the powder. Bubblehead flushed the powder down the toilet and used the 18 rubles 79 kopeks in the following way: he gave 79 kopeks to Mariya for household needs, and 18 rubles he guzzled away...

***

— There isn't any money again, my darling Mariya, — said Bubblehead, — drip some vodka in my eyes.

On the very same day, Bubblehead appeared blindfolded for an appointment with Dr. Powderman. Two nurses led him by the arms, like a bishop. Bubblehead howled and said:

— Farewell, farewell, cruel world! My little eyes are ruined from my labors at the machine...

— The devil knows, what the heck! — said Dr. Powderman. — Never in my life have I seen such an evil inflammation. How did it happen?

— Perhaps I inherited it, my dear doctor, — noted the weeping Bubblehead.

***

For the inflammation of the eyes Bubblehead netted 22 rubles and a pair of horn-rimmed glasses.

Bubblehead sold the horn-rimmed frames at a flea market and distributed the 22 rubles as follows: he gave two rubles to Mariya, and then took one and a half away from her, saying that he would give them back in the evening, and then these one and half and the other twenty he guzzled away.

***

It is not known where the genius Bubblehead filched and scoffed down five packs of caffeine powder, from which his heart started to jump like a frog. They brought Bubblehead on a stretcher to the clinic, to Dr. Syrupwoman, and the doctor gasped.

— You have the kind of heart defect, — said Syrupwoman, who had just graduated from the university, — that you should be sent to a clinic in Moscow where you will be torn apart by the students. It would be shame to allow such a defect to disappear for naught!

***

The defective Bubblehead received 48 rubles and went to Kislovodsk for two weeks. He distributed the 48 rubles as follows: he gave eight rubles to Mariya and spent the other 40 getting to know some unknown blonde, who ran across his path on a train near the Mineral Waters Resort.

— What am I to get sick with now, I cannot figure out, — Bubblehead said to himself, — no other way but to get sick with a huge abscess on the leg.

Bubblehead got sick with an abscess for 30 kopeks. He went to a pharmacy and bought turpentine for these 30 kopeks. Then from an accountant friend, he borrowed a syringe used for arsenic injections, and with the help of the syringe he himself injected turpentine in the leg. The result was such a thing that Bubblehead himself howled.

— Well, now for this abscess we will receive 50 rubles from these blockhead doctors, — thought Bubblehead, hobbling to the hospital.

But a disaster happened.

At the hospital, the Commission was presiding, and in the head of it sat a gloomy and unpleasant-looking man, in gold-rimmed glasses.

— Hmm, — said unpleasant-looking, and through the golden hoops drilled Bubblehead with his eyes, — abscess, you say? OK... Take off your pants!

Bubblehead took off his pants and did not even have time to

look around, as they opened up his abscess.

— Hmm! — said unpleasant-looking, — so it turns out there is turpentine inside your abscess? How did it get there, tell me, dear machinist?..

— How would I know? — said Bubblehead feeling how underneath him opened up the abyss.

— But I know! — said the unpleasant-looking golden glasses.

— Do not let me perish, Citizen Doctor, — said Bubblehead, and wept genuine tears without inflammation.

***

But they still let him perish.
And it serves him right.

The newspaper "Gudok," Moscow, December 25, 1925

Champion of the World (Чемпион мира)

A fantasy in prose

> The debates here at our congress were heated, UDR[1] in his closing remarks, called his opponents clunkheads...
>
> *From the letter of worker–correspondent № 2244*

The hall breathed, every soul was drawn taut as a string. The District Congress was cruising along under full sail. Udeyer stood on the platform and chirped like a nightingale in the woods in the spring:

— Dear Comrades! In summing up my brief four-hour report, I must say, with hand on heart... (here Udeyer put his hand to his vest and made a run with his voice)... that our station has fulfilled its work quota by... 115 percent!

— Wow! — said a deep *basso* voice from the balcony.

— I suppose... (and a warble sounded in Udeyer's throat)... that there cannot be any dispute about the report. Why indeed, debate in vain? I am done!

— Encore! — said Basso from the balcony, and the audience immediately started blowing their noses and coughing.

— Does anyone wish to comment on the report? — asked the chairman in a courteous voice.

— Me! Me! Me! Me! Me! Me! Me! Me! Me! Me!

— Excuse me, not all at once, comrades... Zaichikov?.. Yes! Pelenkin?.. Right now, this second, we're signing up everyone, just a minute!..

— Me! Me! Me! Me! Me! Me! Me! Me! Me! Me!

— Aha, — said the chairman, smiling pleasantly, — now we're cooking, as they say. Excellent, excellent. Who else wishes to speak?

— Sign me up, me Karnaukhov!

— We're signing up everyone!

— What is this... On account of my report, they want to speak? — asked Udeyer and petulantly curled his lip.

— One would suppose, — said the chairman.

— Inte-res-ting. Ve-ry, very interesting, what exactly is it that they may say, — said Udeyer, turning purple, — I am extremely curious.

— I call on Comrade Zaichikov, — continued the chairman and smiled, like an angel.

— Express yourself, Zaichikov, — encouraged the bass.

— This is what I want to say, — began the daredevil Zaichikov, — why is it that these frozen railcars with the rock for the track ballast happened? What are they good for? (Udeyer turned from purple to violet.) — The orator said that everything is 115 percent, yet it is impossible to unload such ballast!

— Are you done? — the chairman asked, pleased with the enlivenment of the work.

— Why should I be done? What are we supposed to do, chomp with our teeth on this ballast?..

— Encore, encore, Zaichikov! — said Basso.

— Would you like to argue with each speaker separately or all together? — asked the chairman.

— One at a time, — with a sinister smile said Udeyer, — I, to each one of them individually, heh, heh, heh, will respond.

He cleared his throat. The hall became quiet.

— Before answering the question as to why the ballast is frozen, let us ask ourselves what is this, this Zaichikov? — thoughtfully said Udeyer.

— Interesting, — the basso reinforced.

— Zaichikov is known to the entire precinct as a dumb bell, — loudly remarked Udeyer, and the hall gasped.

— Sign it, Zaichikov, upon receipt, — said Basso.

— What do you mean? — asked Zaichikov, and the chairman, lord only knows why, played something on a bell resembling the third call to a train, further accentuating the statement of Udeyer.

— Maybe you can explain your words? — with a pale blue voice inquired the chairman.

— With pleasure, — said Udeyer, — what am I, in charge of God's front office? Am I, eh, the one who sent the frost to the site? Well, then, the questions are stupid, there is no need to ask them.

— A clean shot, — observed basso, — Zaichikov, are you still alive?

— Calling the next speaker, Pelenkin, — shouted the chairman smiling confusedly.

— On what basis have you not distributed the gloves? And what are we supposed to do, unload the ballast with our bare hands? That's it. Let him answer me.

— A tricky question, — sounded Basso.

— You have an opportunity to respond, — said the chairman.

— I have seen a lot of asses during the forty years of my life, — began Udeyer...

— An evening of remembrance, — remarked Basso.

— ...But such a one as the previous speaker, as I remember, I have never met. In fact, what am I, a Moscow seamstress? Or am I a glove shop on Petrovka Street? Or maybe I have a factory, according to Pelenkin? Or maybe I can give birth to these gloves? No, I cannot give birth to them!

— A tricky thing, — observed Basso.

— So, why does he bother me? My job is to write, I wrote. Well, nothing more.

— And Pelenkin is defeated with a head capture, — said Basso.

— The floor is open for the next speaker.

— It remains unclear, — said the next speaker, — I'm regarding the 115 percent... We are taught in arithmetic, as well as in the other sciences, that each object can have only one hundred percent, but how is it that we have overworked by 15 percent?

Let him explain.

— I swear, it's more interesting than wrestling at the circus, — a woman's voice said.

— A half nelson, — exclaimed Basso. All eyes were fixed on Udeyer.

— I would gladly explain to this desiring speaker, — convincingly spoke Udeyer, — if he did not give the impression of being clearly a defective person. Why should I explain to a defective? Judging by how he looks at me blankly, he would not understand my explanations!

— He needs to be sent to a colony for the defectives, — replied Basso, who loved to set people by the ears.

— Exactly, comrade! — confirmed Udeyer. — In fact, if you do all the work entirely, then the work attains 100 percent. Right? And if we do something in excess of that, it's still an extra percent? Is it not so?

— *Absolument!* — confirmed Basso.

— Well, it means that we have fulfilled over 100 percent of what we were supposed to! Are you satisfied, deeply esteemed sir? — asked Udeyer of the defective speaker.

— Why are you asking the defective? — answered Basso. — Do not talk to him, ask me. I am satisfied!

— The next speaker is Fiusov, — invited the chairman.

— No, I don't want to, — said Fiusov.

— Why? — asked the chairman.

— Well, I don't feel like it, — said Fiusov, — I withdraw.

— The guy chickened out? — inquired the omnipresent Basso.

— Chickened out! — confirmed the hall.

— Well, then Kablukov!

— I withdraw!

— Pelageev!

— It isn't necessary. I do not want to.

— I don't want to either! Me neither! Me neither! Me neither! Me neither! Me neither! Me neither!

— The list of speakers is exhausted, — said the confused chairman dejectedly, dissatisfied with the weakening of the enlivened work. — No one, therefore, wants to object?

— No one! — said the hall.

— Bravo, — Basso thundered in the gallery, — I congratulate you, Udeyer. You pinned everyone to the mat. You are the champion of the world!

— The round of Greco-Roman wrestling is over, — said the chairman. — Oy, I mean... the meeting is adjourned!

And the meeting noisily adjourned.

Mikhail

Translators' note

1. *UDR* is an abbreviation of *Upravleniye dokumentatsii i raspredeleniya gonorara,* the Director of Documents and Benefits. Bulgakov uses the job title as the name of the character *Udeyer.*

Some snippets of censorship:

20 February 1925. Moscow
From Boris Leontyev (at the Nedra publishing house)
Dear M.A.,

Hurry up, please do everything you can to let us have your story *The Heart of a Dog*. Nikolay Semyonovich [Angarsky] may be going abroad in about two or three weeks' time, and we won't have time to get the thing through the Censorship Committee. And it will scarcely be possible to pull it off without him. If you don't wish the book to be shelved until the autumn, hurry, hurry.

21 May 1925. Moscow
From Boris Leontyev (at the Nedra publishing house)
Dear Mikhail Afanasyevich,

I am sending you *Cuff-notes* and *The Heart of a Dog*. Do what you like with them. Sarychev at the Censorship Committee declared that there was no point in even tidying up *The Heart of a Dog*. 'It's an entirely unacceptable piece' or something similar.

11 September 1925. Moscow
From Boris Leontyev (at the Nedra publishing house)
Your story *The Heart of a Dog* has been returned to us by L. B. Kamenev. At Nilkoay Seyonovich [Angarsky]'s request he read it through and gave his opinion on it 'It's an acerbic broadside about the present age, and there can be absolutely no question of publishing it...'

Of course one cannot put the blame simply on two of three particularly sharp pages: they would scarcely alter the opinion of a man like Kamenev. Nevertheless, it seems to us that your earlier refusal to submit an amended text played a regrettable part in all this.

24 June 1926. Moscow
To the Chairman of the Council of People's Commissars
On 7 May this year representatives of the OGPU [the secret police] carried out a search of my flat (warrant 2287, file 45), during the course of which were confiscated, after they had been duly noted in the record, the following manuscripts which have an enormous intimate value for me:

The story *The Heart of a Dog* (two copies) and my diary (three notebooks).

I earnestly request that these be returned to me.

From *Bulgakov: A Life in Letters and Diaries,* J.A.E Curtiss. Bloomsbury, London, 1991.

The Heart of a Dog was finally published in the Soviet Union in 1987.

1926

The magazine "Smekhach" (The Laugher), № 15, Leningrad, 1926

Encephalitis (Воспаление мозгов)

Dedicated to all the editors of weekly journals.

In the right pocket of my pants lay nine kopeks: two three-kopek coins, a double kopek and a single, and at each step they clinked like spurs. Passersby squinted at the pocket.

It seems that my brains are starting to melt. Indeed, asphalt melts from high temperature! So why can't yellow brains? Admittedly, they are in a bony case and are covered with hair and a white cap. These beautiful hemispheres with convolutions lay inside, silent.

And the kopeks, — clink-clink.

Near the very café of the former Filippov, I read a sign on a white strip of paper: *Cabbage soup, steamed sturgeon, lunch of two courses – 1 ruble.*

I pulled out the nine kopeks and threw them into a ditch. A man wearing a worn-out seafarer's cap, unmatching trousers, and a single boot approached the nine kopeks. He saluted the money and shouted:

— Thanks from the Admiral of the Navy. Hurray!

Then he picked up the coins and started singing in a loud and fine voice:

Ceased bloooo-ssoming long ago-o!
Chrisan-theeee- mas in the gard-en!..

Passersby went past in a stream, wheezing quietly, as if that's how it should be, that at 4 p.m., in the heat, on Tverskaya, an admiral wearing a single boot should sing.

Suddenly, many followed behind me, and spoke with me:

— Compassionate foreigner, please give me nine kopeks too. He's a charlatan. He never even served in the Navy.

— Professor, show kindness…

And a boy, resembling Pushkin's Chernomor,[1] except with a cut beard, leapt two feet in front of me, and hurriedly told me in a hoarse voice:

At the Kalytsi outpost
Lived the bandit and thief—Kamarov!

I shut my eyes so that I wouldn't see him, and began to speak.

— Let's suppose. The beginning: it's hot, and I'm walking, and there is the boy. He leaps in front of me. Homeless. And suddenly the director of the orphanage comes out from behind a corner. An enlightened individual. How to describe him? Well, let's suppose, like this: young, blue eyes. Shaved? Well, let's say, shaved. Or with a little beard. Baritone. And he says: "Boy, boy." And what else? "Boy, boy, aha, boy, boy…" "And wearing an apron," — suddenly said the heavy brains under my cap. "Who is wearing an apron?" — I asked my brains with surprise. "He is, your orphanage guy."

"Idiots," — I replied to my brains.

"You yourself are the idiot. Talentless, — my brains replied to me, — we'll see what you get to feed on today if you don't, this minute, compose a story. Pulp-writer!"

"Not in an apron, but a frock…"

"Why is he wearing a frock, tell us, dumbhead?" — asked my brains.

"Well, let's suppose that he just finished work. For example, he bandaged the leg of a sick girl and went out to buy a pack of 'Trest.' Here one can describe the Mosselprom saleswoman. And then he says:

— Boy, boy… And having said it (I will later compose what he said), takes the boy by the hand and leads him to the orphanage. And so Petka (the boy is called Petka, these kind of freezing-in-the-heat boys always happen to be Petkas) is already in the orphanage, already not telling stories about Kamarov, but reading the ABC-book. His cheeks are fat, and the story is entitled: 'Petka is Saved.' At the magazines, they love such titles."

"The story sucks, — happily swelled under the cap, — and, what's more, we already read it somewhere!"

— Shut up, I am perishing! — I ordered my brains and opened my eyes.

Neither the admiral nor the Chernomor were in front of me and my watch wasn't in the pocket of my pants. I crossed the street and approached a policeman, who was raising a stick on high.

— They just stole my watch, — I said.

— Who? — he asked.

— I don't know, — I replied.

— Well, then it's lost, — said the policeman.

From these words of his, an urge for seltzer water came over me.

— How much for a glass of seltzer? — I asked a woman at a stand.

— Ten kopeks, — she replied.

I had asked her so as to know whether I should be sorry about the thrown-out nine kopeks. I was uplifted and enlivened a little with the thought that I shouldn't be sorry.

"Let's suppose: A policeman. And here, a citizen comes up to him…"

"So what?" — inquired my brains.

"Hmmn… yes, — and he says, — my watch was stolen. And the policeman whips out his revolver and cries: 'Stop!! You stole it, scoundrel.' He whistles. Everyone runs. They catch the recidivist thief. Someone falls. Shots."

"That's it?" — asked my fat yellow ones, swelling from the heat in my head.

"That's all."

"Remarkable, nothing less than genius, — my head burst out laughing and started to tick like a watch, — but only they won't accept this story because there is no ideology in it. All of this, i.e., to cry out, to whip out a revolver, to whistle, and to give chase, could be done by an old-regime policeman. *N'est-ce pas,* Comrade Bienvenutto Cellini?"

The thing is that my penname is Bienvenutto Cellini. I thought it up five days ago in the same heat. And for some reason, all the cashiers at the journal office loved it to death. All of them placed Bienvenutto Cellini in the advance book next to my last name. Fifty rubles, for example, after B. Cellini.

"Or the following: Taxi Driver № 2579. And a passenger forgot a briefcase with important papers from the Sugar Trust. And the honest taxi driver delivered the briefcase to the Sugar Trust, and the sugar industry soared, and they rewarded the class-conscious taxi driver."

"We remember this taxi driver, — bitchingly said my inflamed brains, — long ago in the supplements to the Marxist *Niva.* About five times we met him there, typed in either Times New Roman or Courier. But the passenger did not work in the Sugar Trust, but in the Ministry of Internal Affairs. Time to stop talking. Here's the editor's office. Now let's see what you have to say. Where is the story?.."

I entered with a cocky attitude, via a rickety staircase, singing loudly:

And I for Senya!
And for bricks,
Fell in love with a brick factory.

In the editor's office, turning green from the heat in the cramped room, sat the chief of the editorial office, the editor himself, a secretary, and also two flunkies. The birdlike nose of a cashier poked out from a wooden window, like in a zoo.

— Bricks are bricks, — said the chief, but where is today's promised story?

— Can you imagine, such a grotesque occurrence, — I said,

smiling gaily, — my watch was stolen today on the street.

Everyone was silent.

—You promised to give me money today, — I said, and suddenly, in the mirror, saw that I resembled a dog under a tram.

— There isn't any money, — replied the chief dryly, but on the faces I saw that there was money.

— I have the plot of a story. What a dullard you are, — I began in a tenor tone, — I will bring it to you on Monday, by 1:30.

— What kind of plot?

— Hmmn... In one house there lived a priest...

Everyone became interested. The flunkies lifted their heads.

— Well?

— And he died.

— Is it humorous? — asked the editor, furrowing his brows.

— Humorous, — I responded, wallowingly.

— We already have humor. In three issues. Sidorov wrote it, — said the editor. — Give us something rapscallion.

— I have, — I replied quickly, — I have it, I have it, of course!

— Tell us the plot, — said the chief, softening.

— Ahem... One Nepman[2] went to Crimea...

— Keep going please!

I pushed on the sick brains in such a way that juice dripped from them, and murmured:

— Well, bandits stole his suitcase.

— How many lines is it?

— 300 lines. Well, admittedly, I can... make it less. Or more.

— Write an advance for 20 rubles, made out to Bienvenutto, — said the chief, — but be sure to bring us the story, I ask you seriously.

I sat down to write out the advance with delight. But the brains wouldn't have any part of it. They were small, shrunken, and covered with black parched fissures instead of convolutions. They had died.

The cashier, as it happened, tried to protest. I heard his star-ling-like voice:

— I won't give anything to your Cinizelli.[3] He has already swilled down 60 silver rubles like this.

— Give it, give it to him, — ordered the chief.

And the cashier loathingly gave me a single crisp, mint condition ten-ruble banknote, and another, dark with a fissure in the middle of it.

After 10 minutes, I was sitting in the shade of 'Filippov' under palm trees, hidden from the gaze of the world. They placed a sizeable mug of beer in front of me. "Let's conduct an experiment, — I said to the mug, — if they don't revive after the beer, it means, it's the end. They died, my brains, as the consequence of writing stories, and they will never awaken. If it is so, then I will eat through the 20 rubles and then die. We will see then how they will recover the advance from me, the dearly departed."

This thought amused me. I took a gulp. Then another. With the third gulp the life force suddenly started swarming in my temples, the veins engorged, and the shrunken lobes stretched out in the bony case.

"Are you alive?" — I asked.

"Alive," — they responded in a whisper.

"Well then compose a story!"

At that moment, a lame man approached me with penknives. I bought one for a ruble and a half. Then came a deaf mute, who sold me two postcards in a yellow envelope with the inscription:

Citizens, help a deaf mute.

On one postcard, a Christmas tree stood in cotton snow, and on the other was a rabbit with airplane ears sprinkled with beads. I feasted my eyes on the rabbit. Foamy beer blood coursed through my veins. The heat shone in the windows. The asphalt melted. The deaf mute stood in front of the entrance to the café and angrily said to the lame one:

— Skate out of here sausage, and take your knives. Who

gave you the right to do business at my 'Filippov?' Leave and go to the 'Eldorado!'

"Let's suppose, — I began, flaring up, — a street rattled, a motorcyclist with a nightingale's whistle went off. There is a yellow twisted coffin with mirrored glass (a bus)!.."

"Now we're cooking, — remarked the recuperated brains, — ask for another beer, sharpen a pencil, and keep going... Inspiration, inspiration."

A few moments later, inspiration flooded forth from the stage to the tune of a military march by Schubert-Tauzig, to the clapping of cymbals, and to the tinkling of silver.

I was writing a story for *The Illustration* and the brains sang to the military march:

> *Well, My liege,*
> *Inspiration is given to me?*
> *What's your view?!*

The heat! The heat!

Translators' note

1. *Chernomor* is a very short villain from Pushkin's fairy-tale-in-verse *Ruslan and Lyudmila*. His distinguishing characteristic is a long beard.

2. *Nepman* is slang for a private entrepreneur. Nepmen (plural) emerged under *NEP*, the *Novaya ekonomicheskaya politika*, the New Economic Policy, which was an economic program initiated by Lenin in 1921 that allowed for private ownership of small business while preserving state ownership of banks, large industries, and exports.

3. The *Cinizellis* were a famous circus family. Benevenutto Cellini was a famous Italian sculptor and author.

Radio Peter (Радио-Петя)

(The notes of a victim)

Day 1

I met Peter, who lives in our communal comradeship. Peter is a boy of exceptional ability. All day long he sits on the roof.

Day 2

Peter visited me. Brought me a small black box, and the following conversation occurred between us.

Peter (enthusiastically): Ah, Nikolai Ivanovich, mankind has been searching for thousands of years for the magic crystal enclosed in this box.

Me: I'm very glad that it finally found it.

Peter: You surprise me, Nikolai Ivanovich, how you, an intelligent man with a marvelous living space in the form of your room, could do without a radio. Imagine how you, at half past two in the morning, lying in bed, will hear the bells of Westminster Abbey.

Me: I'm not sure, Peter, that bells can afford pleasure at half past two in the morning.

Peter: Well, if you do not want the bells, you will be receiving currency reports in the morning from the New York Stock Exchange. Finally, if you do not want New York, in the evening you will hear, sitting in your dressing gown, the singing of *Carmen* at the Bolshoi. You will close your eyes and: *Through the midnight sky an angel flew, and a soothing song he sang...*[1]

Me (seduced): How much will the angel cost me, my dear Peter?

Peter (joyfully): For eleven rubles, I will install a simple radio for you, and for thirteen, one with a loudspeaker for twenty-five people.

Me: Well, why for so many? I'm a bachelor...

Peter: Smaller ones do not exist.

Me: Okay, Peter. Here's three... Three more... six and seven. Thirteen. Install it!

Peter (flying out of the room): You will gasp, Nikolai Ivano-vich.

Day 3
I did actually gasp, because Peter broke the wall in my room, as a consequence of which a huge layer of plaster fell off and broke all the dishes on the table.

Day 4
Peter announced that he would do all the work himself: ground it through the water pipe, and a plug from the electric lamp fixture. Peter ended the conversation with the words:

— Now I'm going to the roof.

Day 5
Peter fell off the roof and sprained his ankle.

Day 10
Peter's leg was patched up and he started to work in my room. One wire was stretched to the sink and another to the electric lamp fixture.

Day 11
At 8 p.m., the electricity went out in the entire apartment building. There was an incredible scandal, which ended with a meeting of the house committee, which suddenly issued a deci-sion that I am a self-employed person and will be paying 1 ruble per square yard. The electricians repaired the electricity.

Day 12
Done. In my room the gaping maw of a grey loudspeaker is still silent. It's missing some kind of a screw.

Day 13

This is monstrous! An old woman, the mother of the chairman of the house committee, went to get water from the sink, and the sink said to her in a bass voice: "The Cross and the Gun"[2]... Furthermore, the old fool seemed to have heard the sink add: "Grandma," and the old lady is now bedridden with fever. I'm beginning to repent my undertaking.

In the evening, I read in the newspaper: "Tonight is a broadcast of the opera *Faust* from the Bolshoi Theatre on wavelength 1,000 meters." With a sinking heart, I pushed the lever, like Peter taught me. The midnight angel spoke in a wolf's voice inside the maw:

"I am speaking to you from the Bolshoi Theater, from the Bolshoi. Are you listening? From the Bolshoi, listen. If you want to buy shoes, then you can do so at the Government Universal Market (*GUM*). Write down in your notebook: the *GUM* (nasally), in the *GUM*."

— A strange opera, — I said to the maw, — who is performing it?

"There you can also buy samovars and underwear. Remember underwear. I'm speaking from the Bolshoi Theatre. Underwear is only at the *GUM*. I am now turning you over to the opera hall. I am turning you over to the hall. I am turning you over to the hall. So I turned you over to the hall. The lights extinguished. The lights extinguished. The light is back on again. The intermission continues for another ten minutes, in the meantime listen to an English lesson. *Do svidaniya*. In English: Goodbye. Remember: Good-bye..."

I pushed the lever to the side and all sound extinguished in the maw. Fifteen minutes later, I placed the lever to wavelength 1,000 meters, and suddenly there was a spitting in the room, like from a frying pan, and a strange bass voice started singing:

You tell her, my flowers...

Howling and crackling accompanied this aria. Passersby stopped on the street near my apartment. I could hear that the inhabitants of my apartment had gathered in the hallway outside my room.

— What's going on, Nikolai Ivanovich? — asked a voice, and I recognized the voice of the chairman of the house committee.

— Leave me alone. It's the radio! — I said.

— At 11 p.m., I'll ask you to stop it, — said the voice from the keyhole.

I stopped it earlier because I could no longer endure the howling of the maw.

Day 14

Last night I woke up in a cold sweat. The maw said cheerfully: "Take two steps back." I jumped out of bed barefoot and walked backwards. "Well, how are you feeling now?" — asked the maw.

— Very badly, — I replied, feeling my bare feet freezing on the cold floor.

"Stop and Azerbaijan," — said the maw.

— What do you want from me? — I asked plaintively.

"It's me, Kaluga, — replied the maw, — stop, and with a capital letter. Police fired into the air, stop, and demonstrators, stop..."

I banged a fist on the lever and the maw fell silent.

Day 15

A polite gentleman appeared in the afternoon and said:

— I am the inspector. Have you had this thing long?

— Two days, — I replied, anticipating misfortune.

— You are, therefore, a radio-freeloader, and even worse, you have a loudspeaker, — said the inspector, — you must pay a twenty-four-ruble fine and obtain a permit.

— It's not me who's a radio-freeloader, but it's Peter who's a radio-dickhead, — I said. — He didn't warn me about anything and, moreover, spoiled the entire room and relationships with my neighbors. Here are the twenty-four rubles and an additional six rubles that I'm giving to someone who will fix this thing.

— We will send you a specialist, — said the inspector, and gave me a receipt for twenty-four rubles.

Day 16
Peter disappeared and never showed himself again...

Mikhail

Translators' notes

1. A line from *The Demon*, an opera in three acts by Russian composer Anton Rubinstein. The opera was composed in 1871 based on Mikhail Lermontov's poem "The Demon."

2. The "Cross and the Gun" ("Krest i mauzer") was a 1925 film by director Vladimir Gardin.

The newspaper "Gudok," Moscow, July 8, 1926

A Diamond Story (Бубновая история)

1. A DREAM AND THE STATE BANK

Mokhrikov had a dream in his hotel room about a huge ace of diamonds on legs, with ribbons on its chest on which were written disgusting slogans: *After Finishing a Deal - Walk Boldly!* and *Tuberculosis Patients, Do Not Swallow Your Phlegm!*

— Such ridiculous nonsense! Phooey! — said Mokhrikov, and woke up. He dressed cheerfully, took his briefcase, and went to the State Bank. At the State Bank, Mokhrikov wandered around for two hours, then exited with a briefcase filled with nine thousand rubles.

A person who receives money feels completely special, even if it is state-owned. On the Kuznetsk Bridge, it seemed to Mokhrikov that he had even grown taller.

— Do not shove, citizen, — roughly and politely said Mokhrikov, and he even wanted to add: — I have nine thousand in the briefcase, — but then changed his mind.

The action on the Kuznetsk Bridge boiled like a teapot. Plush cars flew by every second, the display windows sparkled, shimmered, and glistened. Mokhrikov, walking with his briefcase, reflected in them, first upright, then upside down.

— Moscow is a delightful little town, — Mokhrikov began to reflect, — simply an elegant town!

Sweet and criminal dreams suddenly began to boil in the brain of Mokhrikov:

— Imagine for yourselves, dear comrades... the State Bank suddenly burns down! Hmmm... How does it burn down? Very simple, it isn't fireproof, is it? The fire brigades arrive. Firefighters put it out. Only there's no way in hell you're going to put it out if it has been properly lit! Just imagine, it's all burnt to hell. The accountants burned and the accounting records... And, as a result, in my pocket... Oh wait!.. What about the letter of credit from Rostov-on-Don? Ah, the hell with it. But, then, let's say I go to Rostov-on-Don and our Red director who signed the letter has died of heart failure! And moreover, another fire, and all the interoffice, outgoing, and incoming correspondence all burned to the dogs. Hee-hee! Find and seek. And then the orphaned nine thousand will be in my pocket. Hee-hee! Oh, if our Red director knew what Mokhrikov dreams about. But he will never find out... What would be the very first thing I'd do with it?..

2. SHE!

...First of all...

She emerged from Petrovka Street. Skirt to the knees, plaid. Legs, slenderness beyond belief, in cream stockings and patent leather shoes. A hat resembling a blue bell sat on her head. Eyes like, you know what I mean. And her lips were crimson and glowed like fire.

"I finished a deal, now I can walk boldly," — Mokhrikov remembered the dream for some reason, and thought, — What a babe. Ah, what a city this Moscow! If only the Red director had burned... Whew! What a waist...

— Pardon me! — said Mokhrikov.

— I don't talk with men on the street, — she said proudly, and glanced from under the blue bell.

— Pardon me! — said the stunned Mokhrikov, — I didn't mean to!..

— A strange custom, — she said, swaying her plaid hips, — to see a lady and immediately start hitting on her. You're probably a provincial, aren't you?

— Not at all. I'm from Rostov, madam. On the Don. Do not take me for some kind of bastard. I'm a cash courier.

— Nice name, — she said.

— Pardon me, — said Mokhrikov in a sweet voice, — it is my position: cash courier from Rostov-on-Don.

My surname is, in fact, Mokhrikov. Allow me to introduce myself. I'm from Lithuanian nobility. My main surname, the one my ancestors once wore, is Mohr. I even studied in a gymnasium.

— Sounds like *MOPR.*

— Oh please! Hee-hee!

— And what does 'cash courier' mean?

— It's a responsible position, madam. I receive money from the banks: nine, twelve thousand or even more. It's hard and difficult, but that's OK. I'm a trusted man...

"I told myself to buy striped pants. Am I really wearing these pants while speaking with a lady on Kuznetsk Bridge? What a disgrace!"

— Oh money, you say? That's interesting!

— Yes, hee-hee! What's money! Money is dust!

— Are you married?

— No, but you're so young, madam, and single, like...

— Like what?

— Hee-hee, a feather.

— Ha-ha!

— Hee-hee.

....

— Sukharevskaya–Sadovaya, № 201... You're an awfully cocky cash courier!

— Oh, what are you thinking! *Merci.* I just need to stop by my room to change. I have so many outfits in my room. You'd die. This one is for the road, so to speak, don't pay attention to it, it's trash. And what kind of a charming hat are you wearing? And what is that embroidered on it?

— Cards. A three, a seven, an ace.

— Oh, how lovely. Hee-hee!

— Ha-ha!

3. THE TRANSFIGURATION

— Shave me, — said Mokhrikov, clutching the nine thousand to his heart in a mirrored hall.

— Krrch... What do you want to do with your hair?

— Whatchamacallit, comb it.

— Vanya, the device!

After a quarter of an hour, Mokhrikov smelled like lily of the valley. He stood at the counter, and said:

— Show me the patent leather shoes...

Half an hour later, at a store on Petrovka, under a golden sign *Men's Clothing*, he said:

— Perhaps you have a room somewhere, some kind of separate room, where I could change my pants?..

— Please.

When Mokhrikov walked out onto Petrovka, the crowd turned around and looked at his feet. Cabbies from the buggies said:

— Pleeez, pleez, pleeez...

Mokhrikov reflected in the windows and thought to himself: "I look like an actor from the imperial theaters..."

4. AT DAWN

...When all of Moscow was blue, and the cats, who hang out God knows where during the day, crawl like snakes from one alley to another, Mokhrikov stood clutching his briefcase to his chest on Sukharevskaya–Sadovaya, and staggered and muttered:

— Hmmm... If I do not get a drink of seltzer water or beer, I will die, dear comrades, and the street sweepers will pick up the nine thousand... Hold on, not nine, gimme a second... No, not nine... This is what I can tell you: the shoes were forty-five rubles... Yes, but where did the ninety golden rubles go? Yes, I shaved, a ruble and fifteen... It's turning out to be embarrassing... Actually, I can get an advance and I'll take it. And how could he not give it to me? I get back and, bang, they say he died of a heart attack and they have appointed a new guy. Then it becomes a funny story. Dear Mokhrikov, they ask, where are the two hundred and fifty rubles? Did you lose them, Mokhrikov, or what? No, it's better if he doesn't die, the cat of a bitch... Coachman, where can one drink beer in your mangy Moscow at this hour?

— Pleeez, pleez, pleeez... At the casino.

— Hey, what's it called?.. Pull up here. How much will it be?

— Two and a half.

— I... er... well, here, what's up? What's your name?.. Drive!

5. OH, THE CARDS!..

A man in a chocolate suit and dazzling white shirt, with a ring on his finger and an anchor tattooed on the back of a hand, scattered round metal chips and money on a table using a long white blade and a magician's dexterity, and said:

— *Banco suivi!* Pardon, Monsieur, the game continues!..

At the round tables, three guys were sleeping with their heads on their hands, like homeless children. Gray tobacco smoke floated in the air. Bells rang and porters with purses ran back and forth exchanging money for chips. After a few Gorshanovsky beers, it was brightening a bit in Mokhrikov's head, as much as it was brightening outside the windows.

— Monsieur, why are you standing there? — the man with the anchor and ring addressed him. — There is a seat, I invite you to take it. *Banco suivi!*

— *Merci!* — said Mokhrikov dully, and suddenly and automatically flopped into the seat.

— The 10 is available, — said the man with the anchor, and asked Mokhrikov:

— Would you like it, monsieur?

— *Merci!* — said Mokhrikov in a wild voice...

6. THE END

A worried and very polite man was sitting behind a desk in an institution. The door opened and a courier let Mokhrikov in. Mokhrikov had the following appearance: on his feet he had patent leather shoes, a briefcase in his hands, feathers on his head, and under his eyes were greenish rotten shadows, as a result of which Mokhrikov's snub nose looked like a corpse's nose. Before Mokhrikov's eyes flickered black shoals, and black stripes looking like snakes cut through them occasionally. Whenever he rolled his eyes to the ceiling, it seemed to him that the ceiling was strewn with diamond-studded aces, like stars.

— I am listening to you, — said the man at the desk.

—A very important incident occurred, — said Mokhrikov in a low bass voice, — such an incident, just indescribable.

His voice quivered, and suddenly turned into a thin falsetto.

— I am listening, — said the man.

— Here is a briefcase, — said Mokhrikov, — please take a look, there is a hole, — Mokhrikov reported and then demonstrated. Indeed, there was a small hole in the briefcase.

— Yes, there is a hole, — said the man.

They were silent for a moment.

— I got on a tram, — said Mokhrikov, — got out, and there (he pointed to the hole a second time), — they cut it with a knife!

— And what was in the briefcase? — the man asked indifferently.

— Nine thousand, — said Mokhrikov with a childish voice.

— Yours?

— State-owned, — mutely replied Mokhrikov.

— In which tram did they cut it? — asked the man, and in his eyes appeared compassionate curiosity.

— Er... er... in that, what was it, in the twenty-seventh...

— When?

— Just now. I received it at the bank, got on the tram, and...

straightaway, a perfect nightmare...

— So. What is your last name?

— Mokhrikov. A cash carrier from Rostov-on-Don.

— Your parents?

— My father works in a factory and my mother at a cooperative, — said Mokhrikov in a plaintive voice. — I just want to die. I have no idea what to do.

— The bank is closed today, — said the man, — it's Sunday. You're probably confused, citizen. You got the money yesterday?

"I'm dead," — thought Mokhrikov, and again aces flashed in his eyes, like swallows, then he added in a hoarse voice:

— Yes, it was me yesterday who this... m... money received.

— And where were you the night before? — asked the man.

— Er... er... Well, naturally, in my room. In the hostel where I stayed...

— You didn't stop by the casino?

Mokhrikov smiled palely:

— What are you saying! What are you saying! I didn't even... didn't... I wasn't there, no...

— You better tell me, — said the man with kind eyes, — because everyone comes in and says, the tram, the tram. It's even getting boring. Here's your deal, one way or the other, it's better to speak directly, after all, you know, you wouldn't have feathers on your head, for example, etcetera. And you didn't ride any tram...

— I was, — Mokhrikov said suddenly, and sobbed.

— Well, that's much simpler, — the man at the desk perked up. — And it is easier for me and for you.

And having called someone, he said to the opening door:

— Comrade Vakhromeev, you need to escort the citizen...

And Vakhromeev led Mokhrikov away.

Mikhail

What kind of person was Bulgakov? There is a quick answer to that. Fearless, always and in everything. Vulnerable but strong. Trusting but incapable of forgiving any deceit, any treachery. Conscience incarnate. Incorruptibly honorable. Everything else in him, significant as it may have been, was secondary, contingent upon the crux of it all, the thing that drew people to him like a magnet.

Bulgakov's friend Vitaly Velenkin
In the book, *Mikhail Bulgakov and his Times,*
Progress Publishers, Moscow, 1990, p 91

A FINAL CHORD

We hope that you have been entertained and enlightened, dear reader, by this gentleman–writer, who carried the golden flickering torch of Russian humanism through a long and deadly night... unflinchingly, unwaveringly. Who was, is, and always will be remembered, simply and fondly, as *The Master*.